Masque of Deceptions

Shadows book 2

STELLA RILEY

Copyright © 2024 Stella Riley
All rights reserved.

ISBN: 9798333711960

Cover by Larry Rostant
Typography by Ana Grigoriu-Voicu

*In loving memory of my dear friend
and invaluable proof-reader,
Corinne Carter*

CONTENTS

	Page
Prologue	1
Chapter One	5
Chapter Two	18
Chapter Three	30
Chapter Four	40
Chapter Five	50
Chapter Six	60
Chapter Seven	74
Chapter Eight	88
Chapter Nine	101
Chapter Ten	110
Chapter Eleven	121
Chapter Twelve	129
Chapter Thirteen	139
Chapter Fourteen	146
Chapter Fifteen	156
Chapter Sixteen	167

	Page
Chapter Seventeen	177
Chapter Eighteen	188
Chapter Nineteen	198
Chapter Twenty	210
Chapter Twenty-One	224
Chapter Twenty-Two	234
Chapter Twenty-Three	246
Chapter Twenty-Four	255
Chapter Twenty-Five	266
Chapter Twenty-Six	276
Chapter Twenty-Seven	285
Chapter Twenty-Eight	298
Chapter Twenty-Nine	309
Chapter Thirty	318
Epilogue	332

PROLOGUE

January 1781, Reculver Court, Prior's Norton, Gloucestershire

For most of his life, Daniel Shelbourne had been aware that the family finances were at a low ebb. By the time he left Eton, he'd known that the estate was barely showing a profit ... and during his last months at Oxford everything had continued to slide still further downhill. There wasn't enough money to make the necessary repairs to the tenants' cottages or replace the rotting window-frames at the Court; staff had been drastically reduced and Mama seldom entertained any more.

Attempts to persuade his father to discuss the problem hit a brick wall of resistance and Daniel's tentative suggestions for what might be done to improve matters fell on deaf ears. As a consequence, he had no idea how *truly* bad the situation had become until he sat down with the lawyers in the wake of his father's funeral and learned about the debts.

'Debts?' he echoed. 'What debts? No money has been spent here that I'm aware of. And my father hasn't been away from home to spend it elsewhere for more than three years.'

The lawyers, father and son, exchanged glances before looking at him. Then Mr Longhope senior explained that, against all advice to the contrary, his late lordship had been 'borrowing from Peter to pay Paul'. In short, he had taken out a second loan to pay the interest on the first one.

Loans? What loans? For a minute, due to the roaring in his ears, Daniel was beyond speech. But eventually, he managed to say, 'And the original loan ... what was that for?'

'His lordship did not see fit to share that information,' came the prim reply.

No. Of course he didn't. Stupid of me to ask, Daniel thought. But said, 'I see. However, presumably you *do* know how long all this been going on?'

The answer to this caused his stomach to sink still further. The appropriate documents were laid before him. They showed that the first loan had been taken out during his final year at Oxford; and the second, four years ago. His father, it seemed, had been punting on the River Tick for eight years.

'And how much,' he asked, 'is currently owing?'

This time, Longhope's reply almost made his eyes water. It made no sense. The estate might not be profitable but it just about scraped by – or he'd thought it had. So why had Father needed to borrow so much? And for what – since it clearly hadn't been spent on repairs or improvements?

The lawyers went on talking, advising him to retrench.

Retrench? he thought wildly. *How? We don't spend a penny we don't have to.*

They moved on to delicately suggesting items he might consider selling. The land, of course, was entailed. But paintings and other decorative objects … some of the horses? And perhaps Lady Reculver's jewels? They were sure, they'd said encouragingly, that he could raise this quarter's interest in that way.

And what about the next quarter? And the quarter after that?

But he didn't bother to say it. There was no point, after all. He merely rose, thanked Messrs. Longhope for their time and bade them farewell. Then, because he couldn't bear the thought of facing his mother and sister yet, he went instead, like a sleep-walker, to the library where his friends, since their first days at Eton to their last ones at Oxford and now closer than brothers, waited for him.

* * *

Christian, Lord Hazelmere, Benedict Hawkridge and Anthony Wendover looked at him, the same unspoken question in all of their eyes. Then, apparently interpreting his expression, Anthony rose to drop a hand on to his shoulder and press him into a seat; Benedict crossed to pour brandy and put a glass in his hand; and Christian said quietly, 'When you're ready, tell us how we can help. Anything at all. You need only say.'

Daniel nodded and, staring sightlessly into the glass, murmured, 'Thank you.' Then, realising he had to do better than that, he summoned a travesty of a smile and added, 'I appreciate the offer.'

All three gentlemen looked at him. Benedict said what they were all thinking.

'He appreciates the offer but won't take us up on it.'

Since this was true, Daniel didn't bother denying it. He said, 'It's can't, not won't. I *can't* take you up on it. Father's affairs ... well, things are a bit worse than I expected.'

'Meaning they're much worse,' translated Christian. Then, 'Daniel ... you don't need to name the problem. We can guess what it is, if not the scale of it. Why not at least let us make it smaller?'

He pressed his lips together and shook his head.

'Don't be so stiff-necked,' Anthony admonished.

'I'm not.'

'Yes, you are. If you weren't, you'd *talk* to us. There may be more than one way of approaching this and – '

'There isn't.'

'You can't know that,' objected Christian. Then, sighing, 'All right. You won't accept financial help for the same reason you've always refused it in the past. But bottling it up and brooding over it on your own isn't going to solve anything. Anthony's right. Talk to us.'

'Unless,' suggested Benedict deviously, 'you don't trust us?'

Daniel swore under his breath. 'You know it isn't that.'

'He does. Just as he knew it wasn't that when he used the same tactic to make me confess *my* dark secret,' said Christian calmly. 'But that doesn't make him wrong. You said the situation is worse than you anticipated. Worse how?' And after a few moments when Daniel continued to say nothing, 'You may as well tell us. There's no way we're going to leave you to sink or swim on your own.'

This time the silence was a long one. But finally, on something resembling a groan, Daniel muttered, 'All right. If you *must* know, my father left ... unexplained debts.'

'Go on,' encouraged Benedict.

'He – he took out not one but two loans which are still outstanding.' And shoving a hand through his hair, 'I can't begin to imagine what possessed him. He was struggling to pay the *interest* – so there was no chance in hell he'd ever be able to repay the capital.'

He didn't add, *And neither can I*, but his friends heard it anyway.

'Who are the lenders?' asked Anthony. 'Someone reputable, I hope?'

'Firms in the City. Fleetwick? Fleetwood?' He rubbed a hand over his eyes. 'The one who advanced the larger sum was something like that. I can't remember exactly.'

'How much?' asked Benedict bluntly.

Daniel shook his head. 'No. I've already said more than I meant to. I know you'd all offer a loan and I'm grateful. But I can't accept. If I can't repay the loan companies, I can't repay you either. And I refuse to be in debt to my friends.'

'Your friends,' said Christian quietly, 'won't be demanding interest. And they won't force you from your home. Think about it, Daniel … and about your mother and sister while you're at it. Then perhaps then we can talk about this again.'

CHAPTER ONE

June 1781, Hawthorne Lodge, Upper Wick, Worcester

By the time her mother appeared at the breakfast table, Anna Hawthorne had read both of the letters awaiting her, slipped one into her pocket and made certain decisions about her day.

'Good morning, Mama. Did you sleep well?'

'For the most part. The wretched peacocks started calling as soon as it was light. I've never understood why your father wanted them – noisy creatures.'

'He wanted them because they're beautiful,' Anna replied. 'And because he was incorporating peacocks in his design for Lord Ashley's dinner service ... and the next season's collection of scent bottles.'

Mrs Hawthorne huffed an impatient breath. 'He didn't need real birds for that.'

'Of course he did. How *else* was he to develop the correct colours?'

Six years ago, Papa had spent hour upon patient hour in the garden, luring the peacocks with food and teaching them to trust him while he mixed endless paints until he finally found the shades he wanted. Whenever she could escape Mama, Anna had joined him there, absorbing everything he told her, not only about the complexities of creating precisely the required shades in porcelain manufacture, but a great deal else. And since his death, the year before last, she had continued to spend time with the birds who, by now, were as tame as pets.

Now, setting her napkin aside, she began paving the way for something else Mama wasn't going to approve of. Usually, she didn't bother to do this, preferring to head directly for the argument which was sure to follow. But today, since she had a bargaining chip, she decided she might as well use it.

Taking up the letter lying beside her plate, she said, 'An invitation from Lily Anstruther to the house-party celebrating her betrothal to Lord Lycett. I shall – '

'My goodness! She has finally said yes, then?'

'Lily was *always* going to say yes, Mama. She just wanted to enjoy a third London Season. However, regarding the house-party ... I shall send our regrets, of course. Unless you think that Lady Anstruther might be extending an olive branch at last?'

'Augusta Anstruther and I have been at daggers drawn since we made our come outs together, so I sincerely doubt it,' replied Mrs Hawthorne. 'The only thing we can agree upon is that we cannot abide each other. But the fact that *I* will not attend the party is no reason why *you* should not. Lily is a dear girl. And her elder brother counts a number of unmarried, titled gentlemen amongst his friends, some of whom are bound to be present, don't you think?'

'I would imagine so, yes.'

'So you must go. Who knows *who* you might meet or what might come of it?'

'Who indeed?' murmured Anna, knowing the answer would be no-one and nothing but also knowing better than to say it.

Just as she'd expected would be the case, Mama was seizing an opportunity to fulfil her ambition of seeing Anna married to a title. In the eyes of the world into which she'd been born, Mama herself had married beneath her and, so far as Anna knew, had never regretted it. But from the moment of Anna's birth she had been determined that her daughter would do better ... and been hugely disappointed when Anna's London season at the age of nineteen had not only failed to deliver the required result, but any result at all.

Mama had sought help from those old friends and relatives who still received her. And in return for substantial remuneration, her cousin, Cordelia, Lady Maybury, had undertaken to obtain invitations for Anna and to chaperone her at balls to which she would not otherwise have been invited. Papa had leased a house in the best part of Town, paid for extravagant wardrobes for both his wife and his daughter and then stepped back to remove, as best he could, the stigma of trade. But it hadn't been Hawthorne's Porcelain that had made Anna's Season a failure. It had been Anna herself.

Neither Worcester society nor Mama's many lectures on what was proper had prepared her for the people she would meet in the ballrooms of London. Young ladies whose lives appeared to revolve around the newest fashions, the latest gossip and which gentleman was the most handsome, the wealthiest or the owner of, or heir to, the most prestigious title. As for young men, most of *them* seemed to be whiling away their days at various sporting events or over cards and wagers at their clubs whilst living off their expectations. None of them, either male or female, ever talked about anything *interesting* and when Anna had tried to do so, they looked at her as if she had two heads. She seemed to baffle them as much as they baffled her; and the result was that she frequently said something tactless or unintentionally scathing.

In no time at all, she'd become known as the Hedgehog Heiress. After that – and when added to the fact that she wasn't a beauty – even her rumoured excessively large dowry hadn't been sufficient to tempt potential suitors. Anna had told herself she didn't care; that her real life was at home with Papa and Hawthorne's; and, once back there, she thanked God that she'd never need to brave London society again.

Mama, still dwelling happily on the forthcoming Anstruther house-party, cut across her thoughts by saying, 'Make my excuses and say that Miss Draper will accompany you in my place. She may be a *trifle* odd but her connections are excellent. No-one can possibly object to the cousin of a marquis, can they? And we must visit Madame Lavalle. You should order at least two new evening gowns. It won't do to appear to be behind the mode.'

'Indeed, not.' Anna rose in preparation for making a brisk exit if necessary. 'Very well. I'll write an acceptance, after which I have one or two errands to complete in Worcester this morning. Is there anything I can do on your behalf whilst I'm there?'

Immediately, her mother's expression hardened.

'*What* errands? Please tell me that you are *not* visiting the manufactory?'

'The manufactory is certainly one of them,' replied Anna calmly. 'There are matters Mr Lowe wishes to discuss with me – and I with him.'

'But it is highly inappropriate! How many times must I say it? A young, unmarried lady should not be involved in business matters at *all* – let alone doing so in a workplace. What people would say if they knew, I cannot imagine! It's quite bad enough that everyone knows your father left Hawthorne's to you and – '

'To whom else might he have left it?' cut in Anna. 'To second-cousin Malcolm, perhaps – along, of course, with the income from it?'

'Well, no. But – '

'Exactly. You may prefer to ignore it, Mama, but the porcelain works made Papa a rich man and continues to pay for the many comforts you and I enjoy.'

'I am aware of that. But it can continue to do so without – '

'No. It cannot. Papa left it to me because it *mattered* to him and because he knew he could trust me to take care of its future success along with the wellbeing of our eighty-three employees. Meeting with Mr Lowe on a regular basis is an integral part of that.'

Mrs Hawthorne huffed an irritable breath.

'Then, if you *must* speak with him, at least have him wait on you here.'

'It is more convenient to do so at the manufactory.' Seeing her mother open her mouth on further argument, Anna held up a hand to stem the flow and said, 'Please stop. I have agreed to spend a week with the Anstruthers next month. I have agreed to keep an open mind with regard to the gentlemen I'll meet there. And, in the unlikely event that one I think I might be able to live with shows signs of serious intent, I will even agree to consider marriage.'

'And so you should! You are twenty-three, you foolish girl. If you don't marry soon, you never will. Don't you *want* a husband and family of your own?'

'Not enough to marry any man who offers merely for the sake of getting one,' returned Anna coolly. 'But all this is beside the point. I am going to the Anstruthers because you wish me to, not because I want to. But in return, I must ask you to accept that my involvement in the running of Hawthorne's is necessary to the company and important to me personally. Or if that is beyond you, to at least stop arguing about it – since doing so will change nothing. And now I'm afraid you must excuse me or I shall be late.'

* * *

Sitting in the carriage on her way to Worcester, Anna reflected on how very tired she was of Mama's attitude. It had begun on her thirteenth birthday with a decree that it was time she began learning to be a lady and therefore visits to the manufactory must stop forthwith. Prior to that, Papa had been taking her there since she was six and gradually, over the years, teaching her all the various stages of manufacture for each of Hawthorne's wares. He'd let her watch them being born at the designers' tables, take shape at the workbenches of the modelers and gather beauty in the hands of the painters. She'd gazed, entranced, as vases rose magically under the hands of potters at their wheels and waited in breathless anticipation for articles to emerge from the kilns. And when she was ten, Papa had allowed her to make something of her own.

'A potter never stops learning,' he'd told her. 'New ideas and new techniques are being born every day, all of us looking for better ways of doing things. Never think you've mastered it all, Annie – because you never will, any more than I have.'

Mama's edict regarding Hawthorne's was swiftly followed by Anna's departure for a school for young ladies in Bath. Papa made it bearable by sending progress reports on one or other of the manufactory's new lines or asking Anna's opinion on this or that design. Then, during the holidays and unknown to Mama, he had continued to extend her ceramics education at home. He brought samples of everything from china clay to finished products because theory wasn't enough. There was nothing, he said, more useful for judging quality than holding it in your hands. This soft paste was too thin and this one, too thick but this ... *this* one was perfect. This vase *looked* flawless ... but its surface wasn't sufficiently smooth. And the sculpted edge of the plates for a new dinner service which had looked fussy in design proved sensuously elegant when transformed into test models.

So Anna absorbed all the intricacies of her father's business, along with his passion for it. His sudden death rocked the ground beneath her feet; but the annual routine of Hawthorne's was there to steady it again. In January, the two oldest tableware designs were discontinued and replaced with new ones. And in March, June, September and December, the seasonal collection of scent bottles and snuff boxes – three designs of each, only six of which were ever made – was released. Until his death, the scent bottles had always been designed by her father. Now, a team of three talented young men had inherited this honour.

Idly, Anna wondered what had excited Mr Lowe sufficiently to cause him to write asking her to come to the manufactory at her earliest convenience. It was unlike him so there must be a good reason although his letter had given no clue as to what it might be. Not that she minded. An excuse to visit Hawthorne's was always welcome.

The manager met her at the door to the offices with his usual subdued smile. Nathaniel Lowe had been at Hawthorne's for almost three decades having started as an office boy at the age of fourteen. Oliver Hawthorne, who liked to know all his employees personally, had soon recognised the lad's diligence and quick mind – the result being that, before he was thirty, Lowe had risen to the position of under-manager. Anna had known him since she was six. She appreciated the fact that he never treated her as if she still was.

She said, 'Good morning, Nathaniel. Your note said 'at my earliest convenience' and this is it. But if you're busy at the moment, I can occupy myself elsewhere until you're not.'

'No need for that, Miss Anna. I'm glad you've come. Not that it's an emergency ... just something I reckon's worth considering sooner rather than later and risk missing the chance of it. But come along to the office and I'll tell Martha to see about some tea.'

'Don't trouble on my account.' Stripping off her gloves, Anna followed him through the building to his office, nodding a greeting to sundry other workers as she went. 'I'm intrigued. Your note said it was related to something we've discussed previously – but nothing springs to mind.'

Mr Lowe closed the door behind them and, when Anna was seated, said, 'Well, it *was* a while ago – towards the end of last year, if I remember rightly. We'd been talking about the number of genteel visitors we'd had throughout the summer, wanting a tour of the works. You asked if there was some way to make use of it this season.'

'And you suggested creating an exhibition of Hawthorne wares through the years,' chimed in Anna, 'coupled with an opportunity to buy or order.'

'Yes. Only after that we had a series of problems – such as the supply of china clay and the second kiln misfiring – and the idea got pushed aside, then forgotten.'

'So what has brought it to mind again now?'

'A whisper I heard from a friend in Hereford. He's a dealer in antiques and fine art so his clientele and Hawthorne's are similar. He recently bought two paintings he knew had belonged to a certain gentleman. He said that if that gentleman was a customer of ours we might want to think twice about extending credit to him because he's likely in financial difficulties.' Lowe paused and then added, 'He was talking about Lord Reculver.'

A faint frown touched Anna's brow as she tried to place the name. Then, 'Oh. The gentleman who buys the scent bottles?' And when the manager nodded, 'I think I met him once. I must have been twelve ... and he came to see the spring collection on a day when I was here with Papa. He was polite and very ... affable.'

'That'd be him. He hasn't bought anything for the last three years. But before that, he was a collector. I've looked back in the ledgers and every season for twenty-six years, he's bought one of the limited edition scent bottles. At first, he bought the snuff boxes as well he but stopped doing that after four years. And now, as I said, he's stopped buying the bottles as well – which he would do if he's in financial straits.' He stopped and grinned at her. 'Anyway, the whole thing gave me a bit of an idea.'

Anna grinned back. 'Let me guess. That if his lordship is selling paintings, he may also be interested in selling other things – such as his Hawthorne collection?'

'Yes. And if he *is*, limited edition wares going back two and a half decades designed by your father – some of the very earliest even *made* by him – well. They'd make a wonderful feature for our exhibition.'

'Indeed. Do you know how many of our pieces he has?'

'Yes. Twelve snuff boxes and one hundred and four scent bottles.'

Anna stared at him. 'Good heavens! As many as that?'

'A bottle every season for twenty-six years.' Mr Lowe sat back in his chair. 'What do you want to do?'

That didn't require any thought at all.

'Make an approach. Ask if he's interested in selling – subject to condition and valuation, of course. Also, try to find out whether any such pieces have come up for sale recently and, if so, what sort of prices they commanded.'

'I'll investigate further. But we already have some information of that sort in the files. Mr Wicherley of Cheltenham bought all three bottles from the 1776 spring collection – the Muses, if you recall?'

'Euterpe, Urania and Terpsichore? Yes. And?'

'And he sold them last year for four times what he paid. However, a complete set was bound to do well. Lord Reculver only ever bought one of the three … but he had a good eye. He chose Terpsichore that year. And the year before, he bought Flora from the summer collection.' Mr Lowe thought for a moment. 'Of course, he could probably do better by selling the pieces separately at auction rather than as a complete lot to us. But if he's trying to be discreet …'

'As he probably is.'

'An offer from Hawthorne's could be a godsend.'

'Almost certainly, I'd say.'

They shared another smile as they savoured the moment. Then there was a tap at the door and Martha's head appeared around it to say, 'Sorry to disturb you Mr Lowe, sir – but Donald says there's summat not right with the delivery from Upton.'

'Tell him I'll be with him presently,' said the manager.

'No. Go now.' Rising, Anna said, 'I've taken up enough of your time and should be leaving anyway. But let me know when you hear something further on the matter we've been discussing.'

* * *

A few days later at his home in Gloucestershire, Viscount Reculver's reaction to the letter from Hawthorne's Porcelain was not one of unalloyed joy. How the devil had this fellow Lowe found out that he might be amenable to selling *anything* –

let alone a collection of something he didn't even know he had? Surely his precarious financial position couldn't have become common knowledge already? He'd been careful. It was why he'd sent that pair of indifferent 'school of' van Ruisdael landscapes to be sold in Hereford, rather than in Gloucester where they might have fetched a better price.

The only thing making it possible for him to stay afloat in the last six months had been Christian going behind his back and repaying the loan to Fleetwood's on his behalf.

Be furious with me if you like, Daniel, he had written, *and then put it aside. After what you did for me, how do you think I'd feel knowing I could help but not doing so?*

Well, anger had been some part of what Daniel had felt ... but sick relief was a bigger one. So he'd swallowed his pride and vowed he'd pay Kit back somehow, however long it took.

He still didn't know what that original loan had been for. Mama said his father had mentioned some sort of investment but she had no idea what it might have been. And since there was no paperwork to account for it, Daniel could only conclude that Father had been duped into some fraudulent scheme or other. God knew, there were plenty of them to choose from. And details of *how* the money had been lost didn't change the fact that it had been.

Aside from the paintings, he'd sold the two large Chinese vases from the drawing-room, the travelling chaise and four of the horses. These had been sufficient to tide the household over for the time being and also pay the quarterly interest due on Father's remaining, smaller loan ... but Daniel knew that everything he did was merely putting a temporary plug in the hole. Worse still, he couldn't see any end to it.

He picked up Lowe's letter again.

Scent bottles, he thought. *A hundred and four of them. Seriously? And where* were *they, for God's sake?*

Cudgelling his brain, he finally remembered the pair of glass-fronted curio cabinets in Mama's sitting-room. Both were full of four or five inch high porcelain figurines. He dimly recalled one of a dragon and another which bore a more than passing resemblance to the Queen. Were *those* what Lowe was talking about? And, if they were, could Mama be persuaded to part with them? She couldn't possibly *need* over a hundred scent bottles. Could anyone?

Groaning inwardly, he supposed he'd better find out. When asked, the butler informed him that the ladies were taking tea on the back terrace. Deciding to seize the opportunity to get a better idea of what he'd be talking about, Daniel changed direction and headed for his mother's sitting-room and the cabinets.

His memory hadn't been playing tricks. There they all were, cheek by jowl and all of them different. A mermaid on a rock; a medieval minstrel; Venus arising from the waves … and many, many more; most of the tops were silver-mounted and a few, gold. No two were alike and all of them done in exquisite, miniature detail. He opened one of the cabinets and took out Queen Charlotte. Her Majesty's head formed the stopper to the bottle and was attached to her body by a dainty chain. Daniel gave a tiny, disbelieving laugh and returned her to her place between a dancing gypsy and a skimpily clad goddess, wondering how much it was all worth.

He joined his mother and sister outside. They were sitting in the shade because although Mama's hair was fading to grey now, her skin was still that of the redhead she had been in her youth. It was from her that Daniel had inherited his own colouring. Rebecca, by contrast, took after Father's side of the family; dark eyes, dark hair and a perfectly-defined widow's peak that rendered her face heart-shaped.

Refusing tea and, coming directly to the point, Daniel said, 'Mama … for how long was Father buying those little bottles from Hawthorne's Porcelain?'

'The scent bottles, do you mean?' And when he nodded, 'Since the year you were born until – until three years ago. Four each year; spring, summer, autumn and winter.' She sighed, nostalgically. 'Why do you ask?'

Four every year for twenty-six years? Well, that explains the quantity, he thought. But side-stepped her question with a seemingly idle one of his own. 'Do you ever use any of them?'

'Only the peacock one on my dressing-table. Why?'

'Because I've had a letter from the manager of the manufactory regarding them.'

'Really?' said his sister. At the age of nineteen, Rebecca was doing her best to remain cheerful despite having been robbed of her Season this year due to Father's death and seeing scant chance of having one next year either. 'Saying what?'

He sighed but, realising there was nothing to be gained by prevarication, said, 'Apparently they may be interested in buying them.'

'*Hawthorne's* would?' asked his mother blankly. 'Why?'

'I've no idea, Mama. But how would you feel about selling – or at least looking into the possibility of doing so?'

She was shaking her head before he had finished speaking. 'Sell your father's gifts to me? No.'

Daniel drew a long, tired breath. 'Could you perhaps consider it? I wouldn't ask if it wasn't necessary. But – '

'Sell something else. Sell the Sèvres dinner service, if you must. Heaven knows, we're unlikely ever to use it again. But not my scent bottles.'

'I'll sell the Sèvres, since you have no objection and if I can find a buyer,' he said patiently. 'But in Hawthorne's, we may already have one. Please at least *think* about it.'

Lady Reculver opened her mouth on another refusal. But before she could utter it, Rebecca said flatly, 'You can't just dismiss it out of hand, Mama. You know how things are. Papa left a mess behind and –'

'Stop. I won't have you speaking of your father like that!'

'Why not? It's the truth, isn't it? Dan is at his wits' end trying to make ends meet but he can't do it all on his own. You and I will have to make some sacrifices as well.'

'And what are *you* giving up?'

'Hope that I'll even be able to make my come out next year,' returned Rebecca promptly. 'Because if we can't afford it, I won't.'

Touched and grateful that she had come to his defence, Daniel stretched out a hand to her and said, 'I'll do everything I can to make it possible, Becky. And Anthony's cousin, Lady Colwich, has offered to present and chaperone you if necessary.'

'I know and it's kind of her considering she scarcely knows me. But it doesn't solve the problem, does it?'

'No. Unfortunately, it doesn't.' Deciding it was time to take a firmer line with his mother, Daniel turned to her and said, 'The bottles have sentimental value. I understand that. But when was the last time you really *looked* at them, never mind took any of them out of the cabinet? Can you even remember?'

'I look at them,' she insisted. 'Of course I do.'

'So if I moved a few of them around you'd notice? And be able to put them back as they were? Truthfully now, Mama. Would you?'

'I ... yes. I'm sure I would.'

'That sounds fun.' Smiling, Rebecca stood up. 'Shall we try it?'

'*What?* No!' Her ladyship reached for her handkerchief. 'Stop it, both of you!'

'Very well,' said Daniel mildly. 'We'll speak of it again another time. Meanwhile, all I'm asking is that you *think* about it. Will you do that?'

Dabbing her eyes and sighing deeply, she eventually said, 'Very well. If I must.'

'Thank you.' He bent to place a kiss on her cheek, then turned to his sister. 'Walk with me a little before I must get back to the grindstone?'

She took his offered arm. 'Yes. I'd like that.'

'So would I.' He led her down the steps to the gravel path and then said softly, 'Don't push too hard, Becky. She knows things are bad. But she doesn't want to believe just *how* bad.'

'Neither do I – but what use is that? Sometimes I feel so *angry* with Papa ... leaving us in debt with nothing at all to show for it. Is that wicked of me?'

'No. It's understandable. And sometimes I feel the same.' *Mostly, however, I just feel bloody helpless*, he thought but merely said, 'He never confided in me; never let me help in even the smallest way. It probably wouldn't have made any difference if he had ... except that I'd have been better-prepared for what was to come.'

Rebecca strolled on at his side in silence for a little while. Then, 'Hawthorne's Porcelain, you said. There was an Anna Hawthorne at school, though I didn't really know her because she was older than me. But it's not a very common name, is it? And I'm sure I recall some of the other girls whispering that her father was in trade ... so perhaps he owns the manufactory that made Mama's scent bottles. What do you think?'

'It isn't impossible, I suppose.'

'But it isn't much help.'

'Not really, no.'

'What would be?'

'Buried treasure? The pot of gold at the end of the rainbow? An unexpected bequest from an anonymous benefactor?' He managed a grin. 'A handsome, charming and obscenely rich young gentleman riding up to the door on his white horse and refusing to leave until you promise to marry him?'

Rebecca laughed. 'None of those is remotely possible, more's the pity.' Then, coming to a sudden stop to stare up at him, 'On the other hand, perhaps *you* could sweep an heiress off her feet.'

Keeping his tone light, Daniel shook his head. 'I'm sure I could – if I happened to be acquainted with any heiresses, that is.'

'You're not?'

'No. Sorry.'

'Not even one?'

'Not even one.' He hesitated and then added wryly, 'And if I'm to be honest, desperate as things are, I'm not sure I could bring myself to marry a woman just for her money.'

'Why not? Other gentlemen do it.'

'I know. And that's up to them. But I can't imagine it makes for a very happy marriage. After all, the couple in question would both *know*, wouldn't they? And there would be resentment on both sides. She, because he hadn't married her for herself. And he because, however good their intentions, he'd always feel ... bought and paid for.'

'Perhaps,' said Rebecca reluctantly. 'But it needn't be like that. They might come to love each other.'

It was Daniel's turn to laugh.

'You've been reading too many romances, Becky. If only real life *was* like that. But it isn't.'

CHAPTER TWO

Mr Lowe received Lord Reculver's indecisive letter a week later and wrote to Anna, saying, *Reading between the lines, I suspect he'd like to take up our offer of a valuation but something is stopping him doing it. However, he hasn't said no – so with your agreement I'll give it another week, then write again.*

Anna replied to the effect that she was content for him to deal with the matter as he saw fit. In truth, she wasn't content – she was impatient. Surely, either his lordship wanted to sell or he didn't? She tried to work out how old he must be. She'd been twelve when she met him and he'd *seemed* old to her; but he probably hadn't been much older than Mama was now … somewhere in his mid-fifties … so, eleven years on, he wasn't exactly senile, was he? Or perhaps he was delaying in order to find out exactly how interested Hawthorne's was in acquiring the collection, thus enabling him to calculate how high he could drive the price?

A faint smile lit Anna's face. If it *was* that, he had a surprise coming. She hadn't broached the matter with Mr Lowe yet … but if things got as far as a valuation, she intended to do it herself. Thanks to Papa's tuition, there was no one at the manufactory who could assess quality better than she could; and no one, she suspected, who would drive a harder bargain.

Of course, if she *did* do the valuation, it would mean spending a day or two at Lord Reculver's home near Gloucester … but if she took her maid with her and perhaps a female assistant from the manufactory, it would be perfectly proper. Needless to say, there would be the usual tedious argument with Mama over it but Anna wouldn't let that stop her. She intended to play an active role at Hawthorne's and the sooner Mama came to terms with it, the better.

* * *

At Reculver Court, a few days after he'd written to Mr Lowe, Daniel learned that his mother had taken all the scent bottles and snuff boxes out of the cabinets and was painstakingly cleaning them with her own hands. This, he decided, could be interpreted in two ways. But at least it proved that she wasn't merely ignoring the matter until it went away which meant he could continue hoping for the best.

By the time the second letter came from Mr Lowe, Rebecca was able to tell him that the collection was gradually being put back where it came from.

'To be fair,' she said, 'while Mama was cleaning the pieces, they'd been occupying every available surface in both her sitting-room and bedroom – so she needed to put them away before something got damaged. And the cabinets were her only option.'

'You're saying that it isn't necessarily bad news,' remarked Daniel. 'But neither is it the other sort. Has she said anything to you?'

'No. You?'

'Obviously not. But I've had another enquiry from Hawthorne's so I'll have to raise the subject with her again.' He slouched back in his chair. 'I sent samples of the Sèvres dinner service to Mason's in Cheltenham. They've offered a hundred and fifty pounds for it – less than half what it's worth, I suspect – but better than nothing.'

'So you'll take it?'

'Yes.'

'And the scent bottles?'

He shrugged. 'I have absolutely no idea what Hawthorne's might offer for those. I found an old receipt regarding one Father bought six years ago which cost ten pounds fifteen shillings. If they're not worth less than he paid ... well.'

'A hundred at ten pounds each?' breathed Rebecca. '*Really?*'

'Perhaps.'

'Surely that will sway Mama?'

'We can but hope,' he said, preparing to leave the room. And then, recalling something, 'By the way, Kit writes that Sophie says she'll join Drusilla Colwich in sponsoring your come out if and when it happens. But he won't let her commit to anything until after the baby is born – which will be in late August, they think.'

Rebecca flushed a little. 'Considering Lady Hazelmere has never even *met* me, that is remarkably generous of her. You have very, very good friends, Daniel.'

'Yes,' he agreed, once more heading for the door. 'The best.'

Anthony had visited three times since the day Father's will had been read. He'd toured the estate with Daniel and been a mine of useful, highly practical advice on how to improve matters. Some of this – namely, those parts not requiring capital – Daniel had managed to implement.

Benedict, having been once more sent north of the border by his brother, hadn't managed a return visit yet but promised to come as soon as he could.

Christian, reluctant to spend much time away from home while Sophia was increasing, had been only once – and that well in the wake of his letter admitting what he'd done regarding the debt to Fleetwood's. But he wrote regularly and continued to offer further help if only Daniel would accept it – or if the situation reached crisis point.

Now, on his way to Mama's rooms with the possibility of a thousand pounds dancing in his head, Daniel was hoping crisis point might be averted a while longer.

A single glance was all it took to tell him that all the Hawthorne pieces were back on their shelves. Then Lady Reculver looked up from the letter she was writing and said, 'Do we *really* need to sell my scent bottles, Daniel?'

'Yes. If Hawthorne's offer a good enough price, I'm afraid we do.'

'And the snuff boxes?'

He nodded. 'Those, too. I know you don't like it, Mama. In truth, I'm not happy about it either. But there's little choice. Since Father's death, we've been a hairsbreadth from ruin. And though I hesitate to say it, if he'd lived … it might already have happened.'

She flinched and looked away. But finally, she drew a long, clearly painful breath and said, 'Very well. Do what you must.'

'Thank you.'

'Will they – will the pottery people send someone to fetch them?'

'Not to begin with. Someone will come to value them and make sure none of the pieces are missing or damaged.'

'They are not,' she said indignantly. 'I have always taken the greatest care of them!'

'Of course. But Hawthorne's won't make an offer until they've seen the goods.' He hesitated, unsure how much to tell her or to promise. 'Even if they're worth no more than Father paid for them, they could still bring in a substantial sum of money.'

'And if they are not?'

God, thought Daniel, *please let that not be the case. Give me just one bit of good luck.*

'Let's just hope for the best, shall we?'

Later, glancing at Lowe's letter whilst preparing to reply to it, he suddenly realised that the fellow hadn't expressed his condolences. Was it possible he didn't know that Father was dead? No. Surely not. Anyone meticulous enough to comb through twenty-six years' worth of ledgers to catalogue every piece Lord Reculver had purchased would presumably keep an eye on the obituaries in the *Morning Chronicle* so he'd know if his regular clients were still alive or not. On the other hand, perhaps he'd risen to the position of manager in the three years since Father had stopped buying. And it scarcely mattered, did it? Shrugging the thought aside, Daniel picked up his pen and gave Mr Lowe permission to send someone to examine and value the collection.

Though whether or not I decide to sell, he added, *will naturally depend on your offer.*

Then he signed, folded and sealed it and gave it to the butler for posting.

* * *

Whilst unenthusiastically ordering new gowns for her visit to the Anstruther house-party, Anna waited impatiently for news from Mr Lowe. And when it finally came, she called for the carriage and went immediately to the manufactory to discuss the next steps with him in person.

'His lordship is definitely prepared to sell?' she asked.

'Subject to our offer, he says.'

'Understandable.' She took her usual chair and sat facing him across his desk. 'Do you have some thoughts on that?'

'Yes. Lord Reculver's earliest purchases retailed at around eight pounds and the more recent ones, between ten and eleven. I've made a list of which pieces he bought and how much he paid for each one.'

'Excellent. And their current value?'

'As a general rule of thumb?'

'Yes.'

'Well, then. Limited edition pieces hardly ever come up for resale, so the ones that *do* go for as much – or sometimes a bit more – as half again of the original price,' said the manager. Then, with a slight shrug, 'But that is at auction with more than one interested party bidding. Our case is different.'

'Quite. So we start below that. Thirteen for a piece that cost ten?'

He thought about it and finally said, 'I'd start a bit lower. Say twelve pounds? Then, as necessary, increase in ten shilling increments ... but drawing the line at anything beyond fifteen.'

'That's reasonable,' nodded Anna. Then, in response to his expression, 'There is something you wish to say?'

'Something I feel I *should* say, Miss Anna.'

'Then do so.'

'Even buying back the pieces at their original prices will be a significant investment. Buying them at up to half as much again ...' He paused. 'Well, there's no need for me to spell out the figures. I'm sure you've already thought of them.'

'I have. But, in addition to acquiring the Reculver collection for our exhibition, I would also be buying examples of my father's finest work.' She smiled suddenly, a rare smile that few people ever saw. 'That may be a sentimental reason rather than good business sense – but, to me, it's an added inducement. Sufficient, in fact, to persuade me to support the cost of the acquisition personally.'

Mr Lowe's brows soared. 'You – you'd buy the collection *yourself?*'

'That's what I said.'

'That is extremely generous. Are you quite sure?'

'Perfectly. But I'll want something in return.' The smile faded and she continued to hold his gaze. 'I want to conduct the valuation myself.'

If her offer had surprised him, this made him glad he was sitting down.

He said, 'May I ask why?'

'Because I know I could do it – and, if you're honest, you know it, too.'

'Well, yes. But –'

'Please don't tell me it would be inappropriate or anything else my mother will undoubtedly say. I want to play a more active role in the company and this is one way for me to do so. I can judge quality and condition and you have told me what I need to know regarding price. But I have another advantage over anyone you might send from the manufactory. It will have to be done in Lord Reculver's own home and will take more than a day, which means briefly being his lordship's guest.' She paused to let the words sink in. Then she said, 'I mixed with the aristocracy in London. I know how they behave and how many of them think – which gives me an advantage.'

'I daresay it does,' agreed Mr Lowe uneasily. 'But won't his lordship find it somewhat ... irregular? An unmarried young lady arriving to conduct a matter of business with him?'

'Not when that young lady's name is Hawthorne,' replied Anna flatly. 'And it will all be tediously proper, I assure you. I shall take my maid so that Mama doesn't have an apoplexy. And I would also like to take a senior female employee – Sarah Thompson, perhaps – ostensibly to assist me but, in reality, for the look of the thing.'

Mr Lowe knew he probably ought to nip this idea in the bud but doubted his ability to do so. There was a certain amount of logic to what she said; as for her ability to conduct the valuation as well, if not better, than anyone other than himself, he couldn't dispute that. Despite his wife's opposition, Oliver Hawthorne had managed to teach his daughter as thoroughly as he would have done a son. And the manager had no doubt that if Anna *had* been a son, she'd be sitting in his own chair right now. So he put his misgivings to one side and said, 'When do you want to go?'

'As soon as possible. I'm committed to ten days in Suffolk next month. So any time in the next two weeks would be best if it suits Lord Reculver's convenience.'

He nodded. 'And am I to tell his lordship that the valuer will be yourself?'

'In some respects, that might be best,' she conceded. 'But I'd sooner not give him the chance to delay things by raising objections ... so I think we'll present him with a *fait accompli*.' Rising, she shook out her skirts, then held out her hand. 'I leave the arrangements to you, Nathaniel. Let me know when they are in place.'

* * *

Mr Lowe wrote asking if the following week would suit Lord Reculver's convenience. His lordship replied that it would. Mr Lowe then told him to expect Hawthorne's senior valuer together with an assistant by mid-afternoon, Monday next. Daniel saw little need to reply – so he didn't. Instead, he went to communicate the news to his mother and sister.

'I can't imagine they'll be here more than a couple of days,' he said. 'But we'll need to arrange bedchambers for them, Mama.'

'I'll see to that,' said Rebecca quickly. 'Two of the guest rooms in the east wing can be made habitable quickest. They haven't been used in a while so it's just as well we have a few days' grace for cleaning and airing.'

Daniel smiled his thanks at her and then, looking back at their mother, 'It will also be necessary to move the collection from here to –'

'No!' said her ladyship forcefully. 'I'll give it up when I must and not before.'

'Mama ... they can't examine and catalogue the wares here in your sitting-room. *You* don't want them underfoot. *They* will need space to set the pieces out and separate those they've looked at from those they haven't. Since we never use the formal dining-room, I thought they might as well work there where they'll be out of everyone's way – unless you have some objection?'

She shrugged apathetically. 'No. I suppose not.'

Reaching over to take her mother's hand, Rebecca said, 'I know it's horrid, Mama, and I feel for you – truly, I do. But Daniel wouldn't be doing this if he had any other choice. Unfortunately, he doesn't. Surely you can see that?'

There was a long silence. Then, on a heavy sigh, Lady Reculver said, 'Yes.' And to Daniel, 'Take them away, then. Do it tomorrow while Becky and I are at church so I don't have to watch them disappearing. And now you may both leave me to enjoy your father's gifts while I still have them.'

Once outside the door, Rebecca said, 'Well … that might have been worse, I suppose.'

'Might it?'

'Yes. At least she didn't change her mind.'

'No. She just made me feel as if I'd killed her cat.'

She gave a tiny choke of laughter. 'That's absurd!'

'Is it?' He dragged a hand over his face. 'She blames me, Becky. And if she blames me *now*, what will she be like once those cabinets are empty?'

'She'll get over it. What else can she do?' She gave his arm a squeeze and said, 'Cheer up, Dan. At least *I'm* on your side.'

'I know – and I'm grateful. All this would be even harder if you weren't.'

Rebecca fell silent, wistfully wondering if her brother would ever be quite the same light-hearted man he'd been before. Since Papa's death, he didn't joke any more and rarely laughed either. Instead, he'd grown progressively quieter and more serious.

He looks perpetually tired, she thought. *And older.*

She said tentatively, 'After the people from Hawthorne's have been, why don't you go away for a few days? It would do you good. And if all goes as we hope with the scent bottles you'll be able to relax a little, won't you?'

Daniel pressed his lips together to stop himself telling her just how badly he wanted to get away. Away from the suffocating atmosphere in the house and the seemingly endless problems on the estate. Away from the crushing weight of worry that lived permanently inside him. In the months since Father's death it seemed that scarcely a day had gone by without something needing mending or patching up, all of it done on a shoestring and none of it a permanent solution. And then there was the knowledge that the only thing saving him from disaster had been Kit paying off the loan to Fleetwood's when he had. But Daniel never forgot for a second that the debt existed, that he still couldn't repay it – and that it was now owed to his oldest friend. As to the scent bottles, he didn't dare rely on them and wished Rebecca wouldn't either.

Finally, as lightly as he was able, he said, 'Perhaps. After we have the results of the valuation and if nothing dire happens in the meantime … and *if* Mama doesn't baulk at the idea … I'll think about it. But first things first.' *As usual*.

* * *

Anna waited until Mr Lowe notified her of the dates set with Lord Reculver before informing her mother of her intentions. As expected, she conjured up a storm.

'*What?* You're going to do *what?*' gasped Mrs Hawthorne, horrified. 'Are you *mad?* You can't *possibly* go and stay in a gentleman's home – and one, moreover, with whom you're not remotely acquainted. It isn't decent. Your reputation will be utterly destroyed!'

'No, it won't. Ruth will go with me and also one of the women from the – '

'Your maid and a – a working-class female? You think that makes it any better? It doesn't. And as if all that wasn't quite bad enough, *you* will be working as well – for all the world like a common employee or a tradesperson.'

'Not quite, Mama. I'll be Miss Hawthorne of Hawthorne's Porcelain.'

'That's not what Lord Reculver will see. He'll judge you by the company you keep and the fact you're doing a *job*. Under those circumstances, the last thing he'll see is a *lady*.'

Anna managed to refrain from asking what was so terrible about that. Instead, she said calmly, 'Whether he does or not, his lordship is a *gentleman*. What's more, he must be at least sixty years old, he's been a client of Hawthorne's for over two decades and – since he's preparing to sell a collection gathered over all that time – financially embarrassed.'

'Be that as it may, it is no reason for *you* to take a personal role in the matter. I am appalled, Anna! If this gets out, how are you ever to make a suitable match?'

'Since the only reason Lord Reculver is considering selling to us rather than going to auction is because he doesn't want the world knowing his business, there is no reason why it should *get out,* as you put it,' retorted Anna, fast losing patience. 'And as far as my marriage prospects go, any husband of mine – should there ever *be* one – will need to accept that Hawthorne's is part of my life and destined to remain so.' She stood up and, when her mother opened her mouth on what was undoubtedly further argument, said, 'Enough, Mama. I am going to Reculver Court the day after tomorrow and that is final.'

* * *

As soon as the house was behind her and the carriage turned on to the road, Anna experienced a sudden feeling of exhilaration. She'd *done* it. She had escaped the confines of her usual life, even if only for a few days. And who knew? Perhaps this was just the beginning.

Ruth, her maid, occupied the backward facing seat and gazed through the window in silence. At an inn on the outskirts of Worcester, they stopped to collect Mrs Thompson – a pleasant-looking widow of around forty and one of Hawthorne's most gifted painters. She settled beside Ruth and, while her valise was strapped on, said, 'I'd like to thank you for this opportunity, Miss Hawthorne. It's been a good while since I travelled more than a couple of miles from home … not to mention having the chance to see such a rare collection as his lordship has.''

'Mr Lowe gave you his lists?'

'He did, Miss. They're in my bag. I reckon they'll be useful for ticking off the pieces as we see them and maybe adding a mark regarding condition.'

Anna nodded but said, 'It may be best to make our own lists for that along with an initial suggestion as to value. But we can decide on that once the task is in front of us.'

Conversation after that was minimal and Anna was glad since it gave her an opportunity to consider something she'd said to her mother.

Any husband of mine will need to accept that Hawthorne's is part of my life and destined to remain so.

After her semi-disastrous London season, she had largely given up on the idea of marriage. In the first place, she had never met a gentleman she had really *liked*, let alone one with whom she could imagine any kind of future. And, more importantly, she suspected that a husband's opinions on her involvement with Hawthorne's would be much the same as Mama's. The only difference would be that a husband could enforce his will on her more successfully than Mama could.

Now, for the first time, she took a moment to question that assumption. Because, while it was true that *most* gentlemen probably shared her mother's rigid views on how a lady ought to behave and what a wife should or should not do … surely there must be some who did not? Men with a more modern outlook and an open mind?

In theory at least, Anna supposed that one of those *might* be a better alternative to spinsterhood and a life with Mama. *But where to find one?* she asked herself with wry amusement. *Does the species actually exist? Or might I as well go hunting for unicorns?*

* * *

By the time the carriage turned into the drive of Reculver Court, it was a quarter before four and all three travellers were extremely grateful to reach journey's end.

The butler opened the carriage door and let down the steps … then froze, his eyes travelling to each of their faces in turn before settling on Anna's. He said, 'Pardon me, ma'am. But perhaps there is some mistake? We are expecting two gentle—' He broke off and tried again. 'That is to say —'

'You are expecting the senior valuer from Hawthorne's Porcelain,' cut in Anna, extending her hand in a manner which had him automatically offering his arm so she could alight. 'I am she. My assistant, Mrs Thompson and Jenkins, my maid. And you are?'

'Flynn, ma'am. Lord Reculver's butler.' Clearly unsure of his ground, he helped the other women down and told the solitary footman on the steps behind him to take the luggage to the east wing. Then, once more to Anna and leading the way inside, 'Please follow me, ma'am. I will summon the housekeeper to show you to your rooms. And if I may have your card, I will apprise his lordship of your arrival.'

Stripping off her gloves and mentally kicking herself for not having anticipated the need for a card, Anna said firmly, 'It would be best if I first made his lordship's acquaintance – since, if you were expecting a man, presumably so was he. Is he available?'

'I will ascertain, ma'am. But who shall I say – ?'

He stopped as a pleasant voice from above called, 'Did I hear a carriage, Flynn?'

A tall, auburn-haired gentleman ran down to the turn of the stairs … before coming to an abrupt halt on the half-landing and staring at the trio of women below him.

He wasn't the only one who froze. Anna did, too.

She had seen this man – presumably Lord Reculver's son – before, although not for some time. On perhaps a handful of occasions, she'd watched from an upstairs window when he came to the school to take his much younger, dark-haired sister home for the holidays; had watched him catch her about the waist and whirl her around, laughing, plainly as delighted to see her as she was him. And unseen above them, Anna had thought him, not only the most handsome man she'd ever seen, but something much more. He'd been warm, good-natured and wholly unembarrassed by a public show of affection most other gentlemen were incapable of. With her unwanted debut creeping ever closer, it was natural to wonder, somewhat wistfully, if she might meet him in London because … well, just *because*.

She *hadn't* met him in London; but she was going to meet him now. And judging by his expression it wasn't going to be nearly as pleasant as she'd once thought it might be.

CHAPTER THREE

Daniel's gaze travelled over all three women, two of them clearly servants, and came to rest on the one clad in a smart, dark green carriage dress who was clearly in charge. But who the devil *were* they? Surely they couldn't be from Hawthorne's? *Could* they?

He raised enquiring brows at Flynn, currently staring helplessly back at him. Then, before he could ask the obvious question, the woman in green stepped forward, saying briskly, 'Good afternoon, sir. As I daresay you are aware, Lord Reculver is expecting us.'

Another surprise; two, in fact. She spoke like a lady. And since she clearly didn't think *he* was Reculver, she presumably thought she was here to meet his father. Inclining his head, Daniel made a leisurely descent to the hall, saying, 'And you are?'

'Anna Hawthorne, sir. Senior valuer for the company – and also, for the last two years, its proprietor.'

Mama's scent bottles are worth the owner's time, are they? That's interesting, he thought. But said, 'How do you do, ma'am?' He strolled towards her, held out his hand and when she placed hers in it, bowed slightly before instantly releasing her. 'Please forgive my surprise. I made the obvious but mistaken assumption that the valuer sent by your company would be a man.'

'As might usually be the case, sir. But with his lordship being such a regular and valued client over so many years, I felt that taking care of his collection personally was the least we could do.'

'How very civil of you.'

'Not at all. Might I briefly meet his lordship to introduce myself?'

'You have already done so,' he replied smoothly. 'My father died six months ago. *I* am Reculver now.'

Her colour rose, her mouth opened, then closed and she swallowed.

'Oh. I ... see. I'm so sorry. We had no idea, Please excuse the misunderstanding and accept our condolences, belated though they are.'

'Think nothing of it, ma'am.' He glanced beyond her. 'Ah, Mrs Dawson. Please show Miss Hawthorne and her ... companions ... to their rooms and – '

'Mrs Thompson is here to assist me with the valuation, my lord,' cut in Anna, gesturing to the older of the two women behind her. 'Jenkins is my maid.'

'I see. Well, if there is anything you need, please ask Mrs Dawson. We dine informally at seven. My mother is unlikely to join us but my sister will be there – so you need not be concerned for the proprieties.'

'I'm not.'

The statement had clearly been involuntary because she looked as if she wanted to clap a hand over her mouth, causing Daniel to repress a faint smile along with his inclination to say, *Of course you're not. If you were, you wouldn't be here, would you?*

Instead, and with another slight bow, he said, 'Until dinner, then.' And walked away.

Once upstairs in a pleasant if slightly shabby bedchamber, Anna collapsed on the window seat, groaning inwardly whilst the housekeeper and footman came and went with hot water and trays of tea and sandwiches.

That wasn't the best start, was it? she thought. *Actually, it could scarcely have been worse. And, aside from the good looks Ruth is busy cooing over, that man downstairs wasn't the one I last saw from a schoolroom window four – no, five – years ago.* This time an audible groan escaped her. *But how did we not know his father was dead? At least if we had I'd have been better prepared. As it was, the whole encounter – short as it was – knocked me off-balance with the result that I looked like an idiot. What on earth can he be thinking?* And then, *I need to pull myself together. If I don't, dinner is going to be a nightmare.*

Daniel's thoughts, had she been privy to them, wouldn't have made her feel better.

Medium, was the word that cropped up most. Medium height and build; medium brown hair and eyes that might have been either blue or grey. He rather suspected that if, without seeing her again, he was asked to describe her in twenty-four hours' time, he'd struggle to do it. Not that that mattered in the least. She was here in person and she owned Hawthorne's Porcelain ... so she had the authority to make a commitment without the necessity of gaining someone else's approval. She was also starting with the handicap of arriving ignorant of with whom she would be dealing. All that was to his advantage. Perhaps he ought to dust off what was left of his charm and try using it. One never knew. It might work.

Having changed for dinner, he tracked Rebecca to Mama's sitting-room where she had been trying, so far without success, to persuade their mother to dine downstairs.

'No,' her ladyship was saying for what was probably the fifth time, 'I shall have a tray in my rooms while this – this *female* is here. I would hesitate to call her a lady.'

Daniel blinked. 'Who told you the valuer is a woman?'

'Mrs Dawson. What's more, the assistant she's brought with her works in the manufactory as a *painter*. Can you imagine?'

'Why not?' said Rebecca unexpectedly. 'She must be very skilled at what she does or she wouldn't be employed to do it – never mind coming here to help the lady owner.'

'Don't tell me,' said Daniel. 'Mrs Dawson again?'

'Yes.' She grinned at him. 'The quickest way to find out anything is to ask the servants. You know that as well as I do.'

Ignoring this, he said, 'So you've already worked out that the Anna Hawthorne currently in the green room and the Anna Hawthorne you were at school with are one and the same?'

'Yes. But she won't remember me. She left when I was fourteen.'

'Remind her, then. It may spare us some excruciating silences over dinner.'

* * *

When Anna was shown into what she suspected was actually a breakfast-parlour, she found the viscount and his sister already there, conversing by a window overlooking the garden. Both turned as she entered and, smiling, Miss Shelbourne immediately moved towards her saying, 'Miss Hawthorne ... you won't recall it, I daresay, but we were at Miss Winslow's together. How lovely to see you again.'

Anna blinked. As far as she could remember, they had never exchanged two words with each other; and her reason for remembering Miss Shelbourne wasn't one she could admit to. For want of something better, she said, 'Thank you. It's kind of you to say so.'

Waving that aside, Rebecca plunged into a series of light-hearted '*do you remember?*' reminiscences about school, leaving Daniel free to move away and pour three small glasses of sherry – now, a rarely indulged luxury – whilst listening to Miss Hawthorne's replies. The stiltedness of these suggested that drawing-room small talk wasn't something with which she was very adept. But finally, he heard her say stiffly, 'Please allow me to say how sorry I was to hear of your father's death, Miss Shelbourne. As his lordship may have told you, I was unaware of it until today.'

'I didn't tell her that, as it happens,' remarked Daniel. 'But I'm sure she knows.'

Rebecca laughed. 'My spies are everywhere!' And more seriously, 'We have few visitors and the servants rarely see a new face. So when they *do* …' And she shrugged as if that explained everything.

Still clutching her barely-touched glass, Anna murmured, 'Of course. You have yet to put off your blacks. It is a difficult time.'

'It is. But the only reason I haven't yet come out of black is because Mama becomes distressed every time I raise the subject.'

'Then stop *talking* about it and *do* it,' said Daniel flatly. 'No one outside the estate sees you – and, even if they did, it's been over six months.' Then, without waiting for her to reply, he turned smoothly to Anna and said, 'What is your opinion, ma'am?'

Taken by surprise, Anna narrowly avoided choking over her sherry and managed to say that she had worn black for some ten months following her father's death. Then, 'But it was different for me. I had meetings with lawyers, accountants, suppliers and the senior management of the company. I was twenty-one. I had to look capable … and black made me appear older.'

For the first time, Daniel eyed her with some interest. But before he could speak, Rebecca said, 'That all sounds rather daunting.'

'Not particularly – though I had a great deal to learn about the financial and legal side of the business.'

'And the manufacturing processes?' queried Daniel idly.

'No. Thanks to my father, I was already extremely well-versed in that.'

A tap at the door heralded Flynn announcing that dinner was about to be served.

Daniel nodded, set the empty glasses aside and pulled out a chair for Miss Hawthorne. Then, over vegetable soup, simple but well-cooked roast lamb and a raspberry tart, he set himself the task of behaving more like the perfect, aristocratic host he was supposed to be than a man facing financial ruin on a daily basis. He had even told Flynn to serve wine with the meal – something else they usually did without these days.

By the time they had finished eating, he rather thought he had Miss Hawthorne's measure. To a large degree, the late Mr Hawthorne had reared her as he might have done a son so that, when the time came, she could take over his mantle within the manufactory. But a single, colourless reference to her London season caused Daniel to suspect that *Mrs* Hawthorne had other, loftier ambitions for her daughter ... ambitions that remained, and would probably continue to remain, unfulfilled. As for the lady's *own* ambitions ... he couldn't decide what they were, although he got the impression that her only passion was the porcelain factory. Cynically, he wondered how long it would be before she asked to see the scent bottles.

In the drawing-room, leaving Rebecca to fill what might otherwise have been an awkward silence whilst pouring the tea, he watched Miss Hawthorne without appearing to do so. The mid-brown hair was neatly but not elaborately dressed; her only jewellery was a string of very fine pearls; and the lilac silk evening gown, devoid of all trimming, was discreet enough to pass for half-mourning. Did she always dress so conservatively? Had her wardrobe been chosen for what she'd expected to be a visit to an elderly viscount? Or did she eschew frills and furbelows for the same reason she'd stayed in black longer than was strictly necessary? The need to appear *capable*.

He waited until Rebecca had finished fussing with the tea things before entering the conversation with a question which might, if he allowed it to do so, lead in an inflammatory direction.

'Your assistant, Mrs Thompson ... I understand she is one of your senior painters. Do you employ many women?'

'Yes. Approximately a third of our entire workforce is female ... as are over half of our painters.'

'Interesting. Is there any reason for that?'

Anna's brows rose. 'They are suited to the work and good at what they do.'

'So ... not because women are cheaper to employ?'

Far from annoying her, this won him a small but genuine smile.

'No – because, at Hawthorne's, they aren't.'

Faintly taken aback as much by the smile as by her words, Daniel said, 'You pay the women the same as you pay the men?'

'If they're doing the same job, yes. We always have. There *are* differences in the wage structure throughout the company, of course – but those are based on the level of skill or physical abilities required in the various areas, not on whether a worker is male or female.' She shrugged. 'We like to *keep* our people, my lord. We don't want them cutting their teeth with us, then taking their talent and experience elsewhere. So we pay them fairly and look after them.'

'Look after them in what way?' he asked.

'All sorts of ways.' Happy to be on more familiar ground, Anna allowed herself to relax. 'The areas prone to fumes or dust are kept well-ventilated. The rooms where fine work is done have good light from north-facing windows. The men who work with the kilns are supplied with boots and protective clothing to shield them from the heat.' She paused and, as if finally hitting her stride, added, 'Then there are the more general things. Throughout cold weather, three of our employees' wives cook and serve hot meals on the premises. The workers pay two pence for a plate, the labour and ingredients for which cost around sixpence and the company bears the difference. In the case of illness, we offer assistance. We even have a system in place to provide child care if necessary.' She paused again, spreading expressive hands. 'Some of these things, such as adequate light and ventilation have been in place since my father founded the company. Others began as experiments which proved successful enough to be worth making standard practice.' And with the merest suggestion of a shrug, 'As I said, we look after our people.'

'So you do.' It was Rebecca who spoke. 'It's … impressive.'

'It's more than that,' said Daniel dryly. 'It's unheard of and bordering on revolutionary. One wonders what your business rivals make of it.'

'That is up to them.'

'Indeed.' He surveyed her thoughtfully. All the time she'd been speaking, animation had brought a touch of colour to her cheeks and a spark to her eyes. Having got her talking and in order to work his way around to a particular point, he said, 'If it isn't out of place, may I ask why the items purchased by my father are of particular interest to you?'

'Because of the visitors.'

'The visitors?' echoed Rebecca, unwittingly helping him out.

Anna nodded. 'During the last two summers, Mr Lowe and I have become aware of an increasing number of people asking to tour the manufactory. It's not *just* Hawthorne's, you understand. Spode, Derby and Wedgwood are all experiencing the same thing – as, I believe, are the cotton and woollen mills of the north. Apparently, seeing how things are made is becoming a popular pastime. So we thought to offer an additional attraction in the form of an exhibition showcasing the very *best* of Hawthorne ware over the years. And it occurred to us that your late father's collection would make a splendid addition to that.'

'Why?' asked Daniel. 'Doesn't the manufactory keep examples of everything it makes – or at least have the ability to recreate it?'

'Not in the case of the limited edition pieces. Six of each design are hand-made by the same craftsman … and of those six, no two are identical. Each has some small, unique detail of its own. It's that which makes them so sought after.'

'I'm sure. But why *our* father's collection specifically?' asked Daniel, his mild tone giving no indication of the trap he was preparing.

'All the scent bottles in it were designed by *my* father,' she replied proudly. 'Many of them were also *made* by him in earlier years and those are irreplaceable.'

'I see. And this isn't true of any of the other collectors who buy from you?'

'It's true of some. But none of them are currently – ' She stopped abruptly, aghast at what she'd been about to say.

'None of the others might currently consider selling?' he asked gently. And then, after a brief, uncomfortable pause, 'It's alright, Miss Hawthorne. I won't ask how or from whom you learned that I might be open to offers. Since you are here to value the collection, the way in which that came about is of little consequence now, is it?'

'No.' The damage having already been done and deciding that her best course was to brazen it out, Anna said crisply, 'Very well, sir. Since we are speaking plainly ... the whisper that reached us has not and will not be passed on elsewhere. But, from it, Mr Lowe and I deduced that, if you *were* interested in selling, it was possible – even likely – that you would prefer to do so discreetly and might therefore consider Hawthorne's rather than a public auction. Were we correct?'

His brows rising slightly, Daniel thought, *You really* do *favour the direct approach, don't you? Fortunately, two can play at that game.*

'Yes. But don't also conclude that my preference for discretion will enable you to buy the collection at the lowest possible price,' returned Daniel pleasantly. 'It won't.'

Angry at her own mistake and angrier still with him for exploiting it, Anna stood up. 'Then we understand each other, my lord. I take it that the pieces will be ready for Mrs Thompson and me to begin work first thing tomorrow?'

'They already are. Flynn will conduct you to the formal dining-room where you will have space and be free from interruptions.'

'Thank you.' She gave a jerky nod first to Rebecca and then to the viscount. 'Good night, Miss Shelbourne ... my lord.' And stalked out.

As soon as the door closed behind her, Rebecca said, 'That was wicked of you. I scarcely knew where to look.'

'The gloves were bound to come off at some point,' he replied. 'Better now than later, don't you think?'

'I suppose so – though you might have been a bit more subtle about it.'

He gave a short laugh. 'Becky, that lady is about as subtle as a mallet to the head. She has no idea how to make trivial conversation and is only comfortable talking about business. It's scarcely surprising that her London season wasn't a howling success.'

'How do you know it wasn't?' she countered.

'From her tone when she mentioned it. That and the fact that it hasn't been repeated despite clearly failing to achieve the usual result. She's not married, after all. And she must be – what? Twenty-three? Twenty-four?'

With a slight shake of her head, Rebecca came to her feet. She said, 'I don't think I like you very much in this mood, Daniel.'

In truth, he wasn't sure he liked himself much either. But if he was to drag his family out of the pit it was in, he'd better start getting used to that. He said, 'Go, then.' And with a slightly twisted smile, 'Say goodnight to Mama for me.'

* * *

Anna lay awake replaying that final, disastrous conversation over and over in her mind and thinking of at least six ways she could have taken it in a different direction. Then, abandoning this before she became so agitated that she'd lie awake all night, she contemplated the *really* maddening thing about Lord blasted Reculver; his ability to cut the ground from beneath one's feet with a smile and in such a pleasant tone that one didn't realise what he was doing until it was too late. The man was dangerous.

Well, she knew that now, didn't she? Enough not to make the mistake of taking him at face value in future.

Try that again, my lord, she thought grimly, *and I'll be ready for you. As for what I'll pay for your father's collection ... I'll offer the going rate and not a farthing more. And if you need to sell – which, given that this house is woefully understaffed, it seems that you do – you either take it or advertise your empty pockets to the world by going to auction.*

Yes, Anna assured herself. *That's more like it.*

And she would not – absolutely would *not* let his image creep into her mind. Just because everything about him from the thick auburn hair to the dramatic cheekbones and the merest hint of a cleft in his chin made her want to look and go on looking … she would not think about *any* of it.

Daniel Shelbourne, Lord Devious Reculver was a devil in disguise. And if she forgot that for a minute, there was no saying what folly she might end up committing.

CHAPTER FOUR

On the previous evening, Mrs Thompson had dined with the housekeeper in her private parlour and, according to Ruth whilst dressing Anna's hair, was taking her breakfast in the kitchen with the other servants. So Anna went downstairs alone, was directed to the room where they'd dined last night ... and found it occupied by his lordship's sister and mother.

Rebecca bade her a cheerful good morning and told her to help herself from the sideboard. The dowager viscountess looked her over from head to foot and said nothing. Scowling at her mother behind Anna's back and in a tone clearly conveying the message *Don't be rude!,* Rebecca said, 'This is Miss Hawthorne, Mama.'

'Of course. Who else would she be?' And, as Anna took her seat, 'So ... you are the young woman who will be affixing price tickets to my scent bottles, are you?'

Your scent bottles? thought Anna. *Oh.*

'Not exactly, my lady. Mrs Thompson and I will merely examine the pieces – '

'Examine them for what?'

'Any imperfections or – '

'You mean damage, don't you?'

'Well, yes. But – '

'You won't find any,' said her ladyship. And with the satisfied air of one who knows she has had the last word, turned back to her coddled egg.

Anna sipped her tea and nibbled a slice of toast she didn't really want.

Groaning inwardly, Rebecca wondered if she was destined for two days or more of playing the peace-maker. Wishing she could simply get up and walk out, she said, 'Daniel had the large dining-table fully extended and the pieces all laid out for you in readiness. Don't worry – one of us was there the whole time to ensure every care was taken.'

'Thank you. That all sounds very suitable,' replied Anna politely.

'And if there is anything else you need, please don't hesitate to ask.'

'I won't, though there shouldn't be anything.' She hesitated and then, because the girl was obviously trying to ease the tension in the air, added, 'We brought all the necessary information regarding the original purchases with us to help determine current value. And we'll be wearing gloves to handle the pieces, as is standard procedure.'

'How long do you expect it to take?' asked the dowager.

As long as necessary, Anna thought but said, 'No more than two days, I hope. We won't inconvenience you any longer than we must, ma'am. And to that end, I should go and make a start.'

'Of course,' murmured Rebecca. Once again, her mother said nothing.

The household's only footman showed Anna to the dining parlour where Sarah Thompson had already begun ticking off pieces against Mr Lowe's lists. Anna, by contrast, stopped dead three steps into the room and, taking in the array in front of her, said faintly, 'Good God. This is ... actually, I'm not sure there's a word for it.'

'That's exactly what I thought, ma'am. I mean, we knew how many there were but that doesn't prepare you for seeing all of them together like this, does it?'

'No. No, it doesn't.'

Anna walked slowly towards and then along the table. One hundred and four scent bottles ... every one of them different, every one of them an example of imagination and exquisite workmanship and each with some element linking it to the season for which it had been created. There were urns tumbling with greenery and individually sculpted blossoms. There were animals of every type, both real and fabled. And there were figurines by the dozen. Gods, goddesses and demons from mythology; famous people from history; characters from the works of Shakespeare and the more recent plays of Mr Sheridan. Then there were the pieces, like the couple skating or the young girl at her music lesson which contained more than one figure. Seen separately, each was a miniature work of art. Seen all together like this, she suspected that the display would stop anyone's breath for a moment.

Then Sarah said, 'There's one missing.'

'What?' asked Anna vaguely.

'I began by counting them. The snuff boxes are all there but there's only a hundred and three bottles – so one is missing. We'll know which it is when I've finished checking them against the list.'

Anna gave an absent nod. When she and Nathaniel Lowe had discussed acquiring Lord Reculver's collection she had known she wanted it – or believed that she did on some half-sentimental, half-theoretical level. But now she had actually *seen* it, everything was changed. In some unexpected way she didn't begin to understand, it called to her, making her burningly aware that she didn't merely *want* it. She simply *had to have it* ... whatever it took.

Oh damn and blast, she thought. *I can't let that show. If his lordship suspects, even for a* second, *how badly I want it, he'll have the only advantage I haven't already given to him. He'll win. I'll end up paying whatever he asks ... he'll smile that deceitful, devastating smile and .. no. No, no, no. That can't happen.*

Something else nagged at her. She and Nathaniel had been of the opinion that Lord Reculver could obtain a better return by selling the pieces separately at auction. Now, having experienced the potent lure of the collection when seen as a whole, Anna was no longer sure that was true. There were a number of serious ceramic collectors, some of whom were easily wealthy enough to buy what stood on this table outright; she could even name three of them. And she rather thought that if that particular trio stood where she was standing now, the ensuing bidding war would far exceed what she expected to pay.

'It's the peacock from the summer collection of 1776,' announced Sarah at length. And when Miss Hawthorne gazed blankly back at her, 'The missing scent bottle?'

'Ah yes. Well done. Make a note of it, please.' And dragging her mind back to the task in hand, 'I suggest we start with the snuff boxes, since there are only twelve of them. What figure has Mr Lowe put on this silver-mounted *Orpheus and Eurydice*?'

Just over an hour later the door opened upon Rebecca, who said, 'Tell me to go away, if you wish. I only came to ask if you would like tea ... and to tell you that the doors over there lead to the back terrace, should you wish to take a break at some point and go out for some air.'

Without glancing around, Anna said, 'Yes. Thank you, Miss Shelbourne. As for –'

'Please do call me Rebecca.'

'Rebecca, then. As for the tea ... later, perhaps?'

'Of course.' There was an odd little pause during which Rebecca hovered, twisting her hands together. Then she said baldly, 'Actually, I'd appreciate it if we could have a private word. I promise it won't take long.'

Now what? thought Anna, impatiently. But said, 'Very well. Carry on without me, Sarah – and if there are queries, just put them to one side.' And to Rebecca, gesturing to the terrace doors, 'Shall we?'

Once outside with the doors closed behind them, Rebecca walked a little further from the house in silence and finally said, 'May I count on your discretion, Miss Hawthorne?'

'Certainly.'

'Well, then ... as you heard earlier, the scent bottles belong to my mother, all of them being gifts from my father. Naturally, she is reluctant to part with them – hence her attitude towards you. I wanted you to know that it isn't at all *personal* and that she isn't usually rude.'

'I had assumed as much,' replied Anna. 'But thank you for telling me.' She waited. Then, when Rebecca continued to stand there, hands clenched tight over each other, 'Was there anything else?'

'Yes. Please don't judge my brother too harshly either. He – he inherited unexpected problems which he is dealing with as best he can. He's worried about many things but mostly about Mama and me.' She looked Anna in the eye and added, 'He's doing what he must. And he's finding it hard because it requires him to set aside who he *is* in favour of who he *needs* to be. Do you understand what I mean?'

'I think so ... although I'm not at all sure why you are telling me.'

'I'm not, either,' Rebecca admitted. Then, in a rush as if the floodgates had opened, 'Probably because he's the best brother in the world and I can't bear *anyone* to think ill of him when what is happening to him isn't his *fault!*' She dashed a hand across her eyes and said brightly, 'There. That's all I wanted to say. Thank you for listening.' With a vague wave in the direction of the house, she added, 'I'll go back in a different way.' And sped off.

Anna watched her go, various thoughts jostling each other in her head until just two images remained. A handsome, auburn-haired gentleman laughing and twirling his little sister around below that schoolroom window; and the rare smiles and watchful eyes of Viscount Reculver after dinner last night. The same man ... and yet, as she'd already concluded, not.

He'd asked about Hawthorne's and seemed genuinely interested. That had encouraged her to talk and, as usually happened, she'd let her enthusiasm carry her away to the point where she'd said more than she meant to. She could not, in all conscience, blame him for what she'd done herself.

Thoughtfully, she walked back inside wondering just how bad things *really* were here at Reculver.

* * *

Daniel spent the day as he spent nearly every day. The morning, at his desk, working out which bills he could or should pay and which must wait; and the afternoon riding around the estate dealing with other problems entirely ... often by rolling up his sleeves and doing what he could with his own hands; inept though he was, the tenants appreciated him trying and regarded his efforts with a sort of sympathetic indulgence.

Today he'd been attempting to repair the damaged thatch on Mr Turner's barn roof – Mr Turner himself being laid low with a touch of ague and Mrs Turner worrying about coming rain. Since, as usual, Daniel hadn't known how best to do the job, a couple of old fellows, too ancient to climb ladders themselves, sat below offering the benefit of their experience. Most of this being contradictory, it was less helpful than it might have been. On another occasion, Daniel might have found it funny. Today, however, he was merely aware of it taking twice as long as it should, of the scratches on his hands and the ache in his back. And worse than any of this, that he was going to spend the evening making conversation over dinner with Miss Hawthorne and, for Rebecca's sake, trying not to say anything contentious. He had also, he told himself, better insist on Mother joining them – and being as pleasant as she would be towards any other guest.

He returned home with barely enough time to make himself presentable and took the shortcut across the garden from the stables. It was typical of his luck in general that he swung on to the path leading to the rear terrace and walked virtually straight into Miss Hawthorne.

She had already changed into the same lilac gown as last night.

He, by contrast, was filthy, dishevelled and already not in the best of humours. Unfortunately, common courtesy didn't permit him to simply nod and walk on. He said, 'Forgive both my appearance and my haste, ma'am. I am later than I intended and in urgent need of a bath – but I look forward to – '

'Go, sir,' she said. 'Do not delay on my account. Just go.'

'Thank you,' replied Daniel with real gratitude. And strode away.

Anna stared after him, taking in the state of his coat and hands and the absence of vest or cravat. All these were the answer to the question she'd been pondering this morning after that peculiar conversation with his sister. Titled gentlemen did not normally do manual labour. Those she had met in London, for example, would have been horrified at the mere thought and probably physically incapable of it if they'd tried. Lord Reculver, she suspected, had muscles to match those splendid shoulders and –

She checked her wandering thoughts. She had no business noticing his lordship's shoulders or anything else about his person. What she *could* consider was that if he had spent part of his day working, there was either a need or a very good reason for it. Or both.

Inside the house and passing his sister en route for his bedchamber, Daniel said, 'I'm late, Becky. Please tell Mother that I expect her to join us downstairs this evening and to be on her best behaviour – as I shall be. Make sure she understands that it is *not* a request.'

Rebecca watched him disappear into his room and shook her head ruefully. Mama, she reflected, would do as he'd asked. But she wasn't going to like it.

Returning to the house just in time to avoid the first spots of rain, Anna was informed that she would find the ladies in the drawing-room. She hoped Lady Reculver's mood was better than it had been at breakfast. She had avoided the possibility of a chance meeting throughout the day by asking for a luncheon tray to be served to Sarah and herself in the dining-room. They'd eaten and continued working until around four o'clock. Then she'd insisted on leaving everything tidy for the next day before telling Sarah to go and rest for an hour or two. She herself sat reading through the notes they had made before going upstairs to wash and change – after which, realising she had a little time in hand, she'd decided on a stroll in the garden to clear her head. Her meeting with his lordship had not helped at all in that regard.

When she entered the drawing-room, Rebecca rose and smiled at her, saying, 'You seem to have been hard at it all day. How are things progressing?'

'Very well, thank you.' Anna curtsied to the dowager and added, 'It is a very fine collection, my lady. I don't blame you for wishing to keep it. So would I, in your shoes.'

'If you and my son reach an agreement, you *will* be keeping it, won't you?'

'Mama,' began Rebecca warningly.

Anna stopped her with a quick shake of her head, saying, 'No. Her ladyship is perfectly right. I *do* want the collection on permanent exhibition at Hawthorne's.'

She paused, suddenly seeing a way of making this easier – not just for Lady Reculver but also for her son and daughter – and almost opened her mouth to say so. Then she put the idea aside for consideration later. She'd blurted out something without due thought last evening and didn't intend to make the same mistake again. Fortunately, however, there was something else she could offer.

Looking Lady Reculver in the eye, she said slowly, 'One of the scent bottles is missing – as, I think, you are fully aware.'

'And if it is and I am?' came the sharp reply.

'It's quite all right, ma'am,' returned Anna. 'I know *which* it is and can perfectly understand why you would wish to keep it.'

'What? No. You can't possibly –' She stopped, looking confused. Then, 'Well?'

'It's the silver-mounted peacock. The last bottle your late husband purchased. Of *course* you wish to keep it.'

Entering in time to hear these last words, Daniel said, 'Keep what?'

No one answered him. Rebecca, because she wasn't sure what was going on; Anna and the dowager because they were locked in eye to eye combat. Then Anna dissolved the tension by saying, 'And I see no reason why – even if Hawthorne's *do* acquire the rest of the collection which, as we are all aware, is by no means certain yet – you should not do so.'

'You ... you don't?'

'No. It would be foolish of me to quibble over a single piece of particular sentimental value, ma'am – or even two such. So perhaps you might also like to keep the *first* bottle ... if you can recall which that was?'

'It was the *Music Lesson*,' replied her ladyship promptly, her voice not quite steady. 'The young girl with the lute and – and her tutor looking on over her shoulder.'

'Yes,' agreed Anna simply. 'It was.'

'You are saying that I may have that one, too?'

'Not that exactly – since the piece is yours, ma'am. But it need not be included in the collection for the purposes of the sale. I will send it to your rooms in the morning.'

'That is ... generous. I hardly know what to say.'

'Thank you?' suggested Rebecca.

'Yes. Of course. Thank you.' Lady Reculver dabbed at her eyes. 'Forgive me. I had not expected this and fear that I am a – a trifle overcome.'

Smiling faintly, Daniel broke what might have become an awkward pause by saying lightly, 'Turning the tables on me by taking the moral high ground, Miss Hawthorne?'

'Merely not making this any more painful than it needs to be,' she retorted. '*One* of us should, don't you think?'

'Oh – undoubtedly. And when I find a similarly inexpensive concession you may be sure I will offer it.'

'Stop it, Daniel,' muttered Rebecca.

'No,' said Anna. 'He's right. It *does* cost me very little.' And bluntly to Daniel, 'In due course, I shall be making you an offer, my lord. So perhaps this conversation should be postponed until I do?'

'Oh – quite.' He turned away to pour sherry. 'I take it you have made satisfactory progress today?'

'Very much so. We have valued all of the snuff boxes and eighteen of the scent bottles. I had hoped we might finish tomorrow ... but suspect it may take a further half day. I hope this will not present a problem?'

'It won't.' Daniel handed glasses first to his mother and to Anna, then his sister before picking up his own. 'Mama, is there something in the stillroom that will reduce a fever?'

'Of course. Why?'

'Send some to Turner's farm, please. Harry is laid low at present. And the sooner he recovers, the sooner he can repair his own barn roof.'

'I'll take it,' offered Rebecca. Then, 'Is that what you were doing this afternoon?'

'For my sins, yes – under the critical eyes of Grandfather Turner and Uncle Zachary.'

She laughed. 'Oh dear.'

'I'm glad you find it funny. I wish I could.'

'It *isn't* funny,' said his mother firmly. 'And neither is it either fitting or dignified. I don't know why you do it – it can't be necessary.'

Not in any way you'd understand, thought Daniel. *But it's necessary to me. I can't mend the big problems ... but helping mend the little ones stops me going insane and buys me credit with the tenants by showing that I* care *and would do more if I could.*

But there was no use saying that, so he said instead, 'I know that. But it's cheaper than the alternative.'

'Which is what, exactly?'

'Draining the five acre field at Old Fallow. Lending a hand with the barn will stop Harry Turner asking about it for a week or two.' Daniel drained his glass and summoned a grin. 'It's not all bad news. At least the exercise must be good for me. Now ... Flynn is doubtless ready to serve dinner. Shall we go through?'

* * *

Later, sitting alone by the dying fire, Daniel tried to decide what to make of Anna Hawthorne. He couldn't work out whether her generosity to Mother had been made out of kindness or a desire to wrong-foot him. It could be either one. Unless his reading of her was completely adrift, she was extremely shrewd when it came to matters of business and accustomed to considering all the possible angles.

It occurred to him that, as little as six or seven months ago, she'd have run rings around him. Now, courtesy of his current troubles, he had learned a good many things – enough, he hoped, to hold his own when they started talking money.

As presumably always happened in such dealings, her first offer would not be the best price she was prepared to pay, so he knew he could refuse that one with impunity. The same might also be true of the second. But after that? After that, he wouldn't be sure how far he dared push her ... or whether, in fact, he dared push at all. Everything depended on how badly she wanted the collection and, at present, he couldn't read her well enough to decide that.

He'd thought he had her measure. She was blunt, single-minded and every inch the business woman. But her voluntary surrender of two of the scent bottles had muddied the water. Had she really done that purely in order to make his mother less opposed to selling the rest? Or had she some other, possibly devious motive he hadn't perceived yet? Just because he couldn't figure out what it might be, didn't mean there wasn't one.

God, he thought, tipping his head against the chair back. *I'm so bloody sick of thinking and guessing and* trying. *It's like emptying the sea with a bucket. I know it can't be done but I keep trudging back and forth with the pail regardless. Even if she offers what Father paid and hands me a thousand pounds, plus whatever the snuff boxes are worth ... what is the best use for it and how much good will it do? I can mend some cottages, replace some antiquated machinery and drain that damned field. But none of that will be enough to make the estate pay. And unless I can do* that, *not only will there be no Season for Becky, it will merely be a matter of time before I'm back exactly where I am right now. Trapped in one of Dante's circles of hell.*

CHAPTER FIVE

After breakfast and true to her word, Anna asked Flynn to take the *Music Lesson* to Lady Reculver's rooms. If Sarah Thompson was surprised by this gesture she kept it to herself. Miss Hawthorne was neither stupid nor impetuous so when she did something it was always for a reason.

In the dining-room, the morning passed much as it had yesterday. They continued appraising the scent bottles, consulting Mr Lowe's notes regarding each one's original purchase price and marking down an estimate of its possible current resale value. Anna could see the likely total cost of the collection escalating rapidly but refused to let it daunt her. After all, if it *was* an indulgence, it wasn't one that the company would be paying for. And, as for herself, she could afford it.

Anna was about to ask Flynn to bring a luncheon tray for herself and Sarah when Rebecca put her head around the door and said, 'Miss Hawthorne ... won't you please eat with Mama and me today? Mama is eager to thank you properly. And I rarely get the opportunity to chat with a lady close to my own age.'

Anna's brows rose in surprise. 'You don't have friends in the neighbourhood?'

'I used to. But when Mama could no longer afford to entertain, she also stopped accepting invitations so, in time, they stopped coming. And gradually, so did the neighbours.' Rebecca kept her tone matter-of-fact and free of self-pity. 'Now, of course, we're in mourning for Papa. So ... will you please join us for luncheon?'

'Of course, if you wish it. Thank you.' And turning, 'Do you want a tray in here, Sarah?'

'No need to make extra work, ma'am,' came the comfortable reply. 'I'll eat in the kitchen with the rest of the staff.'

Following Rebecca into the small dining-room, Anna was immediately struck by two things. For the first time, the Dowager greeted her with a smile ... and, turning away from the window and the rain still falling outside it, his lordship said lazily, 'How goes your morning, Miss Hawthorne? Better than mine, I hope.'

'Probably,' she said. 'Is the weather an inconvenience?'

'Somewhat,' he admitted. 'I had errands in Gloucester this morning. I am also hoping that the Turner's barn roof has proved watertight ... or, at the very least, that my attempts at repair didn't make the problem worse rather than better.'

'Hoping isn't enough,' observed his sister. 'Try prayer.'

For an instant it seemed to Anna that his smile, the first genuinely full one she'd seen since her arrival, flooded the room with sunshine. Certainly, it flooded *her* with something unexpected and unidentifiable that temporarily stopped her breath.

He said wryly, 'Thank you, Becky. Your confidence in my abilities is a never-ending source of comfort. I only wish I could share it.'

'Try,' she grinned. 'With a bit of practice, I'm sure you can get the hang of it.'

This time he laughed. And Anna thought, *Oh, don't. I liked you more than I should before I'd even* met *you. I can't afford to let it happen again now that I have – and particularly when I have yet to strike a deal with you.*

'That's better,' approved his mother. 'It's a long time since I last heard the two of you tease each other.' And to Anna as they sat down to a collation of cold meats and cheese, 'I was about to ask if *you* have siblings, Miss Hawthorne ... but first, I must thank you for the *Music Lesson*. Flynn brought it to me earlier and I was *so* happy to have it back.'

'Since it wasn't mine to give,' responded Anna, 'you don't need to thank me. It is still your late husband's gift. And no, sadly I don't have siblings – though I've often thought that I might have liked having a sister.'

'Not a brother?' asked Rebecca, reaching for the basket of rolls.

'When I was a child, perhaps.'

'But not now?'

'No. If I had a brother – whether older or younger – it would be he who inherited Hawthorne's, not me. And that would be a very bitter pill to swallow as the company means everything to me.'

Lady Reculver stared at her, nonplussed.

'*Everything?* Surely not. What of marriage? Is not a husband and family what every young woman wants?'

'Not quite *every* woman, ma'am. I don't, particularly.'

'Why, then, did you have a London Season?'

'That was my mother's idea, not mine. I've no intention of repeating it.'

'At least you could if you wished to,' muttered Rebecca.

Ignoring this, her ladyship said, 'You don't want children, Miss Hawthorne?'

'I *might*, I suppose – but that requires a husband, doesn't it?'

'Not necessarily,' corrected his lordship demurely.

Caught with a mouthful of cheese, Rebecca choked and began to cough.

'Daniel!' exclaimed the Dowager. 'Behave yourself!'

'I beg your pardon, Mama,' he said, not sounding particularly contrite. And to Anna, 'You have something against husbands? Or perhaps men in general?'

'As a species? Nothing. But I have a *great* deal against a woman's property passing to her husband on her wedding day,' replied Anna succinctly. 'And the gentleman who would be satisfied with a generous income from Hawthorne's but leave the management of the company solely in my hands probably doesn't exist – because men always think they know best, even when they don't.' And slanting a glance at Daniel, 'No offence intended.'

'None taken.' He shrugged slightly and added, 'The world is full of idiots of both sexes, Miss Hawthorne. But if what you need is an idle fellow in need of money but of no more than mediocre intelligence, there are any number of them to choose from – younger sons, particularly. You must have met some of that ilk while you were in London. If not, I could probably name you half a dozen.'

'Fortune-hunters who'd try to bleed the company dry?' She shook her head. 'No. That wouldn't do at all.'

'A good lawyer could prevent that eventuality. I'm presuming you have one?'

'Of course.'

'Then the problem isn't insurmountable, is it? Bind your husband hand and foot with legal fetters.' He pushed a small bowl in her direction whilst adding negligently, 'Though for the sake of those future children, you might want to choose one you find physically appealing. Pickle?'

This time it was Anna who choked. '*W-What?*'

'Onion relish. For the ham?'

'Oh. Yes. Thank you.' Annoyingly aware that her colour was rising, she decided that it was time to fight back, said, 'Thank you for your advice, my lord – but what of you? Have *you* no plans to marry?'

'Eventually, perhaps.'

'But not at present?' she persisted.

'No.' He trapped her gaze, a flicker of devilment dancing in his own. 'Why? Were you thinking of offering?'

'*Daniel!*' his mother expostulated again – but this time with an arrested gleam in her eye that only Rebecca noticed.

'Hardly,' snapped Anna. 'That would be ridiculous.'

'Indeed,' he agreed easily. And smiling, 'After all, I don't meet any of your criteria, do I? Stupid, lazy, biddable … and content to be a kept man? I'm none of those, I'm afraid.'

Anna stared at him, only one thought in her head, *No. But you're one of the* other *things you listed, aren't you? And well aware of it, I suspect.*

Since Anna appeared lost for words, Rebecca said, 'That's enough, Daniel. You're being outrageous, as usual. And though Mama and I are used to it, Miss Hawthorne is not. So stop teasing and eat – before the rest of us develop indigestion.'

* * *

As soon as she was able to escape without it looking like flight, Anna returned to the dining-room and work. It took almost an hour before the words, *I don't meet any of your criteria* and *Choose one you find physically appealing* stopped buzzing in her head. No. On the face of it, he *didn't* meet most of her criteria – or not in the way he'd listed them. But he met one to a degree that was truly alarming.

She might have felt better had she known that his lordship had *not* escaped and, instead, had been subjected to his mother's opinions on marriage, Miss Hawthorne and other things he didn't want to talk about.

The Dowager plunged straight in with a meditative, 'It might not be such a bad idea, you know.'

'What mightn't?'

'Considering Miss Hawthorne.'

Suspecting he already knew the answer, Daniel said warily, 'As what?'

'A possible wife.'

For an instant, he didn't know whether to laugh or bang his head against the wall. Deciding on simplicity, he said, 'No.'

'I realise it's premature ...and also a bit bizarre but –'

'Oh, it's definitely both of those.'

'However, perhaps we shouldn't dismiss the notion *completely* out of hand?'

'Just to be clear, there is no 'we' in this, Mama.'

'But only think of the advantages!'

'That would be a waste of time. You heard her. She doesn't want to marry.'

'No – she just doesn't want a husband who would meddle with her business. And you wouldn't, would you?'

'No. But that's beside the point. Listen carefully to me. She does not want a husband.'

'But she'd like children. And she's aware that she needs a husband for that – despite that naughty remark of yours.'

'I doubt I told her anything she didn't already know,' retorted Daniel. 'And I'm not convinced that she *does* want children. It seems to me that the manufactory is her substitute for them.'

'You could change that,' came the stubborn reply. 'Young ladies flock to you and always have'

'Anna Hawthorne falls a world away from the category of young lady you are talking about, Mama. She wants one thing and one thing only. And it isn't a man.'

She sighed. 'Such a pity. Wealthy, presentable ... and too clever for her own good.'

'She's certainly astute,' he shot back. 'Returning a piece of your own property to you has apparently changed her from being a female you wouldn't dine with to a female you'll consider as a potential daughter-in-law. *Seriously?*'

The Dowager sighed. 'Very well. I admit that I'm mostly dwelling on what her money could do.'

'And you think I'm not? For this house, for the estate and – '

'And for Rebecca! She'd be able to have her Season – suitably dressed and from a house leased in a good part of Town. And – '

'I scarcely need reminding of that,' snapped Daniel, his patience rapidly ebbing.

'*And*,' concluded his mother triumphantly, 'if you were married, she could be chaperoned by your wife rather than the wife of one of your friends.'

The picture this created re-established his sense of proportion and he laughed.

'Miss Hawthorne presenting Becky? The lady with few social graces and no interest beyond her manufactory? Yes. I can just imagine how well that would work.'

'Oh,' said the Dowager. Then, reluctantly, 'You may be right, I suppose.'

'Thank you.'

'And if you *dislike* Miss Hawthorne, there's no more to be said.'

'Dislike doesn't come into it. I scarcely know her and neither do you. More to the point, if I wanted to marry purely for money – something I'd much rather *not* do – it would make more sense to look for a suitable heiress in London.'

'Which you can't do until we're out of mourning.'

'Quite.' Mentally adding, *And which I can't afford to do any more than I can afford Becky's Season.*

Apparently concentrating on pleating the folds of her skirt, Lady Reculver said, 'Tell me honestly, Daniel. How long can we go on as we are?'

'I don't know,' he admitted wearily. 'Long enough for things to improve a bit, I hope, though I can't guarantee it. But no more talk of marriage, Mama. I can't contemplate it. Not to Miss Hawthorne and, just at present, not at *all*.'

* * *

Around mid-afternoon, Flynn brought Anna a letter from Mr Lowe at the manufactory. This worsened her mood rather than improving it. Sarah Thompson watched her screw it up and hurl it into the small fire that had been lit to combat the chill brought by the rain ... and glimpsing Miss Hawthorne's dark expression, had the sense not to ask any questions.

As on the previous day, Anna called a halt at around four o'clock, sent Sarah away and settled down to go through her notes. Or at least, that had been her intention. Despite all her best efforts, Lord Reculver's voice kept intruding into her concentration – two words in particular.

Not necessarily, he'd said. Two perfectly innocent words but placed in a far from innocent context and one which had put thoughts Anna really didn't want into her head.

Daniel Shelbourne was dangerous and forbidden, at least to her, and she shouldn't be thinking of him at *all* – let alone in *that* way. But she didn't seem able to stop herself. That she'd thought him wildly attractive when she'd been eighteen, was quite bad enough. That she *still t*hought so at the age of twenty-three was ridiculous.

She gave up trying to form an overall picture of what the figures on the pages in front of her told her. Dropping her head in her hands with a groan, she wondered how she was going to get through dinner if the style of his conversation remained as provocative as it had been at luncheon. She didn't know whether he did it on purpose or she was just reading too much into it. But either way, the result was the same. Her normally calm and objective approach was in tatters.

Have you no plans to marry? she'd asked.

And, *No*, he'd replied. *Why? Were you thinking of offering?*

He'd put the insane notion into her head, damn him – and she couldn't get it out.

* * *

In fact, Daniel resolved to be on his best behaviour throughout the remainder of Miss Hawthorne's stay. When Rebecca asked about the progress of the valuation, he learned that there were nineteen remaining scent bottles – all of them Father's most recent acquisitions – still to be assessed. And when he was informed that this should be completed by noon tomorrow, after which Miss Hawthorne would appreciate him setting aside some time to speak with her, he merely inclined his head and murmured, 'Of course.'

The entire evening might have passed without a ripple had not his mother, for reasons that eluded him, chosen to quiz Miss Hawthorne about her London Season. The brevity of her replies showed how little she wanted to talk about this ... but Mother, having the bit between her teeth, persisted. Even then, however, all might have been well had Miss Hawthorne's glancing reference to her mother's cousin, Lady Maybury, not stirred his mother's almost encyclopaedic knowledge of the aristocracy.

As soon as she heard the name, her eyes narrowed and she said, 'Let me think. Yes. Unless I am mistaken, Cordelia Maybury was a Hawkridge before she married ... a third or possibly fourth cousin once removed to the main branch of the family. Is that correct?'

Daniel's heart was already sinking even before Miss Hawthorne agreed that it was and then, entirely needlessly in his view, added that her maternal grandmother had also been a Hawkridge but even more distant a connection than Cousin Cordelia.

'Dear me.' The Dowager impaled her son on a bright stare. 'How interesting. It would appear that Miss Hawthorne must be related to Lord Benedict. You should write, telling him so.'

'I *could*,' he agreed carelessly, 'except that I already know what he'd say. Something about the Hawkridge family being less a tree than a whole forest.' Then to Anna, 'I take it you've never met Belhaven or his brothers, ma'am?'

'Never,' she said, her tone suggesting that she had no interest in doing so. 'Neither has Mama. She says any relationship is so remote, it barely exists at all. But even were it not, she was cast off by her parents when she married Papa – so I never met them either.' And purely to avoid questions about that, 'Lord Benedict is a brother of the current duke?'

'Yes – the younger of them.'

He decided it was time to change the subject but, before he could do so, Rebecca said, 'But you know Lord Oscar and Belhaven as well, don't you?'

'Oscar, yes ... Belhaven, in common with most people, much less so.' And for Anna's benefit, 'He's almost a recluse.'

'But not *completely* so,' remarked his mother, 'since I understand that he turned up uninvited at Lord Hazelmere's wedding.' And to Anna, 'The gentleman usually referred to as the Lost Earl? You'll have read all about him in the society pages, I daresay.'

'I leave society gossip to my mother,' replied Anna dismissively. 'However, I seem to recall her mentioning something about his lordship's sudden reappearance.'

'Which wouldn't have happened,' cut in Rebecca triumphantly, 'had not Daniel and his friend, Lord Wendover, gone hunting for him all over Turkey.'

Daniel swallowed a curse and said firmly, 'Old news, Becky – which we are absolutely *not* going to chew over again now.' He looked across at Anna and said the first thing that came to mind. 'A letter came for you this afternoon. I trust you received it?'

Her expression grew stormy. 'Thank you, yes.'

'Not bad news, I trust?'

'No. Merely ... annoying.' She might have left it there had she not realised that his lordship would have known from the superscription where the letter was from, so she said impatiently, 'A Bristol glass manufacturer wants to buy Hawthorne's. He has asked twice before and been told that the answer is, and will remain, no. Now, seemingly unable to accept this, he is pressing Mr Lowe to arrange a meeting with me in order to discuss the matter.'

'You won't sell to him ... or at all?' asked Daniel, suspecting he knew the answer.

'At all. Hawthorne's is my legacy from my father,' came the uncompromising reply. Then, on something approaching an explosion, 'And *glass,* for heaven's sake! What does *he* know about the manufacture of soft paste porcelain? Nothing. Or the experiments currently taking place to make the wares less brittle with the addition of ground animal bone? Again, *nothing!*'

She stopped as abruptly as she'd started, pink-cheeked and militant, to find his lordship watching her with a very faint smile.

'Animal bone?' said the Dowager, shuddering slightly. 'How ... unpleasant.'

'I suggest you leave it there, Mama – or risk learning more than you want to know.' Then, 'Just out of interest, Miss Hawthorne, will you meet this glass-maker?'

'To what end? It would be a waste of time.' She drew a long breath. 'Forgive me. Mr Harvill isn't alone in wanting to acquire Hawthorne's – Worcester Porcelain would also like to do so. But *their* interest makes sense. They are in the same business as ourselves and we are both too close by and too successful for their peace of mind. But at least they took no for an answer. I am finding Mr Harvill's refusal to do the same intensely irritating.'

'Yes,' agreed Daniel mildly. 'I believe we noticed that.' He paused. 'I shall be at home all afternoon tomorrow. When you are ready to discuss the collection, tell Flynn to let me know.'

CHAPTER SIX

The rain having stopped overnight, Daniel used the following morning to ride to Gloucester in order to hold two necessary conversations, one with his lawyer and the other with his bank. Neither was encouraging. Mr Longhope laid the quarterly figures before him and asked whether he expected the harvest to be a profitable one. The under-manager at the bank politely enquired when his lordship might be in a position to reduce, if not completely settle, his long-standing overdraft. Daniel answered both vaguely but without actually lying ... and then took himself off to the tavern.

The first mug of ale convinced him that there was no point in dwelling on things he couldn't change. Inevitably, the second brought to mind the fact that, later today, he would learn what figure Anna Hawthorne was prepared to offer for the collection. There was comfort in the certainty that she intended to offer *something*. But his nerves were already vibrating with tension caused by his fear of mishandling the ensuing negotiation. Not only had he no experience of bargaining – he had been brought up believing it something a gentleman just *did not do*. Now, however, he must do it and do it well – neither giving in too quickly nor over-playing his hand and risk ending up with nothing. In short, he would need to walk a very fine line.

It was a pity, he thought, that he would be facing Miss Hawthorne in her usual cool, brisk and wholly business-like persona rather than the impassioned woman he'd seen last evening. Just for a few minutes, she'd forgotten to be careful and let rip. The result had been both interesting and informative ... and, in respect of her looks, surprising. Colour had bloomed in her cheeks and fire had blazed in the usually unremarkable eyes. There was, Daniel reflected, a whole other woman lurking inside the somewhat wooden façade she chose to present to the world. And *that* woman would probably be a lot easier to deal with than the other.

Not for the first time, he wondered just how much she wanted the scent bottles. Was it *really* all to do with her late father? If so, it was possible – even likely – that she wanted them very badly indeed. He hoped she did. In that lay his best chance of success.

Abandoning the second mug of ale half finished, he left the tavern and set off home.

* * *

When they'd handled and listed the last of the scent bottles, Anna rose, stretched and said, 'Well done, Sarah – and thank you. You've been a great help.'

'It's been a pleasure, Miss Hawthorne – a nice change from the usual routine.'

That's one way of looking at it, thought Anna. But she said merely, 'I would like to make an early start tomorrow. The rain has stopped but the roads may be hard going in places and I'd prefer not to have to put up at an inn somewhere.'

'I'll be packed and ready, ma'am,' Sarah assured her. 'Will you be speaking to his lordship this afternoon?'

'Yes.' Out of habit, she extracted just one of their many sheets of paper – one containing just three figures; the total cost of the late viscount's purchases ... and her own lowest and highest offers based on Mr Lowe's advice. 'You can pack everything else. As for the pieces, we'll leave them where they are. If Lord Reculver wants them moved, doubtless he'll give the necessary instructions.'

Conversation over luncheon was more than usually stilted, everyone busy wondering what the afternoon might bring. The dowager's expression was speculative, Rebecca's, faintly worried and the viscount's, inscrutable. Hoping her own face was equally unreadable, Anna swallowed food without tasting it and said as little as possible. But finally the meal came to an end and, laying aside his napkin, his lordship rose, saying, 'Well then, Miss Hawthorne. I suggest we retreat to the library and get down to business.'

'By all means, sir,' she agreed coolly, coming to her feet. And, with a slight curtsy for the Dowager, followed him from the room.

The library, into which she had not previously been invited, proved to be a shabbily comfortable room bearing every appearance of being one he used a great deal. The surface of a large, rather ugly desk was almost hidden beneath numerous neat stacks of correspondence and what appeared to be invoices. And the shelves lining the walls were full of books, none of which looked new or seemed to be arranged in any orderly fashion.

She expected the viscount to take what was clearly his usual seat at the desk but instead he led her to a small table flanked by a pair of chairs near the window and gestured for her to sit, saying, 'This will be a new experience for me, Miss Hawthorne. My first time, in fact. I hope you intend to be gentle with me?'

The innuendo was clear enough to conjure up hazy images of the kind that had never invaded Anna's mind before. She knew he'd done it deliberately; but combined with the closed door and quiet room, empty of everyone save themselves, it created a sudden and shocking sense of intimacy and made her intensely aware of the man sitting no more than three feet away, looking completely at his ease.

Feeling her colour rise, she said curtly, 'Kid gloves, my lord? I doubt you need them.' And swiftly, before he could say anything else to discompose her, 'As I daresay you already know, your father's investment in Hawthorne wares totalled one thousand three hundred and eighty-five pounds and seventeen shillings.'

Daniel's heart gave a single, hard thump. This was more than he'd thought.

'I wasn't aware of that, no. Father wasn't meticulous about keeping receipts.' *Like a good many other things, more's the pity*, he thought. But merely added, 'Doubtless because he regarded the wares less as an investment than as gifts for my mother.'

'Of course,' replied Anna, suddenly aware of a foolish impulse to finish this quickly and escape from Lord Reculver's unsettling company. 'On behalf of Hawthorne's, I am prepared to offer one thousand six hundred and fifty – which is roughly twenty percent above the original cost.'

He tilted his head as if thinking about it and let the silence linger.

After a minute or two, she said, 'A fair return, wouldn't you agree?'

'A moderate one,' he shrugged, forcing himself to appear lazily relaxed despite his racing pulse. 'No more than that.'

She waited and, when he showed no sign of saying anything further, 'You have a figure in mind?'

'Perhaps.' He smiled at her. 'But it would hardly be sensible of me to share it with you, now would it?'

The smile, warm and inviting, had its usual effect ... and Anna strongly suspected that his lordship knew exactly what that effect was. Gritting her teeth and doing her best to ignore it, she wondered how many other tricks he had in his arsenal. Not that he needed tricks with looks like that. Thick, lightly curling auburn hair, golden-brown eyes flecked with green ... and as for those *shoulders* ...

She stifled the thought as it bred another of monumentally stupid proportions from a fragment of yesterday's conversation at luncheon.

'And what of you, my lord? Have you no plans to marry?'
'No. Why? Were you thinking of offering?'

Sternly bidding her mind back to the matter in hand and reminding herself that she'd always known he wouldn't accept her opening gambit, she said, 'Very well. One thousand seven hundred and fifty.'

The temptation to play safe and accept it was almost overwhelming. But Daniel forced himself to remain silent; to take a breath and listen to the tiny voice at the back of his mind which whispered that there was something odd here. He had expected this to take longer, had expected her to make him work for every improved offer ... and for each increase to be a small one. Fifty pounds, rather than a hundred.

What is she doing? he asked himself. *It's as if she just wants to strike a deal and go. Does she? If so, it's to my advantage – and an opportunity I can't afford to waste. But why? Is she less experienced at this than she'd have me believe? Am I unnerving her? Or does she want the collection so badly she'll pay any amount to get it?*

Deciding to test the water, he crossed one leg over the other and said slowly, 'Tempting, Miss Hawthorne ... though not, I'm afraid, quite tempting enough. However, we seem to be making progress. Shall I ring for tea while we both take a moment or two to consider?'

She didn't want tea. She wanted to buy the collection and go. She wanted to get out of this room because being alone with him was making her feel hot and doing odd things to her nerves. Worse still, it was making her think things she should not, under *any* circumstances, be thinking. And so, despite being aware that she was straying well outside Mr Lowe's advised margins, she blurted, 'Two thousand.'

Daniel's breath leaked away. Two thousand pounds. Twice what he'd thought he might get. It wouldn't solve all his problems or even come close ... but it would at least ease the situation for a time. He should just say yes and have done with it. He wasn't a gambler; he'd learned the hard way not to risk the little he had. So all he had to do was nod and agree.

Instead, he said, 'Two thousand five hundred.'

Anna's eyes flew to his and locked. Then she opened her mouth to say one thing and heard very different words come out.

'Just how badly *are* you dipped, my lord?'

For an instant, they stared at each other in frozen silence. Then, turning scarlet, she said rapidly, 'I beg your pardon. I had no business asking that.'

Somehow, Daniel managed to stifle his immediate and furious reaction.

'No. You didn't. But since you have ... badly enough, Miss Hawthorne. As you must already know since I would not otherwise be haggling over my mother's keepsakes.' Then, with the slightest of shrugs and a chilly smile, he said with soft implacability, 'Two thousand, five hundred ... and we have an accord.'

Quite suddenly, Anna decided that, much as she wanted to get away from him before she said something even more potentially dangerous than she already had, she *could* not – *must* not – let him have it all his own way. Recalling the idea she'd had yesterday and straightening her spine, she said, 'Two thousand two hundred.'

'Two thousand four hundred,' replied Daniel, counting on the fact that she wouldn't lose the collection for what, to her, would be a paltry sum.

This time, she frowned and hesitated. Then she said firmly, 'Two thousand three hundred, sir – and that is my final offer. Moreover, I am prepared to exhibit the collection with a notice stating *Courtesy of the Dowager Viscountess Reculver* – or some similar legend. The kind of thing seen in museums when artefacts are on permanent loan.'

Thrown off balance, Daniel said, 'Why? Why would you do that?'

'For your mother. It might help ease the situation.' She hesitated and then added, 'It might also suit you. Hawthorne's would *own* the collection, of course ... but there is no need for the world at large to know that.'

He'd certainly prefer that it didn't. He'd prefer the world to remain unaware that the collection had ever belonged to his family *at all*. But the dratted female was right. Mother *would* like it and it would make the loss less painful for her. Also, two thousand three hundred already exceeded his most optimistic expectations. So he drew a long, slow breath and, holding out his hand, said, 'Very well, Miss Hawthorne. I accept. Two thousand, three hundred it is.'

It had never occurred to her that she would need to shake his hand. Ladies didn't. He knew that as well as she did. But in this scenario, she wasn't a lady, was she? She was concluding a business deal on behalf of the manufactory in her role as its proprietor. So she accepted his hand, refusing to let herself notice how firm and warm and well-shaped it was – but powerless against the charge of sensation that shot through her body.

Apparently not similarly affected and faint amusement once more stirring in his eyes, the viscount said, 'Forgive me, Miss Hawthorne. I assumed that business women such as yourself would customarily seal a bargain in the same way gentlemen do. But perhaps I was mistaken?'

'It is of no consequence, sir,' she said jerkily, 'I'm pleased we were able to reach an agreement.'

'As am I. So ... how do we proceed from here?'

Anna drew a long, steadying breath, still struggling to find her composure.

'As soon as I am home, I shall arrange payment. This can be done in whatever way suits you. By draft, directly to your bank or in cash to you personally, if you would prefer that.'

'I would,' said Daniel. If the money went into the bank, it would be swallowed up by the overdraft. He didn't want that. He wanted to decide how best to put it to use. 'And the removal of the collection?'

'Once the money has changed hands, Mr Lowe will send some of our people to pack the pieces and transport them to the manufactory,' she replied. 'It will take a while to organise and exhibit it. But once that has been done, I will give instructions that you be informed and invited to a private viewing – bringing the dowager viscountess, of course.' Anna rose, shook out her skirts and met his eyes with a calm she did not feel. 'And now, if you will excuse me, I should check that all is in readiness for making an early departure tomorrow. But I shall see you at dinner.'

She was half-way to the door when she thought she heard him mutter, 'Joy over-bounding.'

* * *

In fact, she did not see his lordship at dinner.

'He rode into the village and will probably eat at the tavern there,' Rebecca told her.

Thank God, thought Anna.

'But he said you and he reached an amicable agreement about the collection and have settled a very fair price for it.'

Amicable? thought Anna, a little wildly. He'd taken her hand for no more than a few seconds and she'd felt it in every nerve and sinew of her body ... and continued to do so for almost an hour after leaving the library. 'Yes. We did.'

'He *also* said you promised something very kind for Mama's sake, even though you didn't need to,' continued Rebecca. 'But Mama will want to thank you for that herself.'

The Dowager did more than merely thank her. Much to Anna's alarm, she found herself clasped in Lady Reculver's arms and fiercely hugged while her ladyship said, 'Such a thoughtful gesture! And I will greatly look forward to seeing my treasures properly displayed – as they never truly have been before.'

Anna muttered something suitably self-deprecating and was grateful when Flynn announced dinner. Forcing herself to swallow some of what was on her plate in between making brief contributions to the conversation gradually became a little less difficult ... but she was relieved when the Dowager chose to retire early.

Left alone to take tea with Rebecca, she wondered whether it would be unwise to ask one or two of the questions she could not, under any circumstances, ask the viscount. She still shuddered inwardly at her earlier crass demand.

Just how badly are you dipped, my lord?

Quite aside from being rude and intrusive, that had also been stupid. Rebecca's brother had inherited the family's financial situation along with the title. He wasn't responsible for creating it. But the basic question remained the same. How bad actually *was* it? Insufficient income for anything outside the household's most basic needs ... or was the viscountcy neck-deep in debt? Anna had heard snatches of conversation referring to Rebecca possibly making her come-out next year. That, in itself, would be expensive. Then, if she received an offer of marriage, a dowry would be required; and if that had not already been set aside, her brother would have to provide it. For all of which, he would need a great deal more than two thousand three hundred pounds.

Facing the younger girl across the hearth and accepting a cup of tea, Anna said slowly, 'As you know, I didn't enjoy my London Season. But I think you are looking forward to yours, aren't you?'

'If it happens,' replied Rebecca with a slight shrug.

'Might it not?'

'Daniel will do his best to make sure that it does.'

'Of course.'

'And thanks to his friends, there will be no need to lease a house.' Setting down her cup with just a little more force than was necessary, Rebecca added, 'Papa sold our house in Curzon Street years ago while Dan was still at Oxford.'

'I see.'

'Yes. By now, I imagine you must do.' And then, bitterly, 'As I told you, Daniel inherited unforeseen ... complications. If he hadn't, you wouldn't be here – *oh!* Forgive me. I didn't mean to be rude!'

'There's nothing to forgive. You haven't told me anything I didn't already know or hadn't guessed,' responded Anna gently. 'Feel free to speak your mind. You won't offend me. But don't tell me anything you'd rather not ... although you may be assured that anything you *do* tell me will go no further.'

'Thank you.' Apparently content to accept this, Rebecca fell silent for a moment before saying explosively, 'Debts. Papa left debts that none of us knew anything about until he died. I don't know the details. Dan tried to protect Mama and me from the worst of it and didn't tell us anything at *all* until he had to. As for the estate, it seems *that* has barely been scraping by for years and, though things can be put right eventually, it will take time. And money – which, of course, we don't have. This – *all* of this – has fallen on Dan's shoulders when the fault was Papa's. It's so unfair!'

* * *

Later, in the privacy of her own room, Anna considered what Rebecca had told her. It wasn't an uncommon story these days. Landed gentry whose land no longer showed a profit thanks to antiquated farming methods and lack of investment. If the gossip she'd heard in London was a true indication, the usual manner in which such families mended their finances was through a wealthy marriage or two. That, after all, was how Mama had expected Anna herself to acquire the much-coveted title. And it was a solution which lay open to Viscount Reculver, wasn't it? Not just the obvious one, but one with which he, of all men, would have scant difficulty achieving. His looks alone were sufficient to attract a lady he wanted ... and Anna suspected that, when he wasn't beset with problems, he also possessed a sense of humour and quantities of charm. She herself wasn't exactly seeing him at his best right now, but even *she* wasn't immune to –

She cut that thought off with a derisive laugh.

Why pretend? She wasn't just not *immune* to his lordship's manifold charms, she was more than half way to being bewitched. He'd taken her hand and the instant his skin touched hers she had been flooded with feelings she'd never experienced before but had no difficulty at all in identifying. Hunger; want; and a need to know him utterly. Not solely in a sexual sense, though she wasn't naïve enough to suppose that wasn't a part of it. But to watch him, listen to him, learn to read and understand him; to know that he was hers. All of that and probably more. And all of it, thanks to his precarious financial position, not entirely out of her reach.

He needs an heiress, doesn't he? So why not *me?* she thought. And then checked herself. *Stop. Wait. Before you talk yourself into offering to marry him, just* think *for a moment. What was it he'd said? Something about not wanting to be a kept man? Yes. That was it. Basically, bad as things are, he's too proud to sell himself.*

Anna could understand that. When pride was one of the few things a man had left, she imagined it became doubly precious.

And his lordship's pride wasn't the only obstacle. She knew she wasn't at all the sort of wife he wanted; in truth, she probably wasn't the sort of wife *any* gentleman wanted – something which, until now, she hadn't minded. But three days' acquaintance with Daniel Shelbourne had changed that. *Now*, she'd seen a man she *did* want; a man with whom she could imagine making a life where he managed his concerns and she, hers, each of them supporting the other. So if there was even the slightest chance of having him, regardless of the terms, she'd regret it forever if she didn't at least try.

But you can't just march in and ask him to marry you, she told herself sternly. *You have to be cleverer than that. You have to offer him a bargain he might find tempting enough to consider. Otherwise, he'll simply refuse ... or, worse still, laugh.*

The only questions were whether she was brave enough to make the attempt ... and if she was, how best to go about it.

It took the rest of the night to work that out.

* * *

Having avoided Miss Hawthorne at dinner last night, Daniel realised he couldn't do it again at breakfast. Nor, in truth, was there any reason why he should want to. Their business with each other was concluded and the practical details of payment for and collection of the wares would largely be conducted by Hawthorne's manager. Also, he had to admit that he'd come out of it substantially better than expected. All he had to do now was exchange a few bland sentences over the breakfast table, bid the lady a civil farewell and wish her a safe journey home.

The first part went as predicted until, as everyone was leaving the table Miss Hawthorne asked him if he could spare her a few moments of his time.

Sighing inwardly, Daniel said, 'Of course, ma'am.'

'In private, if you wouldn't mind.'

His brows rose a little at that but he nodded and said, 'The library, then.'

Anna followed, watched him close the door and, when he offered her a seat, she took it in case her knees became unreliable – which she already suspected they might.

This time, the viscount chose the chair behind his desk, effectively placing a barrier between them. Anna wished he hadn't ... then told herself it made little difference. He was either going to hear her out or he wasn't – so where he sat was immaterial.

She said, 'I am going to be exceedingly blunt, my lord – for which I apologise in advance. It would help if you could accept that it isn't my intention to offend or insult you in any way. Far from it, in fact.'

'I'll attempt to bear that in mind,' he replied dryly. 'But, just out of interest, what *is* your intention?'

'To offer you a business proposition.'

'Really? Of what sort?'

'We'll get to that in a little while.' Anna paused, mostly to control her breathing which nerves were making erratic. 'First, I have just one question which – which you may consider impertinent.'

'If yesterday's example was anything to go by, I suspect it is likely to go well beyond impertinence, Miss Hawthorne. However, if you've finished preparing the ground –'

'I haven't, quite.'

'Then please do so and get to the point.'

She nodded. 'Very well. It's clear that you are in financial difficulties or you would not – as you said yesterday – have been haggling over your mother's keepsakes. But your lack of ready funds is very evident. The house is understaffed; you can't afford to drain one of the fields on your land and the land itself isn't producing as well as it might if you were able to invest in more modern methods.' She hesitated briefly as he uncoiled from the chair to loom over her across the desk. 'Then there's your sister.'

'I think,' he said, in a low, hard voice, 'that we will leave my sister out of it.'

'Rebecca hasn't yet made her come-out and that will be costly. An offer of marriage, should she receive one, will necessitate a dowry,' continued Anna stubbornly. 'As matters stand, I don't think you can afford either of those things. And if, in addition to everything I've said so far, there are also debts – '

'That's *enough!*' snapped Daniel furiously. 'What business is *any* of this of yours?'

'As I said, we'll come to that. But first, just tell me one thing. How much do you need? How much would it take to fund your accounts, pay off whatever debts you may have and give Rebecca her Season?'

For a long moment, he subjected her to a long, silent stare. Then, his voice tightly controlled but still dangerous, he said, 'This has gone far enough. You said you had a business proposition for me. Make it now – or leave before my patience snaps.'

'Twenty thousand?' she suggested, her tone lightly conversational. 'Thirty?'

This time he said nothing. Instead, he straightened his back and walked around the desk towards her. Anna sat very still, watching him. Then, when he was no more than two steps away, she checked his advance by saying, 'I have a substantial fortune, Lord Reculver, plus quarterly returns from Hawthorne's. What I *don't* have is as much freedom as I would like, thanks to both my mother's and society's notions of what is proper.'

'Freedom to do what, madam? Drink and gamble? Entertain your friends with bawdy jokes over the teacups? Take a lover or two?'

Colour surged to her cheeks and he saw her swallow hard. Then, keeping her tone very level, she said, 'None of those. Very small things – such as coming and going as I see fit, visiting my manufactory on a regular basis or travelling when necessary; all without argument and the need to consider '*what people will think*'.' She paused. 'Gaining these freedoms would be worth a great deal to me.'

'The point, Miss Hawthorne,' said Daniel, in something approaching a growl.

'The point is that I can only see one way to get them – and it is something I have previously discounted as impossible.' Another pause and then, baldly, 'Marriage.'

Whatever Daniel had expected, this wasn't it. 'Marriage?'

'Yes. But to the right man. One who would not hedge me about with restrictions and, as I've previously said, would leave me free to run my business without interference.' Lifting her chin, Anna attempted a smile. 'However, you were mistaken when you assumed I wanted an idle fellow, happy to live off my money. I don't. I couldn't deal amicably with a man I despise. What I *need* is a man of integrity with matters of his *own* to manage. A man who would pursue his goals while I pursue mine, each of us offering the other counsel and support, as and when required. In short, what I want is less a husband than a – a partner.'

Throughout this speech, Daniel had finally begun to suspect what she was building up to and couldn't decide which of his reactions was stronger. Sheer incredulity that the notion should occur to her or shock that she'd actually have the audacity to suggest it.

He said, 'If we've finally arrived at the point, I suggest you simply make it.'

She nodded, rose to face him and, looking him in the eye, said, 'Everything I have learned here leads me to conclude that you have the qualities I have just described. You are caring for your mother and sister and mending matters on the estate as best you can but without any of the resources you need.' She hesitated briefly, then added bluntly, 'I *do* have those resources. And I would be prepared to put them into your hands to apply as you see fit. I do not believe you would misuse them.'

Daniel's mind was reeling but he murmured, 'You're too kind.'

'No, I'm not. I'm practical. You need money; I have it – enough to pay off any debts you may have, along with the other expenses I referred to earlier – and more.' Another pause and then, rapidly and with a complete absence of expression, 'My lord, I think we could forge a successful partnership from which we would both benefit.'

'Do you indeed?'

'I do. I am aware that your immediate reaction is to disagree. But I ask you to think about it.' She paused, swallowed and added rapidly, 'Consequently, I will increase my offer for the collection to three thousand pounds – irrespective of your final decision – if you will merely *consider* my proposal.'

The second the words were out, she wished them back. Where had they come from, for God's sake? They certainly hadn't been part of her plan. But they were out now and couldn't be unsaid ... so the only thing to do was to avoid his lordship's incredulous gaze and press on.

She said, 'If your answer is a refusal, I shall accept that without argument. If the opposite, a further five thousand pounds will immediately be transferred to you as a gesture of good faith.'

Daniel realised he was beginning to feel slightly dizzy. Seven hundred pounds just to think about it? And a further *five thousand* if he said yes? Was she serious or insane?

He said, 'Why? Why the money?'

Her brows rose as if the answer was obvious.

'Two reasons. To help ease your most pressing obligations ... and to show that, if we were to marry, I would leave you free to manage your own business and with the funds to do it already at your disposal. So there it is. All I ask is that you consider it. Do we have an agreement?'

He continued to look at her for what seemed a very long time. But finally he said slowly, 'Yes. I believe we do.'

'Good.' This time, suddenly desperate to get away, it was she who offered her hand and, when he took it, managed to say breathlessly, 'Thank you for listening, my lord. I shall take up no more of your time. My man-of-law will be in touch. May I expect your decision within a month? Or word, if you feel further discussion will first be necessary?'

'You may,' he agreed, subduing the impulse to tell her not to be too hopeful. 'But for now, all I'll say is that I will ... consider it'

CHAPTER SEVEN

Daniel watched from the window as Miss Hawthorne's carriage disappeared round the curve of the drive. Then he dropped into a chair and communed silently with the ceiling.

He'd say no, of course. The only reason he hadn't already done so was that he'd been incapable of turning down that seven hundred pound carrot – a fact that left him feeling more than a little disgusted with himself. Was this what he was reduced to? Selling his word with scarcely a second thought? What was next? Selling himself? She clearly thought she could buy him if the price was right.

God, he thought, shuddering. *I hope not. I was so bloody determined not to marry for money – and that was when there was a chance the prospective bride might have been a woman I actually liked. On the rare occasions I'm not indifferent to Anna Hawthorne it's because she sets my teeth on edge. Marriage between us would be a disaster. Why doesn't she see that? What is it about me that she thinks is so perfectly tailor-made to suit her purposes? She doesn't know me. All she's seen is that I'm struggling to keep my head above water instead of meekly drowning. And what's so impressive about that? A dog would do the same. So what is it she really wants?*

It *could* be the title, he supposed. That was usually how an impoverished gentleman won an heiress. He got money and she acquired status. A good deal all round. But Miss Hawthorne didn't care about the title If she did, she'd be distancing herself from the manufactory, not insisting on running it. Which left what? Him, personally? Again, he thought that unlikely. True, he'd never had any difficulty attracting women ... but, unless he was completely mistaken, *this* woman didn't have a susceptible bone in her body.

She claims to want a partner but, whether she likes it or not, what she's actually buying is a husband. And is this truly about those so-called freedoms she mentioned? Or is there something I'm missing? Because the only thing I'm certain of right now is that, amongst other things, she's knocked me sideways.

His gaze strayed to the decanter on the other side of the room. He felt like getting drunk ... and might have given in to the temptation had there been sufficient brandy left to do the job. Since there wasn't, he told himself to stop behaving as if he'd received a death sentence and start figuring out how to make the best use of three thousand pounds.

There were so many things he'd like to do – fourteen estate cottages in need of imminent repair, for example. But it made sense to get rid of the quarterly interest charges by paying off the remaining two-and-a-half-thousand pound loan to Henderson & Company, so he'd start with that whilst costing out the cottage repairs.

He tried telling himself that this was something to feel cheerful about but at the back of his mind was still that niggling sense of shame. She was giving him a substantial amount of money to consider marrying her ... and he was accepting it under false pretences, already knowing he wouldn't. How was that different to cheating at cards? In essence, unless he fulfilled his side of the bargain, it wasn't. And already he was *afraid* of considering it; afraid that he'd end up being swayed by what he'd gain – namely, escape from the nightmare of the last six months. If he'd found himself incapable of refusing seven hundred pounds, what was he going to do when a further five thousand was dangled in front of him?

* * *

It might have comforted Daniel just a little had he known that, staring sightlessly through the carriage window, Anna was also feeling ashamed of herself. He was desperate. She'd known that and taken ruthless advantage of it – a fact of which he'd be well aware. He'd probably despise her for it and also himself a little for accepting what he recognised as a bribe. This alone didn't bode well for their future relationship in the unlikely event that he accepted her proposal.

But what else could she have done? If he had been desperate so, in a quite different sense, had she. Overwhelmed by feelings she scarcely understood but couldn't withstand, she had found herself unable to walk away without taking a tiny sliver of hope with her. Another woman in her position ... one with beauty and charm ... would have used those advantages equally ruthlessly. All *she* had was money – so she'd used that. And fortunately, money was what Lord Reculver needed most.

Less fortunate was that his lordship was now probably wondering if she made a habit of handing out bribes in order to get what she wanted. She didn't, of course – but why should he believe that? And the bribe hadn't been her only mistake, had it?

Her father had always taught her to be direct. *Cards on the table and straight to the point,* he used to say. And since plain speaking came more easily to her than subtlety, it was what she always did – today being no exception. But infuriating the viscount by listing all the areas for which he needed money he didn't have had probably not been the best idea.

She suppressed a groan. He was going to say no, wasn't he? He'd probably already decided and dismissed the matter out of hand. What else could she expect? There was absolutely nothing in her behaviour during the entire course of their conversation that he would have found remotely pleasant – let alone endearing. He'd say no. And the sooner she made herself accept that, the better.

Well, there was nothing to be done about any of it now. All she could do was move forward. She would instruct Mr Landry to pay Lord Reculver's three thousand pounds in cash, as promised; and she would visit the manufactory and tell Mr Lowe that he could send whomever he thought necessary to pack and remove the Reculver collection as soon as the purchase had been completed. Then, there would be little else to do but wait.

* * *

She had forgotten one thing but had barely removed her hat when her mother reminded her of it.

'You said you'd be back yesterday. Why weren't you?' she asked. And without waiting for a reply, 'Not that it makes any difference. But thank goodness you're here now. Madam Lavalle sent a note regarding your evening gowns. If they're to be ready in time for next week, you need to go for a fitting immediately.'

'Next week?' asked Anna vaguely. After hours in the carriage, she wanted nothing more than a cup of tea and a few moments of tranquillity. 'What about it?'

'The Anstruther house-party!' said Mrs Hawthorne, throwing up her hands in despair. 'Do you remember *nothing* that isn't to do with the manufactory?'

'I hadn't forgotten the party – only that it's so soon. But I'll go to Lavalle's tomorrow and make an appointment if Madame hasn't time for me immediately.' In fact, she could kill three birds with one stone; the dressmaker, Mr Landry and Hawthorne's. Then, not really expecting Mama to be interested, she said, 'I have made arrangements to purchase the late viscount's scent bottles. It is quite a remarkable collect —'

'The *late* viscount? He's dead?'

Anna felt an uncharacteristic temptation to say, *One would hope so, since they've buried him.* But confined herself to, 'Yes. His son now holds the title.'

Her mother's gaze sharpened. 'Son?'

'Yes.'

'Married?'

'No.'

'Then I hope you were properly chaperoned?'

Cynically, Anna suspected that the opposite was probably true. If it was, Mama would see a way of possibly getting the titled son-in-law she'd always wanted.

'Very much so. By his mother and sister – and the fact that the family is still in mourning. Interestingly, Miss Shelbourne and I were at Miss Winslow's together – although we were scarcely acquainted, since she is much younger than I.' Coming to her feet and managing a smile, she added, 'Forgive me, Mama, but I'm quite tired and must wash and change before dinner – so perhaps any further questions can wait until then?'

* * *

On the following morning, Madame Lavalle greeted her pleasantly, said that of course she had time for Miss Hawthorne and led the way to the fitting rooms. Anna approved the largely finished gowns, one a deep blue figured silk and the other, an embroidered *eau-de-nil* taffeta, both in her preferred *robe à l'Anglaise* style with a minimum of trimming. Mother would sniff and call them plain but Anna disliked unnecessary fussiness. Madame did what was necessary in order to make the final adjustments and promised to deliver the dresses in two days' time.

Anna's second call of the morning was at Mr Landry's small office in Greyfriars. She knew he would have preferred to wait on her at home but this wasn't a meeting that Anna wanted to risk Mama overhearing any part of.

When she gave the lawyer her instructions, his reaction was precisely as she'd expected.

'Three thousand pounds, Miss Hawthorne? In *cash?* That is most irregular.'

'Perhaps so. But it is what Lord Reculver has requested.'

'May one ask why?'

'No,' she said pleasantly. 'One may not. I realise it isn't how you would normally conduct such a transaction and that there are certain difficulties involved. But they are not insurmountable, sir. You can use a reputable courier or you can deliver the money to his lordship yourself. If the latter, I'm sure I don't need to suggest that you travel during daylight hours and hire a couple of outriders.'

'No, indeed! But – '

'There are no buts, Mr Landry. Lord Reculver and I have an agreement. See to it, please – preferably as soon as possible – and inform both myself and Mr Lowe when the transaction is complete. But now I'm afraid I have another appointment and must go. Good day, sir.'

She had deliberately left the manufactory until last, aware that – since the Reculver collection wouldn't be the only subject she and Mr Lowe needed to discuss – their meeting would be a relatively long one.

Smiling a little, Nathaniel Lowe said, 'Mrs Thompson says you got it.'

'Yes. I knew you would ask so I gave her permission to tell you.' Beaming back at him, Anna said, 'It's wonderful! All of it laid out together is nothing less than spectacular. If you can spare the time, go with the packing team and see it for yourself – because it will be a while before we have a suitable room prepared in which to house it and therefore no point in *un*packing it until we do. But, leaving that aside, I should tell you that things were not as we expected. The Viscount

Reculver we knew died six months ago and has been succeeded by his son.'

He winced. 'That must have been awkward.'

'A little. But I explained to the current viscount that we were unaware of his father's passing and said what was proper on Hawthorne's behalf.' Since the acquisition was a private one, Anna knew that Mr Lowe wouldn't ask what it had cost but she decided to tell him anyway. 'I paid two thousand, three hundred for it. A little higher than we anticipated but well worth it – as I think you'll agree when you've seen it. Furthermore, I believe we were mistaken in our assumption that the pieces would achieve a larger figure if sold separately at auction. I suspect that, if offered as a whole and properly advertised, Sir Roland Maudsley, Baron Alderwood and Mr Paxton would be fighting each other for it.'

'Ah. It's as good as that?'

'Better, in my opinion. There's just one other thing I ought to tell you. As we might have deduced, the late viscount bought the pieces as gifts for his wife – now, of course, his widow. Understandably, she is very reluctant to part with them and so, to ease the process, I suggested that she keep two of the scent bottles – the first and the last ones her husband bought – which is why they're no longer on the original list.' She grimaced slightly. 'Unfortunately, one of them was the *Music Lesson*. But there's always a chance we might find a replacement for that elsewhere.'

'Not a very big one,' muttered Mr Lowe. And then, 'You got my letter about Mr Harvill?'

The grimace became a scowl. 'I did. What exactly happened?'

'He marched in without warning and demanded to see you. I told him you weren't here and asked him to state his business. He refused – in words I won't repeat. He's not a pleasant fellow, Miss Anna. He's the rude, bullying sort; the sort who thinks if he says something loud enough and often enough, he'll get what he wants. He's not somebody you should be having anything to do with. But until the penny eventually drops that Hawthorne's isn't for sale, not to him nor anyone else, he'll keep coming back.'

'Let's hope not. But if he does and asks for me again, tell him I have better uses for my time than to waste it repeating myself.'

Mr Lowe nodded. Then he said slowly, 'I got the impression he didn't know where you live – and there's nobody here who'd tell him. But I reckon he can find out elsewhere easily enough. The Hawthorne name is well known in Worcester. Any of the shops or tradesmen you buy from know where to find you – and so might Harvill by now. So I think it would be a good idea to have a word with your butler ... just in case.'

'Yes. I will.' She paused, then added, 'But I don't understand why Mr Harvill is so set on buying Hawthorne's. His business is glass, after all. And though I realise the window tax is something of a blight on it, if he wants to diversify and has set his heart on a pottery there are at least three small ones in or around Stoke-on-Trent that he could probably snap up tomorrow. So why isn't he going after them rather than us?'

'We're successful and they aren't?' suggested Mr Lowe. 'Or in Stoke, he'd be in competition with Wedgwood and Spode?'

'And *here* he'd be competing with Worcester Porcelain – as are we.' Anna shook her head. 'I can't help wondering if there's something more. Aside from loud, brash and persistent, what else do we know about Harvill?'

'Apart from the money and the glass manufactory, not very much. Do you want me to make a few enquiries?'

'It wouldn't do any harm. With luck, he'll set his sights elsewhere. But if he doesn't, any information might prove useful.'

* * *

At Reculver Court, four days after the departure of Miss Hawthorne, Daniel's spirits received a boost in the form of an unexpected visitor.

'Is his lordship at home?' asked the new arrival, stripping off his gloves.

Flynn bowed and permitted himself a smile.

'He is in the library, my lord. And will be very pleased to see you, I'm sure.'

'Pleased enough to put up with me for a couple of nights, I hope. But don't stand on ceremony, Flynn. I know the way and will announce myself.'

Another bow. 'Very good, my lord.'

Half-way through totalling a column of figures, Daniel didn't immediately look up when the door opened so the first he knew of his surprise guest was when the gentleman said, 'I've been travelling for five days, Daniel. The least you could do is say hello.'

At the first words, Daniel's head jerked up and his quill stabbed the paper, spraying ink across it. Tossing the pen down, he rose saying incredulously, 'Benedict? Good God! I didn't think you'd get away from Scotland before September at the earliest.'

'Neither did I.' Lord Benedict Hawkridge strolled across, hand outstretched. 'How are you? Better than when I saw you last, I hope?'

'Somewhat.' Grinning, Daniel gripped his friend's hand. 'And you?'

'Well enough. The weather in Stirling was better than usual and the company isn't bad once one gets used to the accent. But Vere really needs to get up there himself from time to time. The tenants expect it.' Dropping into a chair and seeing Daniel crossing to pull the bell, he added, 'Flynn knows I'm here and will be having my bags brought in by now, so I doubt he'll need telling to bring some wine.'

Daniel halted and turned back. 'You're staying?'

'For a couple of nights if you'll have me.'

'Don't be an ass. Stay as long as you like – I'll welcome the company.'

Benedict shot him a narrow glance. 'Have you seen the others?'

'Anthony drops in from time to time, full of encouragement and useful advice – some of which I've been able to put into practice.'

'There's little Anthony doesn't know about estate management,' observed Benedict. 'It's as if he was born knowing what you and I are having to learn from scratch – you, here and I, in Scotland. But what of Kit? Have you seen him recently?'

'No, although he writes regularly. The nearer Sophie's confinement gets, the more reluctant he is to stir from Hazelmere.'

'Well, you can't blame him for that.'

'I don't,' said Daniel. And with the ghost of a laugh, 'In his position, the thought of what lies ahead would probably turn me into a gibbering idiot.'

'Me, too. Which is somewhat humbling when it wouldn't be us doing the work.'

There was a tap at the door and Flynn entered bearing a tray with wine and glasses. When the door closed behind him, Benedict said idly, 'Have you ever met a woman you thought of marrying?'

'No.' For obvious reasons, this was a road Daniel preferred to avoid. 'You?'

'No. A good many who have fascinated me for a while and a handful I've truly liked ... but so far, no one I could imagine spending the rest of my days with.'

Daniel had said nothing to his mother or sister about Miss Hawthorne's extraordinary proposal and didn't intend telling Benedict either. But he realised that he wasn't going to get away with simply not mentioning her at all. If *he* didn't, Mama certainly would because of that virtually non-existent thread of kinship – and Benedict would find it odd that he'd said nothing. So he opened his mouth to change the subject ... but was interrupted by a tap at the door and the reappearance of Flynn.

'I beg your pardon, my lord, but a Mr Landry is here to see you. He has apparently travelled from Worcester and believes that you may have been expecting him.'

I am *expecting him – just not bloody now!* thought Daniel edgily. But said, 'Forgive me, Benedict. I have to see this fellow but it needn't take long and – '

'Take as long as you need,' responded his lordship, coming to his feet. 'If Flynn will show me to my room and have water sent up, I'd like to remove the dust of the road before inflicting myself on the ladies.'

'Thank you. Flynn, take care of Lord Benedict and show Mr Landry in here, please.'

Alone and damning the lamentable timing, Daniel hoped Landry had taken a room at the village tavern. What he most definitely *didn't* need was to have him as an overnight guest.

A small, spare man with spectacles and clutching a leather case, Mr Landry bowed politely but allowed a note of disapproval to touch his voice when, coming directly to the point, he said, 'Miss Hawthorne was adamant that your lordship required payment in cash – and as soon as possible. So here I am.'

'So you are,' agreed Daniel. 'Shall I ring for tea? Or, since this is clearly inconveniencing you, perhaps you'd prefer to deal with the matter as speedily as possible.'

'The latter, sir.' Placing the case on a table, he unlatched it and withdrew three neat bundles of banknotes. 'These,' he said, 'each contain one thousand pounds. Does your lordship wish to count it?'

'Hardly. That would be adding insult to inconvenience, wouldn't it? But I imagine you require a receipt?'

'If your lordship would be good enough to furnish me with one.'

'My lordship is happy to do so.' Daniel walked to his desk, took up a sheet of headed notepaper and wrote, *Received with thanks, the sum of three thousand pounds.* Then he signed it and passed it to the lawyer, saying, 'Thank you, Mr Landry – and please thank Miss Hawthorne for settling the matter so promptly. I did not, in fact, ask her to deal with this immediately she returned home, neither did I expect it. But perhaps I should have done – since I have never met such an efficient lady.'

'She is that,' agreed Landry in a tone which clearly said, *That's one way of putting it.*

'But perhaps you will tell her that I am glad to know she reached home safely.'

'Certainly, my lord.' He latched the case and picked it up. 'And now, if you have no other instructions for me, I shall take my leave. I have reserved a chamber at the White Hart in Tewkesbury and would like to get there in good time for dinner.'

'Of course.' Faintly regretting his earlier surliness, Daniel held out his hand. 'Have a safe journey, Mr Landry – and thank you.'

When the lawyer had gone, he stared at the parcels of money for several moments before drawing a long breath and putting them out of sight in a drawer. Then he sat down and tried to decide whether his next move ought to be telling Benedict he'd been reduced to selling things or asking his mother to be careful what she said about Anna Hawthorne. In the end, he did neither and, instead, had Flynn inform his mother and sister of their guest's arrival, confident that this would result in both of them taking extra pains – and therefore extra time – with their appearance.

* * *

If Lord Benedict was surprised to learn that a distant Hawkridge connection owned a porcelain manufactory, he hid it well, merely remarking that he and his brothers had lost track of their remote and extremely numerous relatives years ago.

'I told Mother you'd say that – but don't be surprised if she still makes a great deal of it. For reasons that escape me, who is related to whom is a passion with her.'

'Well, everyone needs a pastime of sorts, don't they?' said Benedict absently as he continued to stare at the array of scent bottles covering the formal dining-table. And then, differently, 'Seriously, though … don't struggle on alone, Dan. You have friends. Let us help a little now and again.'

'I already owe Kit five thousand,' returned Daniel tightly. And, gesturing to the table, 'Mr Landry came to deliver the money for this. If it was sufficient – and if I didn't need it more elsewhere – I'd use it to repay at least part of that. As it is, I thank you for the offer. But I don't see the point of settling one debt by creating another. Doing that is largely what created this mess in the first place.'

'I can't argue with that.' Following Daniel back to the drawing-room, he said, 'Did you ever find out what your father's original loan was for?'

'No. I don't suppose we ever will. My best guess is that he invested in some non-existent scheme or other but I've no idea what. There must have been documents relating to it, but God

knows what Father did with them. I've searched everywhere.'
Back in the drawing-room and deciding to change the subject, Daniel poured sherry and said, 'If you're wondering what is keeping Mama and Becky, the fault is yours.'

'*Mine?* Why?'

'You're here.' And handing Benedict a glass, 'The only other company they've had recently was Miss Hawthorne – whose conversation revolves solely around her manufactory. Also, you're better-looking. Or so Becky thinks.'

Benedict laughed and was about to utter something rude in retaliation when the door opened to admit the ladies. Coming immediately to his feet to bow over the Dowager's fingers, he said, 'I hope you will forgive me for dropping in upon you without warning, my lady, but the temptation was too great to resist.'

Dismissing this with a smile and an airy wave of one hand, she said, 'It is always a pleasure, Lord Benedict. You know that you are welcome here at any time.'

'You're very kind, ma'am.' And turning his own smile on Rebecca, 'And Miss Shelbourne. I'd ask how you are, were you not looking particularly charming this evening, thus making the question redundant.'

Daniel might have looked forward to teasing him about spreading the butter too thick if it hadn't happened to be true. For the first time since their father's death, Mama had allowed Rebecca to abandon black in favour of pale grey watered taffeta and it suited her – as did the tinge of colour rising to her cheeks. Unfortunately, what he'd hinted to Benedict earlier was also true; his sister was no less susceptible to his friend's magnetic good looks than were the ladies in London. Sighing inwardly, Daniel made a mental note to tell Becky not to get her hopes up and ask Benedict to be a bit less lavish with his compliments.

Benedict's sojourn in Scotland occupied most of the talk before Flynn summoned them to table and for a little while after it. But eventually, as Daniel had known was inevitable, his mother introduced Anna Hawthorne's name into the conversation by explaining to Benedict why they were dining in the breakfast parlour.

'No need to apologise, ma'am,' he replied easily. 'Daniel has already shown me the scale of the problem. I don't believe I've ever seen anything quite like it.'

'That's a tactful way of putting it,' murmured Daniel into his chicken fricassee.

Rebecca turned a choke of laughter into a cough and Benedict winked at her from the other side of the table ... something *else* Daniel decided he'd speak to him about. For now, however, he tried to change the subject by asking after Belhaven and Lord Oscar.

It didn't work. The Dowager allowed Benedict to reply that, as far as he knew, they were both well and then said, 'When Daniel showed you my collection, did he mention that Miss Hawthorne – the lady who is buying it – is a distant relative of yours?'

'He did indeed. But we have a lot of those – too many to count, I'm afraid.'

'But a *lady*, owning and running a porcelain manufactory – and very successfully too, it seems! Aren't you curious?'

'I'm sorry to disappoint you, ma'am – but no, not really. Should I be?'

'No,' said Daniel. 'She wasn't curious about you either.'

Benedict laughed. 'Good for her.'

'She's going to make my bottles the centrepiece of an exhibition of her late father's work and with a card saying *By Courtesy of the Dowager Viscountess Reculver*,' her ladyship persisted. 'Does that not show great delicacy of feeling?'

'Leave it, Mama,' begged Rebecca. 'Lord Benedict is no more interested in Miss Hawthorne than anyone would be in a relative they've not only never met but never even heard of before.' And, shyly, to Benedict, 'Will you be in London during the Season, my lord?'

'That is more than likely,' he replied. 'And will I see you there?'

Darting a glance at Daniel, she said, 'I hope so.'

'Then I'll look forward to dancing with you.' And not only catching but also understanding the look in Daniel's eyes, he added, 'If I can beat a path through all your brother's other friends, that is.'

* * *

Later, when they were alone, Benedict said bluntly, '*Will* she have her Season, Daniel?'

'If it can possibly be managed, yes. Both Sophie and Anthony's cousin, Drusilla Colwich, have invited Mama and Becky to stay with them, so that is one problem taken care of. Everything else is in the lap of the gods. But there's not much I can do about that unless …' He stopped, shaking his head.

Benedict eyed him shrewdly. 'Unless what?' And when no answer was forthcoming, 'Daniel?'

Daniel gave a short, bitter laugh.

'Unless I accept an offer for the only saleable commodity I have left.' Drawing a harsh breath, he added, 'I *should* accept it because it could fix everything else. But I can't … I don't think I can make myself do it. And no. I won't discuss it further.'

It was a long time before Benedict spoke. Finally, he said, 'How long do you have in which to decide?'

'Another three weeks.'

'In that case, walk away from it for a while. When I leave here, I'll be visiting Kit and Sophie. Come with me.'

Light flared in the hazel eyes, then dimmed.

'I can't. Now the scent bottles have been paid for, there will be people coming to collect them – and sooner rather than later, I suspect. I'll have to be here for that.'

'Fine. I'll stay until that's been done. Then we'll leave. Yes?'

There was another lengthy silence. And then, his voice cracking, Daniel said, 'Yes. Oh God, Ben. Yes. And thank you.'

CHAPTER EIGHT

The Anstruther house-party was neither better nor worse than Anna had expected. Lily was pleased to see her – mainly, as she frequently remarked, because Anna was the only female to whom she could speak her mind without raising eyebrows and also the only one who didn't repeat what she'd said elsewhere afterwards. As usual, Anna gave the impression of being similarly free in return ... and, also as usual, Lily didn't notice that she never was.

The weather remained pleasant, so there were numerous outdoor events. The company was also pleasant, if not especially stimulating. And, at the ball celebrating the announcement of Lily's long-deferred betrothal to Lord Lycett, Anna was asked to dance by no less than four gentlemen – one of them, twice. But even this unprecedented event failed to distract her from worrying about what might or might not be going on in Daniel Shelbourne's head.

Mr Landry had set out for Reculver Court with the money the day before she'd left for the Anstruthers. By now, four days on, it was likely that Mr Lowe was either already overseeing the packing of the collection or at least on his way to do so – which meant that there was a good chance the scent bottles would have arrived at Hawthorne's by the time she returned at the end of the week.

But it wasn't the scent bottles that kept her awake at night. It was her own inner turmoil. She'd plunged into the offer she'd made the viscount based solely on a degree of attraction that she hadn't previously believed could exist. And she'd done it without a modicum of proper consideration – the result being that she wasn't even sure she truly understood her own motivation. Then there were the things she'd said to the viscount ... and the expressions that had crossed his face while she'd been saying them. Anger, astonishment and disbelief, to name but three.

He'll say no. He'll be insulted and furious at what he'll see as an offer to buy him. He may be desperate but he has his pride, she told herself, *and I wouldn't want him if he hadn't. No. So he'll refuse. The only thing that might sway him is Rebecca. Without money, she can't have a Season or a dowry or marriage and he wants her to have all three. He might accept for her sake, mightn't he?*

Then, angry with herself, she pushed the thought away as unworthy. Rebecca was neither a pawn in a game nor a bargaining chip. She was a good-hearted girl who wouldn't want her beloved brother to sacrifice himself for her sake by marrying a woman who had what he needed but nothing he wanted.

* * *

At Reculver Court, meanwhile, letters were exchanged with Mr Lowe and arrangements set in place for collection of the wares. Benedict wrote to inform Lord and Lady Hazelmere that he and Daniel would be descending upon them a few days' hence and passed the rest of his time either riding about the estate with Daniel or persuading the Dowager that her son needed to escape from his responsibilities for a little while. In this, he swiftly discovered that he had a staunch ally in Rebecca.

'His lordship is right, Mama,' she said firmly. 'Dan hasn't been himself since Papa died and it's getting worse. You must see that.'

'Perhaps. But – '

'No buts. He thinks of *us* all the time. Us and the tenants and the estate. Everything he's doing is for someone else's sake – mostly ours. It's time we thought of him for a change. It will do him a world of good to spend a few days with his friends. He *deserves* it. And we can manage without him perfectly well.'

'Well ... since you put it like that,' allowed the Dowager reluctantly. 'I suppose a week or so couldn't hurt. But not until after Miss Hawthorne's people come for my scent bottles. Even, knowing what I now know, I couldn't bear to deal with that alone.'

'And you won't have to,' Benedict assured her. 'It was Daniel's first thought when I suggested he come with me to Hazelmere. So ... may I steal him from you for a while?'

Seeing her mother hesitate, Rebecca said bracingly, 'It's only a week, Mama. You'll barely notice he's gone – let alone have time to miss him.'

'Oh, very well. Yes.' And then, 'I am being foolish. Of course he must go.'

* * *

Having travelled the previous day and spent the night in the village tavern, the team from Hawthorne's arrived bright and early with numerous small crates and quantities of soft packing materials. Shaking hands with Daniel, Mr Lowe said, 'I'm glad to meet you, my lord – and for the opportunity to express my apologies for only belatedly becoming aware of your father's passing.'

'It is of no consequence,' replied Daniel, leading the way into the dining-room. 'Here it is – just as Miss Hawthorne left it.'

Mr Lowe checked on the threshold, took a few steps closer and then stopped dead, seemingly rooted to the spot.

'Good Lord,' he breathed. And with a little snort of laughter, 'She wasn't exaggerating.'

'Had you supposed she might have been?' asked Daniel.

'Yes – though Miss Anna isn't usually a great one for displays of enthusiasm.' The manager paused. 'Might I ask what her opening bid was, my lord?'

Daniel's brows rose slightly but he said, 'Sixteen hundred and fifty. Why?'

'That must have taken some restraint.'

'Meaning what exactly?'

'Meaning that once she'd seen this, there wasn't a chance she'd let it slip through her fingers,' came the blunt reply. 'Two thousand three hundred was a good price, my lord. But I reckon she might have gone higher.'

'In a way, she did,' said Daniel dryly. 'She offered attribution to my mother when the collection is exhibited.'

'Ah. She didn't mention that bit. However … to business. I've brought four experienced packers and all the necessary materials. With a bit of luck, we'll have this done by mid-afternoon. I reckon you'll be glad to have your dining-table back.'

'I'll be glad because I'm going away for a few days and would like to leave tomorrow,' corrected Daniel pleasantly. 'And now, I'll get out of your way. If you need anything, speak to my butler.'

Meeting his sister on the stairs, he said, 'Does Mama know they're here?'

Rebecca sighed. 'Yes. She says she will stay in her rooms until they've gone.'

'And I suppose she expects you to stay there with her?'

She nodded. 'I don't mind. It's only one day, after all. And it isn't as though I was planning to do anything else.'

'You are now. It's a lovely day and you're coming for a walk with me – Benedict, too, if you know where I can find him.'

Rebecca's face brightened. 'He's in the library, I think.'

'Good. I'll get him while you inform Mama that you'll be back to keep her company when you've had a breath of air.' He dropped a kiss on her brow. 'Go and get your hat.'

When he entered the library, Benedict waved a letter at him and said, 'Kit is looking forward to seeing us, as is Sophie. He says that, since Gerald is with them just now, he'll send a note to Anthony in the hope that he's also free to join us.'

Warmed by the thought of spending time with all his oldest friends, Daniel smiled and said, 'Then let's hope that he is. But for now, come for a stroll with Becky and me.'

'Willingly. Any particular reason?'

'Yes. Mama's making sure we all appreciate her sacrifice by moping in her rooms while the Hawthorne men are packing. That's fine. But there's no reason why Becky should do the same – especially when Mama will be her only company while I'm away. So ... let's go.'

Joining them in the hall, Rebecca said despairingly, 'She's sitting there staring at the *Music Lesson* and heaving doleful sighs every now and then.'

'Very dramatic. If only Drury Lane knew what it's missing,' returned Daniel sardonically, whilst throwing an arm about her waist and sweeping her with him. 'Come on. Through the orchard to the village and a glass of cider outside the Crown.'

They chatted about various topics as they walked and lured Benedict into sharing such tales of his doings in Scotland that he'd deemed unsuitable at dinner. But when they were sitting in the sunshine outside the tavern, Rebecca said slowly, 'I thought Miss Hawthorne might come to oversee the packing. In fact, I'm surprised that she didn't.'

'I'm not,' muttered Daniel, thinking, *It's just as well that she didn't. I'm not ready to lay eyes on her again yet.* Then, realising that both his sister and Benedict were looking at him oddly, added with a shrug, 'She made the acquisition. I imagine that's her role finished.'

'I suppose so.'

Benedict eyed Rebecca thoughtfully. 'Did you like her?'

'Not very much to begin with,' she admitted. 'But later … yes. She's different. Interesting. And she cares a great deal for the people who work for her. I admire that.'

Benedict turned to Daniel. 'And you?'

For a number of reasons, Daniel saw the wisdom of saying as little as possible.

'Becky's right about her seeming to look after her workers. For the rest, in my case, liking her or not liking her didn't really come into it. The only thing that mattered was getting the best price I could for Mama's bottles.'

'And did you?'

'I believe so. A profit of nearly as much again as Father paid for them.'

Benedict whistled. 'She must have wanted them very badly.'

'She did. According to the fellow overseeing the packers – and who, incidentally, is the manager of the manufactory – she might have gone even higher. But having no previous experience of bartering I wasn't sure how far to push her. So I played safe.'

'It sounds like gambling,' murmured Rebecca.

'It felt like it, too,' he agreed, 'only somewhat more nerve-wracking.'

'Why?' asked Benedict. 'Surely the worst it could be was a missed opportunity.'

'Not missed … lost. With cards or dice there's always another chance if you choose to take it. If Miss Hawthorne had walked away, my bird in the hand went with her – and I might never have found the mythical two in the bush.'

* * *

As she'd expected, Anna returned home from Anstruther Park neither betrothed nor having obtained a potential suitor. Also as expected, Mrs Hawthorne said despondently, 'You didn't even *try*, did you? You never have and never will. I give up.'

'That would probably be best,' replied Anna absently, heading to her bedchamber so that she could read the notes awaiting her from Mr Lowe and Mr Landry in private. 'I don't enjoy disappointing you, Mama, and I certainly don't do it on purpose. But none of Lily's guests were gentlemen desperate for money. And even if they had been, what do you suppose is going to happen in the space of a week?'

And she walked away, leaving her mother mercifully lost for words.

Mr Landry merely reported that he had personally handed the money to Lord Reculver and obtained a receipt for it. Mr Lowe said he entirely agreed with her about the quality of the collection and looked forward to discussing where to situate the exhibition so they could proceed to the next step without too much delay.

Anna had some ideas about that – the most ambitious being a brand new extension. But that would take time which meant an interim solution was needed and she found it impossible to concentrate on that yet; and wouldn't, she suspected, for the next two and a half weeks.

Mr Lowe's note included the information that Lord Reculver currently had a guest.

A friend since Eton and the brother of a duke, according to the butler, he'd written, *The pair of them are off to visit another such who's an earl as soon as his lordship's shut of us. Another world, isn't it?*

Anna folded the letter and put it away. The duke's brother was almost certainly Lord Benedict Hawkridge; and the earl was probably the so-called 'lost' one that, according to his sister, Lord Reculver had seemingly found.

And friends since Eton? she thought dryly. *No surprise there. Half the gentlemen of the* ton *met at school. More than half, probably. It's how the aristocracy worked.*

* * *

Having made a very early start, Daniel and Benedict arrived at Hazelmere shortly after five in the afternoon. Christian and Sophia immediately appeared at the top of the steps to beam at them. Then Christian ran lightly down to pull first Daniel and then Benedict into a fierce hug.

'Welcome,' he said simply. And, laughing, 'It goes without saying that I'm delighted to see you both. And when we got the letter saying you were coming, Sophie was nothing short of overjoyed. Unnecessarily so, in my opinion. I'm still not sure if I should be jealous.'

'That will be the day,' grinned Daniel. And, trotting up the steps to a very obviously pregnant Sophia, kissed first her hands and then her cheek, saying, 'You look wonderful, Sophie. Positively glowing.'

'Thank you.' She squeezed his fingers. 'Kit and I are *very* glad Benedict persuaded you to come.'

'I didn't take much persuading,' he murmured.

'He really didn't,' said Benedict, saluting Sophia as Daniel had done. 'I'll swear you're lovelier than ever, Sophie. How do you do it?'

'Incantations under the full moon,' she laughed. 'And what I am right now is *enormous*.' She slid an arm through each of theirs, drawing them to the door. 'Come inside. Gerald and Anthony are both here.' And, just to be clear – I *am* delighted that all of you are here for Kit's sake. He's overdue for some male company.'

'And she's hoping your presence will stop me hovering like a mother hen,' added Christian, joining them. 'Your rooms are ready. Bradley will see to your luggage and have hot water sent up. When you are ready, join the rest of us on the back terrace for tea – or something stronger, if you wish.'

When the party reassembled outside and greetings had been exchanged, Anthony took the seat beside Daniel and said quietly, 'How are things going?'

'A little better. We rotated the crops according to the plan you made, two of the three tenants with larger holdings have done the same and the results are promising. Your suggestions about a different way of pruning the apple trees seem likely to bear fruit – literally. And I'm more grateful than I can say for you lending me your land steward for a few days. He was immensely helpful.'

'But?' prompted Anthony.

'But until there's money to replace some of the ancient machinery everything else is pretty much at a standstill.' He summoned something close to a smile. 'I tell myself that things can only get better ... but just wish I knew *when*.'

He looked up as Gerald joined them and, with a little of his old devilment, said, 'And how is Miss Julia? Or is that a thing of the past?'

'She's very well,' came the calm reply, followed by a series of swift hand movements.

Hearing Sophia laugh, Daniel said suspiciously, 'What did you say?'

'I said she'd be here now had her mother not felt that some of the company was undesirable. She didn't name names but ... I doubt she meant Benedict.'

'That is wicked, Gerald – and not at all true,' said Sophia, shaking her head. And to Daniel, 'What Mama *actually* said was that, even with Jane in tow, she couldn't allow Julia to spend a week in virtually all male company – apparently *I* don't count! – unless she and Gwendoline accompanied her. And you can guess Kit's reaction to *that*.'

'Vividly!' agreed Daniel, laughing. 'Am I allowed to say Thank God?'

'You may as well,' offered Anthony. '*I* certainly did.'

Managing to frown, Sophia said, 'May I remind you that you are speaking of my mother and sisters?'

'I know – and I apologise. But whereas Miss Julia is a delight, Miss Gwendoline ...'

Anthony stopped, thus giving Daniel the opportunity to say, '... makes single gentlemen feel like a mouse with an eagle hovering overhead.'

She laughed. 'Oh dear! As bad as that?'

'Worse!'

Some distance away and pouring wine for the new arrivals, Christian handed Benedict a glass and said softly, 'How is he?'

'Not good. He still doesn't know what that loan was for – the one you paid off for him; and the fact that you did so is chafing at him.'

'Better that than the alternative. What else?'

'He's selling things. While I was there, it was his mother's scent bottles – a hundred of them, if you can believe it, bought for her over the years by his late lordship. While they were being packed up for transportation, she spent all day sulking. As for what Daniel got for them, all I know is it was half as much again as they originally cost but less than the five thousand he owes you.' He paused, then added, 'Also, for what it's worth, there's something else on his mind that he won't talk about any more than he'll accept help.'

'He won't accept *money*,' corrected Christian. 'But there are other things we can do – beginning with getting him to relax and reminding him how to laugh. So let's start with those.'

* * *

The following days passed pleasantly. Although recently the five of them had seen little of each other, they slid effortlessly back into the easy companionship they'd always shared ... talking and laughing, riding or swimming and, in the evenings, playing cards for sixpenny points. Within twenty-four hours, Daniel felt the load of the last months slipping from his shoulders; and somewhere around the middle of the week, he realised that he was beginning to recover his sense of perspective.

In trying to keep everything – especially the situation with Anna Hawthorne – secret, he'd bottled it up inside. And as far as his mother and sister were concerned, he still considered that the right course of action.

But these men are my friends, he thought. *I know I can trust them – so I can tell them, can't I? They'll listen, they won't judge ... and they'll give me advice if I ask for it. God knows, I need some.*

But still he hesitated. And while he did so, Gerald announced that he was returning to London to attend to the quarterly accounts.

Christian grinned. 'Seriously?'

Gerald flushed. 'Yes. We're a week into July and – '

'And the accounts will wait a few more days.'

'I daresay. But I like to keep on top of things and – '

Benedict murmured, 'Better not let Sophie hear you put it like that.'

Daniel laughed and Gerald's flush deepened. 'I don't know what you mean.'

'Yes, you do,' remarked Christian calmly. 'You're missing Julia and hoping she's also missing you. Admit it.'

Gerald drew an exasperated breath and then muttered, 'Yes. All right, I admit it. But I'm perfectly aware that nothing will come of it – so can we please *leave* it?'

'Yes. But first let me say this. It *will* come to nothing if you don't try. So on your way back to London, think about whether or not Julia should have some say in this. And when you've decided that she should, for pity's sake *do* something.' Christian smiled at him and added, more gently, 'You have Sophie and me on your side, Gerald. And that counts for something.'

* * *

Gerald left the following morning and that evening after dinner, Daniel said baldly, 'I've been offered marriage by a woman with the means to solve all my financial problems. Since I can't solve them any other way, the sensible thing would be to accept. But I ... I'm not sure I can bring myself to do it.'

Not unnaturally, this produced a deafening silence while everyone stared at him. Finally, Christian said, 'Before we come to *why* you can't, let's be clear on one thing. You say she has the means to solve your problems. Does she also have the willingness?'

'She says so. I don't know her well enough to be absolutely sure but I'm inclined to believe her. And she must know that, if I were to agree, I'd make sure matters were nailed down legally and in every other way.'

'Can you tell us who she is?' It was Sophia who asked. 'We'll understand if you'd rather not. But we might be better able to advise you if we knew.'

'I doubt it. It's unlikely any of you know her – or anything about her, other than what I can tell you.'

'Point taken,' agreed Benedict. 'But we have to start somewhere. And you don't need to be told that nothing you say will leave this room.'

Daniel hesitated. Then, deciding that it couldn't do any harm and continuing to hold Benedict's eyes but choosing his words for the benefit of the others, said, 'Very well. The lady owns a porcelain manufactory and I met her when she came to value my mother's collection of scent bottles. Her name is Anna Hawthorne.'

There was a brief silence. Finally, Sophia said slowly, 'I've met her. She was in London during my first Season.'

'So have I,' said Anthony. 'Trixie was out that year, too, and I was on escort duty. They called Miss Hawthorne the Hedgehog Heiress because she frequently managed to say, not just the *wrong* thing, but something ... prickly.'

Sophia nodded. 'She didn't know how to play the game – by which I mean chatting about the inconsequential things everyone talks about at balls and parties.'

'She still doesn't,' muttered Daniel. 'She is an only child and her father educated her as if she was a son. When he died, she inherited the company. She runs it herself and intends to go on doing so. Basically, she's interested in one thing and one thing only. Hawthorne's Porcelain.'

Sophia shook her head, a tiny, wicked glint lighting her eyes.

'Two things, Daniel. Clearly, she's interested in you as well.'

Christian laughed. 'Undeniably true.'

'Maybe. But why? Why *me*? It's none of the obvious things.' He began ticking points off on his fingers. 'She doesn't care about London society. She doesn't give a fig for my title or the status that would come with it. She doesn't even *really* want a husband – or not unless he matches her precise specifications.'

'As it seems that you do,' remarked Anthony with a hint of amusement. 'So ... what are they?'

'She wants the freedom of a married lady but to a man who'll let her run her company – and, I suspect, the rest of her life – without interference, whilst having fish of his own to fry.'

'The first of which you would do willingly and the second with a degree of caution. The fish, you already have in abundance,' said Christian. 'What else?'

'Nothing really,' shrugged Daniel.

'Children?' asked Sophia.

'I don't think she cares much either way. Her life is completely bound up in Hawthorne's and that's how she likes it.' He drained his glass, then stared into it. 'At present, all she's asked is that I consider her offer, so I've no idea how she sees such a union working. For all I know, she may want a white marriage.'

'She doesn't,' said Sophia, matter-of-factly.

'She might,' argued Benedict.

'She doesn't,' repeated Sophia. 'Although, to be fair, she may not know that yet.'

'Well, don't just sit there looking smug,' begged Christian. 'Tell us why.'

'Daniel's already told you that if you'd been paying attention. He needs money and she, apparently, has plenty of it. She doesn't want the obvious thing that he *does* have – namely, the title. On the surface, all she claims to want is the freedom to run her company; and over the last four years, she's probably met a dozen men who'd let her do that in return for the money she'd bring with her. But she hasn't shown interest in any of them or in marriage ... until now.' She smiled at Daniel. 'So what she wants is obvious because it's really the only thing she'd be getting. You.'

Over a crack of male laughter, he croaked, '*Me?* No. Surely not.'

'Modesty aside, you must know women find you attractive. A very happily married friend of mine once described you as *a particularly fine specimen of masculinity*. I suspect Anna Hawthorne thinks the same. I also suspect she's been struck, somewhat belatedly, with the sort of infatuation that most girls get out of their systems at the age of seventeen.' Turning a quelling glance on Christian, Benedict and Anthony, all of whom were still chuckling, she said, 'That isn't helpful.' And, once more to Daniel, 'But that's beside the point. What *matters* is that you don't have to accept her proposal ... but that, if you do, you would have an equal right to set the terms of your marriage. If you want a purely businesslike arrangement, at this stage she'll probably agree to it.' Sophia paused and then added, 'But be careful what you write on tablets of stone, Daniel. Things can change. And even if they don't, you shouldn't make friendship impossible … or the marriage will be miserable. For both of you.'

CHAPTER NINE

For Anna, the days crawled by.

She suggested to Mr Lowe that a possible temporary location for the exhibition might be achieved by moving the offices of both himself and his secretary to the floor above which, at present, was only occasionally needed for storage. That way, the two ground-floor rooms would provide a convenient location. Mr Lowe agreed that this was as good a solution as any and said he'd set the necessary changes in hand immediately. Anna smiled and pretended an enthusiasm she ought to feel but couldn't.

She wasn't used to this degree of distraction and she didn't like it. Unfortunately, that didn't make it go away. No matter what else she might be doing or what other matters demanded her attention, a part of her mind was always occupied with Viscount Reculver; how soon and in what way he might reply to what she was increasingly beginning to see as an act of impulsive idiocy.

When Simeon Harvill returned to the manufactory demanding to see her, it barely engaged her attention. Even his arrival at the door of her home didn't bother her unduly because, having been forewarned of this possibility, Sedley told the fellow that she wasn't at home. However, when Mr Harvill came again only two days later, Anna decided that enough was enough and said, 'Sedley ... please inform the gentleman that I will not receive him. Not now, not *ever*. And if he continues to plague me in this fashion, I shall lay a complaint against him with the local magistrate.'

Then she put the matter from her mind and attempted to concentrate on making a list of the other Hawthorne wares deserving of a place in the budding exhibition and what colour the rooms should be painted in order to show everything off to the best effect.

There was only a week, just seven days left before Lord Reculver was due to give her his answer. Once she had it, she would be able to function normally again. Wouldn't she?

* * *

Daniel arrived home feeling better than he had in what seemed a very long time. This happy state of affairs lasted long enough for him to greet his mother and sister and answer their numerous questions about his friends. Then he went to the library to look through whatever correspondence was awaiting him there ... and everything came crashing down around him again.

The cause was a polite letter from a man he'd never heard of but who it seemed his father must have known very well indeed.

My lord, I suspect you may be unaware of an interest-free loan I made to your late father last autumn. Enclosed, please find his note of hand, bearing the amount, date and both of our signatures.

We were very old friends and his need of the funds was urgent, it being payment of a debt of honour. He expected to be in a position to repay the loan by March, at the latest, but by then sadly, he had passed away. I have delayed bringing this to your attention for as long as possible out of respect for his memory but, as can see, the sum is no trifling amount and represents funds of which I now stand in need.

I look forward to hearing from your lordship at your earliest convenience.

Yours respectfully,

H. Grimshaw

It was indeed no trifling amount. According to this, Father had owed Grimshaw four thousand pounds.

Daniel felt as if the floor was dissolving beneath him. His stomach rose into his throat and he was barely in time to vomit into the waste basket rather than across his desk. Then, pressing a handkerchief to his mouth and breathing very fast, he shut his eyes and tried, without success, not to think.

Four thousand pounds. For a debt of honour? That doesn't sound like Father. He wasn't a gamester – or, if he was, I never knew of it. And where – and to whom – could he lose a sum like that? Come to that, who is this fellow Grimshaw? I never heard the name before. He attempted to take a long, calming breath. Then thought, *What the* hell *was Father playing at? And what* else *don't I know about yet?*

Nausea was still roiling inside him and he felt icy cold. Crossing to the brandy decanter, he sloshed its meagre contents into a glass and downed it in one swallow.

There having been insufficient time to set his plans for it in motion before leaving for Hazelmere, he had three thousand pounds locked in a drawer of his desk. A few, short minutes ago, that had represented a small start on the road to recovery ... but no longer. He wasn't just back where he'd started. He was drowning.

Five thousand owed to Kit, four to Grimshaw and two-and-a-half to Henderson & Company. A total of eleven thousand, five hundred pounds ... not counting the overdraft at the bank. And even using all the money in his desk, he couldn't clear more than a quarter of it.

Every square inch of Reculver land was entailed. The only property that hadn't been, a small manor in Somerset which had come to the family through his great-grandmother, had been sold by his father almost a decade ago. Daniel supposed vaguely that he could try to break the entail ... there were circumstances in which that could be done, though he didn't know what they were. But selling off even part of Reculver went against everything that was in him; and at best, it would just be another temporary bandage on a wound which continued to bleed.

The bank wouldn't extend his credit; it had been stretched too far and too long already. He could not, *would* not, turn to his friends because the existing debt to Christian was already nagging at him like an aching tooth. But this business with Grimshaw ... Daniel forced his brain to work. The fellow lived in Cirencester, a little less than twenty miles away. If he met the man, he might at least get to the root of *that* and perhaps learn something that made sense of the rest of it.

He briefly considered writing to ask for an appointment, then decided against it. Best to take H. Grimshaw by surprise rather than giving him time to prepare.

But before he thought any more about that, there were two obvious things he could do immediately. He hunted for something bearing his father's signature and, when he found it, set it alongside the note of hand sent by Grimshaw. So far as he could see, the signatures looked the same but for the ink in which they'd been written ... but that small difference wasn't enough to give him hope that the newer one wasn't genuine.

He swore under his breath, pushed both papers aside and strode from the library. Finding his mother in the drawing-room and coming directly to the point, he said, 'Do you know of an old friend of Father's by the name of Grimshaw?'

A peculiar expression flickered briefly across the Dowager's face and she hesitated for a moment. Then she said, 'I know the *name*. I've never met the man himself.'

'But he was one of Father's friends?'

'Yes. For a while some years ago, they used to spend time with each other – most often in the vicinity of Cirencester where I believe Mr Grimshaw lived.'

'He did and still does. They spent time *how* precisely?'

'What do you mean?'

'What did they do together? Visit gaming houses? Go to the races? What?'

'Your father didn't gamble – you know that. For the rest, I – I've no idea how they occupied themselves. Why are you asking?'

'Mostly because I've received a letter from Grimshaw and wanted to know that he is who he says he is. But also because, although you say you've never met him, I sense that you dislike him. Why is that?'

'Dislike him? Don't be silly, dear. How could I? But why did he write to you?'

He didn't miss the evasion but he let it go and was equally evasive himself.

'An apparently unresolved matter between him and Father.' Then, abruptly seeming to change tack, 'I'm afraid I have to go away again.'

'But you've only just got back!'

'I know – and it's unfortunate but inescapable. And brief. I'll leave tomorrow and be back the day after.'

Returning to the library and thankful that, in his absence, someone had removed the offensive waste basket, he dropped his head in his hands and did his best not to contemplate the fact that there was a way out of this entire mess if he chose to take it.

All I have to do is say yes and sign the rest of my life away. Nothing to it, really.

* * *

Arriving in Cirencester around mid-afternoon, he took a room at the Twelve Bells where he ordered a bath and dinner. He also asked for and received directions to Grimshaw's house. Throughout most of a largely wakeful night, he searched for the best means of approaching the problem. Then, next day and with the bare bones of a strategy in mind, he set out hoping to find the fellow at home.

The house was a moderate-sized and well-maintained property on a pleasant street. A trim maid answered the door and Daniel learned that he was in luck. His quarry was indeed at home. Daniel was shown into a small parlour containing a good many indifferent ornaments ... and then a tall, thin man walked in, wearing an expression which was half-wary and half-satisfied before being replaced with a cordial smile.

He's expecting to get his four thousand pounds back, thought Daniel cynically as Mr Grimshaw shook his hand and said what a pleasure it was to meet his old friend's son.

'Thank you, sir,' replied Daniel. 'But I fear you have the advantage of me. I don't recall my father ever mentioning you. From where did you know each other?'

'We met at Oxford,' came the easy reply, 'and stayed close after it. I travel a great deal on business – exporting wool and importing cotton. But between trips, I live here with my widowed sister-in-law, thus close enough that your father and I were able to maintain our friendship. Allow me to say how very sorry I was to hear of his death. I shall miss him.'

Daniel acknowledged this with a polite inclination of his head and said, 'You weren't tempted to attend the funeral?'

'Sadly, I was away at the time.' A pause, then, 'I hope Lady Reculver is well? And your sister?' And when Daniel nodded again, 'But forgive me. I should ring for tea.'

'Not on my account, sir. I would prefer to come to the point. I am sure you know why I am here. And – '

'I'd *hoped* you were here to repay your father's loan. Isn't that the case?'

'No. Permit me to be blunt. My father left a number of debts but one to yourself was not among them. So – '

'Well, it wouldn't be, would it? We had a gentleman's agreement.'

'So your letter intimated. But I'd like to know more about it. For example, exactly what *was* this 'debt of honour'? Cards? Dice? A wager? To whom did my father lose it? And why did he suppose he would be in a position to repay you in March?'

For a few moments, Grimshaw appeared to think this over but then he smiled and, with a rueful shake of his head, said, 'Forgive me, my lord, but I can't answer any of that.'

'Can't – or won't?'

'Can't. All I know of the wager is the amount your father stood in need of to settle it. He didn't say how he lost it or to whom. And I didn't ask because, if he'd wanted me to know, he would have told me; and because, when asked for help, good friends give it without insisting on chapter and verse.'

This, Daniel knew without a shred of doubt, was true of *his* friends. But for some reason he couldn't identify, he wasn't sure it was true of the man sitting in front of him. On the other hand, he could all too easily believe that his father might have withheld the details. Secrecy had been a habit with him.

He said slowly, 'Granted. But there is a problem with this that raises doubts in my mind. My father may have gambled as a very young man but neither I nor my mother have known him do so in later years. And, being already in financial difficulties, it isn't likely that he suddenly started doing so in the months before his death.'

'Aren't the difficulties you mention exactly why he *would* have done so?'

'No. Since you knew him so well, Mr Grimshaw, you must have known that he was not a stupid man. And only a *very* stupid man gambles with money he doesn't have,' replied Daniel, praying that he was right about that but by no means certain of it. 'For this reason, I'd need better substantiation of both the debt of honour and your own loan for the repayment of it. Nothing amongst my father's paperwork supports it – so at present, all I have is your word.'

'And the note of hand bearing your father's signature,' countered Grimshaw.

'Which merely states a sum of money to be loaned by you to my father – and nothing anywhere to prove the loan was actually *made*.'

'Are you trying to squirm out of this by claiming that it wasn't?'

'I'm not claiming anything. I'm merely asking for more detailed information before being willing to add your loan to the others already outstanding. None of these debts were created by me ... but at least there is documentation to support their existence. And, though I'd need to seek clarification on this point, I have a suspicion that debts of honour cannot be inherited.'

Grimshaw's colour rose. 'You are splitting hairs, young man. Your father paid the debt of honour with money loaned to him by me. And that debt *can* be inherited.'

'I don't deny it. But I want proof, sir.' Daniel rose, holding both his nerve and the other man's eyes. 'Since I doubt you keep such large sums by you, doubtless your bank will be able to supply that. Feel free to contact me again when you have it. Meanwhile, I will bid you good day.'

He was half-way to the door when Grimshaw caught up with him and grasped his arm. 'Don't think I'll let you get away with leaving me four thousand out of pocket!'

'Show me some firm evidence of that and we'll talk again.' He shook the other man's hand off. 'For now, this conversation is over.' And he walked out.

* * *

Daniel spent most of the homeward journey going back over his meeting with Grimshaw, weighing up what had been said and wondering why he'd suddenly felt so certain that something wasn't right – or if that had only been born of wishful thinking and his own desperation. He told himself that, if something underhand *was* going on, there was a chance the debt didn't exist at all. And even if there wasn't and it did, at least he had bought himself some time in which to use the money he already had in his hands. He would redeem the debt to Henderson & Company as planned and begin setting some of the cottage repairs in hand. At least doing that would alleviate his feeling of utter uselessness.

* * *

While Viscount Reculver was riding back from Cirencester and mulling over his meeting with Mr Grimshaw, Miss Hawthorne was also on her way home, her head busy with the plans she and Mr Lowe had agreed upon concerning the exhibition. It was the only subject capable of distracting her from what she had come to regard as her current obsession. Today, she was considering the rival merits of knocking the two, now empty ground floor offices, into one versus merely installing a connecting archway between them. There were points in favour of both. The former had the advantage of creating one large space; the latter retained greater wall area for eye-level shelving but would still offer room for at least one large, island cabinet for the scent bottles.

She was vaguely aware of her coachman shouting something and then the coach slowed and came to a halt. Anna let down the window and looked out. There were two men on horseback in the middle of the road ... one well-dressed, the other clearly a groom.

'What is the meaning of this?' she demanded imperiously. 'Clear the way, sir.'

Leaving his groom still blocking the way, the gentleman – if, thought Anna sourly, he could be *called* a gentleman – rode to address her through the window. He said, 'You're a hard lady to meet, Miss Hawthorne.'

Immediately guessing his identity, she replied coldly, 'Not for people I *wish* to meet, Mr Harvill. How *dare* you accost me like this?'

'You've given me no choice, have you?'

'For which, I had my reasons. However, state your business and keep it brief.'

He touched the brim of his hat in token courtesy. 'Simeon Harvill, ma'am. And you know my business. You just won't –'

'Oh for heaven's sake!' she snapped. 'How many times must you be told? Hawthorne's is *not* for sale. Not to you, not to *anyone*. Now get out of my way!'

'I offered your man twelve thousand. I'm prepared to go to fifteen for a quick conclusion. It's a fair offer. More than fair.'

Anna drew a long breath and held on to the remaining shreds of her temper.

'Mr Harvill ... listen very carefully, for what I am about to say will not change – neither do I intend to continue repeating myself. My pottery is not for sale. Not at any time, nor for any price. You could offer twenty-five thousand or a hundred and the answer would remain the same. *I will not sell!* Now tell your man to clear the way ... and don't try this again unless you want a visit from the magistrate.' And she called out, 'Drive on, Hawkins. He'll move fast enough when he realises you won't be stopping.'

She slammed the window shut and the carriage jerked forward, forcing Harvill to pull his horse back. Breathing a little too fast but otherwise perfectly composed, Anna leaned against the squabs and thought, *This is ridiculous. Why does he persist? Surely he must realise by now that he's wasting his time?* And then, *But what if he doesn't? I'd rather not go through that again. Perhaps I should consider speaking to Squire Cranford anyway ... just in case.*

By the time she got home, however, she had talked herself out of it. Now he'd had his answer from her own lips, Harvill would surely give up. And if he didn't ... well, time enough to report him for harassment then.

Inevitably, her mind drifted back to the viscount. Four days left now. Just four. And still all she could do was wait. *She* couldn't contact *him* – and neither should she have to. It was up to him to contact her. A civil little note; something along the lines of, *Thank you for your kind offer, Miss Hawthorne but, after due consideration, I fear I must decline.*

If *she* knew what he was going to do, surely *he* must know too? In which case, why was it taking him so long to do it?

CHAPTER TEN

Daniel was well aware that time had virtually run out with Anna Hawthorne and that he should have sent her an answer earlier. He told himself that he would have done so but for that damned letter from Grimshaw. But now there could be no further excuse. There was barely sufficient time left for a letter to reach her. Yet here he sat, pen in hand, in front of a sheet of paper, blank but for his address, the date and the words, *Dear Miss Hawthorne* ... unable to continue because his situation dictated one answer and everything inside him, another.

He thought of Sophia's advice. If Anna Hawthorne had ideas about how a marriage between them might work, he ought to find out what they were and also remember that he would be equally entitled to set terms. In other words, some discussion between the two of them wasn't just desirable, but necessary – for both their sakes.

His friends had also had opinions.

'Don't do it,' Christian had said flatly. 'No amount of money will compensate for spending the rest of your life with a woman you don't even like very much.'

'Think carefully,' advised Benedict. 'Just because you haven't fallen head over heels for anyone yet doesn't mean you never will.'

And, 'Be sure you know what you're turning down before you do anything,' was Anthony's recommendation. 'Sophie's right. You need to know Miss Hawthorne better than you do now. How else are you to arrive at an informed decision?'

Daniel found the idea of inviting further discussion appealing in one way but slightly worrying in another. It spared him the need to reach a firm decision immediately but could also make a refusal more difficult should that be his eventual choice.

Realising that he was just finding new ways to procrastinate, he ordered himself to stop. At this stage, there was no guarantee that Anna Hawthorne would agree to discussing the matter at all ... and if he delayed any longer it would be too late anyway. But if he *didn't* suggest it, he'd never know, would he? He'd have to come down on one side or the other.

She had offered him a life-line and, much as he wanted to refuse, he was painfully aware that he shouldn't. He was balanced on a knife-edge already. If, in addition to everything else, the debt to Grimshaw turned out to be real ... well, he couldn't think about that yet.

But he could and must think about Rebecca. She would be twenty on her next birthday and needed to make her come-out in the spring. As things stood, he had absolutely no hope of finding the funds he would need to make it possible. Becky rarely complained; but Daniel knew that she could see her chance of having the future she'd been brought up to expect sliding further and further away. It was up to him to ensure that it didn't vanish completely.

Reluctantly, he dipped his quill in the ink and wrote, *I have come to realise that a decision on a matter with such far-reaching consequences cannot be made without each of us having some understanding of the other's expectations. You may have thought the same but felt it inappropriate, under the circumstances, to write to me. If so, perhaps we might meet to discuss this further? I could call upon you unless there is some preferable alternative you can suggest.*

Yours etc.
Reculver

He sealed the letter and gave it to Flynn for posting before he could change his mind. She'd agree or she wouldn't. Either way, it was out of his control now.

* * *

Anna broke the seal on his lordship's letter with hands that weren't entirely steady. Then, pulse hammering, she read the contents three times to make sure she hadn't misunderstood.

He wasn't saying no.

True, he wasn't saying yes either. But his request for further discussion was more than she'd dared hope for and felt, at this late stage, like a reprieve.

I could call upon you ...

No. He absolutely could *not*, for fear of what Mama would make of it. So what to suggest instead? She couldn't meet him at an inn or in any public place where there was a risk of them being seen together and one or both of them recognised. Anna might not care for most of society's rules but she had a very clear idea of what one could get away with and what one couldn't – for him as well as for herself.

Which left what? Only one place that she could think of. The manufactory, under the pretext of … something or other.

My Lord Reculver, she wrote.

Do not think of calling on me at home. My mother's fertile imagination would complicate the issue tenfold. Write to Mr Lowe, asking him to arrange a meeting between us at Hawthorne's. Make it sound like a matter of business – you do not need to be specific. He will give us his office so we may speak privately.

Yours, etc.

Anna Hawthorne

As she laid her pen down, she briefly debated telling Mr Lowe to expect his lordship's letter and then decided that it would be best to say nothing in order to appear suitably baffled but also intrigued when it came.

Summoning Sedley, she handed him the letter for posting.

* * *

Although somewhat surprised by Lord Reculver's request, Mr Lowe didn't hesitate to apprise Miss Hawthorne of it and, when she gave her permission, to immediately make the necessary arrangements with his lordship. The result was that, four days later, Anna and the viscount faced each other across a table in the manager's office.

Having exchanged a polite greeting, both of them seemed at a loss to know what to say next. But finally, Daniel broke the silence with, 'Since this was my suggestion, perhaps I should start?'

'Yes.' He was every bit as devastating as she remembered. Somehow, she had to not only put that aside but also hide how it affected her. 'That might be best.'

'Very well. You'll be aware that you … you somewhat took my breath away at our last meeting. Given your previously expressed views on matrimony, your offer came as a bolt from the blue – to which I may not have reacted well.'

'You were shocked. Naturally. Surprising though you may find it, so was I.'

He stared at her. 'You were?'

'Yes. I'd had the idea and could see the advantages of it on both sides.' She paused and, shrugging, added, 'But I hadn't expected to blurt it out *quite* like that.'

'You hadn't?'

'Not at all.' Difficult though it was, she forced herself to continue meeting his eyes. 'As for – for bribing you to consider it, I don't know where that came from. It demeaned me and insulted you. Please accept my apologies for it.'

This was unexpected. Sometimes, Daniel thought, there was much to be said for a person who habitually spoke their mind. Deciding she deserved no less, he said wryly, 'As to that, I could have refused. But I didn't, did I?'

'No. In your position, neither would I. But that doesn't excuse me for putting you in that position. However ... your letter said that, prior to making a decision on whether to – to take my proposal further, we should understand each other's expectations. I agree but am not at all sure where to begin with it. Are you?'

'Perhaps with the fact that your business is here and mine – if the estate can be called that – is some thirty miles distant? In practical terms, how would you see that working if we were to marry?'

'I do not need to be here all the time. Letters and regular visits – two or three days, once or twice a month, perhaps – would be adequate for most purposes.'

'That doesn't sound ... unmanageable,' he allowed slowly.

Anna nodded. 'And for the foreseeable future, you need to be at Reculver. At least until things are in better shape.'

'Agreed. So you are saying we would live there?'

'That would seem the most sensible solution, yes. Unless you have some objection? Or perhaps your mother ...?'

'I would have no objection – and doubt that she would either.'

'Oh. Good.' She waited and, when he didn't speak, said, 'What else did you wish to talk about?'

He could think of one vital issue but didn't feel up to raising that just yet, so he said, 'You expressed concerns regarding a husband's ownership of his wife's property.'

'I did. And you pointed out that a lawyer could solve that problem.'

'Unless,' Daniel pointed out, 'I refused to sign the necessary documents.'

'And would you?'

'No. But – '

'That's what I thought.' A sudden smile touched her mouth. 'You haven't the remotest interest in the manufactory, have you?'

'If by that you mean that I've no desire to meddle with it – no, I haven't. I've more than enough to deal with at Reculver. But you can't just take my word for that.'

'Actually, I think I could,' she replied composedly. 'I believe you would keep your word, as I shall keep mine. But of course I won't rely purely on that. I'd have Mr Landry tie everything up so tight you'd virtually need a passport to get through the door.'

'Would you indeed?'

'I would.'

In spite of himself, he gave a tiny laugh. 'Good for you. All right. What else?'

'From my point of view? Nothing that I'm aware of. We've established that my interests can be secured legally. As can yours … and my obligations to you.' Anna found herself distracted by a wish that he'd laugh more often. Pushing it aside, she said, 'As I tried to intimate at our last meeting, I would prefer you to be my partner rather than my pensioner, so steps must be taken to make that possible. With your agreement, my suggestion would be clearing any debts you may have and funding your bank accounts. When you have no other encumbrances, tackling the problems on the estate will become your sole priority.'

This was very close to what she'd said before and Daniel still couldn't quite believe that she meant it literally. 'Don't you want to set a limit on how much you're prepared to contribute to that?'

'No. What would be the point? Those things have to be done and it will be easier to take stock once they have been.' She paused and then, holding her head high, went on in the same coolly logical tone. 'There is also Rebecca's Season to be considered. You would need to have money on hand for that. But I understand there are ladies willing to – to take care of her actual come-out and it would be best if one of *them* did so rather than myself.'

Recalling with a tiny twinge of guilt that he'd once said the same thing – or something very like it – himself, he asked cautiously, 'What makes you think so?'

'I was not ... popular ... and would not wish that to damage her chances.'

'You appear to have given all this a great deal of thought.'

'As I would any new venture,' she agreed.

Daniel might have smiled at this were it not for the fact that it was beginning to strike him very forcibly that she didn't seem to be asking for anything more than a wedding ring. On present showing, all the advantages were on his side. This pricked his conscience but also bred a suspicion that she'd ask for the one thing he not only didn't *want* to provide but as yet couldn't even bring himself to contemplate.

He said bluntly, 'Pardon me, Miss Hawthorne ... but it doesn't seem that you would be gaining anything at all from marriage to me. Or am I missing something?'

'Yes. I would be gaining a household of my own along with the increased freedom of a married woman. And a husband who I believe I can respect and like.'

'And that would be enough?'

'It would be a good place to start. And a better one than I might find elsewhere ... or that many women like me ever find at all.'

Daniel frowned slightly. 'Women like you?'

'Yes. Ones who don't fit the correct mould and lack the qualities which might make that unimportant.' Neither her matter-of-fact tone nor the smile that accompanied it invited sympathy. 'A fact which was made very clear to me during my time in London.'

'You don't think you do yourself a disservice?'

'No. I know what I am – and I think you know it, too. So ... have we covered everything? Or is there anything else we should address?'

Groaning inwardly but seeing no help for it, Daniel said, 'Yes. Nothing that has been said so far has given me any understanding of what you would expect or are hoping for on – on a personal level.'

'A personal level?' she said blankly. 'I don't think I – ' And stopped abruptly, her colour rising. 'Oh. You mean in the bedroom?'

'Yes. I'm presuming you *have* thought of it?'

'Not in so many words,' Anna muttered. And thought, *Not ones I'm willing to say out loud anyway.* 'But if you have, please go on.'

He managed not to say, *Do I have to?*

Instead, harnessing every scrap of tact he possessed, he said, 'Correct me if I'm mistaken, but you are approaching the question of marriage exactly as you would a business transaction – in which, of course, you are right because it *is* one, even when the couple believe themselves in love. In our case, not only are we clearly *not* in love, we scarcely know each other. Time would remedy that, of course. But at present I am as short of *time* as of everything else. Therefore, from my point of view, if we *were* to agree to marry we may as well do so sooner rather than later … but on the understanding that, for the foreseeable future, we would not be sharing a bed.'

Her expression did not change but he saw her swallow hard.

She said, 'Of course. I had assumed as much.'

Relief washed over him. 'You had?'

'Yes. Anything else would be … extremely premature. And awkward.' Anna hesitated. Then, closing one hand hard over the other and for the first time looking past, rather than at him, added, 'But I would be obliged if you conducted any – any liaisons you might have with discretion.'

Daniel laughed, albeit aridly.

'That need not concern you. Firstly, I don't approve of men who foul their own doorstep, as it were. And secondly, having been celibate as a monk for the last eight months, I'm becoming quite used to the condition.'

'Oh,' she said weakly.

'Oh,' agreed Daniel. 'Now … unless there is anything else, may I suggest that we both take a little time to digest what has been said? Let's say a week? If you decide to withdraw your offer – '

'I won't.'

'Think carefully about what you'd be getting before you say that,' he cautioned. 'As I was saying, *if* you reconsider or if *I* decline your offer, that can be the end of the matter and settled by letter. But if both of us decide to proceed, clearly the next step ought to be me paying a formal call upon you at your home. Yes?'

'Yes.'

'Good.' Daniel rose and, when Anna did the same, bowed over her hand. 'If you think of anything further, write to me – the same when you arrive at your decision.'

'As will you, I hope.' Clinging tightly to her usual composure, she said, 'Thank you for considering my proposal and for coming here today to discuss it. I didn't think you would do that.'

'Neither did I,' he replied truthfully. 'But for various reasons, sense prevailed ... and I am glad to have had this conversation.' His mouth curled in his usual smile and he added, 'I've a better understanding of who I'm dealing with and, hopefully, so have you.'

* * *

When he had gone, Anna folded bonelessly into her chair and pressed both hands over her mouth to choke back an hysterical laugh. He *still* wasn't saying no. And there was a chance, however small, that he might actually say yes.

When he smiled, it made her heart sing. And when he touched her ... oh, when he touched her everything inside her ignited. She thought, *Oh, please.* Please *let him say yes. I can help him. All I need is the chance to do it. And in return, I'll be able to watch him start to smile again and become the man he used to be. I won't ask for more. It would be enough.*

* * *

Daniel drove home prey to conflicting thoughts.

He'd expected the meeting to be difficult, embarrassing and possibly unpleasant. It hadn't been any of those things ...the credit for which belonged largely to Miss Hawthorne. By the end of it, he'd started to realise that he didn't dislike her. Once or twice, he'd even come close to *liking* her; to admiring that no-nonsense approach of hers.

She'd absorbed the news that he wouldn't be taking her to bed any time soon without turning a hair. He wasn't sure what that meant ... only that it didn't mean what Sophia had thought it did. That was a relief. He hadn't much liked the notion that she was harbouring some kind of hopeful attraction which wasn't ever likely to be reciprocated.

For the rest, her generosity astounded him. His debts, his overdrawn bank accounts and Rebecca. All of it offered so matter-of-factly and as if the cost of it all was of no importance that he'd started to wonder just how much money she had clear access to. Usually a young, single lady's wealth was tied up in a way that meant even *she* couldn't get at it.

Her thoughtfulness regarding Becky had swept the ground from beneath his feet.

I understand there are ladies willing to take care of her actual come-out and it would be best if one of them did so rather than myself. I was not ... popular ... and would not wish that to damage her chances.

That couldn't have been easy for her acknowledge privately, let alone to admit to him. He'd been tempted, at that point, to say something comforting. He hadn't because her manner suggested that it wouldn't be welcome; that she'd regard it as the well-meaning platitude it would have been.

All this and more had to be weighed and measured. But the question was the same one it had always been. Could he actually *do* this? *Could* he trade his whole future and the kind of marriage he'd hoped to have one day in return for financial security for his family and the estate?

Cold reality told him that he should.

Cold reality frightened the hell out of him.

* * *

Anna spent the next four days swinging between hope and doubt.

Daniel spent them trying and failing to reach a decision. Then, on the fifth day, came a second letter from Harold Grimshaw.

My lord, it said.

You asked for proof of the loan made to your late father. Here it is. I will expect to hear from you at your earliest convenience, laying out details of how and when I will receive repayment.

Yours etc.

H. Grimshaw

And enclosed from Hoare's Bank in Cheltenham, a bald statement said, *Paid by H. Grimshaw to Viscount Reculver of Reculver Court, Prior's Norton, Gloucestershire on the fifteenth day of November last, the sum of four thousand pounds.*

The signature was that of P. Wilson, Under-Manager.

Slumped in the chair behind his desk, Daniel stared at it for a very long time as the sense of it gradually soaked in.

It's real, then, he thought numbly. *Well, at least that answers one question. There's no longer any point in going back and forth over what to say to Anna Hawthorne. No choice now but to grasp the nettle and write asking when it will be convenient for her to receive me. However, first ... first I'd better tell Mama and Becky. Presenting it to them as a fait accompli wouldn't be a good idea.*

Finding his mother and sister in the drawing-room, he spoke briefly and to the point. When he had finished, they stared at him in silence for a few moments ... until finally Rebecca said, 'No. Daniel, no. You *can't.*'

He shook his head. 'I can't do anything else, love. And it won't be so bad. She – '

'It isn't *her*. It's *you* having all your choices taken away,' she retorted passionately. 'This isn't fair. Why should you have to pay for all Papa's mistakes?'

'Someone has to. And who else is there?' he asked wearily. 'As for unfair ... it won't be fair if you don't have a Season next year so – '

'Don't you *dare* do this for me!' she cried. '*Tell* him, Mama!'

Ignoring this and looking at Daniel, the Dowager said, 'When we spoke of this – or something like it – before, you were wholly against it. Is there *really* no other way?'

'No.' He drew a long breath and then said, 'She – Miss Hawthorne – is being extraordinarily generous. Father's debts paid, the overdraft at the bank cleared and provision for Becky's come-out next spring, for example.'

'Really? That *is* generous.'

'But why?' demanded Rebecca suspiciously. 'After everything she said about marriage and husbands owning a wife's property and the rest of it – why has she suddenly changed her mind? And why you?'

'I'm not sure – although she seems convinced that I won't meddle with her manufactory.' He decided they didn't need to know that she still intended to make certain that he couldn't. He respected her for that but didn't think Rebecca would. 'The situation is simple, Becky. We can't go on indefinitely as we are and Miss Hawthorne's offer is too good to refuse. I know you don't like it … but it solves a lot of problems. So I'd be grateful if you and Mama could make it easy for me – or at least not more difficult.'

'Of course we will,' announced the Dowager. 'If this is your decision, then so be it. We will do our best to support you.' Then, holding Rebecca's gaze with a very firm one of her own, 'And we shall welcome Miss Hawthorne into our home as befits your brother's wife.'

CHAPTER ELEVEN

Lord Reculver's note requesting permission to call catapulted Anna into a combination of wild joy and incipient panic. If he was coming in person, it presumably meant that he had decided to accept her offer. And for the first time in her life, her appearance suddenly became a matter of paramount importance. She had her maid get out every one of her afternoon gowns and decided that she hated all of them. Why was every garment she possessed so *boring*? And some of them were worse than boring. They verged on *dowdy*. Then there was her hair; always the same, sensible styles – one for day and the other for evening. Fortunately, before insanity set in, common sense returned.

He had seen her before. He already knew what she looked like and how she dressed. So if, the day after tomorrow, he arrived to find her completely transformed he would know far more of what was in her head than she wanted him to.

She would have preferred to merely tell her mother that the viscount was coming and would wish to speak to her privately … but two reasons persuaded her otherwise. Firstly, she had to make sure that Mama wouldn't intrude at the worst possible moment; and secondly, there was a remote chance that his lordship might feel it necessary to broach the subject with Mama first.

Consequently, over dinner the following evening, she announced that they might expect a visit from Viscount Reculver on the morrow.

A piece of fish impaled on her fork, Mrs Hawthorne froze and stared at her.

'Why? What is he coming here for?'

'I believe he may intend to make me an offer.'

'For what? You already bought his unfortunate mother's scent bottles, didn't you? What else can he want?'

'Me,' said Anna. And waited.

The fish dropped back on the plate but Mrs Hawthorne continued holding the fork aloft. '*You?* As in … as in …'

'Marriage. Yes. I think so.'

'But – but he's a – a – '

'A viscount. Quite.'

Her mother's eyes grew round and the fork dropped from suddenly nerveless fingers. Beaming, she said, 'A viscountess, Anna – you'll be a *viscountess!* I can't believe it!'

Neither, in truth, could Anna. She said cautiously, 'Let us not get *too* excited, Mama. It isn't certain yet. And it won't be until – '

'If you weren't sure, you wouldn't have said anything, would you?' Mrs Hawthorne laughed. 'Well. I won't ask what you did to bring this about, Anna. Just tell me that no one knows about it.'

Anna stared at her and then realised how typical it was. Of *course* Mama would assume she'd found a way of forcing his lordship's hand. After all, why *else* would he offer her marriage? On the other hand, it was better if Mama thought *that* than learn the truth.

'Don't worry, Mama. There will be no unpleasant rumours or gossip. Let's just say that Lord Reculver and I have reached an understanding and leave it at that, shall we? And please do not indicate that you know *anything* about this until he and I have spoken and it becomes a reality – otherwise, it may not do so.'

* * *

Next day whilst driving to Worcester, Daniel found himself thinking more about Mr Grimshaw than about Miss Hawthorne. Although he couldn't pin it down, he still had a prickling sense that something about both the man and the so-called 'debt of honour' wasn't right. Yet it had to be, didn't it? There was that letter from the bank to prove it.

It wasn't until he was almost there that a startling possibility occurred to him. What if, as he'd sensed all along, Father had never incurred any such debt? What if Grimshaw was a fraudster? What if … and here was what might be the crux of the matter … what if the letter from Hoare's was no more real than anything else?

It might be forged – and Daniel knew exactly how that could be done. Last year on Christian's behalf, he and his friends had constructed something similar that purported to have come from the English Consulate in Constantinople. If *they* could do it, so could Grimshaw. Daniel and the others had got away with their forgery because no one was going to check with the Consulate. Grimshaw would get away with *his* because Hoare's wouldn't answer questions about one of their clients.

So ... it *could* be done. The question, therefore, was whether it *had* been and, if so, whether there was any way at all of proving it.

Hawthorne Lodge was a large, graceful house situated amidst extensive gardens. As soon as he drew up in front of the door, a groom came to take his phaeton round to the stables and a butler appeared to usher him inside. Taking Daniel's hat and gloves, he said quietly, 'If you will follow me, my lord, Miss Hawthorne is in the library and has instructed that you be taken up directly you arrived.'

She'd probably prefer I didn't run into her mother just yet, he thought. *So would I.*

Anna rose as he entered the room and offered him a cautious smile.

'Welcome, my lord. I hope your journey was a smooth one?'

'It was.' Daniel took her hand, bowed over it and stepped back, reminding himself that he'd resolved to ignore the awkwardness of their situation as best he could and talk to her just as he would any other budding acquaintance. 'From the little I've seen, you have a lovely home.'

'Thank you. My father had the house built thirty years ago.' Sitting down, she gestured to a nearby chair and, when he chose to remain standing, immediately drew an unwelcome conclusion. She said stiffly, 'Perhaps I misinterpreted your coming here today. If so, I apologise. I assumed – that is to say, I had *hoped* that you were doing so in order to accept my offer. Is that not the case?'

'Not exactly, no.' At some point in the days since their last meeting, one thing had become plain to him. She deserved some consideration, however small, in return for what she would be giving him; and there was one simple thing he could offer. But first, pulling a folded paper from his pocket and handing it to her, he said, 'Before we proceed, you ought perhaps to read that. It's a list of my ... liabilities ... along with the name and direction of my lawyer.'

She looked down at the paper but made no move to open it.

Finally, setting it aside, she said, 'No. That isn't necessary.'

'Are you sure?'

'Quite sure.'

Daniel drew a long breath. 'In that case, Miss Hawthorne ... will you do me the very great honour of becoming my wife?'

It was the last thing she had expected. For a moment, first shock and then the sweetness of his words stopped her breath. Unaware of the pleasure slowly blooming in her face, she said shyly, 'Thank you. You ... that was very kind of you.'

'Is that a yes?'

'Yes.' She swallowed and then, without stopping to think, mumbled, 'Why did you do it? You didn't need to.'

'I disagree. You were entitled to a proposal. On such a matter, isn't every lady? So I asked. However, you'll have noticed that I drew the line at going down on one knee. I suspected you might have considered that overdoing it.'

'P-Perhaps.'

He smiled faintly and finally took the chair she'd offered.

'Now ... how shall we proceed? I imagine you will wish to be married from here, so banns in your local church would seem the most logical step. Yes?'

'Yes. If that would also suit you, sir?'

Daniel shrugged. 'Well enough. But do you think we might keep it quite a small affair? Aside from the fact that I have very few relatives who *must* be invited and only a select group of friends who are as close as brothers that I'd *wish* to be there, my family and I are still in mourning.'

'Yes. Of course. I'll do my best to stop Mama getting carried away,' she promised. And thought, *Although it's not going to be easy. She wanted a title for me* – any *title. A baronet would have sufficed. But her seemingly unmarriageable daughter is going to be a viscountess and she'll want to shout it to the world.* 'May I ask if your mother and sister are aware of – of any of this?'

'They are aware that I intended making you an offer of marriage today. They are *not* aware – nor need they ever be – of precisely how it came about.'

'And your friends?' Aware of a slight change in his expression, Anna broke off and added quickly, 'You need not tell me if you'd rather not.'

Just for an instant, Daniel considered lying. Then, deciding against it, he said, 'They know the whole story ... but it will never go beyond the four of them. And it's likely that only three will be at our wedding. Lord Hazelmere's lady is expecting their first child in a few weeks, so he won't let her travel or leave her side himself just now.' He'd have liked Christian as his groomsman but knew that it wasn't going to happen. 'I shall be asking Lord Benedict Hawkridge to stand up with me on the day. The other two who you'll meet are Anthony, Lord Wendover and Mr Gerald Sandhurst. You'll find all the necessary names and addresses there,' he said, gesturing to the paper he'd given her. 'But what about you? Who will give you away?'

'Mama will probably ask Cousin Cordelia's husband, Lord Maybury, to do it. We're somewhat short of male relations.' She sighed slightly, 'And speaking of Mama ... I suppose I had better introduce you to her so we can give her the good news.'

'In a moment. I'm assuming you will be instructing Mr Landry to begin work on the legal side of things. I'll write to my own lawyer tomorrow, giving my instructions. And after we've spoken to your mother, perhaps we might visit the local vicar and arrange banns and a date for the wedding. What do you think?'

Too many things to make sense of, thought Anna a shade dizzily. *It's all happening so fast. Why? So he doesn't have a chance to change his mind? So he doesn't have to see me again before the wedding?* But she said, 'By all means, my lord. Since you are – '

'Daniel,' he interposed. 'My name is Daniel. Please feel free to use it.'

Something warm yet oddly painful stirred in Anna's chest.

'Daniel,' she echoed. 'Thank you. And I agree. It makes sense to arrange matters with the vicar today. First, however, Mama.' Rising and her mouth curling wryly, she added, 'I advise you to beware, sir. She may well fall on your neck.'

If Mrs Hawthorne did not exactly throw herself upon him in gratitude, she did express her delight, refrained from saying anything tactless and rang for sherry so they could toast the happy news. Then she waved them off to the vicarage to set their plans in motion.

By the time Anna returned home, having bade farewell to her fiancé, she found her mother busily writing letters to what looked like everyone she'd ever known.

But instantly laying aside her pen when Anna appeared, Mrs Hawthorne said, 'Heavens, Anna! You might have warned me that he's so good-looking. I expected there to be something wrong with him but there isn't, is there? Handsome, charming, beautifully mannered and a *viscount!* Never did I think you'd do so well for yourself!' Pausing she shrugged and added carelessly, 'He needs money, I suppose. But that scarcely matters. You've plenty of it. Unless he's a gamester?'

Controlling a rare burst of temper as best she could, Anna said coldly, 'No. He is *not* a gamester. For the last seven months, he has been trying to deal with the financial disaster left behind by his late father. And you will not refer to this again, Mama – either in my hearing or elsewhere and never, *ever* in front of Daniel. Otherwise I am very much afraid that we shall quarrel. And now I shall leave you to your correspondence and attend to my own.'

Upon which note, she spun on her heel and walked out.

* * *

The only letter she needed to write was to Mr Landry, apprising him of her forthcoming marriage, instructing him on the measures she wanted setting in place regarding Hawthorne's and giving him the information he would need in order to open dialogue with Lord Reculver's lawyers. The last of these was the reason she finally unfolded and read the paper his lordship had given her.

The page began with a meticulous and neatly laid out list of what Daniel had called his 'liabilities' – most of which bore a few words of explanation.

£5,000 owing to Lord Hazelmere.
Originally my father's loan from Fleetwood's in the City but repaid on my behalf and without my knowledge by the earl on March 2nd of this year.

£1,850 My overdraft at Mason's Bank, Gloucester.

£2,000 – £3,000 Possible expenses at Reculver.
My estimate for the cost of immediate repairs, replacement equipment etc.

£4,000 Apparently a debt of my father's to Harold Grimshaw of Cirencester.
I have doubts about this and will be attempting to either verify or dispute it.

Total of the above: £13,850

In addition to these, there is also the cost of my sister's Season and a respectable but not exorbitant dowry – which I cannot begin to estimate.

And finally, there was also a £2,500 loan taken out by my father which, thanks to your payment for the scent bottles etcetera, I have now discharged.

And below these was the address of Longhope & Son in Gloucester, followed by those of his friends.
Lord & Lady Hazelmere, Hazelmere Towers, Stanton St. John, Oxford
They won't come but I'd like them to be invited.
Lord Benedict Hawkridge, 45 Dover Street, London
Anthony, Baron Wendover, Westcote House, Harbury, Warwickshire
Mr Gerald Sandhurst, Hazelmere House, Berkeley Square
Should you choose, you may also add
Lord Oscar Hawkridge, Belhaven House, Hanover Square
He may come from choice or Belhaven may send him.

Thoughtfully, Anna set the page aside. Lord Reculver – *Daniel* – was plainly efficient and possessed of a deep streak of honesty. She liked that about him. She liked it almost as much as she liked his smile and his pleasant voice … and quite a few other things which she refused to let herself list because contemplating them was dangerous to her peace of mind.

CHAPTER TWELVE

The next three weeks were busy ones at both Hawthorne Lodge and Reculver Court.

Daniel despatched hasty notes to Christian, Benedict, Anthony and Gerald so that invitations to his wedding wouldn't come as a shock and kept a careful eye on the cottages where repairs were taking place. The Dowager – deaf to his protestations – insisted on surrendering the master suite to the soon-to-be-married pair; and, despite the upheaval caused by that, also ordered a mammoth programme of cleaning throughout the house, then left Rebecca with the task of supervising it.

Having ruthlessly cut her mother's list of proposed wedding guests by half, Anna ordered a new gown for the occasion, agreed to Cousin Cordelia's twin daughters being her attendants on the Big Day and gave Mrs Hawthorne a free hand with arrangements for the wedding breakfast. Amongst numerous acceptances to the invitations were ones from Daniel's friends, along with a sincerely regretful refusal from Lady Hazelmere. These, she forwarded to his lordship at Reculver.

Between these two, the lawyers were busy with each other. Both bride and groom had given explicit instructions, one of them being an order not to quibble. But Messrs Longhope and Landry – each of them delighted by one particular clause and appalled by another – did not seem able to help themselves.

Mr Landry did his best to dissuade Miss Hawthorne from making an immediate payment of five thousand pounds into the viscount's bank account and arranging for a draft for a further ten thousand to be sent to his lordship's lawyers on the day of the wedding.

'Do it,' said Anna. 'And do it today. Don't bother me with this again.'

Mr Longhope, meanwhile, strongly advised Lord Reculver against putting his hand to the lengthy and detailed document which placed Hawthorne's Porcelain completely outside his ownership, control or future interference.

'Enough,' said Daniel, pulling the agreement in front of him and, having barely read it, proceeded to sign and date it.

Then, pushing it back across the desk, 'Send it back without further delay. In fact, use a courier. The wedding is in less than two weeks.'

That last fact caused Daniel to write to Anna.

I have signed the documents and instructed Longhope to send them back to Mr Landry immediately. If he doesn't, please inform me. On another matter entirely, it has occurred to me that it would be best for our immediate families to meet each other before the wedding. If you agree – and, like myself, would prefer to keep the occasion brief – might I suggest luncheon at some mid-way point, such as the Swan at Upper Strensham? This would also allow you and I to discuss where to spend the first couple of nights after the wedding. I doubt either of us wants to do so in one of our homes.

The fact that he'd written at all made Anna's pulse trip. Reference to their wedding night accelerated it. She told herself not to be an idiot. He was merely attempting to make what *wouldn't* be happening less visible to either family.

Her reply was carefully matter-of-fact.

The documents have been received. A family luncheon to break the ice is a good idea – as is spending the first nights of our married life on neutral ground. Please arrange both of these in whatever way you see fit. Meanwhile, if you have received no notification from your bank about a recent deposit, advise me immediately. I am quite tired of Landry dragging his feet.

* * *

But finally the wedding eve was upon them. To avoid travelling on the day itself, Daniel had engaged rooms in Worcester. Having settled his mother and sister at the more respectable Talbot, he joined his friends at the Crown and, dropping into a chair, said, 'Thank God for a few hours without lawyers' letters or my sister looking as if I'm about to stick my spoon in the wall. But don't let me enjoy this *too* much, will you? I don't want Thor's hammer in my head tomorrow.'

'Wise fellow,' grinned Anthony, busy pouring claret for everyone. Then, 'Did Kit write to you?'

'Yes. He sent his and Sophia's very best wishes and is sorry that he can't be here but he's convinced that the birth is imminent. I hope for both their sakes that all goes well.'

'There's no reason why it shouldn't,' remarked Benedict. 'However, Gerald and I will call at Hazelmere on our way back to London in case moral support is needed. But your last note said you were bringing the mothers together. How did that go?'

'Not too badly, all things considered – but then, both of them are getting something out of this marriage,' came the faintly caustic reply. 'Mrs Hawthorne wanted a titled son-in-law and my mother is happy to be out of the financial doldrums. The only one who remains unconvinced is Rebecca ... but I imagine when talk turns to plans for her forthcoming Season she'll be reconciled soon enough.'

'And are *you* reconciled to it?' asked Gerald quietly.

Daniel shrugged. 'As much as one can expect. Given my situation and like a lot of other men before me, a wealthy bride was always going to be my only solution. So I've accepted my fate ... but been careful to make the parameters clear.'

'And the lady?' It was Benedict who asked. 'Has she accepted them?'

'Yes. She's a realist, thank God.' He raised his glass. 'And now can we please talk of things other than tomorrow and every day after it? I'm not married yet.'

* * *

At Hawthorne Lodge, Anna's evening was proceeding along predictable lines. No one wanted to talk about anything except the wedding and, in the case Patience and Prudence Maybury, the wickedly handsome bridegroom. By the time they'd sighed and cooed and said, more times than Anna could count, how lucky she was and how much they envied her, she felt ready to scream. And when she said goodnight earlier than she might otherwise have done, the knowing smiles set her teeth on edge.

But her spirits rose the following morning when she looked out on a bright, if breezy, day. And when Ruth arrived with tea and hot water, she said impulsively, 'Lock the door.'

The maid stared at her. 'Miss Anna? Did you say *lock* it?'

'Yes. Otherwise I'll have visitors. And if Patsy and Prue are among them, I may take to the hills.'

Ruth giggled. 'And leave the best looking gentleman in three counties waiting at the altar?'

'Don't *you* start,' muttered Anna. Then, with a sudden smile, 'He is, isn't he? But for the Lord's sake, don't tell anyone I said so. And no matter who comes knocking, do not let them in.'

Mrs Hawthorne was turned away twice and the dreaded twins, three times by the time Anna was standing fully-dressed before the looking glass examining her reflection. For the first time, she'd allowed Madame Lavalle to have her way and been persuaded into a dusky rose watered taffeta, cunningly embroidered with paler silk thread ... and she was forced to admit that the dressmaker had been right. The gown was beautiful and the soft shade became her much better than the somewhat chilly blue silk she would otherwise have chosen. Also, Ruth had piled her hair in a much more complex and flattering style than usual and secured it with crystal-headed pins.

Without turning from the mirror, Anna said, 'What do you think, Ruth? Will I do?'

'You will indeed, Miss.'

'Even for the handsomest man in three counties?'

'Even for him. You look lovely. And he's lucky to have you.'

'Thank you – but much though I appreciate your loyalty, let's not get *entirely* carried away,' said Anna. Then, 'Ah well. I suppose it's time I lowered the drawbridge and put in an appearance downstairs. I shan't need you again until later, so if you wish to join the other servants at church, by all means do.'

'Thank you, Miss. From what I've heard, half the village is turning out to get a glimpse of you.'

'To get a glimpse of the viscount you mean.'

'Well, him as well, of course – but mostly you, Miss Anna. You've helped a lot of folk and they don't forget.'

Surprised and a little sceptical, Anna left Ruth tidying away brushes and combs and went slowly down the stairs. In the hall, a glass in his hand, Lord Maybury stood ready to act in *loco parentis* today. He was a large gentleman and, as now, often had a twinkle in his eye. When she got near enough for him to whisper, he said, 'They're all talking forty to the dozen in the drawing-room, my dear, so I left 'em to it – and so should you if you don't want a headache before the ceremony. Come and hide in the library and I'll pour you a drop of sherry.'

Anna smiled, nodded and tiptoed across the hall in his wake. Inside the library but not wishing to crush her gown by sitting, she accepted the glass his lordship offered her and said, 'Thank you for doing this, sir.'

'Standing in for your father – or corrupting you with sherry before noon?'

'Both.'

He laughed. 'My pleasure, m'dear. So ... young Reculver, eh? I've never met him. Seen him around Town, of course, and heard some of what's said of him.'

'And what *is* said of him?' asked Anna.

'Nothing bad, so far as I know. Although there was that duel last year.' Lord Maybury laughed again. 'If the gossips had it right, Hazelmere's muck-raking cousin had a pint of rum punch spilled over him and blamed Shelbourne – as he was then, of course – for it. Called him a liar when he denied it and threw a glass of wine in his face.' He shrugged. 'Well, there was only one answer to that and Shelbourne made it. But then he turned the thing into a Drury Lane farce.'

'He did? How?'

'He had the choice of weapons. He chose whacking at each other with paddles on the Serpentine bridge in Hyde Park – whichever of them took a ducking to be the loser. Apparently it drew quite a crowd.'

'Yes. Yes, I imagine it might.' Anna's brow creased as she struggled to picture serious, responsible Lord Reculver playing the clown. 'And?'

'Selwyn fell in. Forty or fifty men there and not one of them offered to pull him out. He could have drowned. He *would* have if Shelbourne hadn't dived in after him.' Maybury paused and drained his glass. 'Says a lot about him, don't you think?'

'Yes. Yes, it does.' Anna smiled at him. 'Thank you for telling me, sir.'

'Oh, you'd have heard it elsewhere eventually. It was the talk of the town for more than a fortnight – best joke anyone had heard in a long time.' He glanced at the clock and set his glass aside. 'And, talking of time, we should be leaving. Ready, m'dear?'

* * *

The groom's party arrived at the church in good time and were surprised to find a sizeable knot of villagers already assembled outside it and more still on their way across the green.

A good-natured voice called, 'Which of you gents be the lucky man?'

Daniel blinked, bowed and said with a grin, 'That would be me, sir.'

And was answered with a jumbled chorus of, 'Then good luck to you, milord. To you and Miss Anna both!'

Startled but oddly warmed, Daniel thanked them with a wave and continued on his way. Benedict murmured, 'Surprised?'

'Somewhat.' Then, finding the vicar waiting in the porch to shake hands with him, 'Good morning, Reverend. I hadn't expected a welcome party.'

'Miss Hawthorne does a lot for the village, my lord,' replied the cleric. 'Supplying what's needed for the school and paying for a teacher, for example. Everybody wants to wish her happy today.'

'I'm sure she'll appreciate it – as do I on her behalf,' he murmured. And, to Benedict as they continued into the church, 'What next, I wonder?'

The rear pews of the bride's side were already half-full, the groom's, almost empty. Daniel and Benedict took their places in the front pew; Anthony and Gerald sat behind them. Benedict said, 'I'd have thought Oscar would be here by now.'

'Surely, if he was coming he'd have joined us last night?'

'No. He planned to spend a day or two with a friend in Cheltenham; someone else obsessed with Greek battles. But perhaps –' He stopped, as fresh parties of guests arrived – among them, Daniel's mother and sister. Rising with the others to greet them, he said, 'Good morning, ladies. How very charming you both look.'

Rebecca beamed shyly and thanked him. The Dowager replied with a nod, a smile and a murmured response, her attention already fixed on Daniel.

'No second thoughts?'

He kissed her cheek but said, 'Don't be silly, Mama. I wouldn't have let things get this far if there had been. But tell me. Was everything satisfactory for you and Becky last night at the Talbot?'

'Yes. Perfectly comfortable.' She looked across the aisle. 'Another carriage was drawing up as we came in – probably Anna's mother, since she isn't here yet.'

'Very likely.' He pulled Rebecca into his arms for a brief hug. 'Ready to tell me you love me and wish me happy?'

'Of *course* I love you,' she muttered against his cravat. 'And of *course* I want you to be happy.'

'Good,' said Daniel. 'Let's leave it at that, shall we?'

The Shelbourne ladies were just settling in next to Anthony and Gerald when the first of the bride's party arrived. This was composed of Mrs Hawthorne, Lady Maybury and two other ladies, so there was a further round of introductions and greetings. And just when everyone was once more sitting down, Lord Oscar Hawkridge strode down the aisle ahead of three more Hawthornes and everyone got up again.

'Musical chairs,' murmured Daniel.

And, 'You're late,' said Benedict to his brother.

'I'm not,' replied Oscar. 'The bride's carriage was held up by the crowd outside wanting to offer her their good wishes. Popular lady by the look of it.'

But eventually everyone settled down again and the organ started to play.

In the porch, Anna let Prudence and Patience fuss around her, twitching this and straightening that until their father said, 'Enough, you two. Much more of this and the groom will think his bride has changed her mind.'

'She'd have to be mad to do that,' giggled Prudence.

'All done,' said Patience. And encouragingly to Anna, 'You look very nice.'

Mostly because it was what people expected of bridegrooms, Daniel turned to look back along the aisle. Then he grew still.

She looked … different. Not pretty, exactly, and certainly not beautiful. But not ordinary or instantly forgettable either. Today both hair and gown suited, even flattered, her and there was a delicate hint of colour in her cheeks. Then, as the gentleman whose arm she held whispered something to her, warmth lit her face and she looked suddenly softer, less chilly and unapproachable. Daniel discovered that he felt mildly disorientated; then he hoped that this new incarnation would last and wasn't merely an illusion born of the moment.

As for Anna, she handed her prayer book to Prudence, turned and finally allowed herself a very brief glance at her bridegroom. He smiled. As always happened when he did that, her heart lurched and she wondered, for perhaps the hundredth time, whether marriage to Daniel Shelbourne was going to be a blessing or a curse. Given how she felt about him and how he didn't and never would feel about her, she supposed it could go either way. Then she told herself she was being ungrateful. She was being given more than she could have dared hope for a couple of months ago. To want more was greedy.

The service began and she ordered herself to pay attention so that every moment of it would live in her memory. The rich tones of Daniel's voice as he spoke his vows; the steadiness of his gaze; and eventually, the ring sliding on to her finger, warm from his hand. And then it was done. She was his wife.

In no time at all, it seemed, they were outside in the sunshine with the villagers cheering. She smiled and waved back, touched that so many had turned out to wish her – no, to wish them *both* – well.

Her mother, the twins and some of the other ladies came forward to hug her. Daniel's mother was one of them; his sister, although she managed a smile and said all that was proper, wasn't. Anna felt a growing sense of unreality creeping over her.

Meanwhile, a number of gentlemen – one of whom had been Daniel's groomsman and must therefore be Lord Benedict – surrounded him to shake his hand or buffet his shoulder and offer their congratulations. Daniel responded to these with easy grace and took the first opportunity to present them to *the newly-minted Viscountess Reculver; my bride.* All of them smiled, bowed over her hand and behaved as if they didn't know perfectly well how this wedding had come about – or that Daniel wasn't marrying her from choice. She hoped her own performance was equally flawless.

Daniel handed her into the carriage, then paused on the steps to scatter handfuls of coins on the road. The cheers increased in volume. He grinned, gave a mock-salute ... and joined her inside.

For want of something better, she said, 'That was kind.'

'It's customary.' And realising he'd sounded brusque, 'Or so I'm told. May I say how delightful you look?'

She managed not to observe tradition dictated that *all* brides looked delightful.

'Thank you, my – er – Daniel.'

That seemed to ease at least some of the tension.

Amusement tugging at the corner of his mouth, he said gravely, 'A pleasure, my – er – Anna. At least, I'm assuming I may now call you that?'

'Of course! Did I not already ...?' She stopped. 'Oh. Probably not. I'm sorry.'

'Don't be. As for my rather trite compliment, I meant it. That colour suits you.'

Somewhere at the back of Anna's mind was a hazy notion that this was one of those times to keep her mouth shut. Instead, she heard herself say, 'My dressmaker chose it – insisted on it, in fact. Perhaps I should listen to her more in future.'

'You usually don't?'

'No. I – I have a habit of thinking I know best.'

'I am duly warned.' Silence fell. But presently, when a glance through the carriage window told him they were nearly at Hawthorne Lodge, he said swiftly, 'Unlike you, I'll be obliged to make something resembling a speech. Other than that, I shall smile, listen more than I talk and avoid answering questions I don't want to answer. You may wish to do the same.'

She nodded. 'If I can. But your friends? Might they not – ?'

'Don't worry about them. Anthony and Gerald are good at averting potential embarrassments; and the Hawkridge brothers will almost certainly fall victim to my mother's determination to discuss genealogy.' He gave her an encouraging smile. 'Two hours – three at the most – and we can leave. Agreed?'

'Agreed,' she said weakly. And wondered if what came *after* the wedding breakfast was going to be any less fraught with pitfalls.

CHAPTER THIRTEEN

Daniel had reserved a pair of comfortable bedchambers separated by a private parlour at the Anchor in Upton-on-Severn. They arrived in time for a belated tea after which – conversation between them throughout the journey having grown increasingly stilted within ten minutes of leaving their wedding breakfast – Anna gratefully accepted Daniel's suggestion of a stroll along the riverside.

Looking about her with appreciation, she said, 'I haven't been here for years and had forgotten how pretty it is.'

'A good choice, then?'

'Very good.' They walked on in silence for a few minutes until Anna said abruptly, 'I'm sorry that Rebecca isn't happy about us marrying. I hope she'll change her mind because I'd like us to become friends.'

'And I'm sure you will do so.' He hesitated briefly. 'Her attitude isn't personal, Anna. It's the situation she's angry about. She can't forgive Father for leaving the family on the verge of ruin. To my shame, neither can I.' He stopped, then immediately added, 'And that's enough of that.'

Anna disagreed and, without stopping to think, said, 'Forgive me, but I don't think you have anything to be ashamed of. Your resentment is natural and is not purely on your own account. You are angry on behalf of your mother and sister and the tenants on the estate – towards all of whom your father failed in his responsibilities. Had my father died leaving a similar situation, I'd feel the same. Anyone would, I believe.'

'Perhaps.' Although a part of him appreciated that her words were well-intentioned, another part recoiled from any notion of sharing his innermost feelings. He said, 'Shall we continue as far as the bridge before returning to the inn? By then it will be almost time to change for dinner.'

And, recognising the quietly but firmly closed door, she nodded. 'By all means.'

* * *

Sitting before the mirror while Ruth re-pinned her hair, Anna mentally searched for acceptable topics of conversation during dinner and came to the depressing conclusion that there weren't many. He'd made it clear that there was an invisible line she wasn't permitted to cross and behind which he kept everything personal. He didn't mind telling her how Rebecca felt but wasn't remotely comfortable talking about how *he* did.

I need to remember that, she thought. *This is a business arrangement. Nothing more than that. And if I trespass too far or too often, he'll strengthen his defences.*

Daniel, meanwhile, told himself to be more careful, not just about which boxes he opened, but how far he opened them. At best, this marriage was supposed to gradually become a pleasant but undemanding friendship; polite but not close ... at least until they were more used to each other and perhaps not even then. And already he appeared to have accidentally invited her to offer him comfort which he neither wanted nor needed and had therefore resulted in him immediately and none too subtly shutting her out.

What possessed me to ask for dinner to be served up here? he asked himself. *What on earth are we going to talk about?* Then, with rising desperation, *And how the devil are we going to get through the whole of tomorrow? There's a limit to how many questions I can ask about the manufacture of porcelain – and an even greater one on my attention span for the answers. But what else is there?*

When Anna presently joined him in the parlour, she had resumed her usual air of cool self-possession and, accepting the glass of wine he offered her, said simply, 'Perhaps it would be a good idea if you told me about Reculver.'

Daniel blinked. 'In what particular?'

'Since I have neither experience nor knowledge of life on a country estate, all of them. But suppose we start with what will be expected of me as your wife.'

'Expected by whom?'

'By you,' she replied patiently, 'and your tenants and the villagers? At first I supposed that it wouldn't be so very different to Hawthorne's ... but I've realised that isn't true. *There,* I see the people I employ in their workplace. At Reculver, I'm more likely to be visiting tenants in their homes, am I not?' She paused and, when he said nothing, 'But perhaps you'd prefer that I consult your mother about that? Or simply not interfere at all in matters which have always been her province? I have no desire to usurp her position or to encroach where I should not.'

He eyed her thoughtfully for a moment. Then, 'You won't.'

'I might. I wasn't brought up to be lady of the manor.'

'If what I saw outside the church this morning is any indication, you know as much as you need to,' he replied. And, with a glimmer of humour, 'Certainly more than my mother does. She means well, of course, but she's never had an easy rapport with the tenants. If you care for my people as well as you've cared for your own, I doubt there will be any complaints.'

Colour bloomed in her cheeks and she sought refuge in her glass. Finally, she said dispassionately, 'I hope not. But I'm a stranger to them. So if I make mistakes, you must point them out to me – because *they* won't feel able to do so.'

Finally recognising that she was genuinely concerned, Daniel said, 'What is it you're afraid of getting wrong?'

She thought for a moment.

'Mostly, intruding where I'm not wanted. If I see a need, I'm likely to *act* on it instead of waiting for people to ask. It ... it doesn't always go down well.'

'It doesn't?'

'No. Some consider it interference. Others are insulted by what they see as charity. As I said, your tenants don't know me. Getting used to me – *trusting* me – will take time. Meanwhile, I don't want to make your life more difficult than it is already.'

Daniel found her honesty touching. He said, 'I think you're worrying needlessly. So why don't we just take it one day at a time and see how it goes?'

He stopped, as a tap at the door heralded the arrival of their dinner. Then, when the table was laden with various platters and covered dishes, he drew out a chair for her saying lightly, 'Did you by any chance invite company and forget to mention it?'

She shook her head and then, struck by a sudden thought, 'Do the people here at the inn know that we were married today?'

'Well, *I* didn't tell them but that doesn't mean they don't,' replied Daniel, taking his own seat. 'I'll serve us both, shall I? Stop me if you see anything you don't like ... and meanwhile you can tell me what else you wanted to know about Reculver.'

'Numbers,' said Anna, watching him lay neat portions of trout and vegetables on her plate. 'How many cottages and tenant families, for example.'

The hazel eyes flicked to her face, then back to his hands as he filled his own plate.

'Fifteen families and nineteen cottages, four of which have been empty for over a year now. Those and eleven others are currently undergoing long overdue repairs – thanks to the scent bottles etcetera. So – '

'Could you please *not* go on referring to the – the etcetera part?' Anna burst out. 'It was badly done and – '

'On both our parts.'

'If you say so – though I disagree. And everything is awkward enough already without that and without you thanking me at every turn.'

'I wasn't aware that I had been,' he replied equably ... and closed the subject by turning back to his dinner.

Feeling her colour rise, Anna followed his example and let the silence linger. Then, abandoning the trout, she said, 'I'm sorry. I only meant that – '

'I know what you meant.' Sighing, Daniel laid down his knife. 'You would prefer that our relationship, such as it is, was not mostly based upon gratitude. I understand and respect that, but ... we have to start with what we have. The vows we exchanged this morning brought me massive advantages. Unless I'm missing something, all you got was my name – which doesn't seem a very fair exchange, does it?' He waited and when she said nothing, 'Quite. I'm grateful, Anna – as I should be. But I'll express it less often if that is what you would prefer.'

'It is, yes. Thank you.'

'Then let's consider the subject closed.' Turning back to his plate, he ate a little more before pushing his plate aside, saying, 'Returning to your questions about Reculver, we have a flock of sixty-something sheep and approximately a third of our acreage is under cultivation. Both of those need to increase substantially if I'm to begin dragging the estate some way back towards profitability, so they'll be my priority for the foreseeable future.' He investigated another of the covered dishes, 'Chicken in some sort of sauce. Since, like me, you appear to be finished with the fish, may I help you to a little of this? And perhaps we could discuss what you'd like to do tomorrow.'

* * *

Later, lying sleepless in bed and forbidding her mind to stray to the man who was now her husband sleeping two rooms away, Anna reminded herself how important it was to be careful. She must never let him suspect for a single moment how she felt about him. He'd be horrified if he knew that, in the space of those two meetings since she'd left Reculver, what had begun as strong but manageable attraction had blossomed into a wild conflagration of something she'd never believed possible and was still afraid to name, even to herself.

Aware that even thinking about it was dangerous, she turned her mind to debating the point of spending a further day in Upton-on-Severn. Certainly, it had done little so far to ease the tension ... and it was never going to while Daniel remained intent on keeping her on the other side of that invisible door.

We may as well bite the bullet and get on with settling into everyday life, she thought. *At least that way we'd both have something to do instead of being trapped with each other and nothing to fill the time. If we went back, he could throw himself into his improvements and I'd be able to talk with his mother about what needs doing in the house – refurbishments and staffing, for example.* She turned over and thumped the pillow for the fourth time. *Being here isn't achieving anything. Being at Reculver would. As for concealing the truth of our marriage from his family, Daniel is deluded if he thinks we can do that for more than day or two. And what does it matter? Under the circumstances, they'll hardly be surprised, will they?*

* * *

Daniel, meanwhile, was standing at his bedchamber window staring broodingly out into the dark. When he'd first thought of it, the idea of spending the first two nights after the wedding somewhere nobody knew them had seemed a good one. Now, with tomorrow yawning emptily ahead of them and nothing to fill it but more stilted attempts at conversation, he gloomily recognised that it might have been a mistake.

And it's not the only one is it? he admitted wearily to himself. *This morning, we made a lifetime commitment but we scarcely know each other. Yet while she's groping for ways of mending that – of finding places where we can communicate – I'm throwing up barriers. That has to stop. I ought to be at least* trying *to meet her half-way. But for now, being here without other company or anything to occupy us isn't working. I wonder what she'd say if I suggested we go home earlier than we planned?*

* * *

The question of how to spend the day after the wedding was further complicated when the morning dawned on intermittent drizzle. Entering the parlour to find Anna gazing on the wet world outside, Daniel said, 'I suspect this may have set in for the day.'

'So do I.'

He waited for a moment and, when she merely continued staring through the window, said, 'I haven't rung for breakfast because I didn't know what you would like. But it also occurred to me that you might prefer to take it in the coffee room rather than here.'

'Yes.' She turned to face him. 'I would. Thank you.'

'Good. So would I.' Smiling and offering his arm, he said, 'Let's go.'

Downstairs, only two tables were occupied; a solitary gentleman at one of them and two middle-aged ladies at the other. All three nodded a polite greeting to which Anna and Daniel replied in kind before settling at a table by the window.

Having asked Anna's preference and given their order to the serving maid, Daniel came directly to the point.

'If the rain continues, we'll be trapped inside the inn. So I wondered – though it isn't ideal weather for travelling – whether we might consider cutting our stay here short and setting out for Reculver. What do you think?'

'Even without the rain, I had been thinking exactly the same. Neither of us are accustomed to being idle, are we? And I'm sure that you have matters awaiting your attention.'

'Always,' he admitted wryly. 'That's what we'll do, then. I'll order the carriage as soon as we've eaten. And, with a bit of luck, we'll out-distance the rain.'

CHAPTER FOURTEEN

Once inside the carriage and on their way, Daniel came directly to the point. He said, 'I wasn't very easy company last night, was I? Or at all helpful. The situation is awkward for both of us but you were trying to make the best of it and I did the opposite. I don't have any excuses for that but I'll try to do better in future. And to prove my good intentions, if you have questions you consider important, ask them.'

'About anything?' Anna asked. 'Literally?'

'Well ... within reason.'

By whose interpretation? she wondered, able to think of at least half a dozen questions she'd wanted to ask but which, even with this new spirit of conciliation, she suspected he was unlikely to answer. Finally, settling for what she hoped might be amongst the least contentious of them, she said, 'Very well. Here's something that is not at all important but which intrigues me. Lord Maybury said you and Lord Hazelmere's cousin fought a duel on the Serpentine bridge. Is it true?'

He groaned. 'I hoped I'd lived that down by now. But yes. Perfectly true.'

'Am I allowed to ask why?'

'Why the duel?' And when she nodded, 'Have you ever met Basil Selwyn?'

'No. But since he is your friend's cousin, then surely ...' She hesitated before adding doubtfully, 'Unless it was a sort of joke?'

'It was certainly meant to *look* that way.' Daniel paused, unsure how much to tell her. Then, deciding he might as well be honest, 'To put it bluntly, Basil Selwyn is a vicious toad who deserved much, much worse than to merely be made a fool of in public.'

'And yet Lord Maybury *also* said that, when Mr Selwyn fell into the water, it was you who pulled him out.'

'Well, somebody had to. Being the idiot that he is, Basil fell in wearing his coat and boots, whereas I'd stripped down to my shirt and breeches.' He shrugged. 'Since I couldn't let him drown, hauling him out was necessary, not heroic.'

Anna nodded, mentally reviewed the other things she'd wanted to know and decided to find out just how far she could go before he pulled up the metaphorical drawbridge.

She said slowly, 'On the list of your various obligations was four thousand pounds owing to a Mr Grimshaw about which your note said you have doubts. Why is that?'

Not having expected this, Daniel eyed her thoughtfully for a moment. His most immediate reaction was to dodge the question ... but then he thought, *Why not tell her? She isn't stupid. And talking it through with someone could be helpful.*

Finally, he said, 'Before I tell you, I should explain that my mother and sister know nothing of that and, for the time being at least, I would prefer it to remain that way.'

'Then it will do so,' came the simple reply.

'Thank you. Well, then ... it's probably best if I begin with the case as Grimshaw stated it.'

Anna listened without interrupting as he spoke of the initial letter he'd received, of his meeting with Grimshaw and the subsequent letter from the fellow's bank. When he stopped speaking, she said, 'And you'd never heard of him before this?'

'No. My mother recognised the name as that of someone Father had known at one time. But that's all.'

'And what strikes you as odd about it?'

'A number of things – starting with the so-called debt of honour. I take it you understand what that is?' And when she nodded, 'To the best of my knowledge, my father didn't gamble. So if he staked four thousand pounds on the turn of a card or the outcome of a wager, it would have been out of character. Then there's the concept of a large, interest-free loan made several months ago by a fellow it appears Father hadn't seen in some years. I'm struggling to believe in that. Why would Father ask or Grimshaw agree? And having met the man, something about him didn't ring true.' Daniel hesitated, then added, 'The whole thing just doesn't add up ... and not *purely* because I don't want it to.'

'I believe I can understand that,' said Anna. 'But there's also the letter from the bank. That can't be ignored, can it?'

'No. But it's not beyond the realms of possibility that it isn't genuine.'

'Really?' Her brows rose. 'What makes you think that?'

'Because I know how he could forge it.'

'You do?'

'Yes. But please don't ask *how* I know.'

She nodded, calmly accepting this.

'Very well then. Going back to Mr Grimshaw ... he didn't tell you to whom your father had lost this money?'

'No. He said Father hadn't told him – which I admit is all too possible. Secrecy was a habit with him,' replied Daniel bitterly. 'He hid things from my mother, from me and even from his lawyers. Hence the shock of what came out in his will.'

'Very well. What about his signature on the note of hand ... does that appear genuine?'

'Aside from the type of ink it's written in, yes.' He slanted a glance at her. 'Not looking very hopeful, is it?'

'On the face of it, no. However, if your suspicions are correct and the debt never existed, Grimshaw is attempting to commit fraud – and for a spectacularly large sum of money. Unfortunately, however, I don't see any easy way of proving it.'

'Neither do I,' sighed Daniel. 'Also, if I'm wrong and it *does* exist, it will have to be paid eventually. So far, I've delayed doing anything about it but that can't go on much longer. In fact, I'm surprised Grimshaw hasn't turned up on the doorstep by now because he strikes me as the persistent sort.'

'In which case perhaps it's just as well you and I are returning earlier than we originally planned. Since you want to keep it from your family, it would be ... unfortunate ... if he paid a call in your absence.'

He winced. 'Yes. It would.'

* * *

They reached Reculver at a little after noon and the first person to see the carriage draw up was Rebecca. Rising swiftly from the window-seat, she said, 'Good heavens, Mama – they're back already!'

'Back?' echoed the dowager. 'Daniel and Anna? Why? They weren't supposed to come home until tomorrow.'

'Well, clearly they've changed their minds,' said Rebecca, heading for the door. 'A good sign or a bad one, do you think?'

Below in the hall, Flynn had the door open and stood waiting at the top of the steps. Then, the instant Daniel handed Anna from the carriage, he said, 'Welcome home, my lord – my lady. And many congratulations to you from myself and the rest of the staff.'

'Thank you, Flynn. Rain at Upton this morning caused us to revise our plans.'

'Rain, my lord? There's been none here.'

'So I see. Doubtless my mother is – '

He stopped as Rebecca came skimming across the floor to throw her arms about his neck, saying, 'Not that I'm not pleased to see you – but that must be the shortest bridal trip in history! Couldn't you last even *one* more day?'

Daniel dropped a brief kiss on her hair and set her away from him in order to draw Anna forward. He said, 'We *could* have but we decided not to.'

His tone was light and pleasant but contained the merest hint of reproof which neither lady missed. Seeing Rebecca flush, Anna said quickly, 'It was raining and spending the day tied to the inn wasn't very appealing. So here we are.'

'Yes, indeed,' observed the dowager, arriving at the half-landing in time to hear this. 'And a very nice surprise it is, too. Welcome to your new home, my dear, and allow me to show you to your rooms while the luggage is brought in. Flynn, luncheon in an hour, if you please. And Daniel … there are letters on your desk, one of which is from Lord Hazelmere. Perhaps it brings the news that you have been waiting for.'

'I certainly hope so,' he replied. And to Anna, 'You'll excuse me?'

'Of course.'

She smiled at Rebecca in passing and walked away to where her new mother-in-law awaited her, looking faintly anxious. A few steps further on, the dowager said, 'As is only proper, we have had the master-suite readied for you both – though I don't know why we call it that when, this house being so old-fashioned, it's the *only* suite. But I'm afraid that it – it is a *little* shabby. I hope you won't mind it too much.'

'Not at all,' responded Anna smoothly. 'Indeed, I suspected you might feel the house was due for some refurbishment and was rather hoping it might be a project that you and I could tackle together.'

'Refurbishment?' Her hand was taken in an unsteady clasp. 'Oh Anna! If you only *knew* how much I've longed to be able to put things to rights and how *horrid* it's been keeping the state of things from my friends and neighbours!'

'Well, we can start mending that right away, ma'am. Perhaps tomorrow you can show me around the house? We can begin a list of what needs to be done and in what order. Indeed, I'm sure you already have ideas on that score.'

Below in the hall, Daniel looked at his sister and said quietly, 'You liked Anna once, Becky It doesn't make sense to *stop* liking her now when she's done nothing to deserve it. She wants to be your friend ... so why don't you let her? It would make life easier for everyone.'

Rebecca sighed and leaned her brow against his shoulder.

'I know. I just hate that you married her for everyone's sake but your own.'

'Everyone's *including* mine,' he corrected. 'There's a lot to be said for not lying awake at night, worrying. And if it hadn't been Anna, it would have been some other wealthy woman – assuming I could have found one who considered me adequate value for money.' He gave her a brief hug, then moved away. 'Be pleasant to her, Becky. And now I'm going to find out what Kit has to say.'

Christian's letter was brief and somewhat incoherent but also jubilant.

We have a son, Daniel. Michael Francis, born two days ago. A beautiful, healthy boy with his mother's eyes and possibly my hair, we think. And Sophie is well, thank God. More than well. She's crowing with pride over her achievement. As she should be. Visit when you can – don't wait until the christening. We think of you often and can't wait to introduce you to the miniature Viscount Farndon.

Laughing a little, Daniel sat down to dash off an equally brief reply of congratulation. Then, that done, he flicked through the other handful of letters awaiting his attention. Most were of little or no consequence so he set them aside to read later. However, mystified as to what Longhope & Son could be writing about this time, he opened the one from them. Three minutes later with it still in his hand, he was taking the stairs at a brisk pace in search of his wife.

He found her in the master-suite's sitting-room with his mother, discussing the curtains. Cutting ruthlessly across their conversation, Daniel said, 'Forgive me, Mama – but I need a few private words with my lady wife. Now, if you wouldn't mind.'

'You want to – oh. With Anna. Yes. Of course.' And patting her new daughter's hand, 'We'll continue this later, dear.' And she bustled out looking a lot happier than she had half an hour ago.

Anna, by contrast, eyed her husband warily. 'Is something wrong?'

'Not wrong, no.' He waved the letter at her. 'But my lawyers inform me that a bank draft in my name for ten thousand pounds was delivered to them yesterday. Naturally, I can't help wondering when you were planning to mention that.'

'I wasn't.'

'You weren't? At all?'

'No. It's only what was agreed, after all.' And, when he continued to stare at her, 'Five thousand on the occasion of our betrothal to meet your most immediate needs; and a further ten on the day of the wedding to take care of other things – such as the debt to Lord Hazelmere, for example. As for what else will be necessary, I thought we could discuss suitable arrangements for that later.'

Shaking his head as if to clear it, Daniel said, 'Anna ... you ask me not to thank you, then do something like this without even telling me? What am I to say to you?'

Her colour rose and she turned away, tugging at the ribbons of her hat.

'Nothing. Since I was merely fulfilling my side of our agreement, what else can possibly need to be said about it? And right now I'd much sooner know if Lord and Lady Hazelmere's child has been born yet.'

For a few moments, Daniel continued looking at her in silence. But finally, he said, 'He has indeed.'

Anna spun back to face him, smiling. 'A son? They have a little boy?'

'They do. Michael Francis. Mother and baby both doing well, Kit says.'

'That's wonderful. I'm so glad.'

She looked it, he realised. Genuinely happy for people she'd never met. He said, 'When Sophie has got over the birth and they are ready to receive, I'll be paying a brief visit. Would you like to come with me?'

'*May* I?' The words were out before she could stop them and instantly regretted. 'But no. Not this first time. Neither they nor you will want additional company just yet ... but perhaps I could go with you on some future occasion?'

It would be so easy to agree and part of him wanted to. What stopped him was the realisation that, if he continued keeping her out of the important parts of his life, she would let him do it without argument – which spoke a lot better of her than it did of him.

My good intentions didn't last long, did they? he thought grimly. *If you want to spend your married life behaving like a selfish bastard and letting all the sacrifices be on her side, she won't stop you. So be a man and take responsibility for yourself.*

He said, 'You aren't additional company, Anna. You are my wife. Kit and Sophie will want to know you – and I'd like you to know them. So, if at all possible, we'll go in four or five weeks' time. Yes?'

'Very well,' she murmured weakly. And thought, *Don't. It may have been frustrating and a bit annoying when you were throwing up barriers ... but watching you trying to be* kind *will be worse and I'm in enough trouble already.* 'If you're quite sure.'

'I am. And by then I daresay Mama will be knee deep in new curtains and the like so she'll hardly miss us. That *was* speedy work, by the way.'

'Not really. I guessed she would want make some improvements. She shouldn't feel she has to apologise for the condition of her home.'

'Is that what she did?'

'Yes. It's one of the reasons why the neighbours have been dissuaded from calling.' And before he could comment on this, 'From the little I saw when I was here before I was already aware that some work is needed and was looking forward to it as something upon which your mama and I might find common ground.'

Daniel regarded her thoughtfully. 'That's really how you look at it?'

'Yes. Why not?' She hesitated. 'And that reminds me of something else. Your mama can have her personal bills sent to you ... or she may prefer to have her own allowance. You should find out which. And Rebecca must have pin money to spend as she chooses. Not an enormous amount since you will be paying for her clothing and so forth – but enough for her to buy a book or a few yards of ribbon when she wants to do so. Otherwise, how is she to learn the value of money or how to manage it?'

Daniel folded his arms and leaned against the window-frame, a faint smile lurking behind his eyes. He said, 'You seem to have done an inordinate amount of thinking.'

'I'm sorry. I did warn you that I tend to go too fast at times and – '

'Don't be sorry. *One* of us should think of these things and *I* certainly hadn't got around to it. However ...' He gestured to the stack of trunks and valises in the corner. 'Yours, I presume?'

'Yes. My things from home. Everything was packed before the wedding and Mother had it sent by carrier yesterday. My own chaise and Blake, my personal groom, should be arriving tomorrow. Perhaps you would warn the stables of that and ask them to make provision?'

'That won't be a problem. Two carriages and several horses were sold some time ago so there's plenty of room. I suppose we should consider what, if anything, needs doing to remedy that.'

'That's your department, not mine,' responded Anna. 'Do what you think necessary.'

'Thank you. I will.' He offered his arm. 'But for now, why don't you join me downstairs for a glass of wine to toast our homecoming? Everything else – even more thinking – can wait an hour or two.'

* * *

On the following morning, while Daniel dealt with matters relating to the estate and wrote instructing Longhope & Son to settle both his obligation to the Earl of Hazelmere and his bank overdraft, Anna and the dowager toured the house together and began a list that, in less than an hour, had arrived half-way down its second page. Feeling left out and rather sorry for herself, Rebecca wandered around the garden for an hour before belatedly arriving at the conclusion that the only person making her miserable was herself.

Daniel's right, she thought. *I did* like Anna. *And she's done nothing wrong – quite the reverse. Daniel had to find money from somewhere and how else was he to do it? Also, though I don't know the details, it seems Anna is being generous. Last evening, I was* sure *she was about to suggest a trip to the modiste in Gloucester before Daniel somehow managed to change the subject. And Mama is bubbling over with plans for redecorating the house and already talking about holding a small dinner-party for neighbours we've scarcely seen in the last year. Everything is different now. Although it hasn't been mentioned since before the wedding, it seems that I'll even have my Season next spring. And if I do, it will be thanks to Anna, won't it? But the real issue here is Daniel. He's done something he'd rather not have done but is trying to make the best of it. And I should be helping, not making it difficult.*

Spinning on her heel, she hastened back to the house and, on being informed that the ladies were currently inspecting the formal dining-room, followed them there and said brightly, 'You've been at this all morning. I suppose it's too late to offer to help – even if only by ordering tea?'

'Tea is a splendid idea,' said her mother absently. Then, 'Anna?'

'Yes. Tea … and a little while to sit down and evaluate our progress thus far. But first, this room.' She gestured to the table, still fully extended as it had been when she'd valued the scent bottles, its army of chairs arrayed side by side against the walls. 'It needs very little. The curtains are slightly faded and could be replaced at some point. But the upholstery on the chairs is almost as good as new.'

'Because they're scarcely ever used,' murmured Rebecca.

'Exactly. And it seems a great pity.'

'That may be true,' remarked the Dowager dubiously. 'But with only four of us ...'

'Of course,' nodded Anna. 'But if some of the leaves were removed from the table, reducing the seating to eight rather than twenty, it would be adequate for most purposes but not completely dwarfed by the size of the room. What do you think, Rebecca?'

'Me?'

'Yes. This is a lovely room and the panelling is quite beautiful. Would it not be pleasant to dine in here, regardless of whether or not there are guests?'

Rebecca looked around her. She said slowly, 'Yes. It would.'

'Also, when there *are* guests,' finished Anna, persuasively to the Dowager, 'a room needs to feel lived in ... as, currently, this one does not. And last evening you spoke of holding a small dinner-party, did you not, ma'am?'

'Yes. Yes, I did. Oh dear. If you are both set on this and Daniel has no objection, I suppose we might at least try it.'

'If I have no objection to what?' asked Daniel from where he leaned, arms folded, against the door jamb.

'Dining in the dining-room,' responded Rebecca. 'What do you think?'

His brows rose. 'Well, it's a somewhat radical notion ... but I imagine I could probably get used to it.'

His wife smiled and his sister laughed. His mother sighed and remarked that it would make more work for the maids who were over-stretched as it was.

'Not for long,' promised Anna. 'I'd planned to speak to you about hiring more staff and whether there might be girls or young men in the village who'd be glad of the work ... but today's priority was deciding about renovations, wasn't it?'

'And have you?' asked Daniel. Then, when he received no answer, 'Mama?'

'Yes. I believe we have. Enough to make a start, anyway.'

'Excellent.' He grinned at Anna. 'So you'll be free to drive out with me this afternoon and meet some of the tenants, won't you?'

CHAPTER FIFTEEN

Anna's first week as Viscountess Reculver was an extremely busy one. By the end of it, the household had two more housemaids and a second footman, work had begun on the rotting window-frames in the east wing and the refurbishment of the drawing-room was already well under way. The dowager hovered between bemusement and delight; Rebecca roamed the house carrying orders and lists; and Daniel spent as much time as possible elsewhere.

Fortunately, he had plenty to occupy him, a good deal of it away from the house. He checked regularly on the cottage repairs. He arranged for hire of the equipment necessary to drain the field at Old Fallow, purchased a new plough for the home farm and visited a couple of livestock sales, returning with a dozen ewes and a ram that Rebecca insisted had a squint.

The result of all this activity was that, aside from the afternoon they had driven around the estate together, the only time Lord and Lady Reculver spent more than five minutes in each other's company was at dinner. At first, Daniel didn't notice this. Anna did ... but she chose not to remark upon it in the hope that neither the dowager nor Rebecca would do so either.

The other thing Daniel failed to notice was that, although Anna received letters nearly every day, he never saw her answering them. However, this changed on a night when, having retired later than usual and then sat up reading for an hour before climbing into bed and snuffing the candle, he saw a ribbon of light glowing beneath the door to the parlour.

It was almost one in the morning so someone – presumably Anna's maid – had forgotten to douse the lamps in there. Sighing, he sat up and swung his legs out of bed. He was three steps from the door when it occurred to him that, in the unlikely event that either Anna or her maid was still up, he'd better put on his banyan rather than risk one of them screaming the house down at the sight of a naked man. Then, semi-respectably covered, he stalked into the parlour and stopped dead at the sight of his wife, wrapped in a simple chamber-robe, busy with a stack of paperwork at the table by the window.

For the too-brief instant before she turned to face him, her hair was a straight, glossy waterfall tumbling over one shoulder while, etched against it, her profile was cameo-pure. Then she was looking at him out of seemingly fathomless eyes and he had the peculiar sensation of never having seen her before.

The pen falling from suddenly nerveless fingers, Anna stared at him – or more specifically, she stared at the deep vee of bare chest that the dark robe left exposed. Her brain ceased functioning properly. All she could think was, *Why is he here? He never uses the parlour.* And, *Is he wearing anything underneath that?*

'My apologies,' said Daniel. 'I saw the light and thought lamps had been left burning by mistake. It didn't occur to me that you might still be up at this hour.' And when she didn't say anything, 'Is something wrong?'

'No.' She gestured to the papers. 'Just a few outstanding matters at Hawthorne's requiring my attention.'

A *few?* he thought. She'd retired some two hours before him. Had she been working all that time? *Here*, only yards away from where he'd been reading? *Here*, her warm, smooth skin gilded by the lamplight? Alarmed by the direction his mind was taking, he cleared his throat to say, 'And you're doing this now because …?'

'Because I was too busy earlier.' The word 'obviously' hung ghost-like in the air. 'And even if I'd had the time, I wouldn't have been able to concentrate with Ruth bobbing in and out, tidying things and talking.'

And that was when Daniel identified the real issue. Like him, she needed a place in which to work. He had the library. All she had was this room, sandwiched between their bedchambers. He said, 'I'm sorry. I should have realised that you'd need an office of your own. I wish you had told me. And if there are other such things, I hope you *will* tell me. But we'll address this one first thing tomorrow. There is a room leading off the library – not large but pleasant and unused since my grandmother's time. Presumably you've seen it?' And when she nodded, 'Will it do?'

She smiled at him, turning a little pink. 'Very well indeed.'

'In that case, give whatever orders are needed and make it your own. And for God's sake, do *not* thank me. This is your *home*, Anna. Treat it as such. Goodness knows you're pouring enough money and effort into it. Time, as well – if the fact you're working at one in the morning is anything to go by. Is it?'

'Partly. With regard to the house, I want to get as much done as is feasible in as short a time as possible and with a minimum of discomfort for everybody – so organising and scheduling is crucial and time-consuming. But it's only temporary. In a few weeks, everything will settle down.'

'And meanwhile you're burning the midnight oil?'

'No. Meanwhile, I'm enjoying myself.'

'Away from *Hawthorne's?*' he asked, half teasing, half not. 'Really?'

'Surprising as it may sound, yes. I want – I would *like* you to be proud of your home. Proud enough to invite your friends to stay.'

Not for the first time, Daniel was made faintly uncomfortable by her thoughtfulness. Also not for the first time, he wondered just how much money she had at her disposal and quite how much of it marrying him had, and still was, costing her. But these weren't questions he could ask; and, even if they had been, the middle of the night, with both of them dressed for bed and the air around them swirling with inappropriate suggestions, wasn't the best time for that or any other conversation.

He said, 'I'm sure I shall be. But sufficient unto the day, Anna. Leave what you were doing and get some sleep. You won't enjoy anything if you're dead on your feet tomorrow. Don't forget the lamps. Good night.'

And with a nod and a smile, he left her.

She watched the door close behind him and click shut. Still staring after him, she realised something odd. This was the first time that she'd actually felt married.

Back in his own chamber, Daniel shed the robe and slid back between the sheets. He was uneasily aware that something indefinable had shifted in the last half hour ... but he wasn't sure he wanted to know what it was. So he waited until the ribbon of light beneath the parlour door went dark and then settled down to sleep.

* * *

Ten days later, Anna declared the refurbishment of both drawing-room and entrance hall almost complete and Daniel found himself summarily evicted from the library and installed in the little-used winter parlour. To Anna's surprise, he objected to this less than she had anticipated ... and instead informed her that, following her advice, he'd opened an account for his mother at her former dressmaker in Gloucester.

'Like Rebecca, Mama will receive a quarterly allowance but she prefers that larger bills be sent to me.' He grinned wryly. 'And since both she and Becky know this, I doubt they'll waste any time taking advantage of it.'

'They won't,' admitted Anna. 'But that's understandable. When did either of them last have a new gown?'

'I dread to think. Two years, at least – probably more.'

'Then you can expect their first visit to be an expensive one.'

'I'd guessed as much.' Daniel hesitated and then said, 'But after it, perhaps we can begin repairing our fractured relationship with the neighbouring families?'

'Yes. For a long time, from your mother's point of view, everything has been about her inability to keep up appearances. It's why I felt superficial improvements in the main reception rooms should be accomplished without delay.'

'*Superficial* improvements?' he queried gently.

'Yes. New curtains here, a coat of paint there and plenty of polish,' replied Anna. 'We can do better than that later. But for now, the house looks less ... tired. So when there are also new clothes, perhaps your mother and Rebecca might begin paying calls and receiving visitors.'

He nodded. 'You and I could prepare the way for that. As soon as is feasible, I want to go to Hazelmere. But before that I'd like to introduce you to at least some of the local families.'

'Bride visits in reverse, you mean?' she said doubtfully. Then, 'Well, it sends the right message, I suppose. The one that says Lord Reculver and his family are ready to rejoin the world.'

'Exactly. So, with that in mind, will you wish to join Mama and Rebecca at the modiste's after all?'

'No. I don't need new clothes. And I've other plans for the coming days – the most pressing being to ensure that your exile from the library is as brief as possible.'

'For which you'll have my undying gratitude. But don't deny yourself a day out on account of it.'

'I'm not. And when I said I had other plans, I meant it.'

Daniel eyed her thoughtfully. 'Your choice, of course. But may I ask what you consider preferable to shopping?'

'Visiting some of the tenants in order to get to know them better. And if you have no objection, I'll also call in at the school. I helped with the one at home so I won't just be meddling for the sake of —'

'Anna, stop. I know you won't be meddling indiscriminately. And you don't need my permission for things of this sort. If you continue seeking it, I'll feel obliged to retaliate in kind by asking *yours* for every penny I spend before I spend it.'

'No. I don't want that.'

'So you've said. As *I* have repeatedly reminded you that you are my wife and *this* is your home now. So regarding the school and any other similar matter, do what you feel is necessary. I – and the tenants and villagers – can only be grateful. And I imagine the school always has need of something.'

'Reading books, usually,' she nodded. 'Ones for each level of age and ability. Being shared by numerous children means they wear out quickly, so there's a constant need for replacements. Depending on what I find and how well the schoolmistress and I get on, I'll probably offer a quarterly contribution for books as I did at – in Upper Wick. Later … well, we'll see.'

Daniel nodded and, deciding to turn the subject slightly, said, 'If you're going to any of the outlying farms, take the gig. Most of the lanes are too narrow for your phaeton.'

'I'd take the gig even if they weren't,' she replied. 'I don't want to arrive like visiting royalty. It wouldn't be a good start.'

* * *

On the following morning, a letter arrived from Harold Grimshaw.

Daniel stared at it for a long time before walking through to his wife's office, saying, 'Do you have a moment?'

Anna laid down her pen. 'Of course. What is it?'

He held up the letter. 'Grimshaw. If he doesn't hear from me very soon, he's threatening to come here – which is the very last thing I want.'

She waved at the chair on the other side of the desk and, when he sat, said, 'So?'

'I'll go to him. But I'm also thinking of involving the lawyers. There may be questions they can ask that haven't occurred to me – not just of Grimshaw, but of his bank. The officials there won't talk to me but they may talk to Longhope. What do you think?'

'It's worth a try.' She pondered for a moment and then added, 'We could even add Mr Landry, if you like. I could instruct him to write to Grimshaw querying the debt. Receiving letters from my man-of-law as well as yours may make him wonder if the game is worth the candle.'

Quite slowly, Daniel grinned at her. 'And if none of that works?'

'I suppose we either pay him or think again. But for now, you'd better stop him turning up on the doorstep. Go and see him. Tell him he'll be hearing from your lawyers and coming here won't aid his cause – oh, and tell Flynn not to admit him if he does.'

Laughter lit his eyes. 'Anything else, ma'am?'

'Not that I can think of.' She pulled a couple of sheets of paper towards her then glanced up as if wondering why he was still there. 'Was there something else?'

'No. Yes. I've been very self-absorbed, haven't I? Involving you in my problems but never sparing a thought for any you might have.'

'I have none of any consequence.'

'So that fellow Harvill has stopped plaguing you?'

'It seems so.' She picked up her pen, preparing to get back to work. Then, just as Daniel turned to go, she muttered, 'Since he held up my carriage, at all events.'

Spinning on his heel, Daniel snapped, 'He *what?*'

Anna sighed and laid the pen down again.

'He'd stopped pestering Nathaniel for an appointment and took to trying to see me at home instead. That failed as well because I'd given orders he wasn't to be admitted. But he persisted so I had Sedley tell him that if he came to my door again, I'd report him to the local magistrate for harassment. And that seemed to end it.'

'Seemed to – but didn't?'

'No. I was on my way home from the manufactory. He and his man blocked the road so my coachman was forced to pull up. Harvill made yet another – and frankly ridiculous – offer for Hawthorne's. Yet again I refused and repeated my threat about the magistrate. He let me pass then and – '

'*Did* you report it?' cut in Daniel, sitting down again.

'No. Because he stopped bothering me so there wasn't any need.'

'Thus far. And mostly because you're no longer there for him to bother.'

'All right, I take the point,' she conceded with a note of faint irritation. 'But all I wanted was for him to accept that no means no and he finally appears to have done so.'

'You thought that before and he accosted you on the road,' he pointed out. And then, said, 'I'm guessing that, if he wants a porcelain manufactory, there are others he could buy.'

'There are.'

'So why not settle for one of them? Why has he fixed on Hawthorne's?'

'I have no idea.'

'You haven't ever wondered?'

'Well, of *course* I've wondered. But – '

'You don't think there's something peculiar about this level of persistence?'

This time she didn't reply but merely sent him a look that suggested it was *his* level of persistence she found most annoying. Ignoring this, Daniel said mildly, 'You've never considered having him investigated?'

Anna blinked. 'Not *that* exactly – though I did ask Mr Lowe to see what he could find out. But since Harvill hasn't actually done anything illegal, it's hardly a case for Bow Street, is it?'

'No. But there are other avenues.' He stood up. 'I know a gentleman who I believe is accustomed to handling that kind of thing. If Harvill surfaces again, we can discuss that option.' He sent her a fleeting grin, then glanced at the clock. 'And now I'm leaving for Cirencester . I can be there before dark, call on Grimshaw first thing tomorrow and be home in time for dinner.'

* * *

This time Grimshaw's door was opened by an attractive, middle-aged woman who – since she was wearing her hat – was presumably about to go out.

Bowing politely and offering a slight smile, Daniel said, 'Good morning, ma'am. I was hoping to see Mr Grimshaw. Is he at home?'

'Why, yes – both of them are,' she replied, stepping aside so that he could enter and seemingly both flustered and confused. 'Were you looking for my brother-in-law or my son, sir?'

'The former. I haven't the pleasure of your son's acquaintance, ma'am. Perhaps you would be good enough to tell Mr Grimshaw senior that Viscount Reculver is here and would appreciate a few minutes of his time?'

If she had looked flustered before, her reaction to his name was one of something akin to fright.

'Reculver?' she breathed. '*Oh*. Oh ... of course. You are ... you must be ...'

'Still here, Alice?' Grimshaw appeared from a door further down the hall. 'Were not you and William going to the charitable event at All Saints?'

'Yes. But Will forgot the letter he was to take to the rector so he – '

'Is doubtless trying to recall where he put it.' Opening the door to the same room in which he'd received Daniel last time, Grimshaw said, 'Please take a seat, my lord – I will be with you in just a moment.'

Finding himself inside with the door shut behind him just as hurried footsteps sounded on the stairs, Daniel wondered why Grimshaw was so determined to separate him from his relatives. Because they didn't know what he was up to? Or because they did?

He listened to the sounds of feet on the stairs, of brief, low-voiced conversation and finally of the door to the street opening, then closing again. As soon as it had done so, Grimshaw joined Daniel in the small parlour and said, 'This is unexpected, my lord. Dare I hope you've seen the wisdom of paying what you owe?'

'Not exactly,' replied Daniel calmly. 'I've seen the wisdom of placing your persistent demands in the hands of both my own lawyers and those of my wife. Henceforth, they will be handling the matter on my behalf and consequently, turning up at my home will do you no good at all.'

'Keen to keep me away from your mother and your new bride, my lord?'

'As keen, let us say, as *you* appear to be to keep me away from *your* family.' Daniel sighed. 'The situation is very simple, Mr Grimshaw. I'm loth to settle a debt I'm not convinced ever existed. Unless you can give my lawyers adequate proof that it *did* you won't see a penny from me. And that, I am afraid, is my last word.'

'You might regret that – as might your lady wife. And yes, I *do* know who you've married. You did well there if what I've heard about her is true.'

'Let's stick to the point, shall we?' snapped Daniel.

'I *am* sticking to it. I'm pointing out that there's worse things than being a few thousand out of pocket.' Grimshaw smiled, but not pleasantly. 'If you're wise, you won't risk finding that out the hard way.'

'And if *you're* wise, you won't resort to threats. I can assure you that I don't respond well to them.'

'That wasn't a threat, my lord. That was a piece of good advice. A threat would be me asking whether, now your father's gone, you won't mind the truth coming out.'

Daniel frowned. 'What the hell are you talking about?'

'Something you'd be much happier not knowing.'

If that's the case, why mention it? thought Daniel. But he said, 'What, exactly?'

'Something your father kept quiet for twenty-five years – and not just from the world. Mostly, he wanted it kept from your mother and you and your little sister. That was my deal with him, you see. Maybe you should think on that before you start talking about lawyers and the like ... because once things come into the light, it can be hard to put them back in the dark.'

Understanding arrived like a punch to Daniel's stomach. He said incredulously, '*Blackmail?*'

'That's an ugly word. I prefer to call it ... keeping your father's secret. And, in return, he's helped me look after my sister-in-law and her son when my own finances were over-stretched.'

'Blackmail,' said Daniel again. And then, 'For *twenty-five years?*'

'Keeping his secret. And I'll go *on* keeping it for one final payment of four thousand pounds.'

He won't, said a voice in Daniel's head. *If I pay once, there will never be an end to it. He'll come back, over and over again – as it seems he did to Father.* And then, hard on its heels, *Is* that *what those loans were for? To pay off this little weasel? And for* what, *for God's sake? What could Father have done that was so terrible he'd pay to keep it hidden for two-and-a-half decades?*

'No,' he said coldly. 'I'll be damned before I pay you another penny.'

'Not even,' murmured Grimshaw slyly, 'to know what it was your father thought worth protecting you from all these years?'

That was so tempting that Daniel hesitated briefly. But his previous thought still held. Blackmailers never stopped unless their bluff was called.

'Wouldn't that be breaking your 'deal' with my father?' he taunted. 'And no. Not even for that. Do your worst, Grimshaw – and be prepared for me doing the same. There will be no more money. Instead, I'll be doing my damnedest to bring a charge of extortion against you. Good day.'

And turning on his heel, he walked out.

Once in the fresh air of the street, he took a moment to think about the woman who had answered the door. She must be Grimshaw's widowed sister-in-law, with whom he'd said he lived from time to time. Yes. And she had a son – who, given her current age, wouldn't be a child. Daniel wondered whether there was anything to be gained by talking to them. Judging by the widow's reaction, his name had meant something to her. It might be interesting to find out what. Where had Grimshaw said she and her son were going? A charity event at All Saints Church? Yes, that was it.

Daniel strode back to the main road and asked the first person he met for directions.

* * *

The centre of the church was busy. There were little stalls selling home-made cakes, jams and handicrafts in every available space and what looked like half the ladies in the town either buying or selling. Daniel dropped two guineas on to a collection plate just inside the door, then paused and took a long look around, hoping to spot Grimshaw's sister-in-law. What had she been wearing? He tried to see her in his mind's eye. Dark hair with a few strands of grey and a trim figure. A black straw hat tied with blue ribbons and … and a short grey cloak over a blue-and-grey striped gown? Yes. Fairly confident that was right, he sauntered onwards.

There were a lot of black hats; hats with feathers, with flowers and with ribbons, none of them the one he was looking for. And then he saw it – saw *her*, near the altar end of the nave, deep in conversation with a fellow in a cassock who was presumably the rector and a tall fellow in a dark coat. Her son?

Preferring, if possible, to remain unseen, Daniel moved closer through the shadows of the north aisle and halted, half concealed by a pillar. The vicar clapped the young man on the shoulder, said something that made both him and his mother laugh and walked away. Mother and son exchanged a couple of sentences, then turned to go, thus giving Daniel his first proper look at them … or more specifically, at *him*.

One look was all it took to paralyse his brain and suck the air from his lungs.

Oh my God, he thought. *So that's it.*

CHAPTER SIXTEEN

On the morning of the following day and the one on which she expected Daniel back from Cirencester, Anna decided to make a preliminary visit to the village school.

It was a four-roomed cottage and was as clean and neat as anywhere housing a large number children had any chance of being. Although initially mildly flustered by the unexpected arrival of the viscountess, Mrs Jenson, the schoolmistress, quickly composed herself and welcomed Anna with a cautious smile and a curtsy.

'It's a pleasure to meet you, my lady.'

'And mine to be here – though I should apologise for not giving you any warning. I hope my visit isn't ill-timed?'

'Not at all, my lady. How can I help you?'

'I'd like to look around the school, if I may,' said Anna. 'But actually I'm hoping there are ways in which *I* can help *you* – as I was used to doing in my former home.' She smiled suddenly. 'Don't worry. I've no intention of interfering or of upsetting your routine with constant visits.'

Relief flitted through the schoolmistress's eyes.

'Then may I ask what your ladyship has in mind?'

'I won't know that until you've shown me around. So … shall we?'

At the end of an hour, Anna had learned everything she needed to know.

There were currently a total of nineteen pupils, varying in age from five to eleven years and divided into two classes. Mrs Jenson taught the older pupils and fourteen-year-old, former pupil, Daisy Carter, the younger ones. Parents who could afford it, paid sixpence a week for the first child and fourpence for any subsequent ones but there was no regular funding – merely occasional donations from the nearby better-off tradesmen or farmers. The cottage in which the school was housed was Mrs Jenson's home; having already been repaired far too many times, virtually all the classroom furniture needed replacing; and there was an urgent need for new slates, paper, pencils and books.

In short, the only thing Anna *didn't* know was how the school was surviving at all.

Rising at the end of her discussion with the schoolmistress, she said, 'My congratulations, Mrs Jenson. You are doing sterling work in less than ideal conditions and without the support you need and deserve. However, there are a number ways in which I can mend that, if you will allow me?'

'*Allow* you?' echoed the other woman faintly. 'My lady ... anything you can do, however small, would be deeply appreciated, I assure you.'

'Very well. The first thing must be a regular quarterly allowance, sufficient to cover repairs, replacements, day-to-day running costs such as fuel and also to provide *you* with a steady income. I shall instruct my man-of-law to set that in hand immediately. Regarding the other possibilities I have in mind, I shall need to speak with Lord Reculver about those and when I've done so, you and I can talk again.' Pulling a purse from her pocket and handing it to the schoolmistress, she added, 'Meanwhile, this should cover any immediate needs until the first payment arrives from my man-of-law. And now I've taken up more than enough of your time and will take my leave.'

'B-But – I – I hardly know what to say, my lady,' stammered Mrs Jenson, overcome.

'Then don't say anything, ma'am,' replied Anna easily. And with a sudden smile, 'There really isn't any need.'

And she walked out, leaving the other woman to drop weakly into a chair feeling as if she'd strayed into the path of a tidal wave.

* * *

Leaving Cirencester immediately after walking out of the church, Daniel arrived home with ample time to bathe and change but less interested in doing either than he was in telling Anna what he had learned.

On his way to find her, a glance into the library told him that it was his own again. The windows gleamed and had been hung with new curtains; furniture had been given a thorough polishing, leaving the air scented with lavender; and balding rugs had been replaced with others which, though not new, were in better condition. Everything on his desk had been replaced exactly as he liked it. It was an altogether pleasanter room than it had been a fortnight ago.

Inevitably, Anna was in her own office, compiling what looked like lists. But as soon as he poked his head around the door she looked up, saying, 'How was it? Or shall I ring for tea before you tell me?'

'Wine, if you wouldn't mind,' he replied, dropping into a chair. 'It may take a while ... and very little of it is good. Has anything happened while I was away that I should know about?'

'Nothing of any great consequence.' She pulled the bell for Flynn and, when he appeared, asked for wine for his lordship and tea for herself. 'I went to the school this morning. It is in desperate need of just about everything, so I promised the schoolmistress a quarterly allowance. And I have another idea that I'll need to discuss with you.'

'Go on, then.'

'Now? There's no particular hurry.'

'I daresay.' *Give me a few minutes respite from what has been going round in my head since this morning.* 'But what I have to tell you requires privacy and no interruptions.'

'Oh. Well, in that case ... are you aware that the school is housed in the schoolmistress's home and that it receives no regular funding at all? That, aside from the occasional small donation from local folk who can afford it, there's no real provision for *anything?*'

A frown touched his eyes. 'No. I wasn't. And I should have been. What else?'

So Anna explained about the number of pupils and Mrs Jenson's weekly charges, leaving him to work out – as she had done – the meagre income this produced.

'I see.' A tap at the door heralded Flynn bearing wine and a footman with the tea tray. Daniel said, 'Set it down, please. We can manage the rest ourselves.' And when the door closed behind them, he rose and, gesturing to the wine said, 'We'll come back to this presently, Anna. Meanwhile, are you sure you won't join me in a glass of wine?'

'You think I'll need it?' she asked lightly.

'No. But I certainly do.'

'Then yes. I'll join you.'

He filled two glasses, handed her one of them and downed half of the other, before refilling it and sitting down again. Then he said abruptly, 'There is no debt. There never was.

What there *has* been is blackmail, stretching back over twenty-five years.'

'As long as that?' gasped Anna. 'No. Surely not?'

'It doesn't seem possible, does it? But Grimshaw admitted it. He said he and my father had a deal. His part in it was keeping Father's secret from both his family and the world at large. And today, he offered to go *on* keeping it in return for one last payment of four thousand pounds.' Daniel's mouth curled derisively. 'He must think me an idiot. Because it wouldn't have been 'one last payment', would it?'

She shook her head. 'I doubt it. You refused?'

'I refused,' agreed Daniel. 'So then he offered to *sell* me the secret for the same price. I refused that as well and for the same reason – much as I wanted to know what Father could possibly have done that justified him plunging deeper and deeper into financial ruin.'

'Are there no clues?' asked Anna. 'No other way we can find out?'

For what seemed a long time, he stared silently into his glass. Finally he said, 'I may already have done so. I could be wrong, of course … but I don't think so.' He paused again. 'Grimshaw lives with his brother's widow. I met her today. She's on the shady side of forty but, in the right company, could still turn heads And later, I saw her son. Tall fellow, a few years younger than myself; dark eyes, dark hair … and a pronounced widow's peak.'

Anna's eyes widened and her hand crept to her mouth.

'Like Rebecca?'

'*Just* like Rebecca,' he replied grimly. 'Sufficiently so to be our brother … which is presumably what he is.'

For a moment, she said nothing. Then, 'But surely your father can't have been …' She stopped and then, sighing, said, 'But he was, wasn't he?'

'Having an affair with Grimshaw's brother's wife – or widow if that's what she already was? Yes. Stupid not to see that, once he began paying Grimshaw for his silence, he'd be doing it for forever? Again, yes.' Daniel drained his glass and refilled it. 'To be fair, it may have begun with payments for the boy's upkeep and later on, for his education and so forth. But it wouldn't have taken Grimshaw long to realise that as long as Father wanted it kept from *us* – his family – he'd go on paying.'

'The loans your father had taken out … do you think they were because of this?'

'Since I've never been able to account for them any other way, what else could they be?' asked Daniel bitterly. 'He gradually beggared the estate rather than acknowledge an affair and the result of it. How irresponsible … how monumentally *stupid* is that? Did he think the gradual slide into bankruptcy would be easier on Mama than standing up to Grimshaw and telling her the truth of what he'd done before she could hear of it elsewhere? But perhaps, as the years went by, it didn't bother him too much since *I* was the one who was going to have to pick up the pieces. *God!*' He shoved a hand through his hair, dislodging the ribbon. 'Anna … you cannot imagine how utterly bloody *furious* I am.'

'Oh, I think I can. And you've every right to be.'

Inevitably, unhappily, she couldn't help recognising – as Daniel must be doing – that had the late viscount refused to allow Grimshaw to continue blackmailing him, Daniel might not have been left with no choice but to marry for money; to marry *her*.

In fact, Daniel was thinking something quite different and was surprised that the notion hadn't occurred to him before. His father had been a superb horseman. Far too good to misjudge a jump or set his horse at a wall without knowing what lay on the far side of it. But on that day in December it appeared he'd done one or the other … and it had killed him. For the first time, Daniel found himself wondering uneasily if that fall hadn't been a tragic accident at all but Father finally reaching the end of his tether and taking the quickest and, perhaps to him, the easiest way out. Discovering that he felt slightly sick, he did his best to push the idea aside at least for the time being. Everything was quite bad enough already without having to wonder if his father had committed suicide.

He took a couple of slow, bracing breaths and then said, 'We have to decide what to do. We may have a few days' grace while Grimshaw hopes curiosity will get the better of me and I'll go back, prepared to pay – not four thousand perhaps, but *something* for the truth. However, at some point soon, he's going to bring it all out in the open; perhaps by word of mouth or letters to various acquaintances ... or, more likely in my opinion, by selling the tale to one of the scandal sheets.'

'How many people are likely to care about an illegitimate child sired a quarter of a century ago?' asked Anna reasonably. 'Not many, surely. Perhaps if your father had left the child and his mother to starve ... but he didn't. It's a commonplace enough story in its way and, by now, very old news.'

'To you and me, perhaps. But that won't stop the gossip.'

'All right. I can't deny that. But while Grimshaw is blackening your father's name, he'll also be ruining his sister-in-law's reputation and branding his nephew a – a –' She stopped, unwilling to say it.

'A bastard,' supplied Daniel. 'Yes. But then he *isn't* his nephew, is he? He's no blood relation to Grimshaw at all – which is the only thing in all of this that, if I was him, I'd be grateful for.'

'True. But he and his mother are the ones who will suffer most if his true parentage is revealed to the world. Cirencester isn't a large place. Everyone who knows them will hear of it. Imagine what that will do to their lives. And you say that Grimshaw lives in the sister-in-law's house. She's hardly likely to let him continue to do so when he's set her and her son in the public pillory, is she? Surely that's enough to make him hold his tongue?'

'It may be, I suppose. But I daren't rely on it. If it's all going to come out, I can't risk it hitting Mama out of the blue,' he said wearily. 'I'm going to have to tell her so that, if the worst happens, at least she's prepared. Rebecca, too. They'll both be devastated. Despite everything else Father did, they at least had the comfort of believing him faithful, loving and, above all, honourable.' He shut his eyes for a moment and then, opening them, 'You'll notice I haven't *begun* to think of what it will mean for you and me. Particularly you – since you didn't marry me expecting to find yourself in the eye of a scandal. If it helps at all, I'm sorry for it.'

'You have nothing to apologise for. None of it is your doing. And if Grimshaw makes it public, we'll deal with it.' Anna rose and, to his surprise, refilled his glass. 'In fact, the first thing we should do is alert the lawyers. If there is the smallest chance of bringing a charge of extortion against Grimshaw, we should take it.'

'I already threatened him with that. But he knows we haven't any proof.'

'As yet, we haven't tried to find any.' The merest germ of an idea stirred at the back of her mind but she put it aside to consider later and said instead, 'Don't say anything to your mother just yet. It may be unnecessary. Given the destruction it would wreak in Grimshaw's own home life, there's a good chance he won't make the story public. But you said your father was paying him to keep it from this house as much as from the world. To me, that suggests Grimshaw will be much more likely to try telling your mother. That way he gets what he's doubtless thinking of as his revenge without any inconvenience to himself. But with a bit of care, we can stop that happening.'

'How?' asked Daniel edgily.

'Describe Grimshaw to Flynn, giving orders that, if he comes here and regardless of anything he may say, he is not to be admitted,' replied Anna. 'And for the next few weeks, have all correspondence addressed to your mother brought to you first. Meanwhile, keep a close eye on the newspapers – here, in Cirencester and in London. I honestly don't believe Grimshaw will go down that route but it's still best to take what precautions we can.' Unable to help herself, she reached out to lay her hand over his, 'We can weather this, Daniel – and we will.'

He turned his hand over and gripped hers. 'I hope so. And … thank you.'

'No need for that.'

'I think there is. So … finish what you were saying about the school.'

She shook her head, relishing the warmth of his fingers around hers. 'As I said, there's no hurry for that. Tomorrow will do.'

'I daresay. But now will give me something else to think about. So … tell me. For example, is there *only* the schoolmistress or does she have an assistant teacher?'

'Sort of. What she has is Daisy Carter; a fourteen-year-old former pupil who teaches the youngest pupils in return for a shilling a week and extra lessons. But now Daisy's father has heard that we've been taking on extra staff here, he's decreed that she is to go into service when she turns fifteen – which is in three months' time. Not only does Mrs Jenson not want to lose her, she says it would be a waste of a promising mind.'

Frowning a little, he said, 'Is there more?'

'Do you *need* more?'

'No. But if there is, I ought to hear it.'

'Well, then. The furniture is dropping apart, as are most of the books but my donations will be sufficient to take care of that and a few other things, too. However, for years, Mrs Jenson has been using half of her home as a school – for which she hasn't been paid or even compensated for things like coal or candles. It's a disgrace. Either the school should be situated elsewhere or Mrs Jenson should have another cottage to live in. And that is where you come in.'

'I rather suspected that it might be.'

'You told me that there were empty cottages on the estate.'

'I did and there are.'

'Might any of them be suitable?'

'For the schoolmistress to live in? Or to become the school-house?'

'Either.' And before he had a chance to reply she blurted out, 'Apparently your father never took any interest in the school. The village accepted that, at least in recent years, he couldn't afford to do so. But *now* they know that things have changed. You and I can make a difference, Daniel. And one way to do it is by giving the village the school it needs. Mrs Jenson has been charging her pupils because it was the only way to keep the school open – but that means some children don't attend. That is easy enough to change. But, as I've said, there's also the question of proper premises and –'

'Stop. I take the point.' He managed something resembling a smile. 'You want a cottage?'

'Yes please.'

'Then I'll see what I can do.'

* * *

On the following afternoon, Daniel handed Anna the key of the empty cottage lying nearest to the village.

'It was repaired along with the others so it's ready for use. If Mrs Jenson wants to live there I'll make it the official home of the school principal – at a peppercorn rent so that the estate retains ownership and is thus responsible for its upkeep. Her own cottage would continue to be the school-house and she could either rent it to the estate or sell it to me outright.'

'That's generous. And if she prefers to stay in her own home?'

'The empty cottage becomes the school-house,' he shrugged. 'Now ... regarding Daisy Carter. I'll inform her father that, provided she continues at the school, she'll be added to the roll of household employees and receive the same wage as a junior chambermaid.'

Anna laughed. 'There's not much he can say to that, is there?'

'Nothing at all, I hope. I leave Mrs Jenson to you. Take her to see the cottage tomorrow morning, ask her for a decision and tell her that I'll call in a couple of days to answer any questions she may have before having Longhope deal with the legalities.'

* * *

Mrs Jenson toured the empty cottage in silence. At the end, with tears in her eyes, she said, 'There is a garden. It's been so *long* since I had one because the children needed space to play. And I've missed it dreadfully.'

Anna smiled. 'Does that mean you might like to live here?'

'I would *love* to live here, my lady, truly I would! I can't thank you enough.'

'Thank his lordship. I merely brought the situation to his attention. And for you to have a home of your own and while the school remains where it is seems an ideal solution.' Anna held out the key. 'You may as well have this now. Let me know when you've moved in and tell your pupils that they'll be having a little holiday while the school is redecorated, given new furniture and probably a host of other things I haven't thought of yet. Oh – and expect to hear from my lawyer, Mr Landry. He'll be arranging financial matters with you. As for the cottage,' she finished with a smile, 'his lordship and I hope you'll be very happy here. And now you must excuse me. I'm told there's illness of some sort at Reynolds' farm and want to find out if there is anything they need.'

CHAPTER SEVENTEEN

When Anna arrived at the Reynold's farm, there was such a pandemonium of shouting and wailing coming from within the kitchen that no one heard her knock.

'Where's Johnny gone *this* time?' someone demanded over the din. 'Joan, pick up the baby and stop him screaming will you? *Harry!* Where's John?'

'Dunno. Gone off with his pup, I 'spect.'

'Well, *find* him. He's not ill now and he's supposed to be *helping*. I can't do *everything!*'

Two young voices, presumably those of Joan and Harry began talking at once and the baby's screams grew louder.

Oh dear, thought Anna. Then, not without a certain amount of dread, opened the door and let herself in to a shambles of dirty dishes, unwashed pots and baskets of laundry.

'Enough!' she said crisply and with sufficient volume to be heard over the din. Then, when everyone but the baby fell silent to stare at her, 'Thank you. Joan, do as your sister said and quiet your little brother. Now ... how is your mother? And who else is sick?'

Swallowing hard and managing something resembling a curtsy, twelve-year-old Tess whispered, 'Mam's still poorly, milady. And Robbie's worse. Can't stop coughing, neither of them.'

'Yes. I can hear them.' She could and the coughs sounded severe. 'How long has it been?'

'More'n a week now.'

'Has the doctor seen them?'

'No, milady.'

'And your father?'

'He didn't have it as bad, ma'am. He's back out digging the turnips now.'

Taking a florin from her purse, Anna beckoned the younger boy and, handing it to him, said, 'Give that to your father and tell him I said to fetch the doctor. If you see John, tell him to come home.' And when the boy sped off, 'Now, Tess ... I suppose you've been trying to look after your mother and brother and keep everyone fed and I'm sure you've done splendidly. But it's far too much for one person – so while we wait for the doctor, I'll help you clear all this up and then – '

'*You*, milady?' gasped Tess. 'No. That wouldn't be right.'

Anna laughed. 'Why not? I can wash dishes as well as anyone if you'll just find me an apron. But first, make your mother and brother a warm honey drink. Do you know how to do that?' And when the girl nodded again, 'Good. Do it and then put more water to warm.'

By the time Mr Reynolds arrived with the doctor, the kitchen was looking a little less like a battle zone. Aghast at the sight of the viscountess hanging her apron on a hook and rolling down her sleeves, Jack Reynolds said helplessly, 'My lady ... I'm so sorry. Girls – what were you *thinking?* Her ladyship shouldn't be – '

'Don't blame the girls, Mr Reynolds,' said Anna firmly. 'When something I *can* do needs to be done, I rarely wait for permission.' And offering her hand to the doctor, 'How do you do, sir? I'm sorry to call on your services before we've even been introduced.'

'Not at all, Lady Reculver. Doctor Weatherall, at your service. And if Mrs Reynolds has the nasty infection I've seen elsewhere, you did right to send for me because it doesn't clear up on its own.' Then, to Tess, 'Now, child ... take me to the patients.'

Left facing Mr Reynolds, Anna said crisply, 'Looking after the rest of you is too much for Tess to manage on her own. If you've no neighbours who can help, I'll send someone from the Court for a couple of hours each day.'

'That's kind of you, my lady, but I reckon Meg Grant from the next farm over will help us out for a bit.'

'Good.' And to Harry, 'No John?'

He shook his head. 'Didn't see him nowhere, Miss – I mean, milady.'

'Well, if I see him on the way back I'll tell him to go home directly.'

'No need to worry about John,' said Reynolds dryly. 'He clears off with his dog every chance he gets but turns up safe in time for dinner.' He hesitated, then added, 'Thank you for your kindness, my lady. It's much appreciated.'

'I'm happy to help,' she replied, 'and will send a basket of whatever Cook thinks may tempt the invalids. But now I must go or there will be search parties out looking for me. I promised the dowager viscountess I'd be back by luncheon and it's long past that.'

* * *

Despite what she'd told Mr Reynolds, Anna took the long way home – less to look for young John than because, after three consecutive days of rain, today was a fine one and, even in a lowly gig, she enjoyed driving. The road took her past the field at Old Fallow, the bottom of which, prior to the recent rain, the team of men engaged by Daniel had been attempting to drain. They weren't there today – though *why* they weren't, Anna couldn't imagine. She pulled the gig to a stop, wondering if Daniel knew. And it was then that she thought she heard a voice in the distance and, a moment or two later, a feeble bark.

She immediately thought of John Reynolds and his dog but could see no sign of either. Then another, more distinct, cry reached her. 'Help!' it said.

Anna twisted the reins about the bar and jumped down from the gig. She couldn't see anyone and assumed the cry must have come from behind the straggling bit of hedge near the drainage site. Distantly wishing she was wearing different shoes, she set off towards the lower end of the field.

She saw the dog first. It was frantically floundering in the mud and making its situation worse by the minute. Then, a few feet away from it, she saw the boy, lying flat out on the mud and virtually indistinguishable from it.

'Miss,' he called weakly. 'Please, Miss. Help me reach him.'

Several thoughts made their way rapidly through Anna's mind. The first was, *How?* And the second, *Shoes are going to be the least of my worries.*

'Don't move, John,' she called, picking her way gingerly over the increasingly sodden ground. 'And try to calm your dog. Thrashing about like that isn't helping.'

'I know. B-but B-Bertie's scared.'

And so are you, thought Anna. Getting as close to the boy as she could without joining him in the quagmire, she assessed the problem and didn't see any obvious solution without a rope or something that would serve as one. Without much hope, she said, 'I don't suppose Bertie's wearing a collar, is he?'

'Sort of. I tied one of Mam's k-kerchiefs round his neck with my best knot.'

'Well, let's see how good it was. But you'll have to get a bit nearer. Can you?'

'A bit, mebbe. I lay down 'cos I thought I could reach him better and 'cos I dunno how deep the mud is.'

'Not very,' said Anna with more confidence than she felt. 'It's a field, John. There's a slope but no big holes. So ... this is what we're going to do. Somehow, you have to get hold of Bertie and not let go. If you can do that, I'll grab your ankles and do my best to pull you both out.'

'It won't work,' moaned John, miserably. 'Not without rope.'

'Well, the only alternative is leaving you and Bertie while I go for help. And – '

'*No!* No, Miss. Don't leave us! *Please!*'

'Then grab Bertie and hang on – or I'll have to try hauling you out without him.'

He's right, she thought, dragging up her skirts. *This isn't going to work. The best I can hope for is not to end up as stuck as the blasted dog is.*

* * *

Arriving home far too late for luncheon and having asked Flynn to send a tray to the library, Daniel found his mother in a state of agitation. Catching him in the hall while he was still removing his gloves, she said, 'Anna should have been back two hours ago. Something must have happened to her.'

'Not necessarily, Mama. She was going to Reynolds' farm and the school. Something at one or the other must have delayed her – most probably the former since there's sickness in the house. She'll have stayed to help.'

'Perhaps. But I have A Feeling.'

He groaned inwardly. It had been some time since his mother had had one of her intuitions but he was more familiar with them than he wanted to be. He said reasonably, 'What could possibly have happened to her in the village or on our own land? And if something *had*, we'd have heard about it by now.'

'Perhaps. Perhaps not,' came the stubborn reply. 'I think you should look for her.'

'Very well. If she isn't back by the time I've had a bite to eat – '

'*Food* is more important than your *wife?*'

'Not normally, no. But right now I'm hungry so – '

'Take a piece of pie with you,' suggested Rebecca, grinning down on him from the turn of the stair. 'You may as well. You'll have no peace until you go.'

'Oh for God's sake!' he muttered under his breath. And then, calling, 'Flynn! Send somebody to stop Barker unsaddling Cicero.'

'And your luncheon, my lord?'

'Will have to wait – since I draw the line at eating on horseback.' And snatching up his hat and gloves, he strode out.

He went to the school first because it was nearest and he supposed there was *some* chance that he might find Anna there. But the schoolmistress assured him that Lady Reculver had taken her to see the empty cottage, brought her back home and left for the Reynolds' farm at a little after eleven o'clock. Then she went into raptures over her new home and thanked his lordship a great deal more than he either wanted or had time for.

At Reynolds' farm, Tess said, 'She was here a while, milord – helping me wash the pots and clean the kitchen up. And she stayed until the doctor came to see Mam and Robbie. But she set off home a good bit ago now, milord – said she was already late. More than an hour, it must have been.'

Although he smiled and thanked her, Daniel was beginning to have A Feeling of his own. He had taken the direct route to the farm from the village and hadn't seen any sign of Anna along the way – as, had there had been some mishap to either horse or gig, he would have done. This left only one other possibility; that for reasons of her own, she'd taken the other route by the field at Old Fallow ... although, even allowing for a little extra distance, she still ought to be home by now. Daniel turned Cicero's head and nudged him into a canter.

* * *

Anna, meanwhile, was up to her elbows and nearly up to her knees in mud. On his umpteenth attempt, John had finally managed to get a grip on Bertie's 'collar' whereupon, with extreme reluctance, Anna had taken the four steps necessary to take hold of the boy's ankles. The mud was cold, sticky and disgusting. Heavy with it, her skirts made it difficult to move. As for her shoes, one of them had already come off – which, she told herself, was no loss since nothing she was wearing was going to be worth saving. And she was still no closer to dragging John and Bertie free of the mire. She'd probably been trying to shift him for less than ten minutes but it felt like an hour.

'We ain't moving, are we, Miss?' panted John miserably.

Anna ground her teeth. 'No. I'm still … trying.'

For reasons best known to himself, Bertie recommenced barking. John told him to 'stow it' but Anna, still pulling for all she was worth, panted, 'No. Let him. Somebody might hear … and come.'

Already reining in at the top of the field beside the gig, Daniel stared down at the peculiar sight of what *might* have been a boy, what he *knew* was a dog because it was barking … and a female he *thought* was his wife, all of whom were apparently wallowing in mud. Dropping swiftly from the saddle and looping Cicero's reins about the gatepost, he raced to the edge of the safe ground and, taking in the situation at a glance, snapped, 'Do not *move* – either of you!'

Weak with relief, Anna let go of John's ankles and cautiously straightened her back.

'Thank God,' she breathed.

Tearing off his coat and tossing it aside, Daniel briefly considered also removing his boots. Then, realising he'd have a better chance of staying upright with them than without, he sighed and stepped into the ooze. Two steps took him close enough to clamp an arm about Anna's waist and he muttered, 'Don't struggle or you'll have us both on our backsides.' Then he set about yanking her free.

His first attempt scarcely shifted her so he braced himself to try again. Then, with a single, huge heave, he dragged her free and swivelled to deposit her unceremoniously on the firm ground behind him.

Partly from relief and partly thanks to the weight of the mud clinging to her skirts, Anna's knees gave way and she crumpled into a heap to watch anxiously as her husband fought his way further into the sludge in order to get a better grip on John. She saw him register the fact that the mud was a mere two or three inches away from the top of his boots and heard him say, 'Hold on to the dog ... because I'm not doing this again.'

Wisely, John kept his mouth shut.

Bit by bit, Daniel began inching backwards, towing the boy with him. When he felt the ground growing firmer, he speeded up until he could drag John, arms full of Bertie, to safety. As Anna had done, John folded into a heap on the ground; Daniel walked past both of them to inspect the damage to his boots; and, finding himself free, Bertie planted all four paws firmly on the ground and prepared to—

'*Stop him!*' shouted Daniel. But too late.

Bertie launched into a violent and prolonged doggy shake. Mud flew in all directions. It landed in clods and splashes all over Anna and Daniel, including their faces and hair. It even reached Daniel's previously clean coat, lying on the grass some yards away.

Daniel looked at it for a moment. Then, still in silence, he contemplated his wife's mud-spotted face ... and raised one eyebrow.

'Oh dear,' murmured Anna, for want of something better.

'*Oh dear?*' he echoed. 'Is that all you have to say?'

She thought about it. Then, tentatively, 'Thank you?'

Something happened then; something that surprised Daniel as much as it did Anna. He suddenly saw the funny side. His mouth twitched and then, without warning, he dissolved into helpless laughter.

It was the last thing Anna expected. More than that, it was a revelation. She had never seen him, or indeed anyone, laugh like this ... the sound rich and full of genuine amusement at something that few people would have found funny because it actually wasn't. But Daniel laughed until he cried and then, still hiccupping a little, he said, 'If I look even *half* as bad as you do, I hope we don't meet anyone we know on the way home.'

Anna eyed him uncertainly. 'You aren't annoyed?'

'What use would that be?' he managed unsteadily.

'None. But that wouldn't stop most gentlemen.' She hesitated, making a vague gesture to the state of her clothes. 'Aren't you even going to ask how ...?'

'No. That's clear enough. You found John and his misbegotten hound and couldn't resist *helping*.' Having, without much success, tried wiping his hands on the grass, he stood up and reached for his coat. Then, somehow managing to banish any hint of laughter from both face and voice, he turned to John, saying, 'But *you* can explain to me why you aren't at school. Well?'

'I've been ill, haven't I?' the boy mumbled. And, seeing the look in his lordship's eye, added quickly, 'Pa said I could stay off to help Tess, my lord.'

'And yet here you are.'

John picked at the mud beginning to dry on his face and remained silent.

'Very wise.' Offering his hand to Anna, Daniel pulled her up beside him but, continuing to address John, said, 'You got here on your own, so presumably you can get back the same way. However, I strongly suggest that both you and your dog take a dip in the stream by the corn mill – because if you go home like that you'll be in even more trouble than you already are.'

'Yes, m'lord.' Poised for flight, he halted when his lordship spoke again.

'Is there nothing you'd like to say to her ladyship?' asked Daniel gently.

'Oh. Yes. Thank you, milady. For coming to help and not going away and leaving me. And – and I'm sorry about your clothes and – and everything.'

'That's quite all right, John,' Anna replied gravely. 'Just go home and make up for playing truant all day, leaving Tess to manage.'

He nodded earnestly and ran off, Bertie bounding at his heels.

Daniel watched Anna scowling down at her skirts and doing her best to hold them away from her legs. Repressing another impulse to laugh, he set off towards the lane, saying, 'Best to avoid the village, perhaps?'

'I would think so,' she agreed, trudging along beside him. 'Likewise, the front door if you don't want the novel experience of having it shut in your face.'

'It wouldn't be *that* novel. I've had doors slammed in my face before – though admittedly not by my own butler.'

'There's a first time for everything.'

'Trite but true.' Daniel slanted a grin at her, then stopped. 'Why are you limping?'

'I'm not limping. I lost one of my shoes back there and – '

'Then why didn't you say so?' Without warning, he scooped her up and, ignoring her startled squawk, said provocatively, 'You're heavier than I expected.'

Made breathless by a mixture of shock and delight, Anna said, 'Of course I am. I'm wearing half a ton of mud.' And felt renewed laughter coursing through his chest. 'You're taking this remarkably well.'

'There's another way?' Depositing her into the gig, Daniel untethered his horse and climbed into the saddle. 'So ... while we slink home, why don't you tell me about the rest of your day? Unless cleaning kitchens and rescuing dogs is the entirety of it?'

'Not quite. I showed Mrs Jenson the cottage and she fell in love with it. And – '

'I know. I saw her earlier whilst retracing your steps.' And when she looked questioningly at him, 'Mama had one of her *Feelings* and was convinced you'd come to a sticky end.' He grinned. 'Which you had – though I doubt she could have predicted *this*.'

Anna swallowed. His mother had been worried about her. More remarkable still, he'd come looking for her in case she was in trouble. It made everything about the last hour suddenly worthwhile. Keeping her tone carefully light, she said, '*No* one could have predicted this. However ... tell me about your morning. What did Mr Longhope say?'

'The same thing we knew already. We can't bring a charge of extortion against Grimshaw without proof. Basically, we need a witness.'

Anna drove on in silence for a minute or two, then said, 'I had an idea about that.'

This won her a sharp glance. 'Go on.'

'Grimshaw doesn't know me, does he?'

'He knows *of* you – that is to say he knows you are a wealthy woman in your own right. He congratulated me on marrying you; said I'd done well for myself – to which I might have taken offence, had it not been true. And I'm not just talking about money, Anna. I *did* do well. A lot better than I realised.'

Not unnaturally, this rendered her temporarily speechless. Her colour rose and she finally managed to say, 'That is very … gallant of you.'

'No, it's the truth. But we're getting side-tracked. You said you had an idea?'

'Yes. Grimshaw doesn't know what sort of person I am. He doesn't know I'm not the sort of female to be frightened at being caught up in a scandal; or to go behind my husband's back in order to make the possibility of it go away.'

Daniel's expression hardened in an instant.

'No. He doesn't know those things. But you aren't going anywhere near him. So whatever you're thinking – don't.'

'Please just hear me out. If I wrote to him hinting that a meeting between us might be mutually beneficial –'

'No.'

'And went to see him, accompanied by one of Mr Longhope's clerks playing the part of a footman … I haven't thought that part through properly yet but I'm sure you get the idea … and I act the part of a silly, tearful wife, perhaps I can lure Grimshaw into saying things that will incriminate him.'

'No.'

'No, it wouldn't work?'

'No, you're not doing it.' He lifted a hand as if to push his hair back and then, seeing the mud still clinging to his fingers, thought better of it. 'I know you want to help but – '

'Yes,' she cut in. 'I do. And the way I see it, I'm the only one who can.'

'You do more than enough already.'

'And you don't?'

'Don't what?' he asked, sounding baffled.

'Help. Take what happened this afternoon, for example. You saw what was needed and you didn't hesitate.' She paused briefly. 'How is what happened today different to you pulling Mr Selwyn out of the Serpentine?'

The shadows in his eyes cleared and he gave a short, genuinely amused laugh.

'The Serpentine was cleaner. But in other respects? Not very much, I suppose.'

CHAPTER EIGHTEEN

Two days went by during which Anna managed to persuade Daniel to settle for putting measures in place to prevent Grimshaw gaining access to his mother either in person or by post but, for the time being at least, say nothing to either her or Rebecca about the possible threat.

On the third day, Anna received letters from Mr Landry and Nathaniel Lowe. She was about to break the seal on the second of these when she became aware of the change in Daniel's expression as he read a letter of his own.

'What is it?' she asked.

'Longhope telling me we can't make a charge of extortion stick without any proof – which we already knew. And that, from this point, I should cease all communication with Grimshaw and leave the matter in his hands.'

'And will you?'

'What choice do I have?'

'You could consider my suggestion,' she replied without much hope. And when he said nothing, broke the seal on her own lawyer's letter instead of the one from Mr Lowe. After a moment, she said, 'Mr Landry has found something peculiar at Hoare's ... although, knowing what we now do, I don't know how useful it's likely to be.'

'Tell me anyway.'

'There's only one account in the name of Grimshaw – but the initial on it isn't H, it's W.T.' She continued reading. 'Mr Landry's helpful friend hasn't the authority to access the account itself, so he can't check the address. But this at least proves that the letter Grimshaw sent you from Hoare's confirming the payment to your father wasn't genuine.'

'So it would seem,' agreed Daniel. 'I'll pass that on to Longhope and suggest he asks Hoare's to confirm no such letter was sent. What the bank does about Grimshaw's forgery is up to them. Meanwhile, perhaps we could instruct Longhope and Landry to deal with each other directly on this rather than through us?'

'Good idea.'

'Does Landry say anything about Harvill?'

'No. Perhaps I should do as you suggested and ask him to find an investigator.'

'Definitely – although he may not find one in Worcester.'

'Well, we won't know until he tries.' Anna began gathering up her papers and then, realising Mr Lowe's letter remained unread, sat down again and broke the seal on it. For a few moments she read in silence, a frown gathering on her brow. Then she said, 'I'm going to have to go to Hawthorne's.'

'Trouble?' asked Daniel.

'Yes. The worst kind. Something is wrong with one of the kilns though Nathaniel doesn't say what. But it's out of action – and that will affect everything. Production, fulfilling orders, *everything*.' She stood up, clutching the letter. 'Nathaniel is dealing with the situation, of course, but I need to know precisely what is going on. It's time I went, anyway. I've left it longer than I meant to.' She turned to go, then hesitated and said a shade awkwardly, 'You won't mind?'

'Of course not.' Daniel eyed her thoughtfully, turning his next words over in his mind. 'Perhaps I could come with you ... but only if you wish it. Otherwise not.'

For a instant or two, shock rooted her to the spot and froze her brain.

Then, *Why? Why is he suggesting this? It isn't to spend time with me or because he's interested in Hawthorne's. So why?*

She said bluntly, 'Given the current situation, will you be comfortable being from home just now?'

'I don't see why not. I can't do anything that Flynn isn't already doing,' he shrugged. 'And I'm curious to see your manufactory. I'm also conscious of how much effort you're putting in here. It's time I gave something back – even if it's only understanding enough about your business not to make it a waste of your time talking to me about it, should you ever want to. At the moment, I'd wager your maid knows more about porcelain than I do.'

Anna smiled. 'She does. Her brothers are both employed at Hawthorne's. And if you *truly* wish to visit the manufactory and have the time, please come. I would welcome it. But I'd like to go soon – the day after tomorrow, at the latest.'

'That isn't a problem,' said Daniel. 'We can leave tomorrow if you want to.'

'Really?'

'Yes. There's nothing urgent requiring my personal attention and if some such *should* arise, I can be back within a few hours. I imagine we'll be staying with your mother?' And when she replied with a faintly gloomy nod, 'I see the prospect fills you with delight. But ought you not to warn her?'

'No need. Father insisted that guest rooms were always kept ready and that hasn't changed. Also, unless things at the manufactory are a good deal worse than Nathaniel says, we need not stay above two or three days; too short a time for Mama to try to pull us into her social circle – which she would do if she knew we were coming.' Anna stood up. 'Since we will be able to visit Mr Landry, there's no point in writing to him. But I *do* need to remind your mother that the new bedchamber hangings are due to be delivered tomorrow … and I think there's a shop in Worcester that may have the lace she's been looking for if she'd like me to try.'

When she had left the room and he was about to reply to Mr Longhope, Daniel found his mind dwelling on his wife. Thus far, he admitted to himself, marriage hadn't been as bad as he'd feared it would be. Anna had somehow settled into Reculver with scarcely a ripple despite simultaneously setting in hand the improvements his mother had long wished for. She didn't make demands on his time, being seemingly far too busy with projects of her own and was, in fact, independent to a degree that he suspected many gentlemen would find alarming. Daniel didn't. He found it convenient and also rather admirable. He also found discussing situations and potential problems with Anna was very much like discussing them with Anthony or Gerald; insightful, clinical and productive.

Anna, meanwhile, spoke to the dowager, told Ruth to pack for a stay of three or four days and said she wouldn't need her since, when necessary, she'd borrow her mother's maid. Throughout it all, she tried not to read too much into Daniel's desire to accompany her to Hawthorne's. This was difficult because, despite them both being plastered in mud at the time, she still treasured and all too frequently relived those brief moments in his arms. The coming days would be the most time they had spent together since that awkward evening at Upton-on-Severn. But this would be different. Things were comfortable between them now; they had shared goals. And that, she told herself optimistically, was something on which to build ... as long as she was patient.

* * *

It was these thoughts that were responsible for Anna failing to notice the odd gleam that lit the dowager's eyes when she learned that her son and daughter-in-law would be from home for at least two nights, possibly three. Anna was also unaware that, on the following morning, the dowager rose much earlier than was her usual custom and, still clad in her chamber-robe, watched the carriage disappear around the bend in the drive before she sent for her daughter.

Rebecca, also still *en deshabille*, came in yawning but anxious.

'What's wrong, Mama? You aren't usually up for hours yet.'

'Well, I am today. We have a lot to do and must start immediately.'

'On what?' asked Rebecca, mystified.

'On a surprise for Anna. The new hangings for the master-suite will arrive today and she chose the paint for the walls a fortnight ago. So if we summon extra help from the village, we may be able to have at least *her* bedchamber redecorated before they come home. What do you think?'

'Perhaps. But it will still reek of new paint.'

Her mother smiled. 'I know.'

Rebecca's gaze sharpened. 'Mama? What are you up to?'

'Nothing.'

'Yes, you are. I know that look!'

The dowager hesitated and then said, 'I'm just ... giving things a little nudge.' And when Rebecca continued to stare at her, 'Oh very well. You are aware, I presume, that though Daniel and Anna share the master-suite they don't share a bed?'

'Oh. Yes. I should think the whole house knows it. But – '

'Well, it's time that changed. And *this* is how we can change it.'

Rebecca stared at her. 'Mama – you can't interfere in Dan's life like this. Don't you think he's been dictated to enough already? He'll be furious – and rightly so. And then there's Anna. You must have realised by now that she's in love with him?'

'Of course I've realised it – which is even more reason to help things along. It isn't as though they don't get on with each other. Clearly, they do.'

Rebecca shook her head and turned towards the door. She said, 'I can't stop you. But I'm having nothing to do with it.' And she walked out.

The dowager watched her go, her mind still made up. But it was as well, she decided, that Rebecca didn't know that Daniel and Anna's private arrangements had been shared with Anna's mother.

* * *

By means of their early start, Daniel and Anna hoped to arrive in Worcester between one and two in the afternoon. This, they agreed, would make it possible to go directly to Hawthorne's – from where Anna would have a message sent to her mother.

'Purely,' she explained, 'so she will be expecting us for dinner.'

Daniel grinned but said, 'I assume you'd prefer to talk with Lowe privately?'

'Not at all. Why would I? There will be nothing you can't hear. But you may not find it very interesting, in which case Nathaniel will find someone to give you the basic guided tour we devised for visiting members of the public.'

'You'd be surprised at the things that interest me these days. And, I suspect I would prefer the less-than-basic tour that I feel sure *you* would give me – when you can spare the time, of course.'

Pleasure brought a hint of colour to Anna's cheeks but she said awkwardly, 'Of course. I'll be happy to. But only if you promise to stop me the instant you've had enough or I lose you in technicalities.'

'I promise,' he said solemnly. 'I also promise to pay attention … in case there should be questions afterwards.'

* * *

Despite being surprised to see them, Mr Lowe wasn't noticeably discomposed. He led the way up to his office, asked for tea to be brought and then, coming directly to the point, said, 'I hadn't expected you to come, my lady, but I can't pretend I'm not glad you have.'

She nodded. 'Tell me about the kiln. What's wrong with it?'

'Extensive internal damage to just about everything. I've got a team of men working on repairs but it will take time.'

'What exactly happened – and how?'

Mr Lowe drew a heavy breath and said grimly. 'The pulley to the crown damper wasn't functioning. It couldn't be closed.'

'*What?* No. That can't be right.'

'So I thought. But it is. Paddy was fireman that night. By the time he realised what was going on inside, it was too late to do much about it other than stop feeding the fire – which was already at temperature and still rising.'

They stared at each other in wordless horror for so long that Daniel eventually dared to ask a question. He said, 'Excuse my ignorance … but what is a damper? And what does it do?'

'A kiln is heated slowly and takes roughly twenty-four hours to reach temperature,' said Anna tonelessly. 'At first, the dampers are opened to draw the fire. But once the temperature has risen to the right level, they are closed – and largely remain so, except when the duty fireman feels some subtle adjustment is required. I imagine you can guess what happens if one or other of them is left open.'

'The furnace burns too hot and the temperature rises above acceptable levels?'

She nodded but looking at Mr Lowe said, 'What was being fired?'

'Pieces of the new Pembroke tableware. All gone, of course.'

'Bulk orders?' asked Anna.

'For the Pembroke? Six so far, only two of them filled.' He paused, then added, 'But that isn't the worst of it, as I'm sure you've realised.'

'Quite.'

Daniel waited and when nothing further was forthcoming, said, 'So what *is?*'

There was what seemed a long silence. Finally Mr Lowe said, 'The business with the damper. The pulley must have been disabled *before* the clammin – the brick wall that seals the kiln – was built. After that, there's no access to the mechanism itself.'

Daniel immediately understood what was making Anna look so sick. He said slowly, 'Meaning that it could seemingly only have been done by one of your own workers?' And when she nodded, 'Could it have been an oversight?'

'Possible but unlikely. Everything is supposed to be double-checked,' she replied. And to Mr Lowe, 'You've investigated, of course?'

'Immediately, my lady. I've questioned everybody who works with the kilns or has access to them. They were as horrified as you and me. Nobody knows anything.'

'You believe them?' asked Daniel.

'Aside from the fact that this didn't happen by itself, I've no reason not to. But as well as finding out how it happened, there's the problem of being down to one working kiln. And it's not just replacing the Pembroke. It's all the *other* orders ready and waiting for firing and how we're going to meet the delivery dates.'

'Clearly we're not,' said Anna, rising and shaking out her skirts. 'Give me the list of clients and I'll write apologising for the delay. For the rest, we'll talk more when I've had a chance to think about it.' And to Daniel, 'I'll show you around tomorrow. But if we leave now, we'll just have time to catch Mr Landry before he closes his office for the day.'

During the short drive into the centre of Worcester, Anna stared silently through the carriage window. Unable to think of anything he could usefully say, Daniel watched her without seeming to do so and considered what he'd heard so far.

Their business with Mr Landry was swiftly concluded. To Anna's surprise, he said he not only knew of but had previously employed a man who undertook private investigations.

'He is not cheap but I found him reliable. He charges ten pounds a week, plus expenses. And since, in this case, the obvious place to begin with this man, Harvill, is Bristol, there will undoubtedly be the latter.'

'Engage him,' said Daniel briskly before Anna could speak, 'and send the bills to me. No, Anna – please don't argue. If, as seems likely, you're going to be travelling back and forth between home and Hawthorne's in the coming weeks, I want to know that Harvill won't be lurking in the shrubbery somewhere waiting to accost you.'

Once back in the carriage and en route for Hawthorne Lodge, Anna said shyly, 'You didn't need to do that, you know.'

'I disagree – but we won't argue the point.' He smiled at her. 'Humour me. Can your other kiln work harder to partially make up for the one that's under repair?'

'No. A kiln can only be fired once a week because that's how long the process takes. Two days to get the temperature up, two for the actual firing and two more for it to cool down sufficiently for the wares to be removed.' She paused before adding disapprovingly, 'Some pot banks save a day by sending the men in to retrieve the wares after only twenty-four hours – at which stage, the oven is still glowing. It's not only dangerous but also very bad for the men's health. Responsible manufactories always wait at least twice that.'

Daniel absorbed this and then said, 'Ah. Not quite like baking a pie, then?'

In spite of everything that was on her mind, she gave a little choke of laughter.

'Not quite, no. Is that what you thought?'

'Something along those lines. Bear in mind that I've never even *seen* a ... what did you call it just now? A pot bank? And to me, kiln just translates as big oven – hence the baking connotation.'

Catching the expression lurking behind the hazel eyes, Anna finally realised that he was probably less ignorant than he pretended to be and that the point of this conversation was to distract her. But a glance through the window told her that they were nearly at the house, so she said merely, 'I generally find it best not to talk about the manufactory in front of Mama.'

He nodded. 'Then we'll restrict the conversation to things at Reculver; speaking of which, I hope it doesn't need saying that you must invite her to stay whenever you wish.'

'I *must* ... or I *may?*' retorted Anna. And was warmed by his laughter.

* * *

Inevitably, Mrs Hawthorne had a great deal to say about having been given only a few hours warning of their arrival. When he could finally get a word in, Daniel apologised for this and claimed responsibility. His lawyers and Anna's appeared to be at an impasse over a trifling matter which could quite easily be resolved by speaking to Mr Landry in person ... and a rare few days of quiet at Reculver had suddenly made this possible.

'And naturally we have both been eager to see how you are faring, ma'am,' he added with his most disarming smile. 'Anna has been a little anxious, if needlessly so. Clearly, you are flourishing.'

Watching her mother preening and fluttering, Anna felt faintly bilious ... but this was nothing to how she felt when Mrs Hawthorne accompanied her upstairs and turned, not towards the blue suite as Anna had expected, but towards the other guest bedrooms.

'Wait.' Anna laid a hand on her mother's arm. 'Where are we going?'

'To the Venetian room. It's the loveliest one in the house and it has the best view.'

This was true. The problem was that it wasn't a suite; it was a bedchamber with, naturally enough, just one bed. But before Anna could make any objection, Mrs Hawthorne continued onwards saying, 'There's a suspicion of damp in the blue suite so I've had the hangings removed until it can be dealt with.' And opening the bedchamber door, 'You'll be perfectly comfortable here, I'm sure.'

'I daresay.' Anna was struggling to get around this without giving too much away. 'But Daniel and I are accustomed –'

'And besides,' continued Mrs Hawthorne without waiting for her to finish, 'A newly-married couple? And his lordship doubtless eager for his heir?' A slyly enquiring look, then, 'No sign of that yet, I suppose?'

'No sign of what?' asked Daniel silkily from the doorway. He watched his mother-in-law turn almost as scarlet as his wife and, advancing a few steps, added, 'We have been married but a few weeks, ma'am. It is perhaps a *little* early to be setting up our nursery, don't you think?'

His cool expression and even cooler tone, had the desired effect. Mrs Hawthorne muttered something about needing to speak to the cook and beat a hasty retreat.

Shutting the door behind her and summoning a faint smile, Daniel said, 'We could tell her that I snore – or that you do. Or we could say nothing and manage the situation.'

'I'm sorry. She caught me off guard and I couldn't think quickly enough.'

'It isn't your fault. Just out of interest, what excuse did she give?'

'Damp in the suite, causing her to remove the hangings,' replied Anna bitterly. 'I'll wager she only did that after receiving my message. But goodness knows what she thinks she's doing.'

'That's easy enough,' he shrugged. 'Forgive my bluntness ... but she's achieved her ambition of seeing you married to a title so now she's looking forward to being grandmother to the seventh Viscount Reculver. And in the fullness of time, when we're ready for that step, doubtless she will be.' Reaching out, he gave her hands a quick squeeze and said, 'Anna ... you've enough on your mind already. Don't worry about this. It's a big bed. If it makes you feel better, we can always try the equivalent of bundling.' And when she stared at him blankly, 'Laying the bolster between us as a barricade.'

CHAPTER NINETEEN

If dinner was a somewhat strained affair, the thought of what lay after it was sending Anna's nerves into spasm. Apparently sensing this and aware that she would need a maid to help her undress, Daniel announced his intention of taking a glass of port while reading another chapter of the book on Chinese porcelain he'd taken from the library. Wanting to leave the dressing-room free for him and to be safely under the covers herself, Anna scampered through her night-time ritual with a speed that left the maid hiding a grin at what she took for eager impatience. As soon as she'd gone, Anna laid the bolster lengthways down the centre of the bed. Then, since she had no idea how her husband preferred to sleep, she dithered about which side to occupy until she heard his step outside the door and was forced to plunge into the one nearest to her.

Daniel entered the room to find her sitting bolt upright clutching the sheet to her chin, with her hair lying over one shoulder in a single, very long braid. A faint tremor of amusement stirred but he quelled it and said, 'I hope you didn't hurry on my account?'

'Not at all,' she lied. And awkwardly, 'I don't know which side you prefer …'

'It's of no consequence – either will do,' he replied, disappearing into the dressing-room.

It wasn't until he got there that amusement was banished by a thought that hadn't occurred to him until now. Since he rarely wore a nightshirt and hadn't expected to need one tonight, he hadn't brought one with him. This made him wonder if it wasn't time he engaged a valet. But mostly he realised that, even if Anna hadn't been sitting there looking the picture of maidenly modesty, he couldn't sleep naked tonight.

She wouldn't be the only one blushing, he thought ruefully.

Well, the shirt he was currently wearing would have to do. It was long enough to cover the essentials and, provided he stayed tidily under the covers and on his own side of the bolster, all would be well. He pulled his chamber-robe over it and strolled back into the bedchamber, checking the fire and extinguishing a couple of candles on his way to the bed. Anna, he noticed was lying down, eyes shut tight and fingers still gripping the sheet. Daniel removed his robe, tossed it on to a nearby chair and, sitting on the side of the bed, said conversationally, 'Relax, Anna. Nothing is going to happen. Or, to put it another way,' he added, a smile evident in his voice, 'I won't pounce if you don't.'

'I know,' she mumbled. And to herself, *He doesn't want you, you stupid creature. He never has and he never will. Wishing it was different won't change that.*

In fact, as he settled into bed and lay for a moment on his back, Daniel was conscious of a flicker of interest created, he thought, by a faint but pleasant scent of something he couldn't identify. Then, telling himself this was merely the natural result of an extended period of celibacy, he turned over, wished Anna a 'goodnight' and composed himself for sleep.

On the other side of the bolster, Anna lay rigid, miserably unable to ignore his presence a mere two feet away in the dark. She listened to him breathing and wondered how on earth she could possibly sleep knowing that, if she but reached out her hand, she could touch him. The night was going to seem endless.

* * *

When she woke it was still early but the other side of the bed was empty and the open dressing-room door told her that Daniel was elsewhere. Anna slid from the bed, donned her robe and rang for the maid. Tea and hot water arrived promptly, along with the information that his lordship was exploring the grounds. This, Anna knew, was something he sometimes did at home on fine mornings. But she groaned at the thought of what Mama was likely to make of it.

In fact, Daniel joined her in the breakfast parlour before Mrs Hawthorne appeared and, for the benefit of the footman standing near the door said, as though this wasn't the first time they'd spoken that day, 'I met the peacocks. I think they expected to be fed.'

'They did. Papa got them in order to perfect his design for the peacock scent bottle. He spent hours taming them and now they'll eat out of your hand.'

'I was a disappointment to them, then. Perhaps tomorrow,' he said, sitting across from her and reaching for the coffee pot.

'However ... what is our schedule for today? Back to the manufactory, of course, but then what?'

'I want to see the damaged kiln, speak to the men who work it and have further discussion with Nathaniel about the other recent problems.' Then, smiling a little, 'That done, we'll see what progress has been made in the rooms set aside for the exhibition ... and I'll give you the half-crown tour – which, as the cost will tell you, is vastly superior to the sixpenny one.'

Daniel fished the necessary coin from his purse, slapped it on the table and pushed it towards her. 'Done. Cheap at twice the price, I'm sure.'

* * *

Daniel found the kiln both fascinating and impressive. It was housed in a large brick-built structure resembling a squat bottle and, internally, was like nothing he had ever seen before. After his fifth question, Anna introduced him to the foreman while she spoke to the men who had been working with the kiln at the time of the disaster. She came away no wiser. Daniel walked away with a head full of unfamiliar terms and technical information that only increased his curiosity. As he and Anna walked back across the yard to the main building, he said, 'I suppose you know all about saggars and blow-holes and bonts, don't you?'

'Yes. Papa started teaching me about the firing process when I was eight.' She glanced sideways at him. 'I didn't think you'd be particularly interested.'

'Neither did I,' he shrugged. 'But until today I had no idea how dangerous and complex the work is – such as the business of temperature, for example. I understand you use Mr Wedgwood's invention for that.'

'Yes. It isn't always entirely accurate but it's the best method anyone has come up with so far.'

'So Roberts said. I asked if I could see inside the undamaged kiln but he said it's sealed and mid-way through firing. Something which,' he gestured to the black clouds billowing through the air above them, 'I might perhaps have noticed for myself. Does it *always* generate so much smoke?'

'Pot banks burn coal so, yes. With only Hawthorne's and Worcester Porcelain, it's not too bad here. But in Stoke-on-

Trent where there are numerous potteries cheek-by-jowl, the people say it's a fine day if you can see across the road.' And, with a wry smile, 'Like most things, pot banks have their downside.'

Inside, the two former offices were now linked by means of a large archway. Glass-fronted cabinets were already being fixed to the newly painted walls in one of them and Anna was informed that the larger showcases that would sit below them were almost ready for delivery.

She smiled, nodded and then, leading Daniel into the second, as yet empty room, 'This is where your mother's scent bottles will live – pride of place, I thought, in the centre of the floor, allowing visitors to see them from all angles.'

'Mama will be delighted with that, I'm sure. What else will you put in here?'

'We're still deciding. But, if you want to see everything, we'd best get started. There's a great deal of ground to cover.'

She took him first to the design rooms where some dozen men and women drew, discarded and re-drew everything from tableware to grand urns in the Chinese style. But none of them, Daniel noticed, were designing scent bottles. He said so.

'That work is for limited edition wares and thus confidential. So the designers, master-potters and painters who do it occupy a separate area, off-limits to visitors and the rest of the workforce.'

'And me?' he asked.

'Perhaps.' She gave him an oddly disquieting smile. 'If you last the course, I'll think about it.'

At the end of an hour, Daniel had seen storehouses containing everything required in production, from china clay to paint pigments and been educated in the six stages of clay. He'd watched vases and articles of tableware rising from wheels under the magic hands of potters and walked past vast racks of these drying out prior to firing. At the end of two hours and a lesson on the metamorphosis that took place inside the kiln, he'd seen fired wares being decorated. Much of the tableware was done by means of transfers, virtually everything else was hand-painted; all of it had another drying period before being glazed. And mid-way through hour three, when his mind was overflowing with technical details and his body beginning to wilt, Anna unlocked a door at the end of a corridor and led him into a light, spacious room where three young men sat at large desks resembling those used by architects.

Immediately realising where he was, Daniel murmured, 'I'm honoured.'

'You are,' she agreed.

Meanwhile, the designers had come to their feet, smiling, to bid her a good day. And one, a little older than the rest, said, 'It's always a pleasure to see you, Miss Anna – my lady, I *should* say. Been giving his lordship the tour, have you?'

'I have – and this is the part of Hawthorne's that he most wanted to see.'

'Not *entirely* true. I wanted to see all of it … and my brain and my feet are telling me that surely I must have done so,' said Daniel a shade ruefully, 'But over the years, my late father purchased many Hawthorne scent bottles, so I have a particular interest in them.' Then, turning to Anna, 'But won't you introduce us, my dear?'

The unexpected endearment made her heart turn over even though she knew it didn't mean anything. She said, 'Of course. Meet Messrs Dawkins, Barrow and Spencer; each of them is responsible for creating four designs a year, one for each season. These take time, are frequently revised and, because the actual production is lengthy, have to be begun well in advance. As you'll see in a moment, next year's spring collection is already in the latter stages of production – so it's the designs for next summer that are currently in hand here.'

'A pleasure to meet you, gentlemen,' said Daniel. And gesturing to their work, 'Do you mind if I look?'

'Not at all, milord,' replied Dawkins, apparently the group's appointed spokesman. 'Reckon her ladyship wouldn't have brought you in here if'n she thought you was a spy.'

Daniel laughed and sauntered from one table to the next, chatting pleasantly with each man about the subject he had chosen and admiring their meticulous execution. Finally, addressing all of them, he said, 'Some of your drawings are painted and some not. Why is that?'

'The potters need to see every detail very clear, milord. And the painters need the complete picture. You'll understand better when her ladyship takes you next door.'

'Next door' were two adjoining rooms, the first being occupied by the master-potters. Here, Daniel learned that the scent bottles were sculpted in wax, then in clay and fired before undergoing a process called 'tooling'. This made his head spin since it involved taking the piece apart and remodelling the sections to make the inside as smooth as the outer one and finally fusing them back into the finished article.

'Good Lord,' he said, gazing from the shelves of everything from discarded moulds to the completed bottles and their caps, awaiting final firing. 'I had no idea.'

'People never do,' replied Anna smugly. 'But come to the next room and meet the painters. This winter's collection has been decorated, fired and is being glazed. And leading the way through the door, 'You'll remember Mrs Thompson, I daresay? She is the forewoman here.'

Recognising the female who had assisted with the valuation, Daniel greeted her with a nod and a smile.

Anna said, 'We won't bother you for long, Sarah.' And, again to Daniel, 'As I told you, only three of each are made and no two are completely alike. You may enjoy trying to spot the differences.'

She was right. He *did* enjoy it though he didn't find it easy. Then, since the caps were still separate from the body of the pieces, he said, 'Who attaches these?'

'The silversmith. For obvious reasons, we don't allow the bottles to leave the premises. So when all the pieces of a season's collection are ready, he comes here and completes the work in a secure area which is furnished with any non-transportable equipment he needs. After that, the completed wares are locked away until delivery is due. And that, my lord,' she finished with a small smile, 'is the end of the tour. Thank you for your kind attention.'

Daniel grinned back. 'Is it customary to offer the guide a gratuity?'

'It's not obligatory. But you could reward me with tea at the Talbot where they will also be able to supply you with something stronger, if you feel the need for it.'

* * *

A short time later, comfortably ensconced in the coffee room of the inn and holding a tankard of ale whilst watching Anna pour a cup of tea, Daniel said, 'Thank you for that. I really *didn't* have any idea how complex it all is – but also suspect you may have simplified it quite a lot.'

'A little, perhaps, but not so very much. We have a much shorter, watered-down version for chance visitors arriving on a whim.'

'Which excludes the scent-bottles,' he said with a smile.

'Yes. Of course, if you *really* wanted to understand every element of the entire process – and I can't imagine why you would – it would require several visits.' She added sugar to her cup and stirred it thoughtfully before saying, 'The winter collection becomes available on the first of December and is already fully subscribed or I would earmark one for your mother as a Yuletide gift. As it is, the best I can do is reserve the only bottle still available in the spring collection for her … if you think she might like it?'

'Not only would she like it,' he replied, 'she would appreciate the kindness of the gesture – as do I.'

Anna flushed a little and sipped her tea instead of replying, thus giving Daniel the opportunity to say curiously, 'I gather your own mother doesn't collect them?'

'No. She prefers Mr Wedgwood's blue jasperware.'

'Those would be the pieces with white emblems or whatever embossed on them?'

She nodded. 'It's very popular at present – there being nothing quite like it.'

'But the same is true of your scent bottles, surely?'

'Not quite. Other pot banks *do* manufacture those – though naturally we believe ours are superior. And, as with most things, the fact that there are so few available makes them highly desirable.'

'Whose notion was that?'

'My father's. In addition to his manufacturing knowledge and artistic ability, he had a very sound business head.'

'Which it appears you have inherited.' This time his smile had an acidic edge. 'You are to be congratulated on that. And envied.'

* * *

Back at Hawthorne Lodge and the instant Anna was through the door, the butler murmured, 'May I have a word, my lady?'

'Certainly. What is it?'

'In private, perhaps?'

Her brows rose but she crossed to the visitors' parlour. Then, seeing Daniel about to absent himself, she said, 'Don't go. Privacy doesn't exclude you. Well, Sedley?'

'There was an unexpected and – and somewhat awkward development during your absence this afternoon, my lady.'

'Which was?'

'A visitor. A gentleman you had instructed was not to be admitted.'

Before Anna could open her mouth, Daniel said sharply, 'Harvill?'

'Yes, my lord.'

'And precisely how,' queried Anna, 'was that awkward?'

'Because he did not ask for you, my lady,' came the unhappy reply. 'He was here to see Mrs Hawthorne.'

'*What?*' said Daniel and Anna in unison.

Sedley nodded. 'Furthermore, he said his call would not be unexpected ... so I was obliged to ask Mrs Hawthorne if that was so.'

'And she said that it was?' groaned Anna.

'Yes. She demanded that I admit him. And when I explained that your ladyship had previously given orders *not* to do so, she pointed out that – that you no longer reside here.' The butler all but wrung his hands. 'What was I to do? I had no choice.'

'No,' agreed Anna crisply. 'You didn't. Very well, Sedley. Thank you.'

He bowed and made a more than usually hasty exit.

As soon as the door closed behind him, she said, 'Where on earth can Harvill and Mama have met? And, more to the point, what game is he playing now?'

'She can answer the first of those questions. I suspect we know the answer to the second,' he replied. 'Perhaps it would be best if I stay out of the way during your initial foray? And that is not cowardice talking – or not *only* that. I suspect you'll get greater honesty if I'm not there.'

'Probably,' sighed Anna. Then, gloomily, 'They say that these things come in threes. So what next, I wonder?'

'They – whoever *they* are – say a good many frequently unhelpful things.' Drawing her to the door and opening it, he said, 'I'll wait in the library. Good luck.'

As expected, Anna found her mother in the drawing-room and, coming directly to the point, said, 'Sedley tells me that Mr Harvill called and you received him.'

'I did. And why should I *not*, pray? What right have you to dictate what visitors I receive in my own home?'

'At the time I gave orders to deny Mr Harvill it was my home, too and – '

'And now it is not,' snapped Mrs Hawthorne. 'So *I* will decide who is and who is not admitted.'

As yet, Anna could see no way around this so, taking the chair opposite to her mother and hoping she could prevent this turning into a full-blown argument, said, 'Of course. May I ask when and where you and Mr Harvill met?'

'Why on earth does that matter?'

'Humour me, please.'

'Oh, very well. First, at Mrs Denton-West's card party last month and at several other events since then. He is a perfectly pleasant gentleman.'

'I have found him otherwise,' remarked Anna. 'He has been plaguing me to – '

'I *know* what his business was with you! He has told me about it, although he would *not* have done so but for Sedley refusing to admit him today. So I know all about your foolishly obstinate attitude towards him and that he has made several very good offers for Hawthorne's which you've refused to so much as *discuss* with him.'

So that's *it, is it?* thought Anna, unsurprised. *He thinks Mama will help him get what he wants. One would hope that, by now, he might have understood that, the more he pushes, the more determined he makes my refusal.*

She said flatly, 'And I will continue to do so – as you may tell him yourself when, as I'm sure it will, the subject comes up again. Hawthorne's is not for sale.'

'Don't be so foolish, Anna! You are a viscountess now. What do you want with a manufactory? To be associated with trade? Selling is the perfect answer – and I'm sure his lordship will agree with me.'

'No, he won't. I will not sell, Mama. Not to Mr Harvill; not to anyone. You would do well to convince him of that if you intend to continue with this ... friendship. *Is* that what you believe it is?'

'Of course that's what it is. And why not?'

'Well, let's think, shall we? I suppose there's no point in stating the obvious. That he's merely using you?'

'He said you would say that.'

'Of course he did. Sadly, that doesn't make it any less true.' Rising again, she turned to leave. 'I'd recommend that you bear that in mind ... but I don't suppose you will.'

Mrs Hawthorne stared at her. 'You're going? Just like that?'

'There seeming to be nothing else to say,' remarked Anna caustically, 'yes. I'm going. Just like that.' And she walked out.

In the library, she shut the door behind her and leaned against it.

'That was quick,' said Daniel, setting aside the newspaper he'd been reading and coming to his feet. 'How did it go?'

'Much as one would expect. Harvill has worked his way into her social circle, which is how she met him. He's told her about his dealings with me in such a way as to make himself sound perfectly reasonable and me the exact opposite.' Anna crossed the room to sit down facing him. 'And Mama has swallowed it all wholesale. Needless to say, she thinks his offer for Hawthorne's is heaven-sent and that I should accept it. She is also confident that you will think the same.'

'I assume you told her that I don't?'

She nodded. Then, looking down at her hands, 'Are you sure about that?'

'Despite our agreement?' he asked. 'And after today? Yes. Completely sure. Don't doubt that for so much as a second.' He thought for a moment and then said, 'I suggest we call on Mr Landry in the morning before setting off home. He can inform his investigator of Harvill's latest ploy. I also suggest asking Sedley to keep a record of how many times he visits your mother here. It may be of no use whatsoever but one never knows.'

* * *

Their second night at Hawthorne Lodge might have passed in the same way as the first had not both of them forgotten about the bolster because they were too busy analysing the events of the day to remember it. The result was that each of them retired to their own side of the bed – whereupon Daniel fell asleep almost instantly and Anna, though still acutely conscious of his proximity, not very long after. Much later, as dawn was just beginning to creep through the curtains, she awoke to the sensation of a hard, warm body pressed against her back and an arm lying across her midriff trapping her there.

At that point, Anna lay mouse-still, half-afraid to breathe. Then she realised that Daniel must have turned over in his sleep and was unaware of his current position. When she managed to force her brain to work, she came to the conclusion that it might be best if he woke to suppose her equally ignorant. Meanwhile, however, she lay wide awake, determined to treasure these probably all-too-brief but utterly blissful moments of actually lying in his arms.

She knew when he woke ... and also, a scant moment later, when he realised where he was. She lay perfectly still and tried, as best she was able, to breathe evenly as, very slowly and carefully, he uncoiled from her and left the bed. It wasn't until Anna heard the dressing-room door quietly closing behind him that she dared let her rigid muscles relax. Then, groaning, she shoved her face into the pillow and prayed she had got away with it. If she hadn't, the drive home was going to be either embarrassing or several steps beyond awkward if he asked why she hadn't pushed him away.

Shaving in tepid water for the second day running, Daniel acknowledged and tried, with a minimum of success, not to dwell on the surge of pleasure of waking to find himself wrapped around a warm, soft woman; a woman, moreover, he was entitled to wrap himself around. But that wasn't the point, was it? Anna had seemingly slept on, oblivious. But *had* she? Not entirely impossible, he thought ... but unlikely. And if she hadn't, she was clearly intent on making him think she had –

probably to spare them both the embarrassment of having to talk about it. He didn't want to do that any more than she did. Consequently, since she was giving him that option, it would be sensible to take it. Wouldn't it?

Suddenly irritated with himself, he dried his face and reached for a clean shirt. This kind of mental tiptoeing wasn't like him – and over what, for God's sake? He'd cuddled her. Just that. Nothing had actually happened. He finished dressing and walked back into the bedchamber. Anna was sitting up in bed, giving an only slightly overdone appearance of having recently awoken.

'Good morning,' she said, sliding into her robe without looking at him.

And that was when Daniel knew.

But he simply said, 'Good morning. Shall I ring for the maid?'

CHAPTER TWENTY

By the time they were half way back to Reculver, Anna was amazed at how many topics of conversation two people could conjure up when there was something neither of them wanted to talk about. They plumbed the depths of what Harvill expected to achieve by cultivating Mrs Hawthorne and whether it was possible he could have had anything to do with the problem of the kiln. They examined every possibility – and some impossibilities – of what Grimshaw might or might not do and whether there had been any developments during their short absence from home. By the time they moved on to her plans for the village school, Anna could feel desperation snapping at her heels. By contrast, Daniel was beginning to see the ludicrousness of it.

The thing they were both pretending hadn't happened, *hadn't* happened – or not in any sense that mattered. At some point during the night, she'd woken up with him plastered against her backside; and, presumably for reasons of her own, she hadn't done the obvious thing which was elbowing him in the ribs and telling him to get off her.

He chose not to explore *why* she hadn't because instinct warned him that the answer might not be quite so funny. He also chose to ignore the fact that, for the few brief moments he'd allowed it to last, he'd enjoyed it and been tempted to take advantage.

So he joined in the game of 'Let's Pretend' and prepared to enjoy that instead.

By the time the carriage pulled up in front of the house, Anna was exhausted while, for the last five miles, Daniel had been hard-pressed not to laugh.

Back at Reculver, however, his first quiet words were for Flynn.

'Anything untoward?'

'Nothing, my lord.'

'Excellent.'

He nodded and allowed himself to be towed upstairs to see the 'lovely surprise' his mother had been busy preparing for Anna. Daniel didn't find it lovely. He found it deeply suspicious.

His own room hadn't been untouched. But Anna's bedchamber had been stripped of virtually everything but the bed, re-painted in duck-egg blue and equipped with new curtains and bed hangings. It was all very pretty, he supposed grudgingly ... but, even with the windows wide open, the heavy smell of paint was quite intolerable.

Apparently oblivious, the dowager warbled merrily on.

'When the curtains arrived I just couldn't resist!' she said. 'And if we'd had just one or, at the very most, two days, we could have had everything back in place.'

'We?' muttered Rebecca. 'Don't involve me. I had *nothing* to do with this. And I doubt the smell will be gone in less than a week.'

Glimpsing Daniel's expression and aware that his mother had seen it too, Anna groaned inwardly but said, 'This is such a kind thought, ma'am – and it looks just as we thought it would, doesn't it? But there was no need for you to rush, you know. Until it is finished, I shall be perfectly comfortable in the bedchamber I had whilst doing the valuation.'

'Oh. But there's no need for that, surely?' objected the dowager. 'It would mean moving your clothes or – or all the fuss and tripping back and forth, just for the sake of a few days?'

'It would be Ruth tripping back and forth, not me,' Anna pointed out.

'But we can have the parlour straight in no time. And we haven't started on Daniel's chamber yet so –'

'Stop,' said Daniel, flatly. 'Just stop. I don't blame Anna for preferring to lodge in the east wing. If my room smells half as bad as this one, I may do the same myself – because it will take days to clear the air in here. Becky ... have someone make up the green room and the one of the others near to it, please.' And to his mother, 'No doubt you meant it kindly, Mama – and I'm sure Anna appreciates it. But perhaps it might have been better saved until we go to visit Kit and Sophie – if, on present showing, we ever do.'

When the dowager had trailed Rebecca from the room, Daniel closed the door behind them and said grimly, 'This, in the wake of what happened at Hawthorne Lodge, suggests the existence of a plot.'

'I agree,' murmured Anna unhappily. 'The household here and therefore your mother were bound to know about – about us. But my mother couldn't have known unless ...'

'Unless *my* mother told her,' finished Daniel coldly. 'Quite.'

'You're annoyed.'

'Of *course* I'm bloody annoyed! How many times must I say it? It isn't up to our mothers to chart the course of our marriage. That's our business – no one else's – and I'm damned if I'll put up with their attempts to meddle.' He drew a long, calming breath and added, 'Yes, I'm aware that consummation is a legal requirement but, thanks to the night we spent at Upton, no one can be sure it hasn't taken place. Meanwhile – and much more importantly in my opinion – you and I have used these weeks to get to know each other. We aren't strangers any more and have even, unless I'm mistaken, become friends.' He paused and looked her in the eye. '*Am* I mistaken?'

Forcing back the tide of everything she felt for him and of which he, still, seemed completely unaware, Anna shook her head and managed a strangled, 'No.'

'Good.' Daniel eyed her meditatively before proceeding to sweep the ground from beneath her feet. 'Then let's stop ducking around what happened this morning, shall we? At some point during the night, I turned over in my sleep and cuddled up to you. I didn't wake up. But *you* did, didn't you? Unaccustomed as you are to sharing a bed, of *course* you did. But what you *didn't* do was give me a hefty shove and send me back to my own side. Why not?'

'I – I didn't want to wake you,' she mumbled, wishing she could sink into the floor.

'All right. I'll swallow that.' He regarded her over folded arms. 'But how long were you lying there, still as a mouse, until I woke?'

'I don't know.' She lifted her chin and scowled at him. 'Does it matter?'

'It might.' Daniel grinned suddenly, the storm-clouds of mere minutes ago vanishing as swiftly as they always did. 'It might if you were enjoying it ... even just a little bit. Were you?' And when she stood there, scarlet-cheeked and looking anywhere but at him, he added with a gentle hint of humour, 'It's all right to admit it, you know. If it helps, *I'll* admit to enjoying it quite a lot before my brain woke up.'

She shot him a brief, startled glance. 'You did?'

'I did.' Since the fact that any man with a pulse would have enjoyed it wasn't helpful, he didn't mention that. 'And that's a good sign, given where our relationship began and where our interfering mothers would like it to end. It would be an even better one if you enjoyed it, too.' He flashed a sudden and faintly rueful smile and, turning to leave, added, 'Think about it.'

He was almost through the door when Anna finally realised that he was offering her an opening and that, if she didn't take it, he might not offer again. So she said stiffly, 'All right. Yes. I liked it. It was ... pleasant.'

Daniel stopped on her first word and turned slowly to face her on the last.

'Pleasant?'

'Yes.'

No. It was wonderful and I wanted ... I wanted it never to end and a lot of other things I've never wanted before and that I don't understand. But I can't think about that because there's no point in longing for something I can't have, shouted a voice in her head. *But hearing all that is the very last thing you want because you'd be as embarrassed for me as I would be for myself. So let's just stick with 'pleasant', shall we? It's safer. For both of us.*

Daniel eyed her thoughtfully. For the first time, he had a feeling that he was missing something and that it might be important. Briefly, he tried to work out what it could be. But then, when nothing sprang to mind, he shrugged it off as fume-fuelled imagination and said cheerfully, 'Excellent. Now, let's get out of here before we suffocate, shall we? God only knows what Mother expected to achieve by this. If it wasn't so irritating, it might be funny.'

* * *

On the following morning after breakfast, Flynn brought the post to Daniel in the library as he always did but said, 'Amongst your own letters is also one which I don't recognise as being from one of the dowager viscountess's usual correspondents, my lord.'

Daniel nodded, thanked him and broke the seal on his mother's letter first. It proved to be from the modiste, announcing completion of a morning gown and a carriage dress for herself and an evening gown for Rebecca. Catching his sister crossing the hall, Daniel held it out to her, saying, 'Give that to Mama with my apologies, will you? It was mixed up with my own letters and I opened it before I realised my mistake.' He grinned. 'Are you and Mama making up for lost time?'

She laughed. 'Did you think we wouldn't?'

'No. And I don't blame you ... though after making Anna's bedchamber unusable, Mama can count herself lucky I'm not exacting revenge.'

Suddenly serious, Rebecca said, 'I told her not to do it but she wouldn't listen. You know what she's like when she gets one of her supposedly brilliant ideas.'

'Yes. Unfortunately.'

'And I suppose you – you've also guessed what this one was meant to achieve.'

'Yes.' *And I'll be having some strong words with her on the subject*, he thought. But said merely, 'I presume you ordered more than just one evening gown?'

'Three,' admitted Rebecca a little guiltily. 'I hope we weren't too extravagant.'

'If you were, Mama is the one who will suffer the consequences,' he retorted, turning back towards the library and sending her on her way with a wave.

He found Anna going through her own correspondence and, choosing not to interrupt, stood looking through the window until she put the letter she was reading aside and said, 'Did you want to speak with me?'

'Not particularly. Or, then again, yes. Perhaps I did.' Swinging away from the window and dropping into his usual chair, he said, 'Here's a suggestion. Let's leave the lawyers to do what we pay them for and tell Mama to finish what she started in our rooms ... and give ourselves a holiday from *all* of it.'

'But we've only just got back from Worcester,' she objected, half laughing.

'That was no holiday. Like so many other things, it was necessary. So get your hat while I dash off a note asking Kit if this would be a convenient time to visit. And then, while the sun is still shining, we'll pay a couple more bride visits. The Ashworths at Merton Hall first ... and then Sir Horace and Lady Holden at Staverton.' He grinned at her. 'Unless, of course, you have more important things to do?'

More important than spending a couple of hours with you? Hardly, was Anna's immediate thought. But she said merely, 'Not at all. Let's play truant.'

* * *

The Ashworths and the Holdens were delighted to make the new viscountess's acquaintance and equally pleased to learn that the Dowager Lady Reculver was emerging from the semi-isolation of mourning and happy to start receiving visitors once more. Both Mrs Ashworth and Lady Holden vowed to call without delay whereupon Daniel said the same thing to each of them.

'That would be most kind, ma'am – particularly just now as her ladyship and I have to spend a few days away. We would be happier knowing that Mama is beginning to resume old friendships, for my sister's sake as well as her own. They have been alone too much these last months.'

Mrs Ashworth immediately promised to introduce her grand-daughter who would be visiting over the coming weeks. 'And I shall be holding some simple gatherings while the weather holds. Picnics and the like, perhaps.'

Lady Holden volunteered the company of her nieces, the older of the two being exactly Miss Shelbourne's age. 'And I had been thinking of an informal afternoon dance. No one could possibly consider that improper, could they?'

'Improper?' boomed Sir Horace. 'Fiddlesticks! After months of black and no company? The gal's overdue a bit of fun.'

Later, driving home, Daniel said smugly, 'A good afternoon's work, wouldn't you say?'

'And the real reason you chose those particular ladies, I presume?'

'It might have played a part. But I'm happy for you to have the credit.'

'Meaning what?' asked Anna, his innocent tone making her instantly suspicious.

'I'll let you tell Mama and Rebecca to expect callers and invitations ... just before casually mentioning that we may be away.' And laughed at her expression.

* * *

Christian's reply arrived swiftly and in as few words as possible.

Just come, you idiot. What has 'convenience' to do with anything? Come. We'll expect you soon.

'I won't ask if he means it,' murmured Anna, 'because I'm sure he does. But her ladyship would probably prefer something a little less ... casual.'

'No. Sophie won't mind a bit.' He paused, then added, 'Hazelmere is too far to drive in a day so we'll rack up at the Bull in Burford. Can you be ready to leave tomorrow?'

'*Tomorrow?*' And when he merely nodded, 'I ... yes. Probably.'

'Probably won't do. Can you or can't you?'

Anna huffed an exasperated breath. 'All right. Yes. Tomorrow. Fine.'

'Thank you.' Daniel dropped a careless kiss on her hand and headed towards the door before turning back to say abruptly, 'Do you think we dare risk taking a whole week without telling the lawyers where they can find us?'

'I imagine that may be safe enough,' replied Anna gravely, knowing – as he did – that, in an emergency, Flynn would send word. 'Is that what I'm to tell your mother?'

'Yes. And no.' He grinned suddenly. 'Tell her we'll expect work to be finished in our suite by the time we return. And tell her to pay some calls of her own – the Sheltons and Lady Barstow, for example, while we're away. You and I have made a start on re-establishing the family in local society but the rest is up to her.' And he was gone.

* * *

Two days later, roughly four miles from Hazelmere and aware that, for the last hour of the journey, Anna had grown progressively quieter, Daniel said, 'What is it?'

'What is what?'

'The thing on your mind that you can't quite bring yourself to say.'

She glanced at him and away again.. 'I don't know what you mean.'

'So there isn't anything?'

'No.'

He shrugged. 'My mistake, then.'

For perhaps five minutes, Anna watched him gazing through the window as if he'd believed her when every instinct told her that he hadn't. Finally, sighing, she said, 'All right. Clearly, Lord Hazelmere is your closest friend. Equally clearly, as far as the world at large is concerned, there is some mystery surrounding his lengthy disappearance.'

'True, so far. Go on.'

'But it's no mystery to you or Lord Benedict, Lord Wendover or Lady Hazelmere.'

'Or one or two others, if we're being precise,' agreed Daniel. 'But it's water under the bridge now and therefore rarely, if ever, spoken of ... if you were thinking there will be times during this visit when you might be ...'

'In the way?' she supplied bluntly. 'Yes. I had wondered that.'

'Then don't. It won't happen.'

'Not in any obvious way, I'm sure.'

'Meaning what?'

'That you are all too well-mannered to let it show.'

Daniel felt a sudden flash of annoyance. He said, 'I would certainly hope so. I would also hope we are better-natured ... and that *you* aren't going to spend the week storing up imagined slights.'

Her colour rose a little. 'Of course not! That wasn't what I meant at all.'

'Good. This isn't London, Anna. Kit and Sophie are genuinely kind people, both of whom have had their own taste of hell. They won't judge you. So I'd appreciate it if you gave them the same courtesy.'

'Naturally. That didn't need saying.'

'I'm relieved to hear it.'

The remaining miles passed in silence but for the rumble of the carriage wheels. From time to time, Anna snatched furtive glances at Daniel waiting for his expression to relax. For the first time ever, it didn't. Her heart sank still further. Then the carriage was bowling along Hazelmere's drive and it was too late to mend matters.

The great front door swung open. A tall, fair-haired gentleman appeared and was joined a second later by a stunning brunette Anna realised she had seen before. Both of them beamed down at the carriage. Meanwhile, barely waiting for it to come to a halt, Daniel had the door open and was through it. Anna half-expected him to leave her sitting there … but no. He kicked down the steps and offered his hand. He even, she was relieved to notice, offered her a share of the smile that really belonged to Lord and Lady Hazelmere.

She whispered, 'I'm sorry.'

His reply was a tiny nod. Then he was drawing her up the steps towards the earl and countess, saying, 'You said to come soon, Kit. I took that literally.'

'So I see.' Laughing, Christian hauled him into a brief hug. Then, offering Anna a warm smile and his hand, said, 'Welcome to Hazelmere, Lady Reculver. It's a pleasure to meet you at last.'

Anna curtsied. 'Thank you, my lord.' And, aware that two steps away, Daniel was kissing the countess's cheek, added stiffly, 'We had hoped to visit some weeks ago but – but various other matters got in the way.'

'Well, you're here now and Kit and I are delighted.' Beaming, Sophia stepped forward to take both of Anna's hands in a warm clasp. 'You won't recall, I daresay, but I think we may have met in London some years ago.'

'I believe we did, my lady.'

'Goodness! No formalities!' laughed Sophia. 'Daniel is family and so will you be in time, I hope. So call me Sophie, please. And perhaps I may call you Anna?'

'Of course.'

'Upon which note,' suggested Christian, 'might we all go inside so the servants can bring in the luggage and move the carriage? Then, tea for the ladies but perhaps something stronger for you and me, Daniel?'

'Definitely something stronger,' Daniel agreed. 'I'd like to raise a glass to finally *getting* here ... and to meeting Viscount Farndon.' He laughed suddenly. 'It seems no time at all since that was *you*, Kit.'

Presently, in the drawing-room and busy with the tea tray, Sophia said, 'Julia and Jane are here, Daniel ... that is, they're out somewhere with Hamish, right now. Gerald, too, although he insists he's returning to London tomorrow. If he holds by that, Julia and Jane will leave with him – and, in Julia's case, not purely to take advantage of Gerald's escort on the journey.' She handed a cup to Anna. 'Has Daniel told you about my youngest sister?'

'No. I don't think so.'

'Julia is deaf and mute – hence the need for Jane, her hearing companion.'

'Oh.' Anna swallowed. 'I'm so sorry. Has – has she always been deaf?'

'From birth, yes. But, as you'll see, she manages very well. She can lip-read and she 'speaks' using sign language. Jane translates for her.'

'Or you do,' interposed Christian. 'And sometimes now, even Gerald. He's become surprisingly adept at signing.' He gave a tiny laugh. 'Amazing what love can do.'

Daniel grinned. 'Has he plucked up the courage to admit that yet?'

'Yes. He's asked Sophie's permission and mine ... and he and Julia regard themselves as being unofficially betrothed. As yet, the secret hasn't reached Julia's mother – though *how* it hasn't is a mystery since she and Gerald glow like beacons in each other's company.'

'Where Julia is concerned, Mama is wilfully blind,' said Sophia. 'But at present, that attitude has its uses. And I add my mite by encouraging her to put all her efforts into securing a match for Gwendoline – that's my other, less pleasant sister, Anna. But enough about *my* family. Tell me about Rebecca. Will she make her come-out in the spring?'

'Yes. I believe you offered to sponsor her?'

'I did – as did my friend, Drusilla Colwich. And of course we'll both help in any way we can. But that was before Daniel married. Rebecca has you now and – '

'No. Not really.'

Sophia blinked. 'Why not?'

'I am not the best choice. Rebecca will do much better with you and Lady Colwich.'

'Oh. Do you and she not … well, just not get on very well?'

Having listened to this latter part of their conversation, Daniel decided to step in. He said, 'They get along perfectly well, Sophie. The problem is Anna's previous experience of London society. Her own Season didn't go well and –'

'It was a lot worse than that,' cut in Anna, 'as I'm sure Lady – as doubtless *Sophia* will remember.'

'And she's concerned about what effect that might have on Rebecca's,' finished Daniel calmly.'

'It won't have any at all,' said Sophia flatly. And seeing Anna's doubtful expression, 'Truly, it won't. You are Viscountess Reculver. That alone is sufficient to guarantee you respect. But in addition, amongst your husband's very good friends are the Earl of Hazelmere and both brothers of the Duke of Belhaven – even Belhaven himself, if Benedict and Oscar can lure him out of the house a time or two. No one with an ounce of sense is going to risk offending either Daniel or you by turning a cold shoulder on either you or Rebecca.'

'She's right, Anna,' agreed Christian. 'Shallow as it is, society will greet Lady Reculver very differently than it did Miss Hawthorne.'

Anna opened her mouth to speak but, before she could do so, sounds of commotion downstairs were immediately followed by a voice saying, '*No*, Hamish! Mr Sandhurst – *stop him!*' And then the ominous scrabble of paws on the stairs.

'Somebody move the cakes!' cried Christian, setting aside his glass to grab the teapot *en route* for the not-quite-closed door. Then, on a groan as it flew open, 'Too late!'

Hamish burst in, wet, muddy and happy to see so many people. Then, before anyone could stop him, he made a dash for the nearest lap … which happened to be Anna's.

First to arrive on the scene, Gerald Sandhurst unwittingly echoed Christian.

'Oh dear,' he sighed. 'Too late. Again.'

And then, like everyone else, stared when Anna took a firm hold on the dirty, wriggling creature which seemed intent on licking her face ... and laughed. Two steps behind Gerald in the doorway, Julia also started laughing, so it was left to Jane to enter the room apologising.

'I'm so sorry, my lady,' she said, trying unsuccessfully to prise Hamish away from his new best friend. 'There was a duck and Hamish chased it into the mud before we could stop him. Your lovely gown! I'm so sorry. I hope it isn't ruined.'

'Don't worry about it.' Keeping a firm hold on the little dog, Anna stood up. 'However, since I already need of a change of clothes and you don't, perhaps it might be best if *I* carried Hamish to wherever you're going to bathe him?'

'Let her,' said Daniel unsteadily when Jane tried to demur. 'Anna isn't afraid of a little mud. Or even quite a lot of it.'

'The same being true of you,' said Anna, taking a step in his direction. 'So perhaps *you'd* like to bathe Hamish?'

Laughing, he backed away, warding her off with both hands. 'No, thank you. I really wouldn't.'

'I thought not.' And almost but not quite under her breath, 'Coward.'

Glancing with some amusement from one to the other of them, Sophia said, 'Jane, take Lady Reculver to the kitchens, have someone send hot water upstairs and show her to her rooms when she is ready. Kit, you may as well take Daniel to meet his godson while Julia and Gerald explain why, despite what happened last time, Hamish wasn't on his leash when he entered the house.'

* * *

On their way up to the nursery, Christian said, 'She took that rather well, I thought.'

'Anna? Yes. Particularly considering she was a bundle of nerves by the time we arrived here.'

'Was she?' asked Christian, surprised. 'Why?'

'Partly that disastrous London Season I mentioned. But mostly, I suspect, because she wants you and Sophie to like her but is afraid she'll say the wrong thing and you won't.'

'Is she *likely* to say something that bad?'

'No. She's often blunt but never rude.' Daniel glanced at him and added, 'She's more comfortable with her workforce than her social equals. And the pot bank – Hawthorne's – is a remarkably complex affair. She showed me around it and I swear there's not one of the various processes that she couldn't do herself if she had to.'

'So ... it's more than just a lucrative business to her?'

'Much more. It's in her blood.' He came to a halt and lowering his voice, said, 'Kit, I still have no idea what she's worth – not because she won't tell me but because I haven't asked – but it's more than I ever suspected.'

Deciding that this wasn't a conversation to have on the stairs, Christian turned aside from the nursery flight and ushered Daniel into a small, seldom-used parlour, saying, 'Do you *really* want to tell me all this?'

'Yes. She's had her lawyer hand over *thousands*. All my debts are paid, the overdraft at the bank wiped out and yet *more* money for refurbishments to the house, improvements on the estate and personal accounts for Mama and Rebecca. There's no end to it. Half the time I don't know what she's done until I hear of it from either the bank or my lawyer. It ... it's unnerving. And made all the more so because she's getting nothing in return.'

'Has she asked for anything?'

'Only marriage. She has that, of course. But she's paying a hell of a lot for it.'

'Perhaps she considers it worth it,' remarked Christian. 'However ... from what I've seen so far, the two of you seem to get on well enough.'

'We do.'

'Good. So am I permitted to ask how, in general terms, marriage is working out?'

'It isn't nearly as bad as I thought it might be. On a day-to-day basis, both of us are busy with different things. But when there are problems – and we each have some – we've somehow formed a habit of discussing them and looking for solutions together.'

'Well, that's a promising start. And in other respects?'

'Such as what?'

Christian's brows rose. 'Do I really need to spell it out?'

'Oh. That.' A hint of colour touched Daniel's cheekbones. 'We haven't ... and don't. Although it's less unthinkable than it was a couple of months ago.' The realisation that it actually wasn't unthinkable at *all* gave him a jolt. How long had that been true? And why hadn't he noticed until now? Putting the knowledge aside for consideration later, he said, 'I don't think Anna minds. And we'll get around to it eventually. We'll have to. My heir is Cousin Leonard and he's a serving officer of the East India Company in Calcutta.' He smiled suddenly, 'And speaking of heirs ... ?'

Christian laughed. 'Finally. I thought you'd forgotten.' And seeing Daniel opening his mouth to apologise, 'Don't. You needed to talk – and still do, probably. Perhaps Anna does, too, so we'll make plenty of opportunities for both of you. But now come and meet my son.'

CHAPTER TWENTY-ONE

It took less than twenty-four hours for Anna to recognise that her reservations about the Earl and Countess of Hazelmere had been completely mistaken. Christian and Sophia were exactly as Daniel had described them. Never for an instant did they make her feel the interloper she'd been telling herself that she was and, instead, treated her as they might have done had Daniel married her because he'd wanted to rather than because his situation had left him little choice.

Sophia encouraged her to talk about Hawthorne's and how that part of her life fitted in with Daniel, her new family-by-marriage and everything at Reculver. Then, she revealed concerns of her own – principally about how her mother was going to take the news that Julia and Gerald Sandhurst, now on their way back to London, were fathoms deep in love with each other.

'Kit has told Gerald he must ask Mama for Julia's hand – and soon. Even self-absorbed as she is, Gwendoline must eventually notice their attachment; and if she does so before Gerald speaks to Mama … well, let's just say that won't make things any easier.'

'But why would your mother object to Mr Sandhurst?' asked Anna, baffled. 'He is a gentleman and the fact that he's been learning sign language speaks volumes about his feelings for your sister.'

'True. But he's Kit's secretary as well as his friend. Gerald *works*. And there's something else. Mama used to think that Julia's deafness made her unmarriageable but if Gerald offers for her that will change. After all, if Julia can charm *one* man into not minding about it, she can charm another. One who is a better match in the world's – and therefore also Mama's – eyes. Do you see?'

'Only too well. She sounds exactly like my own mother.' Anna smiled wryly. 'She hates my involvement with Hawthorne's – always has. Now, she can't understand why I won't give it up or why Daniel doesn't make me.'

'According to Kit, the latter isn't at all likely.' Sophia paused, her attention on shifting Michael from her shoulder to her lap and adjusting his shawl. 'He says Daniel was fascinated by his tour of the manufactory and would like to visit it again but isn't sure you'll welcome him taking too much interest.'

'Really?' asked Anna, startled.

'Really. Is he wrong about that?'

'Completely.'

'Then perhaps,' suggested Sophia gently and finally looking up, 'you should tell him.'

* * *

However, it was half-way through their stay when the final seal was put on both Anna's feelings towards and understanding of Christian. She entered the library in time to hear him say, 'Eustace has been trying to persuade Alveston to sanction Basil's release. It's been over a year, after all, and Eustace thinks –'

And that was as far as he got before Daniel cut across him saying, 'Later, perhaps.'

'Pardon me,' said Anna, turning to go. 'I didn't mean to interrupt.'

'You aren't,' said Christian. And then, differently, 'Daniel ... you haven't *told* her?'

'No.'

'Why on earth not?'

'It's over and irrelevant,' shrugged Daniel. 'So why rake it all up?'

'Because she's your *wife*, you idiot!' Christian stalked across the room to take Anna's hand and draw her to a chair. 'It's no reflection on you that Daniel hasn't shared my story, Anna. Keeping it strictly between ourselves is a hard habit to break – and it still holds true outside our immediate circle. But you *aren't* outside it. So here is what he hasn't told you.'

And as economically as possible, he explained how Basil Selwyn, his cousin, had arranged for him to disappear, of the three years that had followed it ... and finally of how, thanks to Benedict, Daniel, Anthony and Gerald, he had been rescued and Basil brought to justice.

When he stopped speaking, Anna stared silently at him for a long moment before saying, 'I can appreciate why you prefer to restrict this to as few people as possible. It is at once remarkable and iniquitous. Thank you for telling me … and you may rely on my discretion.'

'I know that,' said Christian. And to Daniel, 'So should you have done.'

'I *did* know it – but that isn't the point!' returned Daniel, mildly annoyed. 'The *point* is that we agreed not to tell anyone who didn't need to know. And since, as you said yourself, it was finished a year ago, it seemed to me that Anna didn't.' He looked at her. 'It was never that I didn't trust you. I know that I can. And I think that *you* know that I do. Don't you?'

'Yes.' She smiled. 'But I'm honoured that his lordship – that *Christian* chose to tell me himself. And we've secrets of our own, haven't we? For example, have you told him about Grimshaw?'

'Oh bloody hell,' muttered Daniel. 'No. I haven't. And now I'll have to.'

Rising, Christian pulled the bell and, when the butler appeared, 'Ask her ladyship to join us, Fallon. And bring sherry, please.'

'Sherry?' queried Daniel. 'Not that I'm quibbling … but isn't it a bit early?'

Christian grinned. 'Not necessarily. Anyone named Grimshaw is almost *guaranteed* to be a villain. However … why do I get the feeling you weren't going to share this?'

'Because he wasn't,' said Anna.

Daniel sent her a mock-scowl. 'I could have said that myself, you know.'

'Yes. But *would* you?'

He opened his mouth then closed it again as Sophia walked in with Fallon hard on her heels.

She said, 'Sherry before noon, Kit? How very decadent. Or are we celebrating?'

Christian waited until the door closed behind the butler, then said, 'Daniel is going to tell us a tale of dark doings – at least, I think he is.'

'*Attempted* doings, thus far,' Anna corrected. 'But, in essence, yes.'

'That sounds intriguing,' said Sophia.

'Doesn't it?' Christian handed everyone a glass and when Daniel remained stubbornly silent, said, 'You may as well tell us, Daniel. If you don't, I'm sure Anna will.'

Daniel met his wife's gaze. 'Will you?'

Sighing, she shook her head. 'Not if you'd rather I didn't.'

'I'd *rather* you hadn't said anything in the first place,' he grumbled. 'However, I'll make a deal with you. I'll tell them about Grimshaw if you'll tell them about Harvill. I imagine I needn't point out that you have the better end of that arrangement?'

'No. Very well.'

'And you can go first.'

Anna cast him a long-suffering look and nodded.

Christian, a note of laughter in his voice, said, 'Anything else, Daniel? Blood?'

'Very funny.' Daniel wasn't laughing. 'Anna?'

So she reluctantly gave a brief account of Harvill's inexplicably persistent attempts to buy Hawthorne's. So brief that, at the end of it, Daniel said, 'Is that it?' And when she nodded, 'No mention of him holding you up on the road?'

'You're making it sound as if he pointed a pistol at me,' she objected. 'He didn't.'

'All right, he didn't. But he *could* have. And what about the business with the kiln?'

'We don't know he was responsible for that.'

'Neither do we know he wasn't.' And, to Christian and Sophia, 'What we *do* know is that he's recently made the acquaintance of Anna's mother and wormed his way into her favour. What would *you* make of that?'

'The same as you, I imagine,' replied Christian. 'What are you doing about it?'

'My man-of-law has is having Mr Harvill investigated,' said Anna, tired of being dismissed. 'There's not much else we *can* do.'

'But Daniel's right to be concerned,' said Sophia. 'It all sounds very peculiar. Perhaps it might be best if you stayed away from Worcester for a while?'

'Thank you, Sophie.' And to Anna, 'Listen to her ... and also to me. If you have to go the Hawthorne's for any reason, I'm coming with you. And that is set in stone.'

The warmth his words created in her heart manifested itself in Anna's cheeks and she said faintly, 'Very well. And if – if you wanted to visit the manufactory again, you would be very welcome to do so.'

The grim expression relaxed and he said, 'Thank you. I'd like that.'

'I, meanwhile,' murmured Christian, 'am still waiting to hear about this fellow Grimshaw – which is where, if anyone can think back that far, this conversation started. So … who is he and what has he done?'

Daniel shut his eyes for a moment and expelled a long breath. Finally he said expressionlessly, 'He's the slippery individual largely responsible for the financial disaster left behind by my father. And now he's trying something similar with me to the tune of four thousand pounds.'

There was an appalled silence into which Christian eventually said, 'Are you talking about what I think you're talking about?'

'Blackmail? Yes. Grimshaw lives with his widowed sister-in-law and her son – which isn't nearly as irrelevant as it sounds.' He paused and then added baldly, 'I've seen the son. He looks more like Rebecca's brother than I do.'

This time the silence was even longer. Finally, Christan rose, picked up the sherry decanter and began refilling glasses, saying, 'I was right about fortification being needed. Go on.'

* * *

Later, alone and able to speak privately, Sophia said, 'Well, we speculated on why Anna asked Daniel to marry her … and now we know. She's in love with him and is walking on egg-shells in case he guesses. He, of course, has no idea – any more than he realises he's well on the way to feeling the same about her.'

Christian laughed. 'I'll give you the first one because it's the only explanation that makes sense. But the second? I doubt it.'

'Weren't you listening earlier?'

'Yes. But don't let his reaction to this Harvill fellow fool you. That's just the in-built instinct to protect what's his.' Then, frowning a little, 'I suspect that discovering he has a half-brother his father spent twenty-five years and a great deal of money to keep secret has hit him harder than he yet realises. He says he won't give Grimshaw a penny – and neither should he. But ignoring the brother's existence?' Christian shook his head. 'That won't last a month. Oh, he'll keep it from his mother and sister. But he won't be able to forget what he knows and he'll be curious about everything he doesn't.'

'What are you saying?' asked Sophia.

'I'm saying Daniel will want to find out about this brother he didn't know he had and doing so will take him closer to Grimshaw's orbit than is wise, given the circumstances. Fortunately, however, there's Anna. If she thinks he's sailing too close to the wind, she'll say so.'

'Undoubtedly,' said Sophia. Then, 'You like her.'

'Much better than I expected,' he agreed. 'When Daniel decided to accept her proposal, I feared it might be the worst mistake of his life. But it's not. Far from it, in fact. He seems to tell her everything ... and he *listens* to her. Listens and, what's more from the little he's told me, takes her advice. This is a good thing because he's always been prone to grabbing the bull by the horns without considering the consequences. It used to be Benedict reining him in. Now Anna's doing it. And she's no fool.' Christian grinned suddenly. 'Although he did tell me a tale about her, a boy, his dog and a muddy field that made her sound mildly deranged and Daniel more like his old self. He *likes* her, Sophie and I'm glad. Relieved, even. But I've yet to see signs of anything more than that.'

'Look harder, then,' retorted Sophia. 'The signs are there. You're missing them.'

* * *

Alone with his wife in their own rooms, Daniel said, 'Since it's bound to crop up later, I'd better admit that I told Kit about the Great Mud Rescue. Hit me now, if you want to and think I deserve it. I'm ready to duck.'

Anna sighed. 'Then I won't bother. But can I ask *why* you told him?'

'The conversation was getting far too serious. I needed to lighten the mood and that was the first thing that came to mind.

However, I did resist the temptation to make myself the hero of the piece.'

'That was noble of you.'

'Yes. I thought so.'

Lounging idly in an armchair, he watched her absently pulling pins from her hair in readiness for Sophia's maid to re-dress it before dinner. Regardless of how it had been styled throughout the day, each lock fell straight within seconds. It was as if, like Anna herself, her hair had a will of its own. He realised that he wanted to touch it.

He said, 'Why did you want me to tell Kit about Grimshaw?'

'As I understand it, you always confided in him and your other friends *before*, so – '

'Before what?'

'Before your father died and your life was turned upside down.' She shrugged and laid a handful of hairpins on the table beside her. 'I didn't see why that should stop just because …' She paused, then said, '… because you have less opportunity now.'

He knew that hadn't been what she'd originally intended to say. He was also becoming increasingly aware that it wasn't only her hair he wanted to touch. He examined that thought. It wasn't entirely new. It had occurred more than once in the last few days. So far, he hadn't acted on it. Now he wondered how Anna would react if he did. Perhaps it was time to find out.

Hesitantly, not entirely sure of his ground, he rose and strolled over to sit beside her and sliding his fingers down one silky strand, said, 'You have nice hair.'

Her eyes locked with his and she was suddenly very still. He wasn't even sure she was breathing. He waited. Finally, she said, 'It's … annoying.'

This was so typical of her that he relaxed and smiled. 'Your hair is? Why?'

'Because it won't curl and needs a hundred pins to hold it in place.'

'Ah. Yes. I can see that might be aggravating. But even so, it's pretty when it's loose like this and it's nice to touch.'

Her mouth opened in shock before she resolutely closed it again and stood up, clearly intent on moving away – though, from what, Daniel didn't know. From him? Or from another self-deprecating remark? Whichever it was, he stopped her doing it by standing up himself to place his hands on her shoulders and gently turn her to face him.

After one startled glance into his eyes, she fixed her attention on his cravat and, without moving or saying a word, waited to see what he would do next.

Not sure what that ought to be, Daniel said, 'I was thinking that perhaps it might be time we tried a kiss ... if that would be acceptable.' And, after a moment, when she said nothing, 'Would it?'

She swallowed hard and nodded. 'Yes. But ...'

'But what?' he asked softly, aware of the pulse beating erratically in her throat.

'I ought to mention that I – I don't know how.'

Distantly and with a glimmer of amusement Daniel supposed he might have guessed, not just that she hadn't been kissed by a man before but that, being Anna, she thought some pre-knowledge was required. He said, 'Well, luckily I do. So why not leave that part to me?'

Still not meeting his eyes, she gave a jerky nod, her shoulders rigid.

Taking this as permission, he lifted her chin with one hand and slid the other around her waist. A tiny tremor which he took for nerves went through her as he drew her just close enough for their bodies to meet. And then, bending his head, he touched his lips to hers and felt, rather than heard, her small, involuntary sound of surprise.

Slowly, lazily, Daniel trailed barely-there kisses over her cheek and jaw until he felt the tension begin to drain out of her and was aware of her hands creeping uncertainly up to his shoulders and, after some hesitation, on around his neck. He gathered her closer, sliding his fingers into her hair to cradle her skull while his lips found hers again, this time moving lightly against them. She sighed and, very tentatively, kissed him back.

Encouraged, he tightened the embrace a little more and lifted his head to look into her face. Her lashes fluttered open and eyes, more blue than grey, gazed dreamily into his.

Daniel smiled. 'All right, so far?'

'Yes,' she whispered.

'Good. Then let's try this.'

And his mouth settling more purposefully over hers, he turned the kiss into a slow, languorous seduction whilst somehow managing to remember not to take it too fast or too far.

Meanwhile, although she'd tried not to let it happen, Anna had been lost since the moment he'd touched her. Now, with the kiss growing ever deeper and little sparks dancing inside her veins and along her nerves, she had only one coherent thought.

Don't stop. I love you and this may never happen again. So please don't stop yet. Give me just a little more time.

Daniel didn't want to stop but knew he'd have to. Inevitably, his body disagreed with this ... which indicated that he ought to have ended the kiss some time ago. But Anna's body fitted beautifully against his; her mouth was sweet and her untutored response, oddly addictive. Slowly, regretfully, he brought the kiss to an end and waited for her to open her eyes so that he could read her reaction.

She looked shy and confused ... and as regretful as he. Sighing, he drew her down on the sofa in the curve of his arm and, with a hint of rueful humour, said, 'I'm wondering why it took us – took *me* – so long to do that. We should try it again ... in fact, I'm already looking forward to doing so. But not just yet.'

'Why not?' whispered Anna.

'Because right now it's likely to become rather *more* than a kiss.' For a moment, she looked blank before belatedly taking his meaning and growing even pinker He grinned. 'Exactly. It's a male thing – one in which we're all basically the same. Don't worry about it.' There was a tap at the door. Daniel laughed and stood up. 'Here's the maid. Just in time to stop me getting into deep water.' Having called the girl to come in, he pulled Anna to her feet, dropping a kiss on each of her hands. 'I'll see you downstairs presently.'

* * *

An hour later, over a glass of wine in the drawing-room before dinner, Sophia immediately sensed that something had changed between them. Whenever he thought no one was looking, Daniel watched Anna ... a very faint smile mingled with an expression Sophia couldn't quite interpret. And Anna seemed distracted and reluctant to meet his eyes at all. Something, Sophia decided delightedly, had moved on apace since this afternoon.

Good, she thought. And tried to find a way of bringing it to Christian's attention.

Anna felt as if she was floating several inches above the ground. Daniel had kissed her – *really* kissed her, not a mere peck on the cheek. That, in itself, was a miracle ... and those moments in his arms had been sweeter and more magical than anything she might have imagined. But, more miraculous still, he'd said he wanted to do it again. She'd tried never to hope that one day he might want her that way. Even now, she reminded herself that it might not mean what she wanted it to mean – merely that he had decided it was time to begin addressing the question of the all-important heir. But still, hope had been born and she could not quite quench it.

Without quite knowing why, Daniel was struggling with surprise. He was surprised by how much he'd enjoyed kissing Anna and surprised by how much he wanted to do it again. He found himself looking forward to the end of the evening when they would be alone. Perhaps he could even go beyond a kiss. Not very *far* beyond it, of course. It was too soon for full intimacy. But perhaps a few caresses, just to pave the way? And then, once they were back at home, they could progress gradually towards the consummation for which, he realised, he was now eager.

He didn't examine his feelings too closely. In some distant corner of his mind was the knowledge that Anna was important to him; perhaps even necessary. But that wasn't a thought he was entirely comfortable with ... so he put it back where it came from.

As for the rest, however, they had waited long enough.

And anticipation of what lay ahead was a pleasure in itself.

CHAPTER TWENTY-TWO

Two days later, Daniel and Anna arrived home in the middle of the afternoon to learn that the dowager and Rebecca were out paying calls.

'Good,' said Daniel. 'And what progress has been made upstairs?'

'I believe your lordship will be pleased,' replied the butler sedately.

'Let's hope so.' And to Anna, 'Do you want to investigate while Flynn tells me if there have been any other developments that I should be aware of? I won't be far behind you.'

She nodded and refrained from expressing surprise that his first thought had been the state of their rooms rather than any activity on Grimshaw's part. She also refrained, as she might not otherwise have done, from asking Flynn to send her maid to her. Since The Kiss, Daniel's behaviour had changed and, whenever they were alone, he frequently made small, affectionate gestures such as putting an arm about her waist and sometimes larger ones which left her pink and breathless.

Upstairs, the refurbishment of their suite was complete. Walls had been painted, new hangings replaced faded old ones and the freshly-polished furniture was back in place. Inevitably, there *was* a smell of paint but it wasn't nearly as bad as before and, with the windows left partly open, ought soon to be gone.

Daniel arrived behind her to slide both arms about her and pull her back against his chest. Looking around his room, he said, 'This is an improvement. Are you pleased?'

'Very. Are you?'

'Delighted. Clearly Mama has had every hand to the pump.'

'Plus some additional help from outside, I should think,' agreed Anna. And before he could remark on it himself, 'The paint smell is strongest in here, I'm afraid.'

'Ah. Well, it if becomes insupportable, you could always invite me to share your room for a night or two.' Aware of the tiny quiver of shock that rippled through her, he released her and moved slightly away. 'We've done it before, after all. But you don't have to say yes. Just perhaps think about it?'

'Yes.' The word left her mouth before it had gone through her brain; before she'd given a second's thought to what he might or might not be suggesting. Then, turning back into the parlour and hastening to change the subject, she said, '*Did anything happen while we were away?*'

'Three letters came for Mama which Flynn wasn't sure about and which I haven't looked at yet. And one of the under-grooms reported a man he didn't recognise hanging around the gates two days ago ... but when Flynn sent Jeffrey out to ask what he wanted, he'd gone. It was probably nothing of consequence. But Flynn's been sending different members of the staff on largely needless errands in case he came back.'

'But he hasn't?'

'Not so far.' Not being entirely sure what she'd said 'yes' to – inviting him to share her bed or merely thinking about it – and suspecting that she didn't know either, Daniel decided to give her time to work it out. 'I'd better take a look at Mama's letters and find out what other matters have arisen during our absence that demand my attention. Presumably, you'll want to check on progress at Hawthorne's?'

'Yes. And meanwhile, I'll have Ruth prepare a bath.'

'An excellent idea. So to save work and since I doubt you are very dirty, you can tell them to save the water for me – and to let me know when you're finished.'

Anna gave a rare and unexpected gurgle of laughter causing him to ask suspiciously, 'What?'

'Ruth puts scented oil into my bath – lavender or rose. Do you have a preference?'

Daniel grinned. 'For myself? No. Do you?'

And walked out before she could answer.

Two of the three letters Flynn had set aside were innocent; an invitation to a card party and a bill from a Gloucester bookshop.

But the third sent a chill down Daniel's back.

If your ladyship wishes to learn the secret that your late husband kept from you for many years and which your son is now also guarding, come alone to Saint Nicholas church in Gloucester at noon on the second day of October.

This offer will not be made again. Tell no one.

A friend.

It wasn't in Grimshaw's hand – or at least, it didn't appear to be – but, like anything else, Daniel supposed writing could be disguised. Thoughtfully, he walked into Anna's office and, placing it on the desk in front of her, said, 'More or less exactly what you predicted might happen.'

She read it and then looked up at him. 'Well, at least we know he's not taking his tale to the newspapers so that's comfort of a sort. Do you know the church in question?'

'Yes. Unless it's changed, there are only services on Sundays – which October the second isn't. And visitors to Gloucester tend to look at Saint Nicholas's leaning spire, then move on to explore the cathedral instead.' He thought for a moment. 'It's an old church, so lots of nice shadowy corners in which to lurk. Grimshaw has chosen well.'

'It's odd, though,' mused Anna. '*This offer will not be made again*, for example. And he doesn't tell her to bring money. Why not? He must still want that, mustn't he?'

'One would think so.' Daniel picked the letter up and read it again. 'You're right. It *is* odd. Aside from *come alone* and *tell no one*, the tone isn't remotely threatening, is it?'

'No.' She frowned up at him, struck by an idea. 'I could be wrong but I've a feeling this isn't from Grimshaw at all. I think ... I think it was written by a woman.'

He stared back at her, his mind making the same leap hers must have done.

'The widow?' And when she nodded, 'Yes. Possibly. Grimshaw's haste in separating us made me think she doesn't know what he's been up to. But, with hindsight, it could equally have been because she *does* know and has an axe of her own to grind – hence this. Unfortunately, the only way to find out for sure is to take the bait.' He held up a staying hand as Anna opened her mouth and said flatly, 'No. I know what you're going to say – and you're not doing it.'

'Well, *somebody* has to and obviously your mother can't. So if –'

'No. We think the widow may have written the note and we could be right. But that doesn't necessarily mean *she* will be the one waiting in the church. It could be Grimshaw himself. So no. You are not going to this meeting in Mama's place.'

Anna leaned back in her chair and eyed him irritably over folded arms.

'What, then? Or let me guess. You are going yourself. You'll arrive early and hide in the shadows until whoever it is turns up. If it's Grimshaw, you'll confront him – with goodness knows what result. If it's the widow, she'll likely flee the church, screaming. No, let me finish.' This as he would have spoken. 'How is any of that better than you hiding behind a pillar while I explain to whoever turns up that the dowager viscountess is too frail to come herself but trusts me to deal with the matter on her behalf? A lie that would work equally well with Grimshaw as with the widow.'

'No, it won't.' Daniel thought he saw a weak spot and pounced on it. 'Grimshaw would believe Mama doesn't know anything about this. He won't believe that *you* don't.'

'Why not? As I told you once before, he doesn't know me. And he doesn't really know you either. How many husbands would confide something like this to their wives? Not many, I'll wager. But how many wives go behind their husbands' backs when they think it necessary? More than those husbands would like to believe.' Anna grinned at him, triumphantly. 'Go on. Argue your way out of *that*.'

It was the grin that did it. Daniel didn't know whether to laugh or shake her. Instead, he hauled her out of the chair and kissed her, long and hard. Then, taking advantage of the fact that she was temporarily speechless, he said, 'You are the most stubborn, impossible woman in the world. What am I to do with you?'

'I daresay you'll think of something,' she replied breathlessly. 'But for now perhaps you could admit that my plan is better?'

'It ... might be,' he allowed.

'Thank you. So let's use the three days we have before the meeting to make sure we've thought of everything, shall we?' *And tell me the paint smell is too strong in your room so I can say you are welcome to sleep in mine because otherwise I won't know how to offer.*

But she didn't say it ... and to her intense disappointment, Daniel said nothing either.

* * *

Anna might have felt less disappointed had she been able to read her husband's mind.

For some little while now, Daniel had been trying to come to terms with an unexpected discovery. He wanted his wife; and he wanted *her* to want *him*, not merely offer to share her bed for some practical reason.

Although still a little shy, she seemed to welcome his gestures of affection and to enjoy his kisses – which was a step in the right direction. The problem was that, for him, those same things had reawakened an appetite for something he hadn't had for a very long time. He'd spent a number of sleepless hours pondering the question that raised. Did he just want sex ... or did he want Anna? And the answer, when he was sure he had it, surprised him. He wanted brave, clever, insightful, straight-from-the-shoulder Anna. Anna of the shy smiles, the rare laughter and the sardonic sense of humour. Anna with the sleek fall of brown hair, the slim waist and the elusive scent of lavender. Anna who never asked anything of him ... or even seemed to want to.

Damn, he thought ruefully. *I've let the situation between us go on too long and become too comfortable. It's high time I changed that ... but there always seems to be some other bloody thing getting in the way. Such as now.*

* * *

Anna entered the church of Saint Nicholas veiled, garbed head to foot in black and glancing nervously around her every third or fourth step. From his vantage point behind a pillar in the north transept where he had been for some time, Daniel watched her tread down the south aisle to the fifth pew from the front and take another look behind her before she sat down, fussing with her skirts. He couldn't help smiling a little. She was the very picture of a lady with a clandestine assignation.

Although it seemed a long time before the church door creaked open again and another pair of feet trod hesitantly down the aisle it was probably no more than ten minutes. Daniel risked a swift peep around the pillar and was immensely relieved to see that the newcomer was female.

Not Grimshaw, then, he thought. *Thank God for that.*

Anna was equally relieved that her instinct had been right. But she merely inclined her head when the other woman sat beside her and waited for her to speak first.

Finally, in a timid voice, she said, 'Lady Reculver?'

'Yes. But not, I'm afraid, the one you were expecting.' Composedly putting back her veil, Anna took a cool look at her companion. 'And you are?'

'Alice Grimshaw. But I don't – ' And then, 'Oh. Of course. You are married to the – the new viscount?'

'Obviously. And I am here on behalf of his mother. The dowager viscountess's nerves are delicate and she was deeply disturbed by your letter – in particular the insinuation that she could not trust her son.'

'Oh. I'm sorry. I didn't intend to upset – '

'You write about long-standing secrets kept by both her husband and her son and you didn't intend to *upset* her?' asked Anna glacially. 'What else *could* you have intended? But let us get this over with. I presume that, in return for this secret, you want money?'

'*Me?* No. That isn't it at all.'

'Then what is?'

'I want to make my brother-in-law stop what he's been doing all these years. And the only way I could think of to do it was to tell her ladyship the truth because then there wouldn't be any secret to keep, would there? I hoped that now Gervase – now her husband is d-dead, she might not find it so *very* painful.'

Wishful thinking or gross stupidity? wondered Anna. But she said merely, 'I have no idea what you're talking about. What exactly *has* your brother-in-law been doing?'

'Making Gervase pay, over and over again for – for an affair that didn't even last three months but which resulted in the birth of a – a child.'

Anna stared at the widow under raised brows. Then, even more coldly than before, she said, 'Let us be clear, Mrs Grimshaw. You are talking about a love affair, an illegitimate child … and, if I understand you correctly, blackmail. Yes?'

'Yes.'

'The affair being with you and the child, yours?'

'Yes.' The widow's eyes filled with tears and she searched frantically for a handkerchief. Then, the words tumbling over each other, she said, 'My husband had not long died and I was lonely. As for Gervase ... he never said it but I think things weren't right at home just then and he took to visiting when Harold, my brother-in-law, was away. He never loved me – I knew that. Only then I was expecting. He promised to look after me and the baby and he did. Generously, too, even though the affair was over. But Harold *knew*.'

She stopped to dry her face and blow her nose. Anna gave her a moment to compose herself, then said, 'Harold knew and used that knowledge to extort money from the late viscount. Is that what you're saying?'

'Yes. At first, he made excuses for needing extra money. He'd say it was for things like paying the doctor and buying medicines because William – my son – was ill. Later, he pretended William's school fees had got a lot more expensive and that books he needed cost four times what they really did. I told Gervase over and over that Harold was cheating him, that the money wasn't for Will and me but he still paid and the longer it went on, the greedier Harold got. Eventually, the amounts of money he asked for got too big to explain away and Gervase finally admitted he couldn't afford them. That was when Harold told him that, if he wanted his secret kept from his wife and son, he'd better find a way.' She hauled in a long, shuddering breath. 'I tried to make him stop, my lady – and I tried to persuade Gervase to bring it all into the open so Harold would *have* to stop. But neither of them would listen. Harold wasn't going to give up such easy money. Gervase said he couldn't bear his Mary to know he'd betrayed her. And so it went on, year after year.'

'And when my husband's father died?' asked Anna. 'What then?'

'I thought that must be the end of it,' replied the widow miserably. 'Only then your husband came to see Harold and something told me it wasn't the first time. That's when I realised that it wasn't *ever* going to stop unless I did something.'

'And that 'something' was to write to the dowager viscountess?'

'Yes. It was all I could think of. I'd rather have gone to your husband but I wasn't sure he'd listen to me any more than his father did. I didn't want – I *never* wanted to upset anybody. Thanks to Gervase, William had a good education and has a promising future in a law office. *I* don't need your family's money. Neither does he. And, by my reckoning, Harold has had more than his share of it.'

'Well, there I must agree with you.' Throughout this entire recital, Anna had been aware of Daniel edging gradually closer in order to overhear their conversation. 'I also appreciate your honesty. However, everything you have told me would much better have been said to my husband. I can assure you that he *would* have listened.'

'And has done so most intently,' remarked Daniel quietly, emerging from the shadows. And when the widow shot to her feet, clutching her throat, 'Please don't be alarmed, Mrs Grimshaw. I am only here because I wasn't sure whether my wife would be meeting you or your objectionable brother-in-law.' He made his way slowly across the nave towards them. 'I don't blame you for anything he has done.'

'You – you don't?' she asked faintly.

'No. I'm merely grateful to you for confirming what Anna and I either know or have guessed.' He smiled, then added, 'But I *am* going to ask something of you.'

'What?'

'Would you would be willing to tell my man-of-law everything you know so that I can bring a charge of extortion against –?'

'*No!*' A look of horror crossed her face. 'I'm sorry – but I can't. I just *can't!*'

Both Anna and Daniel opened their mouths to ask why she couldn't but, before they could do so, a voice from the back of the church said clearly, '*She* won't. But I will.'

All three of them spun around but the widow reacted first with a despairing moan.

'Will? *No!* You mustn't! And what are you doing here? How – ?'

'I followed you.' The young man strolled towards them, his expression grim. 'I knew you were up to something – you've been acting strangely for weeks. I should have known it might be this.' He stopped and faced Daniel across the width of the pews. 'Lord and Lady Reculver, I presume? I didn't hear everything my mother told you but I heard enough and most of it I knew already. So –'

'You can't have done!' exclaimed his mother. 'How could you? I was so *careful!*'

'*You* might have been,' he agreed. And with barely suppressed anger, 'My bloody so-called uncle wasn't.' Then, stiffly, to Anna, 'Forgive my language. But you and his lordship can't possibly hate the man more than I do.' And even more stiffly to Daniel, 'The reason my mother won't help you act against him is that he owns our home. He shouldn't. I'll bet that when your father handed over the money for it he intended the house to be lifetime security for my mother. But it's Harold's name on the deeds, not hers. I know because the law firm I work for handled the purchase and I've seen the documents.'

In the grip of an odd sense of unreality caused mostly by the younger man's uncanny resemblance to Rebecca, Daniel said, 'So he could evict you?'

'He could try – though it might not be as easy as he thinks.'

'And yet you said that *you* would supply the evidence I need?'

'Yes. Even going by just the things I *know* about – which probably amount to less than a quarter of the whole – my existence cost your father thousands over the years so I reckon I owe you that much. And if he throws us out, we'd manage. I've just been made senior clerk so I could afford decent lodgings and – '

'Stop,' said Anna firmly. 'Let us cross that particular bridge if and when we come to it. For now, may I suggest that we take the rest of this conversation to more comfortable surroundings?'

'There's no need for that, my lady,' said Alice hastily. 'People may see us –'

'And if they do?' asked Daniel, crossing to where William stood. 'Admittedly, I haven't yet become accustomed to having a brother ... but that can be mended easily enough. What do you think?' And he held out his hand.

Slowly reddening, William stared into Daniel's face for a moment. Then he gripped the outstretched hand and said, 'Yes. I think it could.'

* * *

'How long have you known about me?' asked William. He and Daniel lounged by the window of the inn's coffee-room with tankards of ale while his mother and the viscountess presided over a tea tray. 'Come to that, how did you find out?'

'Not very long. And I didn't so much find out as guess,' replied Daniel. Then he went on to recount his second meeting with Grimshaw, ending with, 'So that was when I realised he'd been blackmailing Father and knew there was some secret. I had a muddled idea of talking to you and your mother in the hope that you could tell me something useful and I'd heard where you were going so I followed you.'

'But you didn't speak to us. Why not?'

'Because the instant I clapped eyes on you, I no longer needed to. I knew without a shadow of doubt that my father was also yours.'

'How?' asked William, baffled. 'I could understand it if we looked at all alike ... but we don't.'

'No,' agreed Daniel with a wry smile. 'My looks come from my mother's side of the family. Yours, like those of my younger sister, are from my father's. You and she could be twins.'

'Seriously? There's that degree of resemblance?'

'Yes. It's a pity you can't meet her. But I hope you understand *why* you can't?'

'The dowager viscountess?' guessed William.

'Yes. I'd like to continue keeping Father's ... lapse ... from Mother if at all possible. And if Rebecca knows, she's likely to let the cat out of the bag by accident.'

William nodded, drank some ale and then said, 'So how are you going to bring a case against Harold without the cat running yowling through the streets?'

'I can't. But I'll make him believe that I both can and will.'

'You're going to *bluff*?'

'What other choice do I have? My lawyers already have Grimshaw's demands for the four thousand pounds he claimed was owed him, along with a letter from Hoare's bank which I believe is a forgery. Ah. And that reminds me. Do you have a middle name, by any chance?'

Startled by the sudden shift, William blinked and said, 'Yes. It's Thomas.'

'And an account at Hoare's bank in Cheltenham?'

'No. Why are you –?'

'Because there's an account in the name of W.T. Grimshaw there. If I had to guess, Harold falsified your date of birth to make you appear a minor so he can control it as your supposed trustee. I suggest you find out – though perhaps not immediately. Now … going back to everything you and your mother know about Harold's dealings with my – *our* – father; all of that should be sufficient to bring a case against him, shouldn't it?'

'Probably. But what am I to say about our … kinship?'

'The truth.'

'You don't want it hidden?'

'From my mother and the world at large, yes. But if my lawyers aren't discreet, I need new ones.' Daniel pulled out his watch, glanced at it and added, 'It's only a half after one and Longhope's offices are no distance away. If we go there now and I introduce you, you can make an appointment for a time that suits you without me being present.' He paused and added, 'But before you keep that appointment, think very carefully about whether you want to get involved in this – for your mother's sake if not for your own.'

'Try and stop me,' growled William. 'It's time he got what he deserves.'

'Undoubtedly. But –'

'No. Like you, I don't know anything about having a brother but this seems as good a place to start as any.'

'Then, thank you.' Daniel thought for a moment. 'I'll tell Longhope to find and reserve convenient lodgings for yourself and your mother in case they're needed.'

'I can do that myself,' offered William.

'I know. But it covers your tracks better if Longhope does it. I'll instruct him to pay for them and also to act on your behalf if and when things start to get messy. In fact, in the hope of avoiding or at least delaying that, it might be best if we communicated through Longhope for the time being.'

William said slowly, 'You aren't at all like I'd thought you'd be.'

'Better rather than worse, I hope,' said Daniel, still busy scouring his brain for anything he hadn't thought of yet. Then, not finding anything, 'Let's go. If there is anything else I can do, tell me. I have resources that you don't so let's use them. For example, I don't know how you and your mother got here today but after we've seen Longhope, I'll hire a chaise to get you home again.' He grinned suddenly. 'We are in this together, William – and I'm extremely glad to be able to say that.'

CHAPTER TWENTY-THREE

Upon receiving Lord Reculver's instructions, Mr Longhope senior immediately made an appointment for William to make his deposition on the following afternoon. Afterwards, with less argument than might have been the case had it not started to rain, Daniel sent William and his mother back to Cirencester in a hired chaise with a firm handshake and an expression of genuine gratitude.

But once in his own carriage, he stared silently out upon on the rain, his face tight with something Anna couldn't interpret but suspected was the price of maintaining a façade of courtesy and composure throughout what must have been a deeply disturbing afternoon. After a little while, she slipped her hand into his and felt his fingers close around hers. But it wasn't until they were half-way home that he finally spoke.

'Am I doing the right thing?'

'About what, exactly?'

'Keeping all this from Mama. If I told her, I could *actually* prosecute Grimshaw rather than bluffing that I'm going to.'

'True,' she agreed. 'But it isn't just your mother you are trying to protect, is it? There's Rebecca, with her debut just around the corner and William's mother who has to face her neighbours; and finally, there's all the money your father spent to keep it secret. So what you have to decide is whether putting Grimshaw in prison is worth the cost.'

He shut his eyes, sighing. 'When you put it like that … no. It isn't. But I don't like grubbing about in the shadows. It makes me feel no better than Basil bloody Selwyn.'

'That's ridiculous and you know it,' said Anna bracingly. 'You're trying to do your best for everyone with the least possible harm to anyone. Take William, for example. He probably expected resentment, disdain and a blatant wish to have nothing to do with him. But you offered him your hand and called him your brother.'

'Well, regardless of the circumstances, he *is* my brother, isn't he? And none of this is his fault.'

'*No*, Daniel! Don't dismiss it as nothing. It's not. I was proud of you.'

'Were you?' He opened his eyes, revealing a mixture of weariness, surprise and shy pleasure. 'Really?'

'Yes – really.'

For a moment or two longer, he continued to look at her. Then, pulling her into his arms and laying his cheek against her hair, he whispered, 'Thank you.'

* * *

'I presume,' said the dowager, as they sat down to dine, 'you haven't forgotten that our dinner-party is on Saturday? I ask because the two of you seem barely to be here these days.'

'My apologies, Mama,' replied Daniel absently. 'It's been a busy time, one way and another. But of course Anna and I will be here for your party.'

'I'm glad to hear it. And not just in the evening, I hope. I'll need your advice on the place settings, Anna. Mrs Ashworth doesn't get on with the vicar ... and Rebecca is being difficult about sitting next to Reginald Yates.'

'I'm not being difficult, Mama,' said Rebecca. 'I just won't do it. He was at Lady Holden's afternoon dance and his hands go where they shouldn't.'

Daniel glanced up from his plate, 'If he behaves that way here, I'll be having a few words with him. Ones he won't enjoy.'

Rebecca beamed at him. 'Thank you. Can I listen?'

'No.' And he continued eating.

In addition to the air of abstraction that had been clinging to Daniel since they'd said goodbye to William and his mother, Anna became aware of something else. Every time she looked in his direction, his gaze seemed to be fixed on her – though he looked away the instant her eyes met his. The first, she could understand. The second, she couldn't. If something other than the Grimshaw affair was on his mind she had no idea what it might be – unless some new possibility had occurred to him and he was waiting for an opportunity to discuss it.

The latter seemed the likelier possibility when he followed her up to their rooms later – except that, once there, he didn't say anything and neither, as had become his habit since Hazelmere, did he kiss her lightly on the cheek and bid her goodnight. Instead, he followed her as far as her bedchamber door, drew her fully into his arms said softly, 'May I come in and ... perhaps stay?'

Anna's heart tried to leap into her throat. Swallowing hard, she nodded and managed to say, 'Of course.'

He drew a long breath. 'Thank you.'

Inside her room with the door closed behind them, Daniel was suddenly at a loss ... as if he'd never done this before. And in a sense he hadn't, had he? Anna wasn't some woman with whom he was having a fleeting affair. She was his wife; so whatever turn their relationship took tonight would be a significant one. Reaching out to take one of her hands in his, he said haltingly, 'We don't have to make love if you don't wish it, Anna. But I would like to sleep with you tonight – if that would be all right?'

His uncertainty surprised her. His desire not to be alone didn't.

Whatever nerves she might have evaporated.

She said, 'It would be very much all right.'

'It would? Really?'

'Yes. Really.'

Daniel opened his mouth but closed it again when several thoughts collided. He would have preferred to ask her not to ring for her maid and allow him to help her undress but he suspected she wouldn't be comfortable with that. Belatedly, it also occurred to him where doing so was likely to lead ... and that he'd promised her a choice. So he said, 'Then I'll leave you and return in a little while, shall I?'

Anna would have been more than happy to dispense with Ruth's services but didn't quite know how to suggest it – or what his reaction would be if she did. So she nodded and said, 'Yes. Please do.'

When the connecting door closed behind him, she pulled the bell for Ruth and sank down on the stool by her mirror to begin stripping pins from her hair with hands that weren't entirely steady.

Perhaps I ought to have told him that if he wants to do more than merely sleep *with me, I'd welcome it,* she thought. *He doesn't have to know that I love him with every fibre of my being and that I want to lie with him more than I've ever wanted anything.*

Anything? asked a little voice at the back of her mind. *Even Hawthorne's?*

She knew what the answer to that was. Fortunately, Ruth arrived before she was forced to acknowledge it.

The nightly ritual followed its usual course until Anna saw the nightgown Ruth had laid out for her and said, 'No. Not that one. The embroidered lawn with the lace trim.'

The maid froze for a second to stare at her. Then, turning away to hide a smile while she located the required garment, 'Yes, my lady.' And not quite under her breath, 'About time, too.'

'What was that?' asked Anna, sharply.

'Nothing, my lady.' With a perfectly straight face, Ruth cast the nightgown over her head, tied the ribbons and stepped back. 'Although, if you was to want my opinion – '

'I don't, thank you. That will be all, Ruth.'

'Yes, ma'am.' She curtsied and, over her shoulder on her way to the door, 'The braid's a mistake. It'd be better loose.' Then she was gone.

Anna told herself to ignore Ruth's parting shot. She told herself that leaving her hair loose would suggest she was expecting something Daniel wasn't offering. She tried to stay away from the mirror ... but couldn't resist one quick peek. Then, with a groan of self-disgust, she tugged the ribbon away, shook the braid loose and was just reaching for a brush when a tap at the connecting door told her she could do one of two things; smooth her hair or pull on her chamber-robe. She chose the latter whilst telling Daniel to come in; and, when he had done so, realised that she had no idea what to say.

He was wearing the banyan she'd seen once before but, this time – disappointingly – the deep vee of naked flesh was hidden beneath a nightshirt. His preparations for spending the night in her bed were the opposite of hers for wanting him to, it seemed.

Daniel took in the flowing hair and what he could see of the nightgown's sweeping, lace-trimmed neckline and tempting little bows and tried to quell an involuntary quiver of anticipation, sternly reminding himself that those things didn't necessarily mean what he'd like them to mean. A little abruptly, he said, 'I think you should know that my being here is nothing to do with anything except that I *want* to be.'

She shook her head. 'You don't need to explain. I'm *glad* you're here. Today was difficult. What lies ahead of it isn't likely to be any better. So in future, even if there is no particular reason ... perhaps you won't feel you must ask for permission?'

The hazel eyes widened a little and the ghost of a smile dawned.

'You may regret that offer – so I'll accept it before you do. But if I keep you awake, you must tell me to go.'

'And if *I* keep *you* awake?'

I'm fairly sure you will, thought Daniel ruefully, *just not in the way you mean. And there's a simple cure for that which I'm hoping to work my way around to.* But he said lightly, 'I don't think you need worry about that.' He strolled across to give her a brief hug. Then, with what he hoped was a convincing grin, 'But... do you think we might leave the bolster where it belongs?'

Anna managed a tiny laugh. 'Yes. I can't believe I actually thought you were serious when you suggested it that first time at Mama's house.'

'And I can't believe I was *stupid* enough,' he said, only half under his breath. 'Well, then ... with that agreed, let's get some sleep, shall we?'

She nodded, shed the chamber-robe and slid quickly between the sheets, to watch surreptitiously as Daniel moved around the room, extinguishing candles and tossed his banyan aside before blowing out the one beside the bed. Then the mattress shifted as he climbed in beside her ... and unexpectedly reached through the dark for her hand.

A few moments later, he said, 'Thank you for today. You were right about everything and I couldn't have done it without you.'

'You'd have managed. Somehow.'

'Perhaps. If I'd had to. But I'm grateful that I didn't.' There was a long pause. Then, wearily, 'You can't imagine how glad I will be to have Grimshaw out of our lives.'

Lacing her fingers with his, Anna said, 'Oh I think I can. But *"sufficient unto the day is the evil thereof."* So don't think of him now. Goodnight.'

'Goodnight,'

* * *

Both being acutely aware of the other, neither of them expected sleep to come easily and it didn't. But Anna succumbed first and eventually Daniel fell into fitful slumber only to wake an hour or so after dawn to the scent of lavender and a warm, female body pressed against his side. This was so enjoyable that he didn't engage his brain beyond telling himself that he wasn't dreaming. He just sighed, gathered her closer and tried not to become fully conscious. He might have managed this had Anna not slid her leg across his. But she did … and Daniel was immediately wide awake in both mind and body.

He gritted his teeth and, realising that merely remaining still wasn't going to help, started disengaging himself from her so that he could get out of bed. Anna made a little sound of complaint and, still in her sleep as far as he could tell, reached out to pull him back. His breath caught and he froze for an instant before temptation sent all his good intentions into oblivion.

Gathering her into his arms, he set about waking her with butterfly-light kisses along her brow while one hand smoothed a path back and forth between shoulder and elbow. And then, when her eyes fluttered open and focussed on his face, he sought her mouth in a kiss that he somehow managed to make an invitation rather than a demand. And Anna, becoming aware that what she had wanted was within her grasp, tangled her fingers in his hair and kissed him back with all the love that was in her. Daniel gave a tiny growl of approval and turned her slightly so he could explore the intoxicating curve of her waist and hip. Her body arched, pressing against him and making him as aware of his physical state as, presumably by now, so must she be.

Breaking the kiss and, by some superhuman effort managing to stop himself sliding a thigh between hers, Daniel said raggedly, 'I didn't intend this to happen. Do you want me to stop? If you do, tell me and I will. At any point … though it would be easiest for me if you said so now.'

'No,' Anna managed breathlessly. 'I don't want you to stop.'

'Are you sure?'

'Yes.' She locked her gaze with his. 'Don't. Please.'

He gave a shaky laugh and, releasing her, sat up to tug at his nightshirt.

'In that case, you won't mind if I get rid of this thing?' Without waiting for a reply, he pulled it over his head and tossed it aside. 'And, pretty as it is, yours can go too whenever you feel ready. But for now …'

He drew her back into his arms and kissed her again. Oddly, since desire was roaring through his blood with the force of a hurricane, he found he could control it by focussing on Anna's needs rather than his own. He began by learning the landscape of her body through the flimsy stuff of her nightgown; then, by dint of sliding if off a shoulder or up a shapely calf, set about disposing of it altogether.

However, he was increasingly distracted by Anna exploring his chest, shoulders and back with both mouth and hands and eventually, on something half-laugh, half-groan, he said, 'You have an unfair advantage here. Let me even the field.'

And taking hold of her nightgown, tugged it off and sent it in the wake of his nightshirt. Then, pulling her fully against him skin to skin, 'Ah yes. That's better.'

Anna's blood was flowing through silken channels and alive with little, dancing sparks which flared, intermittently, into flame. Everything about him was new and fascinating. The slight raspiness of his jaw and the faint citrus scent of his cologne; the heat of his skin and, beneath it, the play of muscles in his arms and shoulders; and, most of all, that part of him which she hadn't yet seen but which she could feel nudging eagerly at her thigh. She had thought she'd known how much she wanted him. Now, melting in his arms and beneath the clever play of his touch, she realised that she'd had no idea.

Presently, she said, 'What should I do?'

'Whatever you wish,' came the reply as his hands travelled tantalisingly onwards. And, seductively low-pitched as his mouth trailed after them, 'Or you could just leave it to me while I learn what you like best. This, for example.' His tongue swirled around the tip of her breast while his fingers grew bold elsewhere, making her gasp and writhe. 'Yes. That's

... helpful.' Then, a little while later when Anna's hands grew similarly adventurous, 'Ah. Right now, that probably isn't.'

She froze. 'You don't like it?'

'Rather too much,' he managed to say. And hauling in a steadying breath, added, 'I should probably admit that I may not be able to make this last as long as I would like. It's been ... a while. And I want you rather ... ferociously.'

Without warning, the words turned the flames that had been flickering through Anna's blood into a conflagration. The ability to think fled before the tumult of unfamiliar sensations he was creating in her body; sensations that seemed to be multiplying by the second and building towards something she wanted yet was faintly alarmed by.

Twisting restlessly against him, she said, 'Daniel ... I don't ... I can't ...'

'I know, sweetheart. It's all right. Let it come.' Somewhere at the back of his mind, was the realisation that she didn't know what he meant and wouldn't even if he told her, so he used his mouth and hands to better purpose until the storm inside her reached its peak and she clung to him, breathless and shaking.

Although it was killing him, he continued to hold her until the little aftershocks ceased. Then he murmured, 'The next part won't be quite so enjoyable for you, I'm afraid; but only this one time, I promise.'

He was right; and then, in scarcely any time at all, he wasn't.

Discomfort faded and was forgotten.

All that was left was a feeling of completeness; joy of finally being his; and the wonder of knowing that she had given him pleasure.

'God, Anna,' he breathed when he was capable of saying anything at all. 'That was ... I don't know. Thank you.'

* * *

They slept for perhaps an hour and then Anna awoke, still wrapped in Daniel's arms. Grinning down at her, he said, 'Back with me, are you?'

'Yes. How long have you been awake?'

'Not long. I thought about getting up … then asked myself why I'd want to do that when it's so nice here with – ' He came to an abrupt stop, looking appalled. 'Damn. I'm being unforgivably selfish, aren't I? Wallowing in my own well-being instead of asking how *you* are.'

'I'm fine,' said Anna. And thought, *Better than fine. I could dance on the roof-tops.*

'It was your first time.' He surveyed her anxiously. 'I tried not to hurt you but I probably did. Are you sore? Shall I ring for a bath? Or do you want your maid?'

'Stop.' Sitting up, she smoothed a lightly curling lock of auburn hair back from his face and smiled at him. 'I'm fine. Really. No, I don't want Ruth but a bath sounds nice so I suppose I must have her. Will that stop you fussing?'

'I'm not fussing.'

'You are.' And wickedly, 'It's rather sweet actually.'

'*Sweet?*' he echoed, revolted.

Anna nodded. 'Yes. But don't worry. I won't tell anyone.'

CHAPTER TWENTY-FOUR

By Tuesday morning sealed copies of William's and Daniel's affidavits were lodged with Longhope & Son of Gloucester. And on Tuesday afternoon, Daniel received a copy of the letter Harold Grimshaw would be receiving the following day.

In a brisk and no-nonsense fashion, this informed Mr Grimshaw that Viscount Reculver was bringing an action against him for long-standing criminal extortion from his late father and the same recently attempted in respect of himself. An estimated sum of between eight and twelve thousand pounds appeared to be involved. Mr Grimshaw ought further to be aware that Longhope & Son possessed sufficient evidence, not only to prosecute but also obtain a conviction. Then came a veiled hint that the viscount *might* reconsider prosecution if Mr Grimshaw repaid a proportion of the money fraudulently obtained from his father.

And, at the end, *We look forward to hearing from your legal representative regarding this matter without delay. Yours, etc.*

Daniel pushed it across the desk to Anna. When she finished reading it, she said, 'Mr Longhope certainly isn't wasting any time, is he? And not beating about the bush, either.'

'No. I think he's enjoying doing something he can get his teeth into.'

'Good. That's in our favour. What do you think Grimshaw will do?'

'Well, he won't repay the money even if he has it because doing so is an admission that he took it in the first place,' replied Daniel. 'No. He'll deny everything and pin his hopes on me not actually taking him to court. Or he might run – which could be the best solution all round. If he doesn't, he'll probably come here, full of bluster and threats … in which case, I'd be grateful if you can keep Mama and Rebecca occupied elsewhere.'

'I'll do my best – though it will largely depend on how loudly he shouts. Meanwhile, what about William? I know you've had Longhope put safeguards in place but – '

'I did. But as things stand, Grimshaw won't know anything about William's involvement unless matters escalate ... and I'm holding on to the hope that they won't. Now. Enough about that. What news from Hawthorne's?'

'Nathaniel says repairs to the kiln are almost complete and he hopes to have it in working order within the week.'

'Well, that's good news. Did he ever find out any more about what happened?'

'Since he says nothing of it, I assume not. But he writes that all the cabinets and shelves have been installed in the exhibition area and asks what I want putting where.'

'Let me guess,' said Daniel. 'That isn't something you can decide from here?'

'No.' She thought for a moment. 'But this isn't a good time to be away, is it? A lot depends on what Grimshaw does next. So I'll tell Nathaniel to assemble the wares we'd already agreed upon but to leave them crated up until I'm able to be there myself. There's no desperate hurry, after all. I doubt there will be any visitors before the spring; and I'd like to plan and advertise a Grand Opening.' She smiled suddenly. 'The general public may not flood in ... but I'll wager our competitors will.'

'To decide if the idea is worth copying?'

'Yes. And also to find out what, if any, new techniques we've developed,' replied Anna, reaching for Mr Landry's letter which she had deliberately left until last. Then, having quickly scanned the page she looked across at Daniel and said, 'He's had a report from Mr Aldridge, the investigator.'

'Finally. And?'

'Apparently Harvill isn't well thought of in Bristol.'

'There's a surprise. But by whom – and for what reason?'

'The business community in general, I gather. Amongst other things, he has a reputation for underhand dealings.' Anna continued reading. 'Here's something that may be relevant, though I can't see how. The Harvills were originally from Worcester and owned property there. But the whole family moved to Bristol some time in the 1650s, probably on account of damage to property and reprisals following the battle of Worcester at the end of the civil war, he thinks.' She looked up at Daniel. 'I can't see how that helps, can you? Hawthorne's didn't exist until Father bought a piece of semi-derelict land in 1735 and began building the manufactory on it.'

'So is that all Aldridge has to offer? A history lesson?'

'Not quite,' said Anna, frowning over the final paragraph. 'He's heard rumours suggesting that Harvill may be over-extended financially.'

'In which case, how the devil could he afford to buy Hawthorne's – even if you were willing to sell?'

'Mr Aldridge is wondering the same thing and attempting to establish whether or not the rumours are true.' She tossed the letter on to the desk. 'That's it.'

'And none of it any help at all.' Daniel stood up and stretched, then pulled Anna to her feet. 'There doesn't seem much more we can do about any of this for now. It's a little blustery outside but it's dry. Shall we go out for a drive and a breath of air?'

She beamed at him and nodded.

'Perhaps we could look in at the school and then call at Groves' farm?'

He groaned. '*Must* we?'

'Well, not the school, perhaps. But I should call on Emily Groves. The new baby was born four days ago so she will be up and about by now.' A glance at his face told her what he thought of this. Weakening, she said, 'I suppose it can wait until tomorrow.'

'Then let it.' Taking her hand, he towed her towards the door. 'Your dedication to duty is admirable. Usually, I am in awe of it. But right now, I would appreciate having you to myself.' Pausing, his hand on the latch, he whispered, 'I missed you last night.'

She'd missed him, too. He'd slept in his own bed in order, he'd said, to give her time to recover. Anna, who felt perfectly fine, wondered what precisely she was supposed to be recovering *from* but had been either too shy or not quite brave enough to ask … and still was. So she said cautiously, 'And tonight?'

He grinned. 'Is that an invitation?'

'Do you need one?'

'Not *need*, perhaps. But a fellow likes to know he's welcome.' And with a sudden laugh, 'Get your hat and cloak and I'll have them bring the phaeton round. If we dither much longer, Mama will be in here with yet more niggling dinner-party queries and we won't get out at all.'

* * *

After a second night's love-making that, astoundingly, had been even more wonderful than the first, Anna felt as if she was floating a few inches off the ground in a bubble of pure happiness which even the uncertainties of the Grimshaw Affair could not spoil. Daniel might not love her but there was much more between them now than she had ever dared dream there might be and she could be more than content with that.

As for Daniel, he was still not delving too deeply into the nature of his feelings towards his wife but could not help knowing that he was content – even happy – and much of that was due to Anna. Problems were always lessened when he could talk them over with her ... and now there were the added pleasures of the bedroom, made all the sweeter – not just because of the long abstinence which had preceded them – but by Anna's warm and ardent response to his touch.

* * *

It came as no surprise that Wednesday afternoon brought Daniel a copy of the letter of complaint and denial Grimshaw's lawyers had sent to his own. No, they said, their client had neither blackmailed the late viscount nor attempted to blackmail the current one. After all, what possible means could he have to do so? The accusation was a complete tissue of lies and any evidence Longhope & Son claimed to hold could not be other than a fabrication.

'This was to be expected,' Daniel told Anna when she had read it. 'Grimshaw won't have admitted anything and his lawyer is forced to take his word whether he believes it or not. So now I imagine there will be some legal wrangling while Grimshaw's fellow demands to see the evidence and Longhope produces my affidavit but continues to withhold William's for as long as possible whilst still threatening prosecution. In essence, it's bluff and counter-bluff ... and will all boil down to who makes the first mistake.'

'Which is more likely to be Grimshaw, since he's the one who's lying,' she said. Then, 'Do you still think he'll try to see you?'

'I'm less sure than I was. The only card in his hand is Father's affair with Alice Grimshaw and the truth about her son's paternity. But he can't play it even by devious means because, if anything of the sort comes to light now, Longhope will make sure Grimshaw is blamed for it. So all he's left with is making me back down – and I won't.' He paused and then said slowly, 'However, if he *does* come, perhaps I should see him.'

'Not without an independent witness hidden nearby,' she replied promptly. 'And, in my opinion, coming here is more likely to weaken his position than strengthen it.'

'I agree. But perhaps it might be the quickest way to put an end to it. If he believes I'll prosecute and his lawyers consider the evidence strong enough to secure a conviction, they'll advise him to pay me something – anything – rather than let it get that far.' With a grim smile and a shrug, he added, 'Upon which I'll say he can keep his money on condition he leaves this part of England and never returns. That should do it, don't you think?'

* * *

Two days went by with no further developments. On Friday afternoon, Flynn sought out Daniel in the library and said, 'Might I have a word, my lord?'

'Of course. What is it?'

'The fellow young Joseph from the stables saw hanging around the gates some weeks ago is back again – only this time Joseph believes he may have slipped inside the grounds behind her ladyship's phaeton. And I think ... that is I *suspect* he may be the person – '

'How long ago was this?' snapped Daniel.

'Not quite twenty minutes, my – '

'Do you have anyone out looking?'

'All the male staff from both inside and outside the house. But Joseph isn't positive, my lord, and neither am I, not having seen the man myself. There is also the possibility that the intruder may have already left.'

'Equally, it's possible that you and Joe are both right and he's still here. If he is, find him. And don't tell me he's gone unless you're completely sure of it. Where is my wife?'

'Her ladyship came in a short while ago. I believe she is taking tea with the dowager viscountess and Miss Rebecca in the drawing-room, my lord.'

Daniel gave a curt nod. 'Tell her to stay with them – discreetly, mind. I don't want my mother alarmed but until we know whether or not we have an uninvited guest, I'd prefer the ladies were together. I'll be here when you have a definite answer.'

It was some ten minutes later when he was signing a brief letter to Benedict that an unpleasant thought occurred to him, causing him to cast his pen aside and shove back his chair. If someone *had* got into the grounds, they might equally have got inside the house. Several outside doors were habitually in use during the day and therefore left unlocked. And if the trespasser *had* got in … while all the footmen were outside searching … they could be anywhere. Daniel strode out and ran down as far as the half-landing, calling for Flynn.

'Any word from outside?' And when the butler shook his head, 'Search all the rooms on the ground floor in case he got inside. I'll check above.'

He went back up, glanced into both the library and Anna's room to see if everything was as he'd left it and then paused to listen outside the drawing-room door. Since no one was screaming and he could hear the faint rattle of tea-cups, it was safe to assume that all was well. He moved on to the breakfast parlour; it was empty. Pivoting on his heel, he was about to move on when something struck him as not quite right. He looked again, not sure what had snared his attention … and then he saw it. Unless his memory was playing tricks, the Chelsea shepherd and shepherdess on either end of the mantelpiece had changed places.

Had they? Yes, he was sure they had … but that might simply be because a housemaid had taken them down to dust and put them back in the wrong places. Or it might not. It might be a message that someone had been here and wanted him to *know* that they had. Furious now, Daniel spun out and across to the dining-room where three sets of balcony doors led to the rear terrace with steps down into the garden. One pair stood open and, just as the reversed figurines had done, was silently jeering, *See? See how easily I got into your home? And how easily I could do it again.*

Daniel walked outside. Two of the footmen were heading towards the house from the shrubbery and Gregson, his head groom, was trudging back from the other direction.

Gregson saw him and called up, 'Sorry, my lord. Nothing.'

Swearing ferociously under his breath, Daniel stepped back inside, shut and locked the doors before checking the others. It came as no surprise to discover that the key to one pair was missing. Mastering his temper as best he could, he realised that issuing the orders necessary to prevent further intrusions was going to make it impossible for him to keep this from his mother and sister. He didn't have to share quite *all* of his suspicions with them, of course ... but the idea of some nameless fellow creeping about the house was unlikely to go down well.

He ran down the stairs and, finding Flynn in the hall, said rapidly, 'He's been inside. He probably entered through one of the ground floor side doors but he left through the terrace doors in the dining-room and has taken a key. Gather all the servants together. Tell them that we've had an intruder and that, in future, I want all the doors that aren't in constant use kept locked. Make one of the footmen responsible for checking every hour to see that they are. Then talk to Joseph. Find how sure he is that the man he saw today was the same one he saw before ... and, as best you can, compare his description with the one I gave you. Report back to me on that later, please – and tell Joe I'll probably want to speak with him myself.'

'Very good, my lord.'

Daniel gave a curt nod. Then, drawing a long, resigned breath, he went first to the breakfast room to put the figurines back where they should be before going to face his family in the drawing-room. He found them poring over a pile of fashion plates and fabric samples.

'But I *like* pink,' Rebecca was protesting. 'And what's wrong with these sleeves?'

'Too fussy,' said Anna. 'And pink isn't a good colour on you.'

'Perfectly true, dear,' remarked the dowager. And looking up, 'Not that we aren't happy to see you, Daniel, but you are going to be horribly bored if you stay. We are looking ahead to Becky's come-out and listing some suggestions.'

'There's nothing like being prepared,' he murmured. 'But if I may interrupt for a few minutes there is something I need to talk to you about.'

Reading the trouble behind his eyes without difficulty, Anna laid a pattern book aside and said, 'Go on.'

Briefly and making it sound as unalarming as possible by omitting a couple of important details, Daniel told them, finishing with, 'It's unlikely anything of the sort will occur again but it won't hurt to take a few precautions.'

'Are you saying,' demanded his mother, 'that, while we've been in here, some stranger has been roaming the house at will? How is that possible?'

'It appears he slipped into the grounds and then took advantage of an open door to wander inside. He can't have been here for very long because –'

'A thief?' asked Rebecca, wide-eyed.

'Possibly – though, as far as I know, he didn't take anything. It's unpleasant and totally unacceptable, of course, but no harm appears to have been done. I am guessing the man is a stranger passing through the neighbourhood who took the opportunity to take a private tour. But for the time being, can we all please be careful not to leave external doors open as if in invitation?'

'Of course.' Anna stood up, calm and unruffled. 'I take it you've given the necessary orders to Flynn?'

'Yes. He's passing them on to the staff now.' Smiling at his mother and sister, he said, 'Don't worry. It sounds worse than it is. Indeed, I might not have told you about it but for the fact that, for the next couple of weeks, you'll wonder why doors you are accustomed to being open during the day are likely to be locked.' He turned to go and then, as if in response to a sudden afterthought, 'Ah. Anna … do you have a few moments?'

'By all means.' She rose, shook out her skirts and followed him to the door. Then, when he closed it behind them, 'Where?'

'Your office. We're less likely to be overheard there.'

She nodded and led the way without speaking. Once there, however, she said, 'What aren't you telling them?'

'Our intruder wanted me to know he'd been here.' His tone grim, Daniel told her of the figurines, the open door in the dining-room and the missing key. Then he said baldly, 'It's possible it was Grimshaw.'

Anna stared at him. 'How sure are you?'

'Right now, not at all. But Joseph said the same man he saw before was loitering outside the gates again today and slipped into the grounds in the wake of your carriage. Flynn immediately sent all the grooms and footmen out searching for him. I imagine that gave Grimshaw – if it *is* him – his chance to get inside unseen. As yet, I haven't had an opportunity to ask Joseph to describe the man but I will, and hopefully that will give us the answer one way or another.'

Anna stared silently into space, frowning a little. Finally, she said, 'I'm finding it easier to believe our intruder was Grimshaw than some random snooper wandering in by chance. But what I *can't* fathom is what he expects to achieve by it.'

'Other than a rude gesture? One which will make me worry he could do it again?'

'It was a big risk to take just for a rude gesture. And, unless he's completely stupid, if he intended to do it again he wouldn't have left any sign he'd been here. He'd have shut and locked the dining-room doors behind him and pocketed the key. We might not have missed it for weeks.'

Daniel regarded her with an expression that was partly thoughtful and partly something she didn't recognise. Finally he said, 'You know, I ought to find you uncommonly annoying. I'm not sure why I don't.'

'And *I'm* not sure why you should,' she objected. 'Or why you should think so *now*. We were only discussing possibilities, just as we always do.'

'Exactly.' Reaching out, he took her hands and pulled her into his lap. 'And it inevitably ends with you hitting the nail on the head while I'm still hunting for the hammer. It ought to be maddening.'

Allowing one arm to slide around his neck, Anna smiled at him. 'Because you're a man, I suppose?'

'Well, obviously.' He grinned back. 'I'm glad you noticed.'

'I noticed a long time ago.' She hesitated and then, throwing caution to the winds, 'Roughly five years ago, in fact.'

His brows soared. 'Really? We'd met? Before you came to value the scent bottles?'

'No. But I watched through the window when you came to take Rebecca home for the school holidays. Most of the girls were collected by females who were probably their mothers' ladies maids. Rebecca was the only one who was collected by a good-looking young man who always seemed happy to see her.'

Deciding to think about what this might or might not mean later, he said, 'Who came for you?'

'My father. Always. If he'd had his way, I'd have been educated at home but Mama decreed otherwise.' Unable to resist the opportunity, she stroked his hair. 'I met your father once, years ago at Hawthorne's. But even though everyone at school knew Rebecca's father was a viscount, I don't recall anyone ever saying *which* viscount and therefore I didn't make the connection. Consequently, when I came to do the valuation, aside from not knowing your father had died, meeting you was the last thing I expected.'

'I ... see. Were you ever going to tell me any of this?'

She shook her head. 'I'm not sure why I'm telling you now, except ...' She stopped.

'Except what?'

'Except that things are ... different between us now.'

Daniel said nothing for a few moments, playing idly with her fingers. Then, 'Yes. They are. Changes for the better, do you think?'

'Very much so.'

'Good. That's what I think, too.' His thumb made lazy circles on her palm. 'Much though I wish both Grimshaw and Harvill to the devil, there's no denying that they've played a part in forging a relationship between us that I never expected to have.' He grinned wryly. 'As they say, it's an ill wind that blows nobody any good. But now they're nothing but nuisances that I want out of our lives – sooner rather than later.' He sighed. 'And now, pleasant though it is sitting here with you, I'd better have a word with Joe and find out if Flynn has any additional news for me. So give me a kiss and send me on my way. I'll see you later.'

Since nothing either Flynn or Joseph had to say was in any way conclusive, Daniel didn't feel any better informed after he'd spoken to them than he had before. Deciding that safe was better than sorry, he repeated his earlier orders and reconciled himself to living on a knife-edge for the next few days. Then he went back upstairs to find comfort with his wife.

CHAPTER TWENTY-FIVE

On Saturday, a note from Mr Longhope informed Lord Reculver that he had furnished Grimshaw's man-of-law with his lordship's own affidavit some days ago and had no excuse for continuing to withhold that of Mr William Grimshaw. He had warned William of this and advised him to remove to the lodgings in West Street immediately to spare himself and his mother the ensuing unpleasantness.

Regarding the case, the difficulty, as I am sure your lordship will appreciate, is achieving the correct balance between appearing intent on prosecution without actually doing it, he wrote. *However, I am confident that the combination of both affidavits will be sufficient to have the desired effect.*

'Let us hope he is right about that,' said Anna when Ruth was finally satisfied with her hair and left the room.

It was the evening of the dowager's long-awaited dinner party so more than usual effort was required. Anna had chosen to wear her wedding gown for the first time since the day itself. Daniel was unaccustomedly elegant in a suit of bronze brocade which she had never seen before and which complemented the russet tones of his hair. As sometimes happened, he looked so handsome he stopped her breath for a moment.

She said, 'You are very fine this evening. A new suit?'

'No. Merely one I haven't worn since I was last in London. And unless I'm mistaken, *you* haven't had a new gown since that one – which is the one you wore on our wedding day. Am I right?'

'Yes. But that makes it *virtually* new. And none of your mama's guests have ever seen it, have they?' she asked reasonably. 'But if it makes you feel better, I'll buy new clothes when we go to London in the spring for Rebecca's come-out. Until then, I shan't need them.' She twitched the rose silk into the proper folds. 'Shall we go down?'

'In a little while. First, I'd like to rectify an omission.'

'Oh?'

'Yes. Something that's three months overdue.' He took a small leather box from his pocket and handed it to her. 'For you. Open it.'

Startled and a little uncertain, Anna did so. Inside the box, a ring set with an oval-cut sapphire flanked by two small diamonds winked up at her. The breath left her and she looked up at him, not sure what best to say. He'd never given her a gift before. Finally, she managed, 'It's beautiful, Daniel – truly beautiful. Thank you. But I don't know what I've done to deserve it.'

'It's a betrothal ring. And you've *deserved* it – if, indeed, that's the right term – since the day you accepted my hand in marriage.' Smiling at her, he took the ring from the box. 'Give me your hand so we can find out if it fits.' And when she did so, he slid the sapphire next to her wedding band. 'Ah. It does. That's a relief.'

Swallowing the tears that threatened, Anna looked at it, turning her hand this way and that so the stone caught the light. Then, she threw her arms about his neck and whispered, 'Thank you. It – it's a lovely surprise. But you didn't need to do it, you know.'

'Yes, I did.'

Daniel held her so she couldn't see his face just in case there was anything there he'd prefer to stay hidden.

When he'd first realised that he had never given her *anything*, however small, he'd known a betrothal ring was the very least he owed her. Then he'd recognised the problem with that. Nothing he gave her would truly come from him if it was paid for with her money. And whatever little he'd had before their marriage was now completely swallowed up in the funds she'd transferred to him.

The answer, of course, was to sell something. But it had to be something he truly owned – and preferably something Anna would never miss. There wasn't much choice. In fact, so far as he could see, there was only one. The gold pocket-watch his father had given him on his twenty-first birthday. Having a much less grand watch he'd bought whilst at Oxford, he rarely wore the gold one; so in all likelihood, the only time Anna had ever seen it was on their wedding day.

Aside from the embarrassment of selling it to Gloucester's one good jeweller in order to buy the sapphire ring, he hadn't minded its loss as much as he'd thought he might. And now, with her arms around him and his about her, he didn't regret it at all. The way she was clinging to him made him wonder if she was shedding a tear of two and the possibility twisted something inside his chest. It was just a ring. Compared to what she had given him and his mother and would be giving Rebecca come the spring, it was *nothing*. And yet she ...

Shutting down that train of thought, he cleared his throat and said awkwardly, 'It's not very much. But I'm glad you like it. And now I should probably let you go before your gown is completely crushed.'

She sniffed, stepped back from him and turned swiftly to check her face in the mirror. In something almost but not quite her usual tone, she said, 'I think it was probably me holding on to you – but we won't argue. Indeed, we'd better go down before guests start arriving and your mother sends someone to fetch us.'

Nodding, he offered his arm and, as they left the room, said, 'I forgot to ask. Who has the dubious pleasure of sitting by Reggie Yates – he of the wandering hands?'

'He has Mrs Ashworth on one side and me on the other.'

'Well, being seventy if she's a day, Mrs Ashworth should be safe enough. But if his hands stray to you, I want to know about it.'

Anna gave a gurgle of laughter.

'You'll know – and so will he.'

'Ah. That sounds interesting. More so than the rest of the evening promises to be. But at least Mama has grasped the nettle and is entertaining again ... so I suppose we have to start somewhere.'

In fact, the evening was surprisingly pleasant. The guests were all acquainted with each other and happy to gossip, first over sherry in the drawing-room and then over a more than usually elaborate but well-chosen dinner.

At some point during the main course of saddle of lamb, Mr Yates laid his hand on Lady Reculver's thigh. Smiling sweetly at him, she stabbed it with her fork. He yelped and recoiled in a hurry. Looking enquiringly up from his conversation with Lady Holden, reading the situation at a glance and stifling a laugh, Lord Reculver said mildly, 'What is it, Reggie? Been stung by something?'

'Y-Yes,' he managed, grasping the life-line. 'Bee. Must have been.'

'Or perhaps a wasp,' suggested Anna solicitously, aware that Rebecca was trying to turn a giggle into a cough. 'Although one doesn't usually get either of those in October. How very strange.'

'Yes,' mumbled Mr Yates again, dabbing surreptitiously at his injured hand with a napkin. 'Very.'

Later, while the gentlemen were enjoying their port, the dowager cornered Anna and whispered, 'What was that all about? Bees and wasps, indeed!'

'A mere misunderstanding,' replied Anna calmly. 'Nothing that need worry you.'

And later still, when the gentlemen rejoined the ladies and Rebecca had been persuaded to indulge the company with a little music and was playing Bach's *Italian Concerto* with more enthusiasm than accuracy, Daniel asked the same question, albeit more directly. 'What did you do?'

'Stabbed him with my fork.'

'Ah.' He smothered a laugh. 'How fortunate that he was sitting on your left rather than your right.'

'Wasn't it?' She smiled up at him. 'But the evening is going well. I think your mother is enjoying herself and that is all that really matters.'

Vaguely, Daniel supposed that it was. But it was Anna he found himself watching throughout the evening. Although still a little reserved, she was more relaxed in company than she'd been a few months ago. The art of making social small talk continued to elude her but she hid it by listening, smiling and not actually saying much at all. This worked well, thought Daniel cynically, because most people would rather talk than listen. And she *looked* good. When he'd first met her, he recalled thinking her nondescript in the extreme; but she wasn't, was she? Not beautiful, perhaps … but neither ordinary nor mediocre. The warm, brown hair was as soft and shiny as silk. Her eyes were expressive and changed from blue to grey or grey to blue depending on her mood or the circumstance. As for her body, it had been designed to fit perfectly against his; and the pearly smoothness of her skin enchanted him.

It was when his thoughts arrived at the point of wondering how soon their guests would go home and leave him free to take his wife to bed that he realised he'd better call a halt to them before they got him in trouble. Summoning a smile, he sauntered over to Mr Yates and said sympathetically, 'How's the hand, Reggie?'

'Fine. That is ... a little sore. But fine, thank you.'

'Are you sure? I notice you haven't been using it since the ... incident. Someone ought to look at it, for you. Shall I have my housekeeper find a salve?'

'No, no. Please don't trouble.'

'It's no trouble. These things can't be ignored, you know – or there's no saying *what* unpleasant complications may arise.' Still smiling, Daniel held the other man's eyes. 'And we wouldn't want that, would we?'

Mr Yates swallowed and said weakly, 'No. Not at all.'

'Excellent.' He glanced across the room. 'Ah, Mrs Ashworth and her nephew are preparing to leave. Excuse me, will you?'

* * *

As soon as they entered their bedchamber and just as Anna was about to ask what he'd said to Mr Yates, Daniel swung round, trapped her body between his and the door and swooped on her mouth. Minutes later and in between trailing kisses down her neck, he said, 'I thought the Holdens and the vicar were never going to leave. And I've been thinking of this for the last hour.'

'You have?' Anna took the opportunity to free his hair from its ribbon and run her hands through it. 'And there I was thinking you were being the perfect host.'

'I can do two things at once.'

'I know.' And laughing a little as he drew her away from the door in order to begin undoing her laces whilst dipping his tongue into the hollow below her ear. 'You don't need to prove it.'

'Yes. Right now, I do. Damn. I can't move in this coat. Help me, will you?'

She eased the coat off his shoulders, drew it away and was about to lay it tidily over a chair but Daniel seized it, tossed it carelessly aside and returned to make short work of the laces of her gown.

When he'd reduced her to stays and shift, Anna batted his hands away, saying, 'My turn.' And set about unbuttoning his vest.

'I could do that quicker,' he grumbled.

'That, she retorted, 'is true of many things. But speed isn't necessarily of – '

'It is right now.'

'Oh. I ... see.'

'Good.' The vest followed the coat, then her stays and his shirt. In between feverish kisses and his hands seeming to be everywhere at once, Anna fumbled with the buttons of his breeches. On something resembling a growl, he said, 'Much more of that, my lady, and we may not make it to the bed.'

'Oh! How – ?'

'Another time.'

He picked her up, tossed her on to the bed and, faster than she'd have believed possible had she not been watching – which, of course, she was – stripped off what was left of his clothes. For perhaps ten seconds, he stood there looking at her out of hot, hungry eyes ... then, lying down beside her, he took her in his arms and, with mouth, hands and body, proceeded to give them what they both wanted.

Later, as Anna was sliding into sleep, he lay propped on one elbow watching her and letting his mind drift whilst enjoying the satiny skin of her shoulder beneath his fingertips. Distantly, it occurred to him that there was nothing about Anna that he *didn't* enjoy; not even her obstinacy and their occasional arguments. But *this* ... when they came together physically ... this wasn't just sex. It was charged with emotions he'd never before experienced and which made his chest ache with something which, as yet, he was afraid to investigate.

* * *

The following day was one of clear skies, only a gentle breeze and some weak sunshine. Daniel, pursuing his campaign of gradually increasing their flock of sheep and hoping also to acquire an additional shepherd, rode into Gloucester to attend the monthly livestock auction. Knowing this would take the bulk of his day, Anna spent a pleasant hour at the school during the morning and took Rebecca with her to visit one or two of the tenant families after luncheon. The dowager waved them off saying she had letters to write and hoped to take a turn in the garden later if the weather remained pleasant.

It was Daniel who came home first. Whistling cheerfully, he turned Cicero's head into the driveway, his mind occupied with the successes of his day and wondering if Anna was back yet so he could tell her about them. It was pure chance that his eye caught the splash of crimson that was his mother's oldest and best-loved cloak glowing bright against the deep green of the rhododendrons. He smiled and raised his hand to wave. Then he realised she wasn't alone. A dark-clad man was with her. A man who, even at this distance, Daniel recognised.

In one lithe move, he was out of the saddle and, leaving Cicero to make his own way to the stables, took off across the turf at a run, aware that Grimshaw was holding Mother's wrist and talking fast. Somewhere at the back of Daniel's mind was confusion that her expression was one of disgust rather than alarm.

'Get your hands off her!' he yelled. And, reaching them, grabbed Grimshaw's shoulder and hurled him aside so violently that he stumbled.

'Mama ... has he hurt you?'

'He tried,' she replied, brushing off her arm where Grimshaw's hand had been as if removing some filth.

Too furious to ask what she meant, Daniel swung round in time to see Grimshaw regaining his balance and, instead of taking to his heels as any sane man would do, compounding his peril by opening his mouth to say, 'Her ladyship and I were just having a little chat. I expect you can guess –'

Daniel knocked him off his feet with one solid punch before he'd recognised either the intention or all the reasons he shouldn't do it. Sickeningly, he belatedly realised three things. He couldn't, with honour, knock seven bells out of a man twice his age; he certainly shouldn't do it in front of his mother; and Grimshaw's intrusion of his property could be used to his advantage if he kept his temper in check.

Watching Grimshaw get up, one hand cradling his jaw, he said through gritted teeth, 'Go inside, Mama. Ask Flynn to send one of the footmen here to me immediately and send another to tell the village constable that we have an intruder who I'll be holding until he can be placed under arrest.'

The dowager hesitated, 'Daniel, perhaps it might be better –'

'Go, Mama,' he repeated more gently. And, to Grimshaw as she walked away, 'Don't even *think* of running. You won't make it. You *will*, however, give me the excuse I want to hit you again.'

In somewhat muffled accents and still clutching his jaw, Grimshaw told Daniel what he already knew. 'That won't help you now. Neither will having me arrested.'

'Of course it will. A few days ago, you were inside my house –'

'Prove it.'

'I don't need to prove it – because here you are *again*. Repeated invasions of my property only strengthen my existing action for fraud and blackmail. And don't hurl empty threats of telling the world what you know. You can't do that without incriminating yourself still further.'

'I meant, it won't help with your mother. I told her. And that's your fault.'

Ignoring a pang of nausea, Daniel said, 'Told her what?'

'Not everything,' Grimshaw attempted a careless shrug. 'But enough. The last thing your father wanted, of course ... but, as I said, it's your own fault. I don't know how you got to my family but you shouldn't have bribed them to lie about me.'

'They haven't lied and they needed no bribing. They *offered*. The people you call your *family* are about as fond of you as I am. The game's up, Grimshaw. Face it. With their evidence as well as my own, you'll go to prison. And I hope they throw away the key.'

Casting off his pretence of careless confidence, Grimshaw spat, 'You're making a big mistake if you think I won't stand up in court and tell the world your father seduced my brother's wife and –'

'Your brother's *widow*,' cut in Daniel. 'And that isn't how *she* will tell it. So do your worst. All you'll achieve is to deepen the hole you are already in.'

'We'll see. There's a lot I can tell if I choose to. More than you know. But here come your footmen. Two of them. Your butler must think you wouldn't be able to manage with only one.'

'Wrong. My mother thought it might take more than one to stop me damaging you.' Still somehow keeping a grip on his temper, Daniel turned to the footmen. 'This person is our uninvited visitor of the other day. Take him to the stables and have Gregson lock him up somewhere. And check his pockets for the key he took from the dining-room door. Has Flynn sent word to the constable?'

'Yes, my lord. He did it right away.'

'Good.' And, to Grimshaw, 'This has been fun. I'll look forward to seeing you in court.'

And without waiting for an answer, he turned on his heel and walked away.

He was almost at the house when the phaeton bearing Anna and Rebecca turned on to the drive. He waited until she caught up with him and gave the reins to the groom but took his own hand to help her climb down, saying, 'This is good timing. Have you just got back?'

'A short while ago.'

'Who was that man I saw Jeffrey and Thomas taking to the stables?' Rebecca asked while he was helping her down. 'Our mystery trespasser?'

'It would seem so. Mama knows he's here. Tell her I'm having him detained until the constable arrives to arrest him.'

'Good,' she said, heading towards the house and already taking off her hat. 'It will be nice not to have to bother locking doors all the time.'

Anna watched her walk away and then, in a whisper to Daniel, '*Grimshaw?*'

'Yes. There's no time to talk now. I found him in the garden with Mother. He said he's told her so God knows what state she's in. I have to – to ....' He stopped.

'Yes. Do you want me to come with you?' You can say no if – '

He folded his hand around hers and realised that he was shaking – mostly, he supposed distantly, with residual temper.

'I need you with me. I'm not fit to handle it on my own. It's taken every bit of self-control in me not to beat that bloody man to a pulp.' He gave a tiny, derisive laugh. 'Benedict would have been proud of me.'

'*I'm* proud of you,' she said firmly. 'We don't have to go this second. Take a moment. Just breathe.'

He did so, then finally said, 'I don't know what to say to her and – and I'm scared I'll make a mess of it.'

'You won't. Of course, you won't. You managed not to thrash Grimshaw and you can manage this. But perhaps we should decide whether or not Rebecca ought to be told as well?'

He groaned. 'Do you think she should?'

'Yes. Better she hears it from you than from gossip. And, since we don't know what Grimshaw will do next, we can't be absolutely sure there won't be any.'

Daniel nodded, drew another long breath and said, 'True.'

'Also, you shouldn't have to go through it all more than once,' added Anna. 'So … when you're ready, let's go and get it over with.'

CHAPTER TWENTY-SIX

They entered the drawing-room as Rebecca was about to leave it, seemingly unaware that, behind her, her mother's face was a mask of anxiety.

'Don't go just yet,' said Anna, laying a light hand on the girl's arm. 'The four of us need to talk.'

'Daniel – *no!*' exclaimed the dowager. 'There's no need to bring Rebecca into this!'

'Unfortunately, there is,' he replied gently. 'Sit down, Becky. This may take a little while. Now, Mama ... let's start with you. What did he say to you?'

His mother shut her eyes and leaned her head back against the chair. There was a long, airless silence. But finally she said faintly, 'He introduced himself.'

'And then?' Daniel waited and when she showed no sign of continuing, 'I should explain that I know who he is. What did he tell you?'

The dowager opened her eyes and sighed. 'Nothing I didn't already know.'

This time it was Daniel and Anna's turn to be struck dumb. But finally Anna said cautiously, 'I'm sorry ... but I think we need to be very clear what that was. Unless you'd rather Daniel or I said what we *think* it was?'

'You think you can *guess?*' she demanded. 'You can't.'

'Try us,' said Daniel. And less gently this time, 'Mama. What did he say?'

Another pause and then, 'He told me about William.'

Her gaze travelling from face to face in complete bafflement, Rebecca said, 'Who is William?'

This time the dowager pressed her lips together and shook her head.

Again, Daniel waited, his eyes locked with Anna's. Then, in response to her barely visible nod of encouragement, he said, 'He is our half-brother, Becky.'

Their mother shot to her feet. 'You know? *How* do you know that?'

His attention still on his sister, Daniel said, 'Does that matter right now?'

Rebecca's expression was one of utter confusion.

'I don't understand. Our half-brother? He can't be. How – ? Oh.' Her hands crept to her mouth and, from behind them, she whispered, 'Father? Father had ... had ...?'

'Yes,' said her mother tonelessly, dropping back into her chair. And to Daniel, 'How long have you known?'

'About William? Not long. But I've known since June when Grimshaw wrote to me asking for money that there was *something*; and one look at William was sufficient to tell me what that something was.' He sent his sister a faint smile. 'He looks just like you, Becky.' Then, once more to his mother, 'But the real question isn't how long *I* have known. It's how come *you* do – and whether Father knew that you did.'

Seeing Rebecca's initial shock beginning to turn to pain, Anna moved to put an arm about her, saying softly, 'I know it hurts. But it was a long time ago.'

'That doesn't m-make it any better,' said Rebecca tearfully. 'How *could* he?'

'I don't know. But it doesn't mean your father loved you any less.'

Daniel was still waiting for his mother to answer him. 'Well, Mama?'

She swallowed. 'Your father told me.'

Anna could see Daniel fighting to swallow a curse or probably several of them. To give him a moment, she said, 'When did he tell you? And why?'

Wearily, the dowager said, 'He kept it from me for as long as he could but it – it *weighed* upon him. Finally, he couldn't bear it any longer and he told me he'd had a – a brief liaison with a widow and that it had resulted in a child.'

'When?' demanded Daniel. 'When was this?'

'I think William was almost a year old.'

Seconds ticked by in silence. Throughout them, Anna sat very still, her eyes fixed on Daniel and trying to communicate strength and support.

Finally, in a tone of dangerous calm, he said, 'You have known for roughly twenty-four years?' And when she nodded, 'In that case, why the *hell* did Father go on letting Grimshaw blackmail him to keep it from you?'

'Blackmail?' she echoed. 'No. It was never that. Gervase paid for William's care and education and so forth, as was only right but – '

'No. He paid Grimshaw thousands!' snapped Daniel, his temper rising. 'Enough to support a hundred illegitimate children. Year after year, he carried on paying Grimshaw until he was all but ruined and having to borrow money to do it. And all that time, you *knew* because he'd *told* you!' He paused to draw an unsteady breath. 'Was he *completely* insane?'

The dowager didn't answer this. But eventually she said simply, 'It was never me he wanted it kept from. At the time of his affair with Alice Grimshaw, I had been unwell and things had been ... difficult ... between us. He knew I would understand how it had happened and he knew I'd forgive him.' She stopped and then added, 'It was *you* he wanted it kept from, Daniel. You and Becky. He couldn't bear you to know he'd slipped from the pedestal all fathers want to occupy in their children's eyes. He didn't want you to know *ever*.'

Daniel gave a harsh laugh and shoved a hand through his hair.

'Let me get this straight. You are saying Father thought leaving me to inherit a financial nightmare and a blackmailer who wanted *me* to go on paying after he died was preferable to me knowing he'd broken his marriage vows and left Becky and me with a bastard brother? Seriously?' He laughed again. 'He *was* insane.'

'No.' His mother stood up. 'I understand that you are upset, Daniel – '

'*Upset?* Now there's a thundering euphemism!'

'— but I can't listen to any more of this now – and neither should Rebecca. We can talk again when you're calmer. Come, Becky.'

'I'll follow you in a little while, Mama,' said Rebecca, sounding steadier. 'First, there's something I want to ask Daniel.'

'Oh – if you must,' muttered the dowager. And walked out.

Deciding that Daniel's need was greater than Rebecca's, Anna crossed to sit at his side and took his hand in a firm clasp. She said prosaically, 'Well, that was unexpected. All those precautions of ours and not one of them needed. I wonder if Grimshaw is aware that your mother has known about William for almost his whole life?'

'I doubt it.' He drew another calming breath and then said, 'All right, Becky. What is it you wanted to know?'

'Have you met him? William?'

'Yes. And now you know about him, so can you if you wish. But that's up to you.'

'What is he like?'

'We only met once so I don't know him well ... but he's pleasant. And honest.' He hesitated, 'It's important to remember that he's not to blame for any of this. Neither, in truth, is his mother. They haven't had an easy time either, living with Grimshaw.'

Ignoring that, Rebecca said, 'Does he really look like me?'

'Right down to the widow's peak,' replied Daniel with something that was almost a genuine smile. 'You could almost be twins.'

She nodded, pleating and re-pleating a fold of her skirt. 'I was going to ask if people will find out and there will be talk. But if he and I are as alike as you say, there's bound to be, isn't there? If people who know me see him, they'll put two and two together just like you did.'

'That's possible,' he agreed, 'but unlikely. William lives in Cirencester and works in a lawyer's office so you don't exactly move in the same circles. Also, in the spring, you'll be going to London – and who knows where after that if you meet a gentleman you want to marry? I don't think you need worry too much.'

'But what about this man, Grimshaw? Are you *really* going to prosecute him for trespass?'

'Yes. Furthermore, I'm making him believe I'll prosecute him for blackmailing – '

'But if you do that, he could say *anything!*' burst out Rebecca. 'In court. In front of *everyone!*'

'He won't. There's nothing he can say that won't see him convicted of extortion and sent to prison for quite a long time. Trust me, Becky. Anna and I know what we're doing.'

'Don't forget,' added Anna, 'that Daniel wasn't joking when he said that, after your father died, Grimshaw tried to get money out of him instead. He demanded four thousand pounds he claimed your father had borrowed from him to pay a gambling debt. Daniel didn't believe him but couldn't be certain he was lying. It was that as much as anything that made marriage to me seem the only answer.'

'Marrying you is the only good thing to come out this whole mess,' growled Daniel, squeezing her fingers and unwittingly making her so happy she wanted to cry. Then, to his sister, 'Blackmailers don't give up unless they're forced to. Grimshaw proved that today when he came here to frighten and threaten Mama. If I don't stop him, there's no saying what else he'll try. Think about that, will you?'

'And while you do, go and see how your mother is,' Anna suggested in the nearest thing to her normal tone that she could manage. 'You're not the only one who has had a shock today. Daniel and I have, too – and so has she.' She smiled suddenly. 'But when you want to talk about this again, know that we are here and that we love you.'

Rebecca looked at her out of overbright eyes for a moment, before crossing swiftly to the door, saying, 'And I love both of you. I was being selfish. Sorry.' Then she was gone.

Sighing, Daniel let his head sink back against the sofa and, grateful that they were finally alone, slid an arm about Anna.

She said, 'You look exhausted.'

'A bit,' he admitted. 'I used the short time I had with Grimshaw in private to convince him that my original prosecution is not a pretence. I'm hoping that a few days locked up on a lesser charge may make him reconsider his position with regard to the greater one.'

'It should certainly make him hesitate,' she replied. And glancing at the clock, 'The constable ought to be here soon, oughtn't he?'

'I hope so. I'm not leaving the premises while Grimshaw is still here but I need to see Sir Philip Weaver.'

'Who is he?'

'The chief magistrate. I want him informed of the situation so there can be no slips.'

Anna nodded. 'It can wait until tomorrow, can't it? It's turned five o'clock now and will be starting to get dark in an hour or so.'

'True,' he agreed. 'Then, 'Was I too hard on Mother?'

'I don't believe so. She took the ground from beneath you. Anyone would have reacted as you did.' And, leaning her head against his shoulder, added, 'There really is no accounting for your father's behaviour, is there? What on earth can he have been *thinking?*'

'God knows. I certainly don't. He'd confessed to Mother. I was five years old and Rebecca hadn't even been born. Father could have told Grimshaw to go to hell. By the time I went to Eton, it would have been old news. So why he went on –'

He stopped in response to a tap at the door and called, 'Yes?'

Flynn entered, bowed and said, 'The constable has arrived, my lord. What are your instructions?'

Daniel stood up. 'I'll see him. Is he alone?'

'Yes, my lord.'

'Then send orders to Gregson to ready the gig and bring it to the front. He's to have someone tie the prisoner's hands if they haven't already done so, then drive both him and the constable back to the village and see the fellow safely bestowed.'

In the hall and looking supremely uncomfortable, the young constable twisted his hat in his hands.

Daniel said, 'Thank you for coming, Constable …?'

'Benson, my lord. The message said you've a trespasser. Is that right?'

'It is. His name is Harold Grimshaw and he has not only wandered my grounds on several occasions but also invaded my house. I want him charged and brought before Sir Philip.'

'Yes, my lord.'

'Good. We've held him here, pending your arrival. Since you're alone and so that the fellow has no opportunity to overpower you and run, my head groom will drive both of you back to the village. I'll speak to Sir Philip about this tomorrow and put him in possession of the full particulars. Any questions?'

'No, my lord. Thank you.'

'Excellent. Flynn … see the Constable on his way. And you can tell the staff to relax. Our unwelcome visitor won't be troubling us again.'

'That is very good news, my lord.'

'Yes. Isn't it?'

Back in the drawing-room, Anna said, 'Why are you taking precautions to stop Grimshaw escaping? Didn't you say it might be the best solution all round if he ran?'

'I did – and I still think that. But I don't want him to run *yet.*' His smile had a distinct edge to it. 'Not until I've finished frightening him. And ideally, not until running makes him a fugitive.'

Anna stared at him. 'You want him to *escape?*'

He nodded. 'I want him gone for good. So, yes, escape *is* the best solution since it would mean he won't dare show his face near here again.'

'I ... see. And are you by any chance looking for a way to arrange that?'

'I won't say the notion hasn't occasionally crossed my mind,' came his seemingly negligent reply. 'But mostly, I want Grimshaw's only thought to be getting as far away from me as he can. Because if he crosses my path again, the results may be ... unfortunate.'

* * *

On the following morning, Daniel avoided his mother and sister by breakfasting early. Afterwards, he wrote to Mr Longhope, apprising him of recent events and, deciding it was now safe to contact William directly, sent the same information to him. Then he visited Sir Philip Weaver and rode home well satisfied with the outcome of their meeting.

'He's appalled at the notion that any shady character can wander in and out of our hallowed halls at will and feels certain that the gentlemen who share the bench with him, namely Sir Horace Holden and Major Charlton, will feel the same,' he told Anna somewhat sardonically. 'All three are firm believers in we landholders sticking together – an attitude I'm less fond of, particularly when it's applied to poaching. But –'

'Why? What *is* their attitude to poaching?'

'It's illegal and gentlemen take a dim view of losing game they've reared for their own sport. Penalties for poaching range from three months in prison to hanging.'

'*Hanging?*'

'Yes. But few men go poaching for fun. They do it to feed their families and, in my opinion, penalties shouldn't be so harsh. However, on this occasion the gentlemanly attitude to property is to my advantage. Grimshaw can't claim to be innocent when he was actually *caught* here, so he's likely to spend a few weeks in Gloucester gaol. This may give his lawyer pause about fighting the blackmail charge.' He pulled her into a close embrace and said into her hair, 'God willing, it's almost over.'

She hugged him back. 'Let us hope so.'

He released her slowly and said, 'How are Mother and Rebecca this morning?'

'Less fraught than yesterday – as you would already know if you hadn't fled the house at some ungodly hour to escape them,' she replied with mock severity. 'But I took the precaution of giving them something more cheerful to think about.'

'What? Or would I be happier not knowing?'

'Perhaps – though I don't think so. I suggested holding a modest house-party in late November. Around the twenty-seventh, I thought.'

He groaned slightly. 'You want me to have a birthday party?'

'A *thirtieth* birthday party. Yes. But if it helps, think of it as a pre-Yuletide gathering before the weather is at its worst and people are elsewhere with relatives. Your particular friends could be invited to stay for a few days. I think they'd come. And you'd like to see them, wouldn't you?'

'You know the answer to that.'

'So may I start arranging it?'

'I can hardly say no, can I?' He drew her close and leaned his cheek against her hair. 'But it's time you stopped doing things for the family and me. You've done enough.'

She flushed. 'It's only money. That's all I have to – '

Without warning, Daniel swung her around to face her and, gripping her shoulders, said, '*Stop!* Money is *not* all you have to offer. Far from it. And I don't want to hear you say that ever again. Not *ever!* Do you hear me?'

Once more struggling for composure whilst hiding what his words did to her, she said, 'I think they probably heard you in the village tav—'

He shook her. 'I'm not joking, Anna.'

'No. I can see that. But really – '

'No buts.' He pulled her back into his arms. 'I'll have a birthday party and say 'thank you' if that will make you happy. Will it?'

'Yes. But only if it's what you want.'

'God grant me patience,' he growled. 'And what do *you* want?'

I want you to be happy. I want to see you relaxed and laughing, the way you used to be when you fetched Rebecca from school. And I'd like ... I'd like to think that I played a part in making that happen.

But she didn't say any of that. She merely smiled at him and said, 'Right now? The same thing you do. To see the back of Harold Grimshaw, once and for all.'

CHAPTER TWENTY-SEVEN

During the course of the next few days events moved on apace, mostly by letter.

A note from Sir Philip Weaver informed Daniel that Harold Grimshaw had been transferred to Gloucester gaol and his case would be heard five days' hence.

Upon learning that their client was now being charged with trespassing on Lord Reculver's house and grounds, Mr Grimshaw's lawyers informed Mr Longhope that they no longer felt able to represent him in the matter of criminal extortion and had advised him accordingly.

Mr Longhope told Daniel that, this being so, there was a strong possibility that, if the case were ever to be brought, it would go through uncontested. Daniel replied with instructions that, regardless of this, Grimshaw should be notified that the case against him for extortion would still proceed.

After much discussion and debate with the dowager, Anna sent out cards for Daniel's birthday party – first to those who would be house-guests and then to near neighbours for celebrations to be held on the day itself. Acceptances from Christian, Benedict, Anthony and even Gerald came back by return and others followed more slowly. Nobody refused.

William wrote congratulating Daniel on having victory within his grasp and said how much more pleasant the house was now that his 'uncle' was no longer in it. In a postscript, he added, *Although the measures you set in place for mother's protection and my own weren't called upon, I'm grateful to you for the thought. If possible, I would like to express my thanks in person. Perhaps we might meet – just the two of us – at some mutually convenient location? I know better than to come to your home.*

Showing this to Anna, Daniel said slowly, 'But why shouldn't he come here? If Mama and Rebecca don't want to see him, they don't have to. And you wouldn't mind, would you?'

'Of course not. But *just the two of us* is clear enough. He wants the opportunity to get to know you better.'

'I took that to mean he won't be bringing his mother.'

'As well it might. But if he comes here, every servant who sees him will know who he is.'

'Ah. And Rebecca will have a fit?'

'Very possibly.'

'Point taken. I'll suggest a tavern somewhere midway between us. But I'm going to tell him there's only one reason he can't come here – and explain what it is.'

* * *

The week flew by and the day of Grimshaw's hearing arrived. Although they tried to pretend otherwise, everyone at Reculver – from Anna down to the kitchen maid – was on edge. Daniel, of course, wasn't there, being required in court to give evidence.

The dowager said, 'When will we know?' or 'Why haven't we heard?' five times an hour. By two in the afternoon and gritting her teeth until they ached, Anna claimed there were important business matters requiring her attention and fled to her office where she had to stop herself locking the door.

Returning at a little after four, Daniel grinned at Flynn and said cheerfully, 'You haven't seen me. My wife hiding in her office, is she?'

Flynn agreed that she was. Daniel strode through the library to Anna's room, shut the door behind him and locked it. Then, opening his arms to her, he said, 'It's done. He was found guilty and is currently beginning a six week sentence in Gloucester gaol.'

She flung herself on him, laughing with relief. His arms closed about her and, lifting her off her feet, he spun round saying, 'We're finally *free*. I can scarcely believe it.'

'Neither can I,' she whispered, hugging him. 'We should celebrate.'

'My thoughts exactly.' He kissed her with undisguised intent, then stepped back to strip off his coat.

Anna also stepped back, still laughing but with a note of suspicion.

'What are you doing?'

'What does it look like?'

He reached for her again only to be foiled when she stepped nimbly away saying as severely as she was able, 'Is this *always* your first thought?'

'No. Often perhaps. But not always. Come here.'

Shaking her head, she protested, 'Daniel, *we can't.*'

'Why not? You're here; I'm here; the door is locked; there's a sofa. And I can be very adaptable. Let me prove it.'

'No.' She batted his hands away. 'Prove it later, by all means. But your mother and sister are somewhere nearby *fretting* and –'

'They won't know I'm back. I told Flynn he hadn't seen me.'

'And any minute now one or other of them will knock at my door, lift the latch and wonder why they can't get in.' And seeing that he had started undoing the buttons of his vest, 'Will you *stop* taking your clothes off? We can't make love *now!*'

The sense of what she was saying had made its impression some minutes ago but Daniel hadn't been able to resist teasing her. Now, his hands stilled and he muttered sulkily, 'You're no fun.'

'None at all,' agreed Anna calmly as she set about refastening his buttons. 'But you've known that all along. And at times, it's just as well – since you are often completely atrocious.'

He laughed, dropped a kiss on her hair and picked up his coat.

'That's fair, I suppose. Perhaps we'd better go and break the good news. Flynn will do his best to cover my tracks but I'm not sure how long he'll manage it. And don't tell me I shouldn't have asked him. I know that. But I just wanted a few minutes alone with you first.'

* * *

Discovering the butler hovering outside the library door, Daniel said, 'I am now officially home, Flynn. Are the ladies in the drawing-room?'

'Yes, my lord. May I ask if all went well today?'

'It couldn't have gone better. In fact, it's cause to bring out the champagne …and please also see that ale is served below stairs for the staff, many of whom have been put to some extra trouble recently.'

'Thank you, my lord. I'm sure that will be greatly appreciated.'

Inside the drawing-room, the dowager held a piece of embroidery she wasn't working on while Rebecca stared through the window into the garden. Both turned when the door opened and, as one, said, 'Well?'

Daniel grinned and, in as few words as possible, told them.

'Thank heavens!' said his mother. 'So that wretched man will go to prison?'

'He's already there. And I have every hope that the six weeks for trespass will make him eager not to risk a longer sentence for blackmail.'

'He didn't say anything about Papa or William?' asked Rebecca anxiously.

'Not a word,' Daniel assured her. 'We have won the war ... and Flynn is on his way with champagne so we can celebrate the peace.'

A little later, when a toast to the successful vanquishing of Harold Grimshaw had been made and drunk – and more to test the reactions of the other ladies than anything else – Anna said, 'This will also be welcome news to William and his mother – not least because it has been achieved with less unpleasantness for them than we thought might be the case.'

'True,' nodded Daniel. 'I've already told Longhope to continue regarding them as clients for the time being. And I asked him if it's possible to replace Grimshaw's name with William's on the deeds to their house, as would have been Father's wish. He seems to think making it look as though William has *bought* the house may do the trick – even without Grimshaw's signature or consent.' He shrugged and added wryly, 'That was when I said I'd rather not hear any more on the grounds that it might incriminate me.'

'Would it?' asked his mother.

'Only if my name appeared in writing anywhere.' A sudden smile. 'I am learning that Longhope is rather better at what he does than I had previously thought.'

'Excellent,' murmured Anna.

'Yes. I knew you'd like that.' And to his mother and sister, 'As for William ... he has written asking if he and I can meet – immediately adding that he knows he can't come here. I have replied telling him that he would be welcome to do so but, in view of the family resemblance, he can only do it with the aid of a wig, false nose and glasses.'

Anna laughed. 'You didn't *really* say that, did you?'

'Yes. Why not? But on the assumption he'd rather not come in disguise, I've suggested the Feathers at Winstone instead.' And seeing both his mother and sister open their mouths to speak, he added pleasantly, 'I'm *telling* you this, not raising it for discussion. It is William's testimony as much as mine which would put Grimshaw behind bars for extortion if I were to let this go to court. That is more than adequate recompense for anything I can do for him.' He stood up, smiling blandly. 'More champagne anyone? And who is going to tell me exactly what is being planned for this birthday party of mine?'

* * *

Daily life having regained a normality it hadn't had for a while, Anna and the dowager were able to concentrate on the refurbishment of the bedchambers in the guest wing prior to Daniel's birthday. There were six of these, all well proportioned and each having a small dressing-room. Three were allocated to Lord Benedict, Baron Wendover and Mr Sandhurst and two others to Lord and Lady Hazelmere who would have their baby son with them. Anna suggested leaving the sixth vacant in case of unforeseen circumstances. Then, with five weeks at their disposal, new hangings were ordered and a small army of men armed with paintbrushes swung into immediate action.

'Is this really necessary?' Daniel asked Anna. 'With the exception of Sophia, my friends have all stayed here before without finding their accommodation lacking.'

'And would again, I'm sure,' agreed Anna. 'But their visit is a splendid excuse to redecorate the bedchambers and I've no intention of wasting it. So leave us to it, please. And if you're short of something to do, make sure the stables are up to scratch.'

He shook his head and laughed. 'Yes, ma'am!'

* * *

The day on which he had arranged to meet William was cloudy but dry so he elected to ride to Winstone, rather than take the carriage. En route, he took the opportunity to call at one of the outlying farms and, upon receiving an affirmative answer to the enquiry he'd made a couple of weeks before, told Mr Roper to proceed. Then he continued on his way, whistling.

Arriving at the Feathers a little early, he asked for a private parlour and wine and told the landlord that he was expecting a guest and that they would order food in due course.

William was also early and entered the parlour looking faintly apprehensive. This changed when Daniel rose smiling, hand outstretched and said, 'Welcome. I'm glad you suggested this. We *ought* to know each other. And we've something to celebrate.'

'So it seems. Your note said he'd been sentenced to six weeks?'

'Starting immediately,' agreed Daniel, gesturing to a chair and turning away to pour wine. 'All being well, by the time those weeks are up, he'll take to the hills rather than risk receiving a longer sentence for blackmail.'

Accepting the glass he was offered, William raised it, saying, 'I'll drink to that.'

'As will I. How is your mother?'

'Happier, I think, than I've ever seen her. Our home is a different place these days. And speaking of home, did he *really* make his way inside yours?'

'Yes. And wanted me to know it.' Daniel told him about the figurines and the open terrace doors but added, 'I couldn't have proved that had not the stolen key been found on him. That and being caught in my garden rather sealed his fate.'

William laughed and then, growing serious again, 'But I ought to be asking how *your* mother is. I understand he was talking to her?'

'He was. Having, as I thought, a fair idea of what he'd have been telling her, I expected her to be distraught.'

'She wasn't?'

'No.' Daniel drained half his glass. 'As it turns out, she's known about you since you were a year old.'

'*What?* How?'

'Father told her.'

William's jaw went slack. He said weakly, 'You're not joking, are you?'

'No.'

'But ... but he went on paying. All that money, year after year. Why?'

'According to Mother, because he didn't want *me* to know. And if there's any sense in that, I can't see it. Can you?'

'No. None at all.' William fell silent for a few moments. 'Do you think he might have been ...'

'Mildly insane? The idea has crossed my mind. Something else I've wondered is what Grimshaw did with the money? He didn't live like a wealthy man. So where did it go?'

'Aside from the purchase of the house, down the drain – or it might as well have done,' replied William. 'I doubt we'll ever know how much his lordship paid him over the years, mostly a hundred here and a couple of hundred there, I'd guess ... but I've a shrewd idea of what became of it.'

'Go on.'

'Harold isn't a gamester but he *loves* speculation and somehow or other, he wormed his way into an investment group. Wealthy men he wanted to be his friends – which made it a case of keeping up with them. So he bought shares in things he heard them talking about – such as cargoes of this and that or the hind legs of a racehorse.' William shrugged. 'The others might have made money but I don't think Harold ever did. He may have been lucky from time to time but mostly he wasn't. Ships sank and horses went lame ... but that didn't stop him. He just moved on to the next scheme and the one after that.' He shrugged. 'And – and it was our Father's money that funded them all.'

Daniel cursed under his breath. Then, drawing a long breath, he said, 'All right. Enough of that, do you think?'

'Since it doesn't change anything, yes.'

Nodding, Daniel reached for the wine bottle and re-filled both glasses. 'Agreed. And if we're going to get to know each other, we should talk about ourselves instead. My younger days are exactly what you'd expect; Eton, then Oxford followed by years mostly spent in London.'

'No grand tour?' asked William.

'No. There was no money for it. But a couple of years ago I spent several months traipsing around Turkey searching for a lost friend.'

'Did you find him?'

'We did. But that's a tale for another day. What about you?'

William shrugged. 'The village school, followed by grammar school in Cheltenham. After that, I was articled at Fairburn and Grant. They've been good to me – given me time to study and take the examinations; and, as I told you, I was promoted to senior clerk a few months ago – something that I hadn't expected to happen for years yet.'

Daniel regarded him thoughtfully. 'Is there any chance of a future partnership?'

'Perhaps. But ... well, you probably know how that works.'

'You have to buy your way in? Yes.' He paused. 'I could help with that.'

'That's ... good of you. But I think I've taken enough help from you already – albeit indirectly.'

'Even so. However, there's no point in discussing – or arguing – about this further until the opportunity arises. Just let me know if and when it does. Upon which note,' he said rising and pulling the bell for the innkeeper, 'shall we order food?'

A little later over substantial portions of beef and onion pie, William said hesitantly, 'My mother asked if you would give her warmest regards and thanks to Lady Reculver for her kindness the day we all met.'

'Of course. Anna would wish me to return the same, I'm sure.'

'She ... forgive me if this sounds impertinent ... she seems a remarkable lady.'

'She is,' said Daniel. 'And it's not impertinent at all. I'm fortunate – and don't mind admitting it. May I ask if there is a young lady in your life?'

'No. I won't be contemplating marriage for some time yet. I could afford a wife but I'm not ready for the responsibility of children. And even if that wasn't true, I intend to enjoy my freedom for a few more years.'

'I felt that way at your age. But as an old married man of almost thirty, I'm finding that marriage has its compensations. Amongst other things, Anna keeps my mother and sister happily occupied elsewhere. Ah.' He stopped. 'I suppose you guessed that your likeness to Rebecca is the reason I can't invite you to the house? I saw it straight away, so I imagine my household staff would, too. Otherwise – '

'You don't need to explain. I understand.'

Daniel shook his head. 'Not entirely, you don't. If it wasn't for Becky, I wouldn't worry about potential gossip. But she's finally making her long-delayed debut in the spring and is afraid of anything happening to spoil it. In a sense, it's a pity because, when she's got used to the idea of having another brother, I suspect she'll want to meet you.'

'As I would her,' said William. 'It's odd knowing I have a half-sister who looks so much like me. A bit unnerving, actually. What if we were to come face to face in the street?'

'Possible but unlikely. However, we can probably resolve that, given time.' He stood up and stretched. 'Shall we share another bottle of wine?'

'Why not? This is a rare treat for me so I'm inclined to make the most of it.'

* * *

While Daniel was out, Flynn informed Anna that her presence was required in the kitchen. This was unusual but not completely unheard of, so she didn't bother to ask him what was amiss but merely laid down her pen and made her way downstairs. Inside the kitchen, everyone from Cook to the scullery maid were clustered, laughing and cooing, about someone – or something – she couldn't see. Then, belatedly recognising her presence, they fell silent and stepped back to reveal Mr Roper of Heath Farm ... and, in his arms, a squirming bundle of black and white fur.

Anna blinked. 'Mr Roper? I don't quite understand. What ...?'

The tubby little fellow beamed at her.

'His lordship earmarked him a month since but said to hold on to him till he was twelve weeks.' He held the puppy out, giving Anna no choice but to take him. 'He – his lordship, that is – must've been counting 'cause he came this morning, spot on to the day, and said it was all right to bring him to you now.'

Anna, her arms full of warm, wriggling puppy and her chin being licked by a raspy pink tongue, said stupidly, 'He's for me?'

'Yes, m'lady. His lordship said you'd never had a dog but you'd like one. So when I told him my Bess – that's my best sheepdog – was in pup, he said to let him know when the litter was born. Came right off to see them, he did, and he picked this'n.' He grinned at her. 'Lively little fellow, he is. Clever too, I reckon, for all he's funny looking. Still, as his lordship said, looks aren't everything.' He reached for his hat. 'Well, I'd best be off. Doubt you'll have any problems with the little 'un but if you do, you know where to find me.'

And, with an affable nod, he turned and left.

Anna looked down at her new pet. He was a singularly mismatched little animal, the fur of his left ear and around his right eye being white and the other sides, black. She felt laughter bubbling up, fairly sure that Daniel had deliberately chosen the most comical-looking one of the litter. And then, seconds later, tears were pricking at her eyes because he'd remembered an off-hand remark she'd once made and fulfilled a long-forgotten wish. She laid her face against the little animal's neck and blew into his fur. He gave a little yip and wriggled about until he could lick her face. Anna was already in love.

* * *

Daniel arrived home later than he had originally intended to learn that, for once, his wife was not to be found in her office.

'Ah. Roper came, did he?'

'He did, my lord.' Flynn relieved Daniel of his hat and gloves. 'I believe her ladyship and Miss Rebecca are playing with the dog in the drawing-room.'

'And my mother?'

'In her rooms, my lord. She is ... less enamoured of the new arrival.'

'No surprise there,' murmured Daniel.

He found Anna and Rebecca sitting on the drawing-room floor, entertaining the puppy by rolling a ball back and forth between. Shutting the door and leaning against it, he opened his mouth to speak but, before he could get a word out, Anna scrambled to her feet and hurled herself on his chest, saying, 'Thank you – oh, *thank* you! I love him!'

'Already?' managed Daniel, despite being semi-strangled.

'Already,' she agreed positively. 'And I promise he won't be a nuisance.'

He gave a snort of laughter. 'Don't. He's a puppy, so he will be most *definitely* be a nuisance from time to time. But he'll grow out of it.'

'Oh.' She released him and stepped back. 'You know about puppies?'

'Of course he does,' said Rebecca, getting up from the floor. 'Just because there haven't been any dogs here *recently* doesn't mean there never have been. There used always to be two or three of them ... hounds or spaniels, mostly. But the last one died a little while before Papa did. I've missed them.'

'So have I,' admitted Daniel, watching the pup plough an erratic course to his feet, sniff his boots and manage something resembling a bark. Dropping to one knee, he offered his hand. Another sniff, a lick and then an enthusiastic attempt to bite his fingers. 'Well, Anna? What are you going to call him? And *don't* tell me you haven't already decided.'

She sighed, smiled at him and scooped the puppy up into her arms, still a little emotionally overcome.

'Scamp,' she said. 'I'd like to call him Scamp.'

Daniel laughed. 'That sounds about right. Almost a prediction, in fact. Scamp, it is.'

* * *

It wasn't until later when they were alone that Anna had the opportunity to say shyly, 'I can't believe you remembered what I said about always wanting a dog but Mama refusing to have animals in the house. It was just a passing remark, made weeks ago.'

Daniel shrugged, as if it was of little consequence.

'Perhaps. But it reminded me that this house isn't the same without dogs in it and that you deserved to have one of your own before we acquire any others. However, I wanted it to be a *real* dog with some intelligence – not one of these pocket-sized things – so I had to wait until the right opportunity came up.' He gave one of Scamp's ears a gentle tug and let the pup gnaw on his fingers again. 'Roper's sheepdogs have always been excellent examples of their breed – and this little chap's sire and dam are no exception.' He paused and added tentatively, 'Do you really like him? You wouldn't rather have a lapdog? Because if so, I can – '

'No! Scamp's perfect and I wouldn't change him for anything,' said Anna, watching her new pet trot off to explore their private parlour. 'But you'll have to tell me how to look after him properly.'

'As yet, there are really only two things you need to know. Until he gets used to his teeth, chewing will be his favourite occupation. Give him things he's *allowed* to destroy and keep anything he isn't – such as your shoes, for example – out of his reach. And secondly, teach him two words. His name so he'll start to come when he's called; and 'No', so he learns what is acceptable behaviour and what isn't. That's it, really. Has Mrs Dawson hunted out the old dog baskets yet?'

Anna nodded. 'And old blankets. There's one in my office and another in the bed—'

'No,' said Daniel firmly before she could complete the word. 'He is *not* sleeping in your bedchamber – or mine, either.'

'But – '

'*No*, Anna. I draw a line at having him in bed with us – which is what would happen. In here, if you must. But not in the bedrooms. We'll start as we mean to go on, please.'

* * *

So they did. Anna settled Scamp into his cosy basket, gave him an old slipper for company and waited until he curled up and went to sleep. Then she crept off to her own bed, cuddled up to Daniel and, hearing no sounds from the parlour, fell asleep herself.

Peace reigned for perhaps an hour before pitiful little cries and a paw scratching at the bedchamber door woke her. She resisted as long as she could and then, since Daniel slept on, she slid out of bed, donned her chamber-robe and crept into the parlour where Scamp instantly leapt upon her in undisguised delight.

It was perhaps a further half-hour before the bedroom door opened on Daniel, wrapped in his banyan and carrying a lighted candle. Placing the candle on a table, he gazed wordlessly on the sight of his wife, huddled in a shawl and half-dozing on the sofa by the dying fire with Scamp curled up in her lap.

Daniel took in the tableau over folded arms. The dog sat up and looked back at him. Then, clearly deciding that it was *Just Him* and *Nothing To Worry About*, gave Anna's hand a proprietary lick and settled back to sleep.

A minute or so later, Anna also opened her eyes and said, 'Oh. Daniel.'

'Yes. Was I not clear about 'starting as we mean to go on'?' he asked quietly.

'Yes.' In the shadowy light, she couldn't tell if there was a hint of amusement in his face but suspected that there wasn't. 'But – '

'It included you sleeping in your bed and Scamp sleeping in his,' said Daniel, as if she hadn't spoken. 'It did *not* include him sleeping on your lap while you slept on the sofa. But now we've clarified that point, please put him back where he belongs and come to bed.'

'It's just for tonight. He's in a strange place without his brothers and sisters – '

'And you'll be saying the same tomorrow night and the next one if you give way now. Dogs are creatures of habit, Anna. And this,' he gestured towards Scamp, 'isn't one we want him to learn since, aside from anything else, he won't always be this size. Now ... please do as I asked so we can all get some sleep.'

And he walked back to the bedroom, telling himself that he was not at *all* envious of his wife's affection for a dog she'd known less than twenty-four hours. The idea was ludicrous. Of course it was.

CHAPTER TWENTY-EIGHT

For the next two nights, Anna was unable to resist getting out of bed to stop Scamp crying with soothing words and a cuddle before re-settling him in his basket. On the third one, Daniel kept her too busy to think of it; and on the fourth, there was blessed silence until a little after seven when Scamp decided everyone needed to get up.

Consequently, over an earlier than usual breakfast, Daniel read and re-read a somewhat lengthy letter, before looking across at Anna to say thoughtfully, 'The one thing we've done nothing about so far is bringing the stables up to strength.'

'You mean *you've* done nothing about,' she retorted. 'I distinctly recall saying that was your department.'

'I just hadn't got around to it yet.' He waved the letter at her. 'But now might be the time. Lord Atherton is a first-class horse-breeder and he writes that he has more than the usual crop of foals due. Consequently, since his stables are already stretched for space, he has a number of horses for sale.'

'Is he a friend of yours?'

'Not exactly. He's thirty years older than I am, so more of an acquaintance. But he says he recalls frequently seeing me coveting his bloodstock and wonders if I might be interested.'

'Which I gather you are.'

'Very much so. Rebecca's aged mare was put out to pasture months ago. Thanks to your mother's peculiar blind spot on the subject, you don't ride but have admitted that you'd like to learn. So ... two ladies' mounts ... and a pair to draw the curricle which has been languishing unused since February. The family travelling carriage is antiquated and should be replaced before we all travel to London – and a team will be needed to draw it. With luck, Atherton's stables may be able to supply most of those. What do you think?'

'That there's nothing on your shopping list for yourself.'

'Horses for the curricle,' he reminded her. 'For the rest, Cicero is still in his prime and I can only ride one horse at a time. Buying another would be an indulgence rather than a necessity.'

'Perhaps,' conceded Anna. 'But don't let that stop you.'

'We'll see. However, getting back to the point ... this strikes me as too good an opportunity to miss. But I doubt I'm the only fellow Atherton's written to so I want to act smartly. He's set a date four days from now for interested parties to inspect the animals available. I'd like to get there at least a day before that ... and he lives a little way out of Chipping Norton.'

'Where's that?' asked Anna.

'Oxfordshire. Somewhere between thirty and thirty-five miles, I think.' Daniel mentally computed the distance and then said, 'Just over a day to get there and the same to get back ... with probably a full day at Atherton's home while – assuming I'm buying – we haggle over terms. Three nights away if everything goes smoothly. Four if it doesn't.'

She nodded. 'The sooner you leave, the better, then.'

'You wouldn't mind?'

'No.' And with a wicked smile, 'Scamp will keep me company while you're gone.'

'I daresay,' growled Daniel. 'But I'd better not come home to discover he's taken up residence in our bed – or the fur will most definitely fly.'

* * *

Daniel set off two hours later and by the following afternoon, he was being shown around Lord Atherton's stables. Not remotely surprised by his early arrival, his lordship had laughed and said, 'Thought you'd be one of the first, Shelbourne – beg pardon, it's Reculver now, ain't it? Come hoping I might be parting with Jupiter, have you?'

'I didn't dare be that optimistic, sir,' grinned Daniel ruefully. 'But ... are you?'

'Not a chance, m'boy – not a chance. On the other hand, Orion's out of the same bloodline. He might take your fancy. Come and meet him.'

'With pleasure ... although, much as I might like to, I wasn't planning to acquire a hunter.'

'What, then?' asked Atherton, leading the way into the first of three large stable-blocks.

'Ladies' mounts for my wife and sister – sedate rather than spirited. A carriage team. And perhaps a pair suitable for my curricle.'

'Hmmph. Well, I've a couple of mares that might suit the ladies and a very nice pair of greys I'd keep if I had the room. But you'd be better off looking for your team at auction rather than here where their pedigree will cost you more than you ought to be paying for what you need.' He gave a jovial laugh and slapped Daniel on the back. 'How's that for honest trading? Now. Here's Orion. What do you think?'

Orion, a magnificent black, looked down his aristocratic nose and snorted derisively. 'Oh lord,' breathed Daniel, reaching out to pat the glossy, sable neck. 'You weren't exaggerating, were you, sir? He's superb.'

'Like to try him out, would you?'

'I shouldn't. But after I've seen the mares and the pair... may I?'

Atherton laughed again. 'Wouldn't have offered otherwise, young man. But be prepared to be tempted.'

'I'm tempted now,' admitted Daniel weakly. 'So let's move on before I ask what you want for him.'

* * *

With Daniel gone, Anna divided her time between overseeing progress in the guest bedchambers, her weekly visit to the school and starting work on establishing a regular routine of mealtimes, walking, napping and play for Scamp. She had three days, possibly four, in which to astonish her husband with the puppy's progress upon his return.

This worthy plan fell apart on the second morning of Daniel's absence when she received a letter from Nathaniel Lowe which he had taken the unusual step of sending by express courier.

Information has finally come to light regarding the incident with the kiln. Although I can and will take the necessary steps on your behalf, I suspect that – when you are aware of the circumstances – you will prefer to take a hand in the matter yourself.

It turns out that our saboteur was Samuel Price who, as you'll recall, was one of the kiln maintenance team before ill-health forced his retirement. The reasons for his actions and the means by which he was able to carry them out are better left until we can speak in person. However, one thing you should know immediately. There is a possibility that Harvill was behind the entire incident.

The letter fell from Anna's fingers and, for a moment or two, she stared into space feeling oddly chilly. Harvill. Again. And Daniel away for at least one more night, perhaps two. He would want her to wait ... but she couldn't. Rising, she swung into action.

She scribbled a note to Daniel and left it on his desk along with Nathaniel's letter. She told Ruth to pack for, at most, two nights and prepare to travel with her; she informed the dowager that her presence was required at Hawthorne's and she asked Rebecca to look after Scamp. Finally, when her groom brought the phaeton to the door, she gave the puppy one last cuddle and walked out of the house.

* * *

Arriving in Worcester only a little after three in the afternoon, Anna went directly to the manufactory and trod upstairs to Mr Lowe's office without even glancing into the exhibition rooms.

The manager rose from behind his desk the instant he saw her, saying, 'My lady! I hadn't expected to see you before tomorrow at the earliest.'

'If there's any chance at all that Harvill was behind the kiln incident, this is too important to wait even another day,' said Anna crisply, sitting down in a swish of skirts. 'Samuel Price, your letter said. Doesn't his son still work here?'

'Yes. But as far as I'm aware, he has no idea what his father has been up to.'

'So how did you find out?'

'Price was given a thorough mauling in the street and stabbed in the chest. For several weeks, it was touch and go during which he convinced himself he was going to die – at which point he told his daughter what he'd done to the kiln rather than go to meet his maker with it on his conscience. As it turned out, he recovered but by the time he realised he was out of danger, his daughter had already brought the tale to me.' He paused. 'But perhaps I should start at the beginning?'

'Please do.'

'After his retirement, Price missed his old workmates here so he used to drop in to see them on a regular basis. Everyone was so accustomed to seeing him around that nobody thought anything of it. And there might not have *been* anything to it had he not also begun gambling with a shady crowd of fellows down on the riverfront – the sort who make a living doing other people's dirty work – and got into debt.'

'The *idiot*,' muttered Anna. 'Go on.'

'When he couldn't pay, his new friends roughed him up and threatened worse. Then one of them told him there was a man who'd been looking for someone to do a job at Hawthorne's; a job which apparently needed inside knowledge of the manufactory. So stuck between the devil and the deep, Price agreed to do it. As he'd done numerous times before, he wandered in for a chat with Paddy on firing-up day. Whilst waiting for the brick-layers to come in and build the clammin, Paddy went out to answer a call of nature and Price used the time to disable the pulley to the crown damper. It was as easy as that – and Paddy had no reason to suspect anything until much later when he couldn't make the damper work.'

'But why didn't he tell you about Price's visit when you questioned him?'

'He said he forgot about it in all the panic and, even if he hadn't, he'd never have supposed Price might be responsible.' Mr Lowe sighed. 'However, we know now ... some of it, at any rate. It's likely that it was Harvill who wanted a kiln put out of action and paid Price to do it but we've no proof of that because Price never met him. Orders were relayed to him through his criminal friends. But once again it's likely that the second, more serious attack was ordered by Harvill to cover his tracks. My guess is that he meant Price to die ... and Price thought he was going to. Hence his desire to confess – an outcome Harvill couldn't have foreseen.'

For a long time, Anna was silent. Finally, she said wearily, 'What I don't understand is what on earth Price was thinking. Why didn't he come to *us* for help instead of letting himself get sucked into this unholy mess?'

'I think he was too ashamed, my lady. But you'll want to ask him that question – and others – yourself, I'm sure.'

'I will indeed.' Another silence. Then, 'Have there been any further signs of interference by Harvill?'

'Not so far,' replied the manager. 'But that isn't to say that there won't be.'

'Quite.' Anna glanced at the clock. 'I'll go and see Price now, I think. Please send a message to my mother informing her that I'll be with her in the next hour or two and will be staying overnight.'

* * *

In Oxfordshire, Daniel had seen and thoroughly examined the horses Atherton had suggested might suit his needs and expressed serious interest. Atherton waved aside any discussion of price, saying they could get to that later over dinner and a bottle or two and instead led him back to the first stable outside which the head groom had Orion already saddled and waiting.

Although he was by no means blind to his lordship's tactics, Daniel couldn't resist the lure he was being offered. Telling himself that, no matter how much he might want to, he didn't have to buy the horse merely because he'd taken up the offer of a ride. He also reminded himself not to partake too freely of that 'bottle or two' until he and Lord Atherton had reached an agreement. And, if an excuse for that was needed, he could truthfully say that he wanted to leave for home in the morning.

All of this, he soon discovered, was fine in theory but less so in practice. Once astride Orion, the only part of his good intentions to remain intact was concluding negotiations today so that he could set off back to Anna tomorrow.

Orion wasn't just powerful, swift and possessed of enormous stamina. He was also surprisingly nimble, good-tempered and intuitive. Consequently, by the time the two of them returned to the stable-yard, the only thing holding to his resolve was the unarguable fact that he'd be spending enough of Anna's money on horses they actually needed so buying one they didn't was an extravagance.

He reined in to find Atherton still there, chatting with his stable-master. Not even waiting for Daniel to dismount, he said, 'Knew you two would get on. Marriage made in heaven if ever I saw one.'

'Perhaps. But –'

'Never mind that. Come inside and take a glass with me and we'll open talks on the mares and the greys while they fill a bath for you. Anything you have to say about this fellow,' he patted Orion's neck, 'can wait until you've had a chance to think about it.'

This was a surprise. Daniel had expected Atherton to strike while the iron was hot, as it were and he was still in the grip of the inevitable euphoria of the ride. He dropped from the saddle, nodded and followed his lordship into the house.

There, over a glass of extremely good canary, Lord Atherton named figures for the mares and the pair of greys which, though high, were not unreasonably so. Then, once again telling Daniel to give it some thought before saying anything further, he had a footman show him to his room.

* * *

Anna, meanwhile, had a long, painful conversation with Samuel Price during which he confessed what he'd done, apologised over and over again with tears in his eyes and ended by breaking down completely when Anna said, 'I'm disappointed in you, Samuel. Instead of doing something which would damage Hawthorne's and which you knew to be wrong, did it never once occur to you that your best course was confiding in Mr Lowe? That we would have *helped* you?'

'I told him that, the silly old fool,' muttered his daughter. And a little later, whilst seeing Anna out, 'I'm sorry, my lady. I went to Mr Lowe as soon as I found out even though I knew it was too late.'

'I know you did, Lizzie, and it can't have been easy. But I'm grateful. At least I now understand how it happened – which is more useful than you can perhaps imagine.'

Once back at Hawthorne Lodge, she had to explain her impromptu visit to her mother. She kept it as brief as possible. Predictably, Mrs Hawthorne said huffily, 'Doubtless you'll find a reason for laying the blame for this at Mr Harvill's door?' And without waiting for a reply, 'Why isn't his lordship with you?'

'He was from home,' sighed Anna, 'and I regarded the matter as urgent.'

'Will *he?* Or will he just think you're being headstrong as usual?'

Anna knew perfectly well that Daniel would much prefer her to have waited until he was able to come with her but when she returned home none the worse for her brief excursion there wasn't really a great deal he could say about it.

She said, 'What Daniel thinks or doesn't think would surprise you, Mama. And now, please excuse me. I need to change.'

While she washed her hands and face and let Ruth help her into a fresh gown, she reflected on the fact that she probably ought to set off home immediately after breakfast tomorrow ... and that she *would* have done so had not tomorrow been Sunday. The one day of the week when Hawthorne's was empty but for the firemen tending the kilns. She'd have the rest of the manufactory to herself and could spend a couple of hours unpacking the Reculver collection and setting it out in the exhibition room. Two hours, she thought – three at the most – and she could still be home by early evening. After all, there was no guarantee that Daniel would be back himself by then.

Yes, she thought. *Why not? What harm can it do?*

* * *

After a modicum of bartering, more for form's sake than anything else, Daniel bought the pair of greys and the well-mannered mares for Anna and Rebecca but managed to refuse to purchase Orion. When he and Atherton had shaken hands on the deal, his lordship said, 'You've got will-power, Reculver – I'll give you that. But I think you'll regret turning Orion down. Chances like that don't come along very often.'

'I'm all too aware of that, sir,' agreed Daniel a shade ruefully. 'But since inheriting, I've learned a few hard financial lessons and promised myself I'd profit from them.'

'Well, I've got to respect you for that. Pity, though. Orion's a young man's horse. But I'll not part with him to just *anybody*. If the condition of the pair drawing your phaeton is any indication, you'd treat him with respect and give him a good home. Now, I won't try to persuade you against your better judgement ... but I'll knock five percent off the price and tell you something I don't reckon you've thought of yet.'

Daniel stared at him. 'Five percent?'

'Yes. Cutting my own throat, as the saying goes. Must be getting senile.'

'Hardly that, sir. But I wasn't ... I didn't refuse in order to force down the price –'

'I know that. If I didn't, I wouldn't be doing this. But I'd rather Orion went to you than any of the other young bloods I'm expecting to turn up here in the next day or two. And here's the thing you're missing. Have you forgotten I told you Orion came from the same bloodline as my Jupiter?'

'No. But –'

'And have you got any idea how many requests for Jupiter's stud services I've turned down over the years?' Atherton waited, watching Daniel's expression. 'Ah. Penny dropping is it?'

'I ... yes.' Daniel felt oddly dizzy. 'Do you *always* refuse?'

'Yes. Always have. But *you* don't have to. You can earn Orion's price back in stud fees. With the right mare, you could even breed from him yourself. Think about it. And in between, you've got a horse a good many men would kill for. So ... what do you say? Do we have a deal or not?'

Drawing a long, slow breath, Daniel held out his hand, saying, 'Yes. I believe we do. Thank you, sir. And I promise that Orion will have the very best care I can give him.'

'He'd better,' came the gruff reply. 'He'd better or you'll answer to me.'

* * *

Having made arrangements for the transportation of all five horses, Daniel took his leave of Lord Atherton immediately after breakfast. Impatient to be home, it was irritating that the distance required an overnight stop. On the way to Chipping Norton he'd broken his journey at Stow-on-the-Wold. On the return one, he planned to get as far as Coberley, a mere ten miles from home. Even without a crack of dawn start, he could be at Reculver by ten o'clock at the latest.

He amused himself on the drive by wondering how Anna had occupied herself in his absence and whether she had weakened to the extent of letting Scamp into their bed. He hoped not. He didn't want to fight that battle again. And after an absence of three nights, he was looking forward to sharing that bed with his wife.

Next day, he entered the house just as Scamp was racing across the hall with Rebecca in hot pursuit, yelling breathlessly, 'Scamp. *Scamp!* Come *here*, you mad animal!'

Ignoring Rebecca and perceiving the newcomer, the little dog skidded instead in Daniel's direction. Swooping on him and trying to prevent his face being enthusiastically licked, Daniel said laughingly, 'The last few days don't seem to have had much of a calming effect, do they?'

'He's so *quick*,' panted Rebecca. 'And unpredictable.'

'Make the most of it. Where's Anna?' he asked, heading for the stairs with the puppy.

'Not here.'

Daniel was aware of a pang of disappointment. Then, reminding himself that Anna couldn't have known when to expect him, he continued onwards, saying, 'Where, then?'

'At the manufactory.'

This stopped him with his foot on the first step. 'She's *where?*'

'She went the day before yesterday. Something urgent, she said. She left a note on your desk.' And, seeing her brother about to put the puppy down, '*Don't!* He can't climb the stairs yet but if he starts running around here again it will take me an age to – '

But Daniel wasn't listening. He set Scamp on his feet and took the stairs two at a time to the library. Anna's note was brief.

I'm going to Hawthorne's – Nathaniel's letter will explain why. I'll stay with Mama tonight and, barring the unforeseen, will make an early start home tomorrow. I hope your mission prospered.

He skimmed through Lowe's note and grudgingly accepted her reasons for going. But she *wasn't* back, was she? Moreover, if she'd waited a mere day, he'd have gone with her – which she knew perfectly well was what he would have wanted. He glanced at the clock. If she had made an early start, she might be back in the next hour or two. But if she hadn't … if something had delayed her … he wasn't going to sit twiddling his thumbs waiting. He could make the journey quicker on horseback and knew the route she'd take. He'd either meet her on the road or catch up with her at Hawthorne's.

Tossing down both notes, he pulled the bell for Flynn and, when he appeared, said crisply, 'Tell them to saddle Cicero. I'm going to Worcester.'

CHAPTER TWENTY-NINE

In order to avoid returning to her mother's house before driving home, Anna had Ruth with her as well as Blake, her groom, when she drew the phaeton to a halt in Hawthorne's yard. Handing each of them some coins, she bade them take the morning for themselves in Worcester.

'Be back here at one – no, make it two. I shan't want you before then.'

Taking out her keys, she let herself in and locked the door behind her. Then she went first to the office and spent an hour looking through the last quarter's accounts. Once finished there and taking a duster with her, she went back downstairs to stroll through the exhibition rooms, admiring the new cabinets as she went and imagining how it would all look once the various wares were in place.

The crates holding the Reculver Collection stood open but had not been unpacked. Each bottle was wrapped in soft cloth and protected from its fellows by a mixture of straw and torn up newspaper. Unlocking the lid of the large cabinet which stood in the centre of the second room, Anna began methodically unwrapping and dusting bottles before placing them in it.

As she ought to have known would be the case, she completely lost track of time, scarcely hearing the clock in Nathaniel's office when it struck noon. Her entire focus was on the gradually emerging collection and how spectacular it was going to look when every piece was placed to its best advantage. At some point, she thought she detected a faint whiff of smoke but assumed that, somewhere upstairs, a window had been left slightly open, allowing the smoke from the kilns to get in. She'd check on that before she left. Meanwhile, she carried on working, unveiling piece after lovely piece until the cabinet was a dazzling display of shape and colour.

No other pottery will have anything finer on exhibition than this, she thought with enormous satisfaction. *I dare them to try.*

The smell of smoke came again, stronger this time. Anna paused, frowning. Where *was* it coming from? Leaving what she was doing, she opened the door, stepped into the entrance hall and came to an abrupt stop. The smell was much stronger here; and it wasn't the familiar coal smell of the kiln ovens. Neither, she suddenly realised with an unpleasant jolt, coming from outside. It was coming from the other side of the door to the corridor off which lay all the work-rooms.

It was inside the building.

* * *

Roughly half-way to his destination, Daniel halted in Upton-on-Severn to rest and water Cicero. He hadn't met Anna driving in the opposite direction – hadn't, in fact, met much traffic at all, it being Sunday. It was coming up to midday. If he still hadn't met Anna by the time he reached Worcester, she was either staying for a further day because the matter of Samuel Price required it or something else had occurred to delay her departure.

Worry stirred and gnawed at him. Swearing under his breath, he realised he had what his mother would call A Feeling. He didn't like it.

* * *

Anna froze, pulse racing and mind working feverishly.

Aside from the coal for the kilns, the manufactory used numerous other flammable materials. Ingredients for glazes, oils and pigments for mixing paints, quantities of turpentine for cleaning brushes. Then there were the stacks of paper for use by the designers. Large quantities of all of these were stored in two locations, well away from each other, with smaller quantities close to where they were needed. And, in addition to this, the limited editions department had its own storeroom which housed stocks of everything.

Every possible precaution was taken to ensure that fire couldn't start by accident– of that Anna was sure. That this must have been set deliberately was a matter for later. *Now* was for finding it. Unless the fire-raiser had brought more than a tinder-box with him, there were three likely locations. However, finding out which meant opening the locked door at the far end of the hall and she had a feeling doing so might make everything worse.

She needed help; more help than the pair of firemen tending the ovens. She also needed to stop dithering. She flew to unlock the hall door but left it shut, then she raced outside to the huge bell that was rung to announce the end of the working day. It could be heard a quarter of a mile away. Surely hearing it on a Sunday ought to bring a few folk running to find out why? She heaved on the rope with all her might, over and over again, creating an irregular, alarmed clanging. Then, praying it was enough, she fled along the outside of the building until a glimpse through the windows told her where the fire was.

Fires. There were two of them.

One in the paint store on the ground floor, the other upstairs, next door to the limited edition studio. Words she'd once or twice heard spoken but never previously uttered herself escaped her lips. Harvill or some hireling of his was in there, doing his best to destroy everything Father had built ... everything she was sworn to protect ... and the livelihoods of over ninety people.

Let him still be here, doing this himself, thought Anna, soaking her handkerchief in a water-butt and snatching up a long-handled shovel, *because I'm going to kill him.*

She reached the rear door through which she assumed Harvill must have entered and, as she expected, found it unlocked. Thankfully, the kiln firemen were racing towards her from the other direction. Wasting no time, Anna said, 'Saunders – come with me; Baxter – see if help has arrived and start *doing* something.'

Baxter nodded and dashed off. Saunders, horrified on his own account as well as Anna's, said, 'You can't go in there, my lady.'

'Yes. I can.' And pressing the wet linen over her nose and mouth, she wrenched open the door and went through it, not waiting to see if he followed.

* * *

Minutes after Anna left the front of the building, a little group of people from nearby cottages – some of them Hawthorne's workers – began gathering in the yard and were followed soon after by Anna's phaeton.

Drawing the horses to a halt, Blake called, 'What's going on?'

'Dunno,' replied one man, scratching his head. 'Somebody rung the bell so –'

He broke off as an upper floor window shattered allowing smoke to billow out.

'Oh bloody hell,' breathed Blake. And without a second's hesitation, yelled, '*Fire!* Get buckets and water – *now!* And more help. Where's her ladyship? She can't be stupid enough to stay in there, can she?'

Ruth scrambled down from the phaeton wailing, 'She can. It's *exactly* what she'd do – start trying to put it out instead of getting herself to safety. We've got to *find* her.'

'How?' he snapped. 'I don't know the lay-out inside and she could be anywhere!'

'There's two ways in,' one of the neighbours told him as another set the bell clanging again. 'This'n,' pointing to the front door, 'and another round the back. We'll split up – some of us'll get buckets and start filling 'em, the rest can find extra hands. Can't do much without.'

The men dispersed, leaving Ruth wringing her hands amidst a small huddle of women. She said, 'If something happens to my lady, how am I going to tell her mother – never mind his lordship?'

* * *

Inside, her eyes already streaming, Anna heard the upstairs window break and gambled on the likelihood that Harvill – *And please, please let it be Harvill* – had lit the upper fire before setting the lower one and risk being caught in his own trap. Both hands being occupied, she jabbed Saunders with her elbow, then pointed along the corridor towards the paint store and the other rooms beyond it. Trying to shield his mouth and nose with his sleeve, he nodded miserably and followed her.

Upstairs, the fire could be heard gathering pace. Smoke was billowing throughout the building and, against the crackling of flames, Anna could hear bottles exploding inside the paint store where the blaze had a firm hold and was sending out unpleasant fumes. Pointing again, this time to the large, stoneware bottles of water stacked against the far wall, Anna indicated that she wanted Saunders to do what he could. Then, leaving him to it and starting to cough, she lurched onwards. Four rooms ahead of her, something else was burning. But before she got that far, the next open door revealed Harvill, busily piling stacks of paper in the centre of the floor.

'Don't you *dare!*' she choked. And took a wild swing at him with the shovel.

It whacked him squarely between the shoulder-blades, sending him to his knees with a grunt. Standing over him ready to hit him again, Anna managed, between spasms of coughing, to say, 'What is the *matter* with you? Trying to burn the place down because I won't sell? Are you *insane?*'

Harvill didn't reply, choosing instead to put all his efforts into standing up.

Anna was having none of that. She whacked him again. He dropped forward, leaning on his hands and said jerkily, 'Don't want your damned factory. Never did.'

* * *

By the time Daniel arrived, the upstairs fire had spread to the adjacent room and black smoke was pouring out through the broken window. Below in the yard, a brawny fellow was filling bucket after bucket from the pump while a chain of women passed them hand to hand to the men carrying them into the building. The entire scene was like something out of a nightmare and his skin turned icy cold.

Seeing Ruth standing nearby, watching, he said, 'Where's my wife?'

'She ... she ...' stammered the maid. And, unable to frame the words, pointed.

Daniel's breath promptly evaporated. A voice in his head said, *No. No, no, no. This isn't happening.* He croaked, 'Tell me she's not in there.' But the girl's face told him that she was. He spun round and raced to the door. He was vaguely aware that both the chain of women and the men carrying the water inside were operating a system; one bucket went upstairs, the next one down. Further along the building, another window exploded making everyone either duck or jump.

Daniel did neither. He just forced his way through the door, shouting, 'Where is she? Do any of you know? *Where is she?*'

'Not sure, m'lord,' said someone. 'We think she's maybe down here somewhere but there's men checking upstairs as well. Trouble is, there's more'n one fire and they're spreading because a lot of the rooms open on to each other.'

Daniel knew that. He remembered it from the tour Anna had given him.

Dread paralysed his lungs and froze his brain.

The only thought he had was, *Where are you? Where? I can't lose you. Not like this. Not at all. I couldn't bear it.*

And racing down the corridor, where small fires seemed to be breaking out in rooms on either side of him, he bellowed her name over and over again.

* * *

Anna didn't hear him. Eyes streaming, throat raw and still threatening Harvill with the shovel, she managed to say, 'What do you mean – you don't want it? What have all these weeks been about – if not that?'

It was a few moments before he answered her – though whether because he didn't want to or because, like her, he could scarcely breathe, let alone speak, she didn't know.

But finally he gasped, 'The land. I want ... the land. What's in it is ... mine.'

Anna had no idea what he was talking about but knew that this wasn't the time to care. She could hardly see and her chest hurt. But from somewhere outside the room and overhead she could hear hurried footsteps and male voices exchanging staccato remarks. Help had arrived. There was a chance that not quite *everything* would go up in smoke.

Then Daniel was in the doorway, leaning against the architrave for a second to stare at her before storming across the floor to haul her into a bone-crushing embrace.

'Oh God,' he breathed. 'Oh God. Thank you.'

He was holding her so close she could feel the too-rapid thudding of his heart. She let her muscles go slack and leaned into him, weak with the knowledge that he was here ... so everything would be all right.

Daniel gave a long, shuddering sigh, tried to pull himself together and, failing, said less steadily than he would have liked, 'Anna, love ... unless you want to frighten me into an early grave, don't do anything like this again. *Ever.*'

Something inside her lurched. He'd called her 'love'. And even though she knew he might not mean it literally, it still took root in her heart and made it sing.

But they were forgetting Harvill and he, aware of it, was slithering his way towards the door. Daniel checked him with one foot, saying coldly, 'Don't move another inch if you want to leave this room intact.' And to Anna, 'Harvill, I presume?'

'Yes.'

He nodded and, as one of the water-carriers paused in the doorway, said, 'This fellow is the fire-raiser. Tie him up and put him somewhere safe until I can be bothered with him.' And once more to Harvill, 'Be grateful that they're putting out your fires. If the whole place had been going up, I'd have left you inside to burn with it.'

Giving a startled gasp as he swept her up and carried her out, Anna said, 'No. You wouldn't.'

'I might. I *would* if he'd hurt you. But let's just get out of here.'

They emerged into the yard to a ragged cheer which he acknowledged with a wave and something resembling a grin. Then, setting Anna on her feet and allowing himself one brief, fierce kiss, he said, 'Later, I may be able to cherish the memory of seeing you standing over Harvill like the wrath of God. But not just yet. Right now, my nerves are still shredded. Don't be surprised if I chain you to my wrist for a week or two. Or longer.'

Turning to the clucking women surrounding them, he said, 'Look after her ladyship, please. I'll be back in a little while.' Then, knowing that Anna was in good hands, he strode over to the pump and told the sweating fellow operating it to take a break, adding, 'I need to work off the urge to put my hands around a man's throat ... this will help.'

* * *

Unfortunately, the day was far from over. Anna refused to leave until she was sure there was no further danger. Then she insisted on taking a preliminary look at the damage which she eventually declared bad but not catastrophic. The work rooms would need cleaning and redecorating; furniture and various pieces of equipment would have to be replaced, as would most of the stocks of oils, pigments and so forth. But all the finished wares were stored in a separate part of the building on the far side of the offices, so none of those had been lost or damaged – which was a blessing. Finally, she had a note taken to Nathaniel Lowe's home so he would be prepared for what awaited him tomorrow morning.

Daniel, meanwhile, sent for a pair of constables to arrest Harvill, informing them that he'd want to question the fellow himself on the morrow. It occurred to him that he'd recently had a lot more to do with officers of the law than any sane man would want to. He hoped this would be the last of it.

By the time everything was done it was far too late to set off for Reculver – even if either he or Anna were in any fit state to do so. So he told Blake to take Cicero, ride to Hawthorne Lodge and warn Anna's mother to expect them and that they would require baths. He hoped she'd keep her opinions on Harvill to herself.

* * *

Mrs Hawthorne received the news that her gentleman friend was currently under arrest for attempting to burn down the manufactory with a lack of comment which actually said a great deal. Much later, eyes still red and throat a little sore but glad to be clean again, Anna snuggled up to Daniel and, yawning, said, 'It's been quite a day, hasn't it?'

'That's one way of putting it,' he agreed.

Among the other shocks to his system had been one of cataclysmic proportions. A discovery that was simultaneously both new and yet not new at all.

Quite simply, he was fathoms deep in love with his wife – and had been for a long time without recognising it. But today, in those brief minutes when he'd thought he might lose her ... might have *already* lost her ... the truth had hit him. She was his need, his delight and his haven when life's storms threatened to overwhelm him – all things he'd taken for granted.

But no more, he decided.

The mere thought of being without her was too painful to bear. Did she know, he wondered? *Could* she know when he hadn't himself? Probably not. But today had taught him a hard lesson. One about not taking *anything* for granted. Not tomorrow ... and not his wife. Emotion clogged his throat. He swallowed it. This could not wait.

CHAPTER THIRTY

Turning slightly, he said softly, 'Are you still awake?'

'Barely.'

'Hold on for a little longer. I need to tell you something important.'

Another yawn but she opened sleepy eyes. 'Now?'

'Yes, now.' And then, swiftly and simply before his nerve failed, 'I love you. I love you so much I can't imagine what I'd do or be without you. And I don't ever want to find out.'

Suddenly wide awake, Anna sat up. The only candle still burning was the one on his side of the bed so his face was in shadow, making his expression impossible to read. She said wonderingly, 'Are ... are you sure?'

'Completely sure. I don't know why it took arriving to learn that you were inside a burning building with no guarantee you'd come out alive to make me realise it. But it did and ... well, I wanted you to know.' Though she couldn't see his face, he could see hers clearly enough, along with the tears gathering on her lashes. He said uncertainly, 'That's all right, isn't it?'

Anna nodded and, unable to trust her voice, reached out to touch his cheek instead.

He trapped her hand beneath his. 'Then why are you crying?'

'I'm n-not.'

'You are.' Daniel sat up, eyeing her anxiously. 'Dense I may be, but I know tears are never a good sign.'

'These are,' she whispered. 'These are happy tears.'

'*Happy* tears?' he echoed. And was about to ask how he was supposed to know the difference, when the look in her eyes stopped him. There *was* a difference, he realised. Behind the tears, she looked both shy and incandescent. Relief washed through him.

'Oh. For a moment, I thought ... but, good.'

She managed something that might have been a shaky laugh. 'I'm sorry. I – I can't quite take it in.'

'Why? It's not so hard to believe, is it?'

'For me, it is. I'm not beautiful or charming or – '

'Your opinion, not mine. You're beautiful to *me* ... and a score of other things, none of which I'd properly appreciated until I thought I could lose them. I *love* you, Anna ... have done for weeks and I'm an ass for not realising it sooner.' He stopped, then added awkwardly, 'I just wanted you to know. You needn't ... you don't have to say anything in return.'

Anna gave a tiny, unsteady chuckle.

'Yes, I do.' Seeing him about to interrupt, she laid a finger against his lips. 'I was more than half in love with you from the first time I saw you, years before we met. At nineteen, I was weaving girlish fantasies about you. But then I *did* meet you and I fell in love with the real man rather than the imaginary one. You. It's always been you.' She hesitated, then added, 'I never expected you to love me back, though I hoped that one day you might – just a little bit. I knew I couldn't be the wife you wanted but I could perhaps be the one you needed.'

Daniel wrapped his arms about her and drew her down with him.

'You're both. And more. And always will be.'

'It may take me a little while to get used to that.'

'Me, too. God. When I think back ... I was completely against marrying for money.'

'I know. It's why I called my proposal a business arrangement. It was never that for me ... but I didn't think you would accept anything else.'

'I probably wouldn't have,' he admitted. 'But for Grimshaw's demand ...' He stopped, pulling her down into his arms. 'No. I won't give him the credit. I'd rather think that we were meant for each other, you and I. Fated, even.'

'Set in the stars?' Nestling closer, Anna said, 'I like that idea.'

'So do I. If we weren't both so damned tired, I'd show you just how *much* I like it. But there's always tomorrow.'

'Yes. So there is. Tomorrow ... when we're home again.'

And though both of them were aware of it, neither mentioned that tomorrow would bring Harvill. They merely fell asleep holding each other.

* * *

Morning came too soon.

Leaving Anna to sleep a little longer, Daniel rose, dressed and went downstairs. There, he obtained yesterday's left-over sponge cakes and went into the gardens to feed the peacocks. He did it partly because having peacocks eat from his hand was a novel experience ... and partly because he needed some measure of peace to settle on his mind before he looked at the man who could very well have got Anna killed.

He was still there, surrounded by fowl who hadn't yet accepted he had no more food to offer them and were being extremely vocal about it, when Anna found him. She said, 'Greedy, aren't they? And noisy. Mama doesn't like them.'

'What *does* she like?' he asked moodily. Then, dusting crumbs from his hands and rising, he took her in his arms for a kiss, then said, 'Good morning. You look better.'

She searched his eyes. 'You don't.'

'I will when we're on our way home.' He drew her hand through his arm and turned back towards the house. 'So ... today's schedule. Breakfast, bloody Harvill and then brief stops to speak to both Lowe and Landry?'

'Yes. And they *will* be brief. Nathaniel doesn't need me to tell him what needs to be done. But a number of our workers came to help yesterday and I'd like to give them a bonus by way of thanks. As for Mr Landry, we'll need him to handle the case against Harvill. After today, I don't want to hear of that man ever again.'

Daniel nodded. He didn't say that he would be doing his best to make damned *sure* they never heard of him again. But first, he wanted to know the truth behind Harvill's seeming fixation with Hawthorne's because, try as he might, he couldn't see even a grain of sense in it.

* * *

Daniel having made it known that he and the viscountess would want to conduct their own interview, Harvill had been detained overnight in one of a handful of cells beneath the court house rather than in the city gaol. Mr Owens ushered them into an office where a clerk sat unobtrusively in a corner, and offered tea.

'Thank you, but no,' said Anna, calmly removing her gloves. 'As you'll appreciate, yesterday was extremely trying and my husband and I are anxious to get home, so we'd like to keep this as brief as possible.'

'Of course,' agreed Mr Owens. 'Of course. Most understandable and, in a moment, my clerk will have him brought up. But first, two things. He's been ranting like a madman all night so we'll leave the manacles on and I will put a constable outside the door in case he turns violent.'

'If he turns violent,' remarked Daniel in a tone of dark anticipation, 'we won't need the constable. However ... the second thing?'

'Although I shall take no part in it, I'll remain throughout your interview.'

'Why?'

'Facts pertinent to the incident and therefore relevant to the charges may emerge.'

'You mean,' said Anna, 'that he may say things to us that he won't admit to you.'

'Precisely, my lady. If that will be acceptable to you, my lord?'

'As long as you don't interfere, yes. So let's get it over with, shall we?'

Still in yesterday's filthy clothes, his hair mostly untied and his face and hands in need of further scrubbing, Harvill leaned against the wall and glared insolently at them.

Anna looked coolly back at him under raised brows.

Idly crossing one leg over the other, Daniel finally said, 'Well? Nothing to say? Or perhaps you've lost your voice from spending the night shouting?'

Still Harvill didn't speak. Eventually, Anna said, 'I knew this would be a waste of time. Even if he opens his mouth, it won't be the truth. He has neither reasons nor excuses. And even if he *did*, what use would they be? He was caught, red-handed, setting fire to my manufactory – and *that* in the wake of arranging the sabotage of one of the kilns. I don't much care what drove him to do it. I just want him to pay for what he did.' She turned to Daniel. 'Remind me. What *is* the penalty for arson?'

'Hanging,' he replied laconically. And seeing Harvill flinch, decided to let the word linger on the air for a little while before adding, 'Or perhaps – since transportation to the American colonies is no longer an option – life imprisonment with hard labour.' He smiled coldly and shrugged. 'Still nothing to say, Mr Harvill?'

Apparently he hadn't.

'You told me you didn't want Hawthorne's, just the land it stands on,' remarked Anna. 'Why? And why *now?* The obvious assumption is that you think something is buried there. But if that's so, it's been there for at least four decades.'

For the first time, Harvill unlocked his jaws. 'Longer.'

'Over a century?' asked Daniel lazily. And when, once again, Harvill showed no sign of answering, 'Well, since you didn't manage to burn the manufactory down, it isn't going to be dug up any time soon. Not in your lifetime, anyway ... which, thanks to your actions yesterday, may be considerably shorter than it might otherwise have been.'

'I offered to buy it!' shouted Harvill suddenly, making Anna jump. 'More than once, at a fair price, I offered to buy – '

'Buy it with what? According to my information, you don't have the money.'

Ignoring this, Harvill continued ranting, his words coming out faster and faster.

'She should have sold it to me but she wouldn't. And what's underneath is mine. *Mine!* My family owned that land and I want what they left there. I'm *entitled* to it.'

'Not any more,' said Anna calmly. 'Your family don't own it now. I do. The land, the buildings on it ... and anything buried below. However, I very much doubt that there is anything or ever was because – '

'There was. I *know* there was – and I can prove it!'

'Because when the manufactory was being built,' she went on calmly, 'and particularly in the area where the kilns were to be sited, excavations for the foundations would have been quite deep. If anything had been found there, I would know.'

'No,' He shook his head, a sly look entered his eyes and he whispered, 'But *I* could find it. And it's a fortune worth finding.'

Ah, thought Daniel. *Thinks he can make a deal, does he? Imbecile.*

He said, 'Go on. And make it quick. We haven't got all day.'

'There'll be plans,' offered Harvill. 'Plans of the manufactory before it was built. And *I've* got drawings of my family's house and gardens that were there before. With both of those, I can work out *exactly* where my ancestors buried their valuables when they left the city.'

'In that case,' said Daniel, sounding bored, 'why didn't you say so instead of setting fire to the manufactory?'

'Because you wouldn't have listened!' Harvill was yelling again. 'Like you're not listening *now!*'

'To a story that makes no sense?' remarked Anna. 'For example, why did your family leave the city? And why couldn't they take their valuables with them?'

'It's obvious, isn't it? With soldiers everywhere, it wouldn't have been safe.'

'Soldiers?' she asked impatiently. And to Daniel when Harvill said nothing, 'Do *you* know what he's talking about?'

'I assume he means the Civil Wars of the sixteen-forties,' shrugged Daniel with a hint of derisive amusement. 'We'll have pirates and evil fairies soon.'

'Not the first two Civil Wars,' murmured Mr Owens helpfully, 'but the third one. Forgive me, my lord. The history of Worcester is a passion of mine … and in 1651, Charles the Second's attempt to reclaim his throne ended here in a great battle against the forces of the Parliament. Enormous damage was done to the city – both during the fighting and in the confusion afterwards. Many houses had to be demolished and others stood empty for weeks or even months awaiting repair.'

'Thank you,' said Daniel. 'That is helpful. But now we have the context, perhaps Harvill might like to fill in the rest?'

Harvill fidgeted and moistened his lips. He said, 'After the battle, a lot of people left the city until things settled down again. My family didn't. They stayed and they … adapted.'

'Adapted?' queried Daniel gently.

'To the circumstances. And the opportunities. But after a while, there were new difficulties so they decided to leave for a few months, taking only what could be carried easily. It's taken years to find my great-grandfather's diaries – *years!*' His voice started to rise again. 'But the record of how the family prospered and the treasures they had to leave behind is all there.

A fortune in gold and silver plate and jewels! And it's my inheritance. *Mine!*'

There was a long silence. Finally Daniel said, 'What does that sound like to you, Mr Owens?'

'The same thing it sounds like to you, my lord. His ancestors were looters.'

'That's a lie!' shouted Harvill. 'They were nothing of the sort!'

'Looters,' said Daniel flatly. 'And this so-called buried treasure consists of goods stolen during the inevitable confusion after the battle. Looted from damaged houses and shops – perhaps even churches.'

'Definitely churches,' interposed Mr Owens. 'Even, I'm afraid, the cathedral. A relic pertaining to Saint Wulfstan disappeared at that time and has never been seen since.'

Briefly hoping that Owens wasn't going to ask if *he* could dig up Hawthorne's, Daniel turned again to Harvill. 'There was probably still an army presence in and around the city. Your ancestors couldn't risk being caught with their ill-gotten and possibly easily-identifiable gains, so they left them behind when the city got too hot to hold them. They planned to sneak back and collect them later – only for some reason it didn't work out that way. If any part of your story is true, it's that. Isn't it?'

'No. It wasn't *like* that! They only took – '

'It was *exactly* like that,' said Daniel, coming to his feet. 'But why you suppose we'd be interested in recovering stolen property, I can't imagine.'

'Drop the charge of arson, give me the chance to retrieve it,' blurted Harvill, 'and I'll give you half.'

Daniel gave a harsh laugh. 'You think you can *bribe* me? You can't. You were prepared to burn Hawthorne's down for something that was supposedly put in the ground over a century ago and that may or may not still be there. I don't know if you're stupid, desperate or merely insane – though I suspect it's the latter. But because of you, my wife might have died yesterday and –'

'And if she had? You'd still have had her money, so why would —?'

Before he could finish the sentence, Daniel had spun him round and rammed him, face first, into the wall. Then holding him there and in a silky soft tone that Anna thought truly chilling, he said, 'Have you any idea how much, how *very* much, I want to hurt you, Harvill? I mean *really* hurt you? One more word in that vein and I'll do it. For your information, my wife is worth more to me than all the treasures of the earth. If any harm had come to her ...' He stopped, trying to summon some control. 'Let me put your position very simply. You will never be given permission to excavate anywhere at all at the manufactory. You will, however, face a charge of arson and the penalty for it dictated by the law.' Ignoring the fact that Harvill was struggling to breathe and Mr Owens was half-way to the door, presumably to summon the constable, he paused and pressed harder, saying conversationally over his shoulder, 'You know, Anna ...it seems there's been bad blood in the Harvill line for generations – right down to the current sorry specimen. But I think I've heard enough. Have you?'

'Yes.' She laid a hand on his shoulder and said softly, 'Let it go, Daniel. He isn't worth it. Leave him to the courts. And we have other calls to make before we can go home.'

* * *

Ruth and Blake awaited them in the hall.

Drawing Ruth to one side, Anna took off her cloak and wrapped it around the maid's shoulders, saying 'Would you mind riding outside with Blake? I wouldn't ask, except – '

'It's all right, my lady. I understand you and his lordship have things to talk about.' Ruth slid a sideways glance at the groom and whispered, 'As it happens, so do Joe and me.'

Anna blinked. 'Oh. You mean ...?'

'Yes. Only Joe thinks you and his lordship wouldn't like it.'

'I haven't any objection. And I can't imagine why his lordship would either. But I'll mention it to him, if you wish.'

'Oh, *thank* you, my lady! That'd be kind.'

When they were on their way to Hawthorne's and she was sitting snugly in the curve of Daniel's arm, Anna said, 'It seems that Ruth and Blake have an ... understanding.'

'They do?'

'Yes. You wouldn't mind, would you?'

'Why on earth would I?'

'That's what I thought.' She leaned her head on his shoulder. 'Better now?'

'Somewhat.' He sighed. 'If it's any excuse, I don't think I've quite got over yesterday yet. But I'm sorry you saw the evidence of it.'

'Don't be. You were ... formidable.'

He shook his head. 'I lost my temper. I shouldn't have. But what he said about the money twisted a nerve. It was true in the beginning, I admit that. But it isn't true *now* and hasn't been for a long time. You believe that, don't you?'

'Yes, Daniel. I believe that.'

'Thank you.' And after a long pause, 'As for Harvill, he and his deranged obsessions won't trouble us again.'

'No,' agreed Anna. And thought, *Not if he has half a brain and hopes to escape the noose.*

* * *

Mr Lowe greeted them with a grim smile and tidings that the cleaning-up operation was already in full swing. 'Work is at a standstill while everyone lends a hand with that. I've begun ordering necessary replacements and the glaziers will be here tomorrow to see to the windows. I take it you want everywhere freshly painted?'

'Yes. And all traces of yesterday obliterated,' said Anna firmly. Then, 'I was unpacking the scent bottles when it started. Were any of them damaged in the stampede to put the fires out?'

'Not one. You can go and see for yourself if you wish.'

'I'll take your word for it.' She rose from her seat. 'I knew you'd have everything well in hand, Nathaniel. I needn't have come really except I thought it wouldn't hurt to let the workers see me here and in one piece. Did you reward those who helped yesterday?'

He nodded. 'Five shillings apiece, as you suggested. Most of them said they'd have done it for nothing.'

'I know,' said Anna simply. 'And that is the point, isn't it?'

* * *

At Mr Landry's office in Angel Street, the lawyer listened in horrified silence and then said, 'Where is Harvill now?'

'Magistrate Owens will have transferred him to the gaol by now. We've told him that you will be acting on our behalf and will keep us informed of progress,' replied Daniel. 'I'm sure I don't need to tell you that there's no question of leniency. Harvill might have burned Hawthorne's to the ground and people could have died.'

'Quite so, my lord. Rest assured that I shall make that very clear.'

'Thank you.'

'And pay off Mr Aldridge,' said Anna. 'We have no further need for his services – but you can tell him that the information he found regarding Harvill's family turned out to be at the heart of the whole business.' She stood up. 'I think that's everything. Liaise with Mr Lowe regarding necessary expenses for the repairs at Hawthorne's and see that he has what he requires. As always, I have complete confidence in him.'

* * *

They talked very little on the journey home, both of them emotionally drained by the events of the last twenty-four hours. But Anna asked whether Daniel's visit to Lord Atherton had yielded the results he'd hoped for and he told her about the greys for the curricle and the mares for herself and Rebecca.

'A bay for Becky and a chestnut named Juno for you. No carriage horses, so I'll find those elsewhere once we have the carriage,' he told her. And added wryly, 'Also, despite all my good intentions, I let his lordship tempt me into buying one of his prize stallions. But that was less an indulgence than an investment.'

'An investment?' yawned Anna.

'Yes. I'll tell you all about it later.' He settled her more comfortably across his lap. 'Meanwhile, go to sleep. I'll wake you when we're nearly home.'

In fact, although he hadn't expected to, Daniel dozed part of the way himself and awoke feeling even more rumpled and disreputable than he had before.

They pulled up outside the house at a little after four and Daniel was still giving Blake instructions about Cicero who had made the journey tied to the back of the carriage when the dowager appeared on the steps to say irritably, 'Where have you been until now? Riding off with scarcely a word like that! We expected you back yesterday. And Daniel ... what on earth have you been doing? You look an utter disgrace.'

'Thank you. I scarcely need reminding that I've been wearing these clothes since I left Atherton's estate yesterday morning.' He walked past her, taking Anna with him. 'Flynn; tea for her ladyship, brandy for me and baths for both of us, if you please.' And to his mother, 'Excuse us, Mama. There was a situation at Hawthorne's that required our presence and we'll tell you all about it over dinner. But right now, we're exhausted.'

'That's all very well,' she argued, following hard on his heels. 'But what with horses arriving but no arrangements made for them and messages from Sir Phil – '

'Later,' said Daniel, sweeping Anna onward only to be briefly checked by Scamp hurtling at him like a bullet. Scooping the dog up and tucking him under one arm, he muttered, 'Keep walking, Anna. He who hesitates is lost.'

She managed a weak laugh but said, 'Messages from Sir Philip must be about – '

'I know. But they'll still be there in an hour.' Reaching their rooms and closing the door firmly behind him, he set Scamp down, dragged off his coat and dropped it on the nearest chair. 'Let us just have a brief respite before facing the next hurdle – whatever that may be – not to mention the inevitable barrage of questions Mama has in store.'

* * *

Bathed, freshly shaved and wearing clean clothes, Daniel felt a new man and, knowing that Anna would be some time yet, couldn't resist a trip to the stables. Rather than leave Scamp alone to wreak havoc, he found the leash in order to take him with him. That this wasn't going to work became immediately evident. Scamp, deciding the leash was a new game, grabbed it between his jaws and tugged in the opposite direction to the one Daniel was taking. Deciding to leave this part of the pup's education to someone else, Daniel gave up and carried him.

He was just handing the dog over to a footman rather than risk a lot of excited barking around the horses when Rebecca arrived at his side. He said, 'I'm off to the stables – if you'd like to join me?'

'Yes, please! I've seen the new horses. They're all beauties.'

It wasn't true to say that Daniel had made no arrangements for the new arrivals. Gregson had known he'd gone to Atherton's looking to buy and would doubtless have prepared the empty stalls for new occupants. However, what he *wouldn't* have been expecting was Orion ... and Daniel looked forward to seeing his face.

Gregson didn't disappoint him. He said reverently, 'The black, my lord – he's something out of the ordinary, isn't he?'

'He certainly is.' Daniel produced an apple from his pocket, asked for a knife and sliced it in half. Handing one part to his sister and feeding the other to Orion, he said, 'The bay mare is yours. Her name is Flora.' Then, to Gregson as Rebecca danced off, 'This fellow is Orion. Can you believe I almost *didn't* buy him?'

'No, sir, I can't. Its be a crime to pass up a horse like this. They don't come along every day. You've ridden him, of course?'

'I have.' Daniel grinned. 'You'll have your turn, never fear. But put him in the paddock tomorrow and let him settle in. How are the others?'

'The bay has been a bit on the fidgety side ... otherwise, all of them are in fine fettle, my lord. The greys make a nice pair.'

'They do. Over the next few days, perhaps you can have somebody get the curricle out of retirement and polish it up? As for the chestnut, I'll bring her ladyship to see her in the morning.'

'Very good, my lord. I'll have her ready for you.'

Leaving Rebecca in the stables, Daniel returned to the house and collected whatever mail had arrived during his absence. Three notes from three different gentlemen; Lawyer Longhope, William Grimshaw and Sir Philip Weaver. And all of them, as it turned out, bearing the same news. Daniel climbed the stairs, quietly laughing.

He was still grinning when Anna joined him, clad in a pale blue undressing gown.

She said, 'You're looking very pleased with yourself – and not merely on account of a clean shirt, I suspect.'

'You suspect correctly.'

Seeing the letters in his hand, she said, 'Good news?'

'Very good. I'll give you three guesses.'

'I wouldn't know where to start.'

'You will if you think about it. Try.'

'One of the letters is from Sir Philip?'

He nodded.

'So it *is* something to do with Grimshaw?'

Another nod.

'He's admitted to blackmail?'

'Better than that.'

Anna's eyes widened. 'Oh. He's *escaped?*'

Daniel laughed and hugged her. 'That's my clever girl. Yes. He's escaped.'

'When? And how?'

'Three days ago. As for *how*, Sir Philip doesn't know – only that it happened when Grimshaw was being taken back to gaol after answering some questions about the extortion charge at Longhope's office.' He grinned at her. 'The other letters are from Longhope himself and William. William asks how it is possible that yesterday, while he and his mother were out, his so-called uncle had been in the house and taken a sum of money, along with some clothes. And Longhope ... Longhope merely says he can only assume that the guards were slack and didn't take adequate care.'

Anna eyed him suspiciously. He both looked and sounded too innocent.

'But you, of course, have your own theories.'

'I might have.'

Definitely too innocent.

'I don't suppose,' she said slowly, 'that you by any chance had a conversation with Mr Longhope similar to the one you had with me?'

'I doubt it. Longhope doesn't put the same ideas into my head that you do.'

'I'm referring to the one where you said it might be the best thing all round if Grimshaw *did* run but at a point where doing so would make him a fugitive?'

'Oh. *That* conversation.' He frowned, apparently searching his memory and then said, 'No, I don't think so – or not in so many words, anyway. But I suppose I *may* have mentioned something like it … just in passing, as it were.'

Anna folded her arms. 'In passing.'

'Yes. Indeed, if you were to ask him, I doubt you'd find Longhope has any recollection of it at all.'

'Oh, I'm *sure* he hasn't,' came the sardonic reply. And then, on a note of laughter, 'It's probably best if this conversation is similarly forgotten.'

'That,' observed Daniel, pulling her down to his lap, 'is precisely why I've been attempting not to have it. Especially when there are so many more enjoyable things we might be doing.'

Anna smiled at him. 'And you have ideas about those, I suppose?'

'Yes, love. Many, many ideas.' His eyes with their customary lurking smile looked deep into hers, 'Enough to last a lifetime.'

EPILOGUE

November 1781, Reculver Court, Prior's Norton, Gloucestershire

The first guests to arrive in the days just prior to Daniel's thirtieth birthday were the Earl and Countess of Hazelmere, with their four-month-old son, Viscount Farndon. Within twenty-four hours, they were followed by Lord Benedict Hawkridge, Baron Wendover and Mr Sandhurst. Consequently, Anna rose to summon the ladies from table after dinner that evening, saying, 'This being the first occasion that all five of you have been together for some considerable time, gentlemen, you doubtless have a great deal to talk about. So we ladies have agreed –'

'Three of you have,' muttered Rebecca. '*I* didn't.'

'— that you need be in no hurry to join us in the drawing-room – or indeed, at all. Take your port here or repair to the library – the choice is yours,' Anna went on smoothly. And, with a smile, 'Difficult though it will be, we'll try not to miss you.'

Christian and Benedict laughed. Daniel said lazily, 'All that means is that you'll talk about us instead.'

'Don't flatter yourselves,' replied Sophia over her shoulder, following Anna out.

As the door closed behind them, Daniel said, 'The library, do you think?' And when his friends nodded, 'Then go and make yourselves comfortable. I'll tell Flynn to bring brandy and port.'

When they were all seated, glass in hand, around the fire, Christian said, 'I suppose we might begin by catching up with each others' news. Mine, you already know. Michael's christening has been delayed due to the death of the vicar at our family church and the time it's taken to install a replacement. But it will finally take place the second week in January. Sophie and I hope you will all be there – weather permitting.'

'We'll be there, regardless of the weather,' promised Anthony. Then, 'My news is soon told. Lizzie is betrothed to Viscount Cardew's eldest. And that, thank God, will be *all* my sisters off my hands.'

'Enjoy it while you can,' grinned Daniel. 'I'll lay money that, as soon as the Season starts, your mother will turn all her match-making skills to finding a bride for *you*. Rumour has it that mothers do that as soon as their sons turn thirty.'

'Which I won't do for another eight months,' retorted Anthony. 'You are the first of us to reach that advanced milestone.'

'Thank you for reminding me.'

'My pleasure. But enough of that. Your turn, Gerald.'

A slow smile lit Mr Sandhurst's face.

'Julia and I are now formally betrothed.'

'You are?' Rising to grasp his hand, Daniel said, 'That's wonderful news! My sincerest congratulations. Did her mother not object as much as you expected?'

'She did. But Kit and Sophie persuaded her.'

'That's one way of putting it,' remarked Christian dryly. 'Sophie merely told her that, if Julia wasn't allowed to follow her heart, Lady Kelsall could continue husband-hunting for Gwendoline without any help from her. There having been three near misses so far, that did the trick fast enough.'

'Near misses?' asked Anthony, amused.

'So I believe. Lord Chillenden, before Sophie and I were married. Sir Jeremy Worth and Mr Foster-Smythe since. Sophie's theory is that, sooner or later, Gwendoline always manages to give them a glimpse of her true self – upon which, they take to the hills.'

'She stalked Oscar and me for a time,' remarked Benedict. 'It was ... unnerving.' After a scattering of laughter, he added, 'So before anyone asks, I'm not likely to be married or even betrothed any time soon and have no other news of any great interest or importance to impart. Like everyone else, I'm waiting to hear about you, Daniel. How is married life suiting you?'

'Since you ask, extremely well,' grinned Daniel. He paused briefly. 'If you want the truth, I'm happier than I ever thought I would – or even could – be.'

For a moment, all four gentlemen contemplated him in silence. Then Christian said slowly, 'You can tell me to mind my own business if you wish. But while you were staying with us, Sophie insisted that Anna was in love with you and that you, although you didn't yet know it, were close to feeling the same about her. Was she right?'

Daniel's colour rose a little but he replied without hesitation. 'On all counts.'

'Then I think I can safely speak for all of us when I say we're happy for you. And relieved because the omens weren't favourable.'

'The omens were wrong, as was I. Anna is ... remarkable; which, considering what we've been up against since we married, is just as well.'

'Yes,' said Christian. 'I've wondered about that. Have the Grimshaw and Harvill sagas been resolved?'

'They have. So while I tell the others what you already know perhaps you'd play host and re-fill everyone's glass?' And to the others, 'There are two, separate stories here. One of Harold Grimshaw; the man largely responsible for my father dying neck-deep in debt. And the other of Simeon Harvill; a fellow with an obsession bordering on insanity.'

As economically as possible, Daniel spoke of Grimshaw's blackmail and of William, the excuse for it; then about Harvill's inexplicable determination to acquire Hawthorne's.

'That's how matters stood when Anna and I visited you, Kit. But a lot has happened since then. Amongst it, that my mother has known about William since he was a year old.'

'*Seriously?*' asked Christian, stunned.

'Seriously,' agreed Daniel. 'But I'll come to that presently.'

When he arrived at the point of Grimshaw's recent flight, Benedict said, 'And you're satisfied with that?'

'Yes. I can't prosecute for blackmail without the whole story coming out in court, so him disappearing is the best solution. He's gone. And that's all Anna and I care about.'

'That makes sense,' offered Anthony. 'So ... what happened with Harvill?'

Daniel made a sound that wasn't quite laughter.

'He thinks his larcenous ancestors buried their Civil War loot in the land the manufactory now stands on. So, since Anna wouldn't sell it to him, he set fire to it.'

'*What?*' gasped all four gentlemen, more or less in unison.

'Yes. While I was away buying horses, Anna went to Hawthorne's. I got home, found her gone and followed her. When I got there, smoke was pouring out from both the ground and first floor windows ... and they told me that Anna was inside. I'll swear my heart stopped for a moment.' Once again, he tried to laugh but didn't quite manage it. 'When I said she's remarkable, I meant it literally. I don't know how she stays so clear-headed – yet she does. Knowing she needed help quickly, she rang the bell that signals the end of the working day because it was *Sunday* so people living nearby would know something was wrong. I wouldn't have thought of that – but *she* did. Then she went inside a burning building looking for Harvill. When I got to her, he was on his knees and she was standing over him with a *shovel*, for God's sake!'

His friends glanced at each other, unsure what to say. Finally Christian said, 'I take it that – unlike Grimshaw – Mr Harvill *will* face prosecution?'

'Anna might have died,' said Daniel grimly. 'If I could kill him with my bare hands, I would. So yes. He'll be tried for arson.'

'It's a hanging offence,' remarked Gerald quietly.

'I know. And so does he.' Daniel drew a steadying breath. 'Can we talk about something else?' And randomly to Benedict, 'How is Belhaven?'

'No less peculiar than he ever was – though he's been taking his seat in the Upper House more often than he used to. Another departure is that he's started asking Oscar when he intends to find a suitable bride and provide the dukedom with an heir.'

Christian's brows rose. 'He doesn't intend to do that himself?'

'It's beginning to look that way,' shrugged Benedict. 'Needless to say, Oscar is less than happy. He has no objection to marriage but would prefer to do it without Vere's interference – and I can't blame him for that.'

'Belhaven is – what?' asked Anthony. 'Nearly forty?'

'Thirty-seven.'

'And he's never shown a preference for any particular lady?'

Benedict laughed. 'Not that I know of. But you have to attend society events in order to meet ladies – and we all know how rarely he does that. Although ...' He stopped and added slowly, 'Oscar says that just after he left Oxford and the five of us were still in our second year, there were vague rumours that Vere had suffered a Disappointment. But Oscar dismissed them as nonsense – and I agree with him. Aside from Vere not exactly being a gargoyle, what sort of female turns down a duke?'

'True,' agreed Daniel. And with an innocent smile, 'But if *Oscar* doesn't produce the next duke, it will fall to you, won't it? And marriage isn't so bad, you know.'

Benedict hurled a cushion at him. 'There speaks a man besotted with his wife.'

'I don't deny it.'

'Upon which note,' said Christian coming to his feet, 'with the exception of Daniel, will you all please be upstanding for the toast we've yet to make.' And when they had done so, 'Long life and happiness to Daniel and Anna ... and may their future be free of Grimshaws, Harvills and other similar complications.'

'To Daniel and Anna,' chorused his friends. After which Christian added, 'So ... Dan and I are the first to fall, with Gerald soon to follow. Does anyone want to wager on who will be next? Benedict or Anthony?'

'Benedict,' said Anthony, promptly and echoed by Christian.

'Anthony,' said Gerald and Daniel.

'Neither,' said Benedict, raising his glass. 'Oscar. And good luck to him.'